VENEER

VENEER

DANIEL VERASTIQUI

CHANNEL 8 PRESS
Austin, Texas

"You cannot become who are you

while pretending to be someone else."

- From The Reflections of Noetica, Volume IV

"Someone reconciled a penis on all the desks this morning."

Kate laughed into her cup of coffee. She had been scanning the playground and trying to keep track of her kids. Luckily, none of them were in earshot.

"It's not that I mind a penis," continued Liane. "But why so many?"

Kate glanced over to see if she really wanted an answer, but Liane had turned away towards a sudden noise.

"Do you know who did it?"

Liane nodded towards the monkey bars. "Either Jalay," she said, then motioned to the picnic tables, "or Rosalia. They're my only free reconcilers."

"At least you have some," said Kate, thinking back on her struggles with her class. "Mine are all still stuck on active toys."

"Active toys. I doubt they even help." Liane flashed a smile. "Besides, kids learn at their own rate. Jalay only recently clicked, so of the two, I would guess it was his artwork this morning. Typical male."

Kate was watching the foursquare court but managed to shrug in response. "Maybe it wasn't him then. A boy would have drawn boobs, right?"

Liane's veneer shimmered as her eyebrow bounced. "Good point." As they both turned to look at Rosalia, she continued, "But she seems so innocent."

"Never judge a person by their veneer," said Kate, echoing the maxims that adorned the hallways of the school.

"I don't know. Maybe she's bored. She's already mastered this year's curriculum. I don't even know what else to teach her."

"You're lucky you have a gifted." Kate searched out Deron's face in the crowd. He was sitting alone on a bench by the mural wall. "I've got a non-believer in my congregation."

"Which one?"

Nodding in his direction, she replied, "Deron Bishop. He's only reconciled an active toy once or twice and I don't even know how he did it. Everyone else can reconcile the toys, but Deron… It's like he doesn't think it's possible."

"You know what Professor Ghose would say about that?"

Kate nodded. "Controlling the veneer is not a matter of *if*, but of *when*."

"So we just have to find a way to reach him."

Smiling at the offer, Kate replied, "He's got some kind of mental block, but I think one day it's just going to pop for him."

"Sure, and then you'll have wieners all over your desks too."

"At least he'd be reconciling. I don't know what he's going to do when we start on active palettes in the spring." Kate looked down at the palette in her lap. The small rectangle of molded plastic responded to her mental command and displayed a cartoon version of Deron sitting at his desk crying, his active palette broken in half on the floor.

Liane laughed at the image, reached out, and reconciled it away. "Don't worry about it, Katie. If he's still struggling by then, we can put him in an after-school program at Dahlstrom. You know they're always interested in these problem children."

"He's not a problem child," said Kate, feeling protective. She looked at the mural wall again. "He's a good student. I just need to be a better teacher."

"He doesn't smile much, does he?" asked Liane. "Maybe there's something going on at home that we're not aware of?"

"I don't know. His mother seems very caring."

Still, Liane had a point. Deron didn't look like he was enjoying his free time. He was ignoring the other children and focusing on the red ball in his lap. The active toys weren't supposed to leave the room, but Kate couldn't fault him for wanting some extra practice time. She thought he might have reconciled the red color, but if so, why was he so upset?

"I'd better go check on him," said Kate, setting her palette on the bench. She stood and pulled her sweater tighter around her body.

It wasn't a long walk to the jungle gym, but she had to stop every few feet to talk to one of her kids. In the classroom, especially when it was time to answer a question, they would do their best to be invisible. But out on the playground, they all vied for her attention. Kate humored them as best she could, ending each encounter with a reminder that recess would be over soon.

At last, she reached the mural wall and sat down on the bench beside Deron. There were tears at the corners of his eyes, but he made no attempt to wipe them away. When Kate cleared her throat, he looked up for only a moment.

"Did you reconcile that ball, Deron?"

He shook his head minutely and crossed his arms, dropping the ball into his lap. His eyes drifted to the swing sets and when Kate followed his gaze, she saw he was looking at Russo Rivera. The little devil was doing his best not to appear interested.

"Russo turned my ball red," said Deron, as if there were no greater injustice. He picked up the ball again so she could see.

"You don't like red?" asked Kate. "It's like an apple."

"I hate red!"

Kate nodded and waited a moment for Deron to calm down. He wasn't usually a slave to his emotions, but when they took control, the results were difficult to predict. In a soft voice, she asked, "What color do you like?"

He replied without hesitation. "Blue."

Kate leaned forward and put her elbows on her knees. She whispered so that only he could hear her. "You can turn its veneer blue if you really want to, Deron. All you have to do is reconcile a new color. Do you remember what we've been practicing?"

Deron shrugged. "I can't do it."

"Well, let's give it a try, okay?" After a nod, she continued, "Alright, now what kind of blue is your favorite? Is it like the teeter-totters over there?"

"No," he replied, looking up. "Blue like that."

"Light blue," said Kate. "It's a beautiful color, Deron. Good choice."

He nodded in agreement and almost smiled.

"Now, what's step one?"

"Hold the ball." His words were unsure. "I have to be touching it, right?"

"Right."

Deron lifted the ball with two hands and spread his fingers around it.

"What's step two?"

"Um…"

Kate pointed to the sky. "You need to imagine that color in your head. Look at it and then shut your eyes."

It took him a moment, but he finally replied, "Uh-huh."

"Then let's do step three. All you have to do is believe that the ball in your hand is that color. Tell yourself that when you open your eyes, the ball will be blue."

Deron scrunched his eyes tight, but Kate could see that the color was not changing.

"All you have to do is believe, Deron."

She could repeat the lessons over and over, keep telling him that believing was seeing and imagination dictated reality, but it wouldn't be her efforts that made it click for him. Something had to change within Deron, something in the way he viewed the world.

Sensing his frustration, Kate reached out and placed a finger on the ball, turning it blue instantly.

"Open your eyes, Deron."

The smile on his face made a warmth bubble up through Kate's body. "See how easy it is?"

Deron turned the ball over in his hands. Behind his smile was disbelief that made Kate's heart sink. There was no lesson here. Reconciling for Deron wouldn't hold up in the long run and even if he did manage it himself, he still might not believe it.

The smile faded as Deron looked to the swings again. "He's just gonna turn it red when you're not looking."

"Then you turn it back."

"He's better at it than me."

Kate put her hand on Deron's back and gave him a reassuring pat. "Yeah, but I'm better than him. He can only reconcile the active toys. Look what I can do." She reached back and put her hand on the mural wall. New color cascaded from the top of the wall and replaced the cartoonish landscape with a snow-covered hill against a sea of stars. Little green triangles representing trees dotted the hillside. "This is what the wall will look like at Christmas."

"Russo can't change it?"

"Not yet. But one day when you're both older, you'll both be able to change anything you want. You can even change your hair or your face. You like the color blue?" Kate concentrated for a second and reconciled a bluish tint on her eyes. "See?"

"I want to do that."

"Soon," said Kate, cycling back to her normal brown. "For now, you can practice on the active toys. If you want, you can take that ball home. It'll be special homework and no matter how you do, you'll get a star for trying."

"Okay," he replied, though the edges of his mouth still dipped. A veneer would have masked his emotions. Until he learned to control it fully, he would be at the mercy of his true appearance.

"You should go play," said Kate, standing up. She touched the wall again and returned it to the previous Thanksgiving theme. "There are only ten minutes of recess left."

Deron squeezed the ball with both hands. "I'm going to practice."

It's a start, thought Kate. Deron went through cycles of ambition and apathy, neither of which made it easy to teach him. Good reconciliation required a clear mind and a vivid imagination. Kate thought about what else she could do for him as she crossed the playground and returned to the bench. Liane was talking to one of her kids, but she sent the girl away.

"How did it go?" she asked.

"Russo turned his ball red."

"That little shit," whispered Liane.

Kate felt herself nodding. "Deron just doesn't get it."

"He will. One day his mother is going to walk into his room and find all sorts of nasty stuff on his walls." She paused, made a connection in her head. "You're right; boys will reconcile boobs the first chance they get."

"So you suspect Rosalia now?"

"Maybe. I'll just give them all detention until someone fesses up."

Kate chuckled and looked out over the playground again. Deron had gotten up and was now walking towards her. In his hand, he held a red ball. Kate shook her head; it had only been a minute or two since she left him.

"He did it again," said Kate.

Liane followed her gaze to Deron. "Russo?"

"He's been terrorizing Deron, turning all of his toys red." Kate started to stand up, but felt a hand on her arm.

"Wait," said Liane, urging Kate back to the bench. "Look at this."

Rosalia had left her seat at the picnic table and was moving to intercept Deron. They met between the monkey bars and the foursquare court. Their conversation was muted by the distance, but Kate could see that Deron was having a hard time looking Rosalia in the eyes. He kept his head down as he handed over the red ball. Only after she returned it with a bright blue veneer did he look up and smile.

"Aw," said Liane, nudging Kate with her shoulder. "Isn't that sweet?"

"It is," agreed Kate. "Maybe she should tutor him. I'll trade you Samantha."

"Would if I could, but I'll probably have to put her in Talented and Gifted after the winter break. Then I'll only have Jalay." She paused for a moment and sighed. "It's a shame. They do look cute together."

"Yeah." Kate watched Deron's eyes follow Rosalia as she walked away. "I guess it wasn't meant to be."

Deron stood for a few minutes before turning and heading back to the mural wall. There, he studied the ball in his hands, maybe tried to change its veneer if his face was any indication. He only looked up to cast quick glances at Russo.

"Would I be a bad teacher if I had Russo transferred to Glenmore?"

"Not if you think that's best. If he's a special case, then he needs special attention. He'd get that at Glenmore."

"He wouldn't be able to mess with Deron anymore."

"At least not until high school," said Liane.

Kate dipped her head and pulled her palette into her lap. With a quick tap, she reconciled an image of Deron in a graduation gown that bunched up at his feet and a cap that covered most of his face. "Hopefully he'll be stronger by then."

"Which one?"

Liane was right. Little monsters grow up to be big monsters.

"You don't have to decide now," said Liane. "Give him the rest of the year to turn it around. Make him understand the consequences."

"And Deron?"

"If I don't lose Rosalia to TAG, maybe she can work with him."

It might not be enough, thought Kate. She let her doubt bubble up to her veneer.

Liane put her hand on Kate's shoulder. "She can teach him to reconcile little peeners all over your desks."

Kate tried to stifle her laughter.

Across the playground, Deron hadn't made any progress with his ball. It was still Rosalia's blue, not that he seemed to mind very much. She knew he wouldn't even try to change it now. At least not until Russo turned it red again.

Kate smirked.

One way or another, Deron Bishop was going to learn to reconcile.

ONE

DERON

Deron was only faintly aware of the nightmare winding down. The school gym was fading out like a slide show dissolving into the next picture. When it was gone, only the desk beneath him remained, with its glowing portal offering up questions that cycled too quickly to be read, accompanied by answers in a language he didn't recognize. Soon there was no difference between portal and desk, between the veneer and the squiggles that somewhat resembled words. Even in the dream, Deron's mind rejected this divergent form of the veneer. There was no order to it, no control that he could exert. He pushed it away, forced it into the infinite distance.

Then he was alone in an empty construct, left only with a sense of dread at not having answered a single question on his test.

Deron shook himself awake and opened his eyes to his darkened bedroom. Reaching for the wall, he imagined his room lit up in a soft amber color. This thought, combined with the physical contact of his fingers, caused the walls to cycle through the gradient of black to yellow, stopping somewhere in between to match the vague idea of color in Deron's head. He looked to the ceiling, thought of trees, and reconciled a bright sun in a blue sky, surrounded on the edges by the tips of evergreens.

One by one, his decorations loaded, covering the walls with reconciled posters, some of them moving, others static but detailed. Above his desk, a rectangular section exploded from a pinpoint and formed a widescreen portal. It flickered twice before loading Deron's start page—four icons sitting on a background of Rosalia at Gillock Pond.

Though it was as bright as a cloudless day in his room, the world outside remained dark, still awaiting sunrise. He could reconcile light wherever he wanted, but ultimately his body took its cues from the natural cycles of night and day. At that moment, the world was telling him to stay in bed. Deron closed his eyes and embraced a darkness so absolute that if he hadn't felt the pressure of the bed against his back, he could have imagined himself simply floating in the ether, surrounded by emptiness and quiet.

The nightmare came back to him.

He did have a test in third period English that he wasn't prepared for. The text was available anywhere he could reconcile a portal, but he had never gotten around to reading it. In a matter of hours, he would have to sit down at a desk just like the one in his dream and answer questions about the motivations of people who didn't really exist. The only option was to cheat somehow, to bring up the text in small print on the edge of his desk. That was risky though and in the long run it was better to take the zero than take the zero *and* get caught cheating. Rosalia had probably done the reading. Whether she would fill him in on the details was another story.

Deron groaned, tried to force his body into action, but it was set on staying put. There was just no part of him that wanted to get up and go to school. Nothing about it was appealing, not the lectures from the bored teachers, not the stale burritos in the cafeteria, and certainly not the shops—the fabricated images that appeared randomly on the walls throughout the school. Russo's creativity knew no limits when it came to putting Deron's face on obese women or men in overalls fornicating with wildlife. Principal Ficcone had warned him about it a few times, but the shops kept popping up, with Deron unable to do anything but erase them when he found them. Rosalia held that he should respond in kind, but Deron could never summon the energy.

The portal above his desk beeped and when he looked over, he saw a flashing envelope with a *3* superimposed over it. The e-mails were probably unsolicited, a pitch for a short-term loan or a social network for cheating spouses. Rolling onto his side, Deron faced the wall and smiled at the photo stream that flowed in an arc from the headboard down to the middle of the bed. Pictures of Rosalia were plentiful, dating back to junior high and the hazel eyes she used to wear. Her pictures progressed until her hair turned to red flames, collected in a high ponytail on the back of her head. This was how Deron knew her now.

Sebo made his share of appearances too, first showing up in the middle of seventh grade and then gradually coming to dominate the screenshots they had culled from various run and guns. He was tall, like Deron, but he had spent his early years at Dahlstrom Academy where the physical education program was more than just a suggestion. There was no telling what his original colors were since the first time they met he had been wearing some kind of neon veneer copied from a bad anime. It wasn't a strange choice for a seventh grader; everyone was experimenting with something, doing whatever they could to set themselves apart.

A quick double-knock made him roll over just in time to see his mom poke her head through the opening door. There was no sign of fatigue in her immaculate face; the only way someone would have known that Ania Bishop had just woken up was from the robe she wore and the rollers in her hair.

"You're going to be late for school," she said, her feet remaining just outside the threshold to his room. "I made pancakes."

"Can I skip today?" He wrapped his pillow around his face to shut out the world.

"Sure," she replied.

Deron pulled the pillow away to look at his mom. Sometimes it was hard to tell when she was joking.

Ania clucked her tongue at the barely tasteful nudes occupying the corner by Deron's desk. "I thought I told you I didn't want that on the walls."

"It's my room."

Putting a hand on her hip, she replied, "Yes, but it's *my* house. If you want to live like that you can go stay with your father."

"Yeah right," said Deron, swinging his legs over the side of the bed. "He can't even make pancakes."

"Maybe the whore knows how."

For a moment, Deron thought she was referring to Carina, the tall brunette who towered over his desk. It was his mom's eyes that gave her away, that revealed hatred in a flicker of her veneer. Even after all these years, she was still mad that his dad had left her, left both of them.

"Come on," she said, putting her hand on the wall. Carina's tan body shimmered and gave way to a surreal vista under a starry sky.

Deron couldn't say he disliked the new art on his walls, but that kind of virtual tourism was from his mom's generation, not his. He was more interested in the video games, the violent and immersive simulations that molded innocent tweens into poorly veneered anarchists.

"There's bacon…"

"Then I guess I have no choice."

Ania put her nose in the air. "Damn right you don't." A moment later, she was gone, the door tapping shut behind her.

Part of him wanted to get dressed and go downstairs; the air was already thick with the smell of bacon. The other part, the side he almost always listened to, could only think of Rosalia.

Deron reached over and traced a circle on the wall over the headboard. The pale amber faded away and a smaller version of his start page appeared in the portal. He clicked into his mailbox and brought up the three unread messages. The first one was spam, an invitation to a sim parlor that specialized in full-release sensory. Next was a calendar invite from Sebo; he wanted to go to Paramel on Saturday to play the new Destined 4 Death campaign.

The third message was from Rosalia, and his thoughts of her turned the wall surrounding the portal into a collage of photos. Some of them were repeats from the photo stream; others were from a more candid collection. He found himself smiling at one subset where he had tried to reconcile Rosalia stripped down to her underwear, to nothing. None of them looked right, but he was too scared to ask her to help him clean them up.

With a casual swipe, he cleared away the pseudo-nude photos and focused on the message. It was the usual fare: a good morning, a brief description of last night's dream, and a suggestion of what they should do after school. She ended with a statement that made him sigh, just an innocent, "Hope you finished your reading last night." She signed the message with love, as always.

Deron wiped the wall clean and stood up. Stretching, he reached beyond the trees on the ceiling to the simulated heavens above. Somehow, the reconciled but natural colors of a wooded landscape and a blue sky beckoned him into the world. It wasn't a scene that existed in Easton, not with its shiny skyscrapers and malls and carefully manicured micro-parks.

His mind wandered, but too soon he was thinking about school again, about the exam and Rosalia and the shops.

Shaking his head, Deron took the first step and set the day in motion. He grabbed a clean pair of underwear from his dresser and headed for the bathroom. Pausing at the door, he slapped the wall as if it were a malfunctioning vending machine. In the corner, Carina's curves reappeared. With a few well-placed nudges, Deron managed to reconcile a smile onto her face.

"Good morning," he whispered.

TWO
RUSSO

The J. Perion Tower had been vacant for almost a year, victim of an economy that seemed to fluctuate wildly under the mismanagement of the local government. It was one of dozens of skyscrapers whose construction had simply stopped, leaving a building that turned into a skeleton thirty floors up. Some furniture still remained in the few completed offices, though anything worth stealing had long since vanished in the night. The only occupants of the commercial monument were the veneers that brave vandals had reconciled on the inner walls.

Russo Rivera stood in the alley just outside the back entrance and examined the new warning signs posted beside the door. They were the typical nonsense: no trespassing, private property, and a full recitation of occupancy laws. For months, he had been using the empty building as his home away from home, a place where he could practice reconciliation without anyone badgering him about the content. Until now, no one had tried to keep him out.

"You think this means we shouldn't go in?" asked Russo.

Jalay Chapman shrugged without looking up from his palette. His finger darted across the screen, scrolling through a library of static images. He was six inches shorter than Russo and built like a compact bulldozer. Unfortunately, he had no coordination beyond his fingertips. He could draw and shop like no one else, but when it came to physical movement, he was a lost cause.

"Do you want this by Spanish or not?" Jalay asked, irritated. He found a spot on the opposite side of the alley and leaned against it. Behind him, presence-sensing veneers kicked in and displayed a four-by-four grid of muted commercials.

"Maybe someone else wants it for their playground," Russo mused. He put out a hand and turned the warnings into gray boxes and then faded them to match the evercrete background. "If they don't want people going in, they should put up some kind of sign."

Looking up briefly, Jalay muttered, "It's probably locked." When Russo touched the door handle, he added, "And alarmed."

Russo smirked and pushed the door open a few inches.

"Silent alarm?" asked Jalay.

"Let's go inside," said Russo, kicking the door open. He groped for the wall in the darkness and when his fingers connected, he pushed some light down the hallway.

"We'll be late for school." Jalay hadn't moved from his perch.

Russo considered scolding his disciple for putting too much faith in school, but something about the hallway drew his attention inward. In previous visits, the walls had been blank, just floor to ceiling canvasses waiting for their veneers. Now, someone had reconciled them into reflective surfaces; he saw his own face perfectly, black eyes and all.

As if sensing his need, the ceiling above him illuminated, enhancing the facing mirrors effect and allowing him to see deeper into infinity. A red-bordered box grew down from the top of the wall, moving and expanding until it settled over his face and flashed white. Russo smiled when he noticed it was holding his image captive.

Turning on the spot, Russo walked back outside, muttering to himself.

"What?" asked Jalay.

"It *was* alarmed." He paused for a moment, considered the strange occurrence of Jalay being right. "It took my picture."

Jalay smirked. "Good thing you're wearing that face today."

Raising his eyebrows a little, Russo replied, "Yeah. Shit, if they think they're gonna catch me based on that picture, they're out of their—"

Movement at the end of the alley caused Russo's throat to tighten up. People had been passing by all morning, but only now did two figures step out of the crowd and take an interest. They looked just like everyone else, but the way they stared, the way they held themselves, spoke to some hidden danger. It became apparent a moment later when their veneers flared to reveal the black and blue uniform of the Easton PD. Russo's flight reflex kicked in, barely leaving enough time to warn Jalay, and even that took considerable effort.

"Run!"

Russo was surprised to see Jalay keep up with him as they sprinted down the alley. He had an odd, stop-motion way of running that looked awkward and inefficient. It allowed for a burst of speed, but Jalay wouldn't be able to maintain it for more than a couple of blocks. It made Russo smile to see his friend begin to labor as they broke out onto the street. He wouldn't have to outrun the uniforms today; he'd only have to outrun Jalay.

They split up at the end of the alley and Russo headed towards the micro-park on Mills and 28th. There was light pedestrian traffic on the sidewalks, mostly early morning workers stalking their way to their daytime dungeons. Russo slipped between them nimbly, swapping out his appearance every few seconds to create confusion. As far as they were concerned, an entire group of impolite youths were pushing their way through the crowd.

At Cole Street, Russo made a right turn and dashed across three lanes of traffic, prompting a chorus of honking horns from the commuters. Some asshole even stuck his head out of his car to yell at him, but Russo gave him the finger and ducked into an alley. When he emerged on Hancock, his eyes jumped to the flashing red text on the surrounding buildings. He cut left, glanced at the store windows to find notices on all of them, each with a picture of his face and a caption along the top that read *Person of Interest*.

He kept to the alleys after that, darting into the open only when he needed to cross a street. Portaled boxes kept following him through the veneer, most of them blurry and indistinct beneath an overlay of his own face. At Cameron, Russo decided to hide in a news kiosk to catch his breath. There, he tried to calm himself, but his heart was beating too fast. The fight inside his body made Russo double over in pain. Collapsing onto one knee, he wondered how long it had been since he ran from the police.

"Are you going to come out?"

Russo started at the gravelly voice. For the first time, he noticed the shadows on the evercrete sidewalk, two rounded sections of black stretching across the entrance to the kiosk. One of them wavered as the uniform tapped his foot.

"Are you going to arrest me?"

"Yes," said the uniform, drawing out the word. "You made me run. And I just had breakfast."

"Ouch," said Russo, feigning sympathy. He cycled through various ways to escape the clutches of the law, but nothing seemed viable. "That doesn't sound good," he continued.

"Not good for me. Worse for you."

"If it helps, my side hurts." He was on autopilot, making conversation until the moment was right for him to burst out and make a break for it.

"I thought you'd be in better shape than your friend." He laughed to himself.

The sound was unsettling. Its resonance suggested a thick neck and powerful lungs. Easton's finest were notorious for being big and dumb.

"Come on," he urged, "we need to take a ride downtown."

He was playing cordial, but Russo knew it was just a veneer, a way to get him to surrender quietly. With an even voice, he asked, "Whatever happened to 'you'll never take me alive, Copper'?"

"Sounds like a good way to get your ass shot."

Russo hurled himself out of the kiosk in a desperate bid to escape. For a brief and beautiful moment, the outside world seemed welcoming, drawing him from his temporary jail cell into a realm of infinite freedom. But as he moved, a massive forearm broke in from the left side of the frame.

It caught him on the nose, blurred his vision, and sent him sprawling backwards to the sidewalk. He felt a strong hand grip him on the upper arm; it dragged him easily towards the street. A patrol car pulled up on cue and out stepped another brick house of a uniform.

"You look out of breath," said Brick, opening the back door for his partner.

"The little fucker's fast," said the uniform, pushing on Russo's head and forcing him into the car.

Russo held his breath; it smelled like someone had recently puked all over the seat and floorboards. Only after the pain threatened to overwhelm did he venture a tentative gasp.

"What's your name, kid?"

"George," replied Russo.

"What's your last name, George?" There was a palette on the dashboard that showed Russo's face. The uniform reconciled the name into a search box.

"Washington." When he got a tired look in response, he added, "Do you think this'll hurt my political career?"

"I don't think you have to worry about *any* kind of career." Then, to Brick, "What do you say? Failure to present identification?" He got a nod in response.

"I cannot tell a lie," Russo recited.

"What," the uniform asked, turning sideways in his seat, "you think you can just reconcile a veneer, and no one will know it's you? Don't you think more people would be out robbing banks if that really worked?"

Russo considered the question but kept his face neutral.

"I blame the schools," he continued. "They teach kids to reconcile, but they don't teach the limits."

They rode in silence for the next few minutes, giving Russo ample time to imagine what kind of technology they had downtown that would reveal his true identity. Impossible, he thought. Although he'd seen the inside of a police station once or twice, it was for minor infractions. They had never even taken his fingerprints.

Outside, the TNC Bank building loomed as the car pulled up in front of the Easton PD. The uniforms dragged him out and escorted him to an empty holding area. Russo walked casually to a bench along the back wall and when he sat down, he saw the uniform still staring at him. Just for fun, Russo changed his hair color to green, then red, and then zebra. He got into a rhythm, had his whole body cycling through the spectrum. The uniform shook his head and walked away.

The clock on the wall said it was just past eight o'clock. If he had gone to school, he'd be sitting in Geometry waiting for Mr. Holt to finally lose it and start openly groping Tina the Suck-Up. It was easy enough to imagine, to project onto the front of Tina's locker in a drive-by reconcile, but to see it in person? Russo smiled, buried his face in the ample cleavage of his fantasy.

Sometime later, the uniform returned with a man in a dark suit. He had one of those too-square jaws that made him look alien. The fact that he was a full foot taller than Russo didn't help either.

"Mr. Washington, this is Agent Eric Tavarez."

Russo's throat went dry. If they were bringing in an agent…

"Can we hurry this up?" asked Eric. "I've got a thing."

The uniform nodded and opened the cell door. He pulled out his baton and pointed it at Russo. "Now you stay put."

Russo wanted to say something witty, but he couldn't take his eyes off Eric. The agent was staring at him intently, as if trying to see through him. Or through his façade.

"Your palette, please," asked Eric. The uniform motioned to the desk sergeant and had him bring over an EPD tablet. Eric held it for only a few seconds before handing it back. Without another word, he left the room.

The pressure that had been building at the back of Russo's head began to lessen, but the look on the uniform's face kept relief at bay.

The uniform studied the image before turning the palette around and saying, "Mirror, mirror…"

Russo's mouth went dry as he took in the picture. Over the years, he had changed his appearance so many times and the reflective veneers had always backed up the lie. But this picture, it looked so strange, so foreign.

He barely even recognized himself.

THREE
ROSALIA

There was nothing redeeming about the physical education program at Easton Central High School, not when Coach Baird's idea of good exercise was to run in place for half an hour while a pastiche of inspirational landscapes scrolled by on the walls. It would have been better to get outside, have some fresh oxygen instead of the recycled air that smelled faintly of body odor. Still, Rosalia put in her time like an obedient student. If it wouldn't have thrown her off balance, she would have closed her eyes and pretended she was somewhere else.

The pretending part was easy; all she had to do was reach out and reconcile the wall into anything she wanted to see, though at the moment her mind was too foggy to imagine anything worth emulating. It was still early, and her body was mostly asleep, going through the motions for the sake of a good grade. Like most mornings, she was just trying to survive, trying to deal with the aftermath of a night spent reconciling.

Someone had to pay for the self-prescribed sleep deprivation.

She smiled at that, thinking it was worth the trouble if she got to spend the majority of her time doing the things she wanted. The dazed fatigue of waking was better spent on first period P.E. anyway.

The only moment of clarity Rosalia had had since she rolled out of bed that morning had been in front of the school with Deron as he lamented his inability to find time to read. That was typical; he was nothing if not a reliable procrastinator, though she did consider the alternative—that maybe he shared her desire to do the things that mattered, instead of those that had no true bearing on the world. That he hadn't read the story was inconsequential in the larger picture. It was only necessary because he had an exam on it later. Without that test, the story became pointless, just a jumble of words on a palette.

Rosalia nodded as she walked, her rhythmic breathing forcing a *yes* out of her mouth. Glancing at the readout on the treadmill, she saw there were still five minutes remaining. Under some circumstances, five minutes would be a nothing interval. If spent with Deron, perhaps playing a game or just watching the turtles sun themselves at Gillock Pond, the time would have passed in an instant. But with her body breaking down and the pain building in her lungs, each second ticked by like a slow drip from a faucet. The only choice was to look away from the numbers, try not to think about them.

The woods ended as the stationary runners veered right and came upon a clearing. A couple hundred yards away was a welcoming oasis with three palm trees set in an equilateral triangle, the tips leaning in towards the center. A hint of fresh water sparkled between them and Rosalia could almost pick out its aroma over those of her classmates. It was a satisfying image, no doubt, but ultimately it was just a high-tech version of a carrot on a stick, another virtual reward for real labor.

When the machine began to slow, she leaned forward and stretched her legs by letting them slide to the end of the treadmill one at a time, each extension bringing a slight tingle to her calves. Finally, the belt stopped altogether, and she stood up, surprised to find the tightness in her chest gone. Though she hated to admit it, the constant jogging had done wonders for her endurance. Plus, it had kept her slim at a time when no amount of reconciliation could hide a fat ass.

Rosalia grinned when she looked over and saw Deron doubled over next to his treadmill. He had his hands on his knees and was gasping for breath as if he had just run a marathon. She felt the strange sensation of effortless walking as she approached him; her legs still thought she was on the treads and were pushing harder than they needed to. It wasn't until she was right on top of him that he looked up, still gulping air.

"Good jog?" she asked, putting her hands on her hips.

"Sure," he replied, between breaths.

"Come on, stand up. You need to open your airway." With a little prodding, she got him to straighten up. "Put your hands on your head and lean back. That'll help you get some air." She let her hand linger on his shoulder.

"This isn't the alley behind the Y, Ms. Collier," warned Coach Baird.

A chorus of snickering made Rosalia remove her offending hand. There was gratitude in Deron's eyes though and that's all that really mattered. It took a moment for the blush in his cheeks to lessen.

"So you're a doctor now?" he teased.

Rosalia scoffed in reply. "You don't have to be a doctor to know basic things about your body. People spend so much time focused on their veneers that they don't realize what's going on underneath." She touched her sternum, drew Deron's eyes to the center of her soaked t-shirt. "See what I mean?"

He looked away casually, as if her breasts held no sway over him. "Yeah, under your shirt."

"What's that?" She gave him a confused smile.

"I'm interested in… realizing what's under…" He trailed off, then added, "Your shirt."

"Oh," she replied. "This I knew."

"Fifteen minutes, people. Let's hit those showers. I don't want to be smelling you in the halls all day." Coach Baird's voice boomed in the room, a side effect of yelling at the lacrosse team after school.

"Can you get out of next period early?" asked Rosalia.

Deron raised an eyebrow as they shuffled towards the exit.

"I can tell you about the book you didn't read." It sounded too judgmental the second it came out, so she tempered it with a smile.

"Ah yeah, the book." He shrugged. "If you think it'll help."

"Couldn't hurt."

"How are you going to get out of Drama?" he asked.

Rosalia laughed in response, putting her hand on his shoulder again. "Mrs. Hawkins is a pushover. I'll just tell her I'm having *women's troubles*. Seriously, that's what she calls it. As if bleeding—"

"Well," interrupted Deron, "this has been both informative and disgusting. Perhaps we can discuss your biological processes again at a later time?"

"Dork," she replied, kissing him quickly on the nose.

"Once more and I'll be writing you up, Ms. Collier," said Coach Baird. "And you shouldn't encourage her, Mr. Bishop."

"She beats me if I refuse," explained Deron. He gave Rosalia a wink and then disappeared into the boys' locker room.

Rosalia presented Coach Baird with her most innocent veneer, but he didn't seem to find it amusing. He pointed to the girls' locker room and she acquiesced with a giggle. She didn't blame him for his tough demeanor; it was his burden to maintain order amongst a gaggle of hormone-crazed teenagers. She couldn't think of a harder job in the school except for whoever had to clean up after the boys in their locker room. Already their hollering spilled into the hallway.

Not that the girls' locker room was a bastion of civility; the snide remarks and judgmental glances made it a minefield of self-doubt. Rosalia did her best to stay out of it, to ignore the comments about someone's thighs or the contents of their bra. All she had to do was focus on the basic sequence of events that would get her in and out with the minimal amount of fuss. Even the nudity didn't bother her anymore; the desire to get out of her sweaty clothes and into a cool shower outweighed any lingering sense of shame.

There were always a few whispers as she passed the other girls, comments about Deron and conjectures about how far they had gone. Mostly, the talk just put pictures in her head, visions of what it would be like if she ever went to bed with him. Smiling at the thought, she stepped into the shower room and felt a wave of steam pass over her face. In the stalls, a few of the girls were already soaping up, trying to get clean without getting their hair wet.

The first drops of water were cold, but they warmed quickly as Rosalia put her face under the stream. It felt like a soft massage on her eyelids, little pokes and prods around her mouth. She parted her lips, drew in some water, and pushed it out again. The sudden deluge moved down her chin and neck, reminding her of Deron again. Unlike on the treadmill, here she could close her eyes, put away the bright and flashy world for a moment and live just within herself. It was a state of consciousness that she was always trying to teach Deron about, but he seemed more interested in the real and physical, as most boys were. Still, there were moments when he almost understood, when they would sit together with their eyes closed, not talking, hands barely touching, and be satisfied.

Rosalia withdrew from the waterfall and brushed her hands over her eyes. On her right, Ilya's head appeared over the neck-high partition.

"What are you thinking about?" Her veneer was slight at best, making her smile more sincere than its reconciled counterpart. Although they had shared classes for most of the year, it was the first time that Ilya had ever really engaged in conversation.

"Nothing," replied Rosalia, dispensing some soap into her palm.

"My grandmother says that when a woman closes her eyes and sways to music only she can hear, she is always thinking of a man."

"Then you know who I was thinking about."

Ilya smiled thinly. "I heard you guys went all the way," she whispered. "Is it true?"

"What do you think?"

"It's hard to tell," she admitted. "But there has to be a reason you're so calm compared to these other girls." She motioned with her head to the stall across the aisle.

Rosalia glanced back and saw the borderline anorexic body of Vera Delgado covered in suds. She huffed and said, "Not even a good fucking could solve *her* problems."

Ilya giggled as she pulled her hair together behind her head.

"Can you keep a secret?" asked Rosalia, leaning closer to the wall. Her shoulder touched the cold tile, sending a small shiver up her spine. "We haven't actually done it."

"Oh," said Ilya. "So you're using it as incentive. Me too."

"Who are you seeing?" Rosalia was happy to change the subject.

"No one right now."

"Any leads?"

She shook her head, turned away to wash the shampoo from her hair. "I think I've played enough of the Central field. Though Deron's friend is kinda cute, right?"

"Sebo? Have you ever listened to him talk? He's all veneer and no substance."

"Yeah, but we're all that way."

"Maybe," said Rosalia, dialing off the water.

Ilya stepped out of her stall at the same time, but unlike Rosalia, she held her towel in her hand instead of wrapped around her body like a normal person. "Hey," she said, before Rosalia could walk away.

"Yeah?" Even though she told her eyes not to move, they still managed to inventory the slender Ukrainian.

"See you in Pre-Cal?" Her smile didn't match the banality of her question.

"Sure."

Rosalia resumed her trek to the lockers and sat down on the bench facing hers. For a moment, the image of Ilya's body flashed in her head but before a verdict of envy or judgment could be rendered, it was gone. Ilya might have been a model in the making, but Rosalia didn't consider her more attractive than herself. Looking down as she dried her legs, she examined her body, wondered if Deron would ever prefer Ilya's petite European curves to her own proportions.

With a smirk, she pulled her bag from her locker and extracted the plain, unreconciled clothes. They were all the same dull gray, but they wouldn't remain that way. All it took was a little concentration and she could be dressed in any style she wanted. Within reason, of course.

FOUR
DERON

Between classes, the halls of Easton Central were a mix of vibrant colors and positive reinforcement. Every square inch of real estate had a non-threatening image or a piece of sound advice. Sometimes it was overwhelming; Deron wasn't always in the mood to be accosted by virtual cheerleaders or by flashy ads that promoted regular attendance and good citizenship. Now in his third year at Central, he had learned to tune out the audio-visual bombardment.

When classes were in session and the halls were empty, it was as if the school grew depressed. The colors faded, the animated characters shuffled off into the virtual distance, and the maxims of the school's guidance counselor lost their hypnotic luster. It made Deron think there was nothing sadder than a reconciled wall without an audience. They didn't even take notice of him as he walked by.

Getting out of class had been easier than expected. All he had to do was fake an illness, say that he was going to throw up and better to do it in the nurse's office than at his desk. So with twenty-five minutes left in the period, he ventured out into the hallway with the confidence only a signed note from a teacher could afford. At the intersection with the atrium where he should have turned right to go to Nurse Hendricks' office, he turned left and ducked into the dead-end hallway between the two band rooms. The door to the storage room was slightly ajar and Deron took a quick look around before he slipped inside.

In the dim lighting, he could only make out the general shapes of various instrument cases and music stands with sharp edges pointing every direction. Deron made his way around the French horns and trombones to a small alcove hidden around a corner. There, he found an old couch that hadn't been reconciled in years, a dusty piano with a few broken keys, and most importantly, Rosalia.

She smiled at him from the couch and beckoned him to sit down. The cushion made a whooshing sound when he dropped onto it. At Rosalia's level, her smile didn't seem as genuine anymore, as if she were just using it to mask some minor trepidation.

"What's wrong?" he asked, nudging her with his shoulder.

There was hesitation in her eyes and Deron was observant enough to see the flicker of color pass over them. She looked away for a moment and then said, "I've decided to kill Russo."

She was joking, of course, but Deron played along. "Why?"

"He put up another shop," she replied. The palette in her lap was blank, but when she placed her thumb on it, the colors started cycling in from the edges. It took her a moment to reproduce the image, as if she were having trouble remembering it. At last, she angled the palette towards Deron so he could see the finished product.

"Uh oh," he said, taking in the artwork. "It looks like I've spilled peanut butter on my vagina."

Rosalia tried to stifle her laughter.

"And that Terrier looks like trouble," he continued, nodding his head thoughtfully. Suddenly, his face went sad, and he put his hand to his chin. "Can I ask you something serious?"

"Yeah." Her face mirrored his expression.

"Does this picture make my legs look fat?"

Rosalia bit her lip. "Why aren't you mad?"

"What's there to be mad about?"

"This was in the girls' bathroom!"

Deron sighed and stood up. It was just another shop. Disgusting yes, but no more vile than the hundred others Russo had created.

"It's not a big deal," he said, sitting at the piano. He struck a few random keys, thought it sounded like a familiar melody. "There's not a girl in this school that thinks I have a puss."

"Seeing is believing," said Rosalia in a sententious tone.

"So really, the basic premise of the picture is wrong."

"Yeah, but maybe everyone thinks that if you *did* have one, you would put peanut butter on it and try to attract small dogs."

Deron struck a dissonant chord on the left side of the keyboard and threw his hands up in the air in mock outrage. "Who knows what I would do if I had a vagina?! I mean, if you think about it, waking up one day as a girl would probably break me mentally. All bets would be off."

"That doesn't excuse—"

He turned on the bench and put up a finger. "I think it does. A lot of human behavior could be explained away by the phrase 'but yesterday I had a wang.'"

Rosalia's face squirmed; she was cute when she tried not to laugh.

They stared at each other for a full minute before Deron finally said, "Puppy love."

"Gross!" She lifted her palette, threatened to throw it at him.

Deron put up his arms to protect his face as he returned to the couch. They struggled briefly for control of the weapon before he managed to disarm her. As he stared at his new prize, a reminder about the exam popped up in the corner, bringing the reality of school back to the equipment room.

He handed the palette back to Rosalia and asked, "Are you gonna tell me about the story or not?"

"I don't know," she replied. "Can you keep your mind off interspecies sex for ten minutes?"

Deron's eyes narrowed. "Who could really make that promise?"

"A normal person." Rosalia's palette dimmed and then returned with the title of the story in large, baroque lettering. "Now, pay attention."

He tried to listen, really made an effort to concentrate on what Rosalia was saying. She used her palette to help him imagine the characters, gave them faces she estimated from their written descriptions. In the right context, it would have been invaluable in preparing for the upcoming test, but Deron found himself scrutinizing her veneer. He spent several minutes staring at her hands, at her fingers as they moved across the palette, correcting a smudge here or an errant line there. She was a natural talent at reconciliation, always had been.

Although they first met in elementary school, they never even shared a teacher until junior high. It was one day in seventh grade that he found her sitting alone in the cafeteria, her breakfast cooling, untouched. Sitting down beside her, he noticed the faraway look in her eyes.

"You okay?"

Rosalia shook her head and cleared away whatever thoughts had been bothering her. Her face grew more animated and she replied in a normal voice, "Oh, hi."

"You just wake up or something?" he asked.

She gave a nervous laugh. "I had a bad dream last night. Can't shake the feeling, you know?"

Deron nodded, having had his share. "Tell me about it," he said. "I'll tell you what it means." He didn't have the first clue what dreams really meant, but he was confident he could make a joke on any subject and hopefully put a smile back on her face.

"It was strange," she began, her eyes drifting away again. "I was walking in a park or something, at night. There were little lampposts on the sidewalk. Then there was a building, a really old one. It was made of some kind of pink stone. I went inside and it was really quiet."

Deron's mouth opened in amazement. The table under his backpack had begun to shimmer and through it he could see the faint image of an expansive green lawn broken up by a cobblestone path. As Rosalia recounted the dream, the image bent to her narration. He saw the interior of a premodern building where the walls were polished stone instead of reconciled patterns. There was even a wobbly avatar of Rosalia walking through the cavernous rooms like a lost child. When he looked over at her for confirmation, he found that she had closed her eyes.

A crowd formed as Rosalia crested the stairs. Surprisingly, they all remained quiet, entranced just as Deron was by the scene playing out on the large table. The haze disappeared and everything became a level of crisp that rivaled reality. A window came into view, cut right into the stone walls with smaller bricks forming its outline. It was flat on the bottom and angled to a point on the top. Rosalia's avatar paused at the window, put her hands on the sill, and stared out into the night.

In the distance, the ocean swelled with waves too large for the current scale. Above, stars poked out from the black sheet, twinkled in their own carefree way before the brilliance of a full moon blotted them out. It was too close, taking up too much real estate in the infinite sky. Every detail was clear. Every crater and ridge looked dangerously real.

Deron smiled at Rosalia. There was a look of intense concentration on her face as if she were pushing the memory down through her arms and out her fingers. Then, a tremor appeared at the edge of her mouth, followed by a flaring of her nostrils. Deron looked back at the table in time to see the moon crashing into the ocean, sending up an enormous spray that shook Rosalia free of the window. Her avatar struggled to stay on its feet even as the world moved out from under her.

Gravity shifted; trees broke free and floated into the void, their roots still clinging to clumps of earth.

The laws of physics ceased to exist. Staring at the horror in the avatar's face, Deron suddenly understood. He put a hand on Rosalia's shoulder to bring her out of the trance. She looked at him, hesitated, and then shrugged his hand away.

"That was beautiful," said a girl with a pink bow in her hair. When Rosalia didn't respond, she pointed to the table. The image was already fading.

As the crowd dispersed, Deron asked quietly, "How did you do that?"

"Do what?"

"You made it look so real."

Rosalia pulled her bag into her lap. "I don't know. It's just something I can do."

She left him sitting there at the table with the memory of the moon looming in his mind. He had always wanted to ask her about the dream but never got a chance. Now they had been dating since the winter break, and he had almost forgotten all about it.

A pleasant bell ringing in the distance broke Deron from his reflection. Rosalia was still talking about the story and his eyes locked onto her glistening lips as they came together to form sounds. She always wore some kind of lip gloss; Deron thought the Root Beer tasted best. Caught up in the imagined moment, he leaned forward to kiss her.

Rosalia put a hand on his shoulder. "Come on, we should go."

"Do you remember when we first met?"

"At Bowie?" she asked, slipping her palette into her bag.

"No, in junior high. Remember in the cafeteria? You reconciled a whole table."

"Are you sure that was me?" She led him to the door and peeked outside.

"Yeah, you did a moon crashing into the ocean and the Earth breaking up."

"Why would I do that?"

Deron detected a hint of nervous laughter. "It was a dream you had, right?"

She closed her eyes briefly and let out something resembling a sigh and a curse mashed together. When she looked back at him, her eyes were that rare kind of serious. "Yeah, I remember."

"Do you still have that dream?"

"Yeah."

"Does it always end the same way?"

"Always," she replied. Her fingers were soft as she took his hand and pulled him into the hallway.

FIVE
RUSSO

As unquestioned ruler of Easton Central High School, it was Principal Ficcone's job to mete out punishment when one of his students got out of line. How he went about it depended on whether parents were in attendance. If they were, his veneer remained professional and his tone even. If they weren't, if instead the student just happened to be accompanied by two Easton uniforms, then the principal wouldn't even bother with formalities. Whether it was his scowl or tone of voice, the man had no trouble expressing his anger.

Some judge in a black nightgown had issued summary probation for Russo, telling him that trespassing was a serious offense and that if he wanted to occupy the building, he would have to purchase it legally. He then instructed the uniforms to drop him back at campus. That was half an hour prior, and Russo had made the mistake of mentioning an exam in English. They slowed down on purpose, even pretended to get lost when they got close to the school.

Ficcone thanked the uniforms for their efforts and escorted Russo into the school. They crossed one hall and entered the main atrium, but when Russo started drifting to the right, the principal spoke in a tight voice.

"Where do you think you're going?"

Russo paused, pointed towards the hallway. "I have English now."

"No, you *had* English twenty minutes ago. You're tardy."

"But, but, I have an exam!" Russo pretended to bite his nails.

"Save it, Russo. We're going to ISS."

Russo had spent most of his high school career as a guest of the In-School Suspension room and despite his protests, he actually preferred it to regular classes. It was where teachers sent unruly students or those unlucky enough to be in the hallways when the second bell rang. It wasn't that different from any other classroom, except that the teacher changed depending on the period. Russo assumed there was some kind of forced lottery where the losers had to take turns babysitting the delinquents.

Ficcone held the door open for him. "He's all yours, Mr. Lee."

A hidden smile crept onto Russo's face. Mr. Lee didn't give a damn what happened in the ISS room, so long as no one got seriously injured. Turning around to find a seat, his smile turned into a full-blown grin when he saw Jalay sitting at the back of the room. He kicked his chair as he took the seat next to him.

"I see you made it, bitch."

"Yeah," replied Jalay, raising his eyebrows slightly. "What happened to you?"

"Probation," he announced, as if it were some kind of consolation prize.

"I wonder why he chased you and not me."

Russo thought about it for a moment. "Probably had something to prove. You know uniforms; they're just waiting for the chance to beat up on some innocent kid who happens to walk through a door."

"There were signs," Jalay pointed out.

"I didn't see any!"

Mr. Lee looked up for a moment but said nothing.

"So what're you doing in here anyway?" asked Russo.

Jalay beamed.

"You posted the shop?"

"Yeah. I did all the bathrooms on the first floor, but a freshman caught me upstairs. She screamed."

"Just like a bitch," said Russo. He sat chuckling for a moment, thinking about how Jalay's face must have looked when he was discovered. Usually, they just posted the shops on the walls in the hallway, but those never lasted long. Bathrooms made more sense, since teachers shied away from them in favor of the lavish facilities in the teachers' lounge.

"So how was jail?"

"Been there, done that." He waited to see whether Jalay would believe him or not, but he seemed more interested in the palette on his desk. It already had another shop of Deron on it. "But something weird happened."

"Yeah," said Jalay, absorbed in his creation, "I remember the first time I got raped in the butt."

Mr. Lee cleared his throat enthusiastically.

"Shut the fuck up," said Russo, kicking the back of Jalay's leg. "I'm serious."

"It couldn't have been that bad. They don't know who you are."

"They know." He paused, thought back to Eric's inquisitive eyes, and shuddered. There was something invasive about the way they stared into him. "I mean, the regular porkers didn't know shit, but this one guy…"

Jalay turned in his seat.

"He was an *agent*. And he looked all fucked up like some kind of alien or one of those Japbots but with normal eyes." The two orbs flashed in Russo's mind. "He looked at me."

"Lovingly?"

"No. He just kinda stared."

The sound of the door opening got Russo's attention. He looked over to see a girl with long hair and an emo veneer enter the room. She went straight for a desk at the front without a word to Mr. Lee.

Russo continued, "He *saw* me."

"He saw you?"

"That's what I said. The fucker shopped me like it was nothing." Russo turned back to Jalay. "He reconciled the *real* me."

Jalay dismissed the idea with a shake of his head. "Fuck you."

"He's a Seer." It even sounded like a real thing.

"Then you should have *shown* him something."

Russo thought of his palette. They had taken it away when they put him in the cell; it was the first time his personal workspace had ever been in someone else's hands. Pulling the dormant tablet from his backpack, he found foreign fingerprints lining the piano gloss around the edges. He used his shirt to smooth away the swirling dirt, returning it to the pristine condition it deserved. With a quick mental command, he opened a rectangular portal and brought up his start page.

"You're not viewing pornography are you, Mr. Rivera?" Mr. Lee's question made the emo girl in the front row look up and cast a sideways glance at Russo.

"Just studying for next period," said Russo in a voice that wasn't really his. Bringing up a search box, he started querying the network for cases of people who could undo veneers without having to touch the surface. Most of it was bunk, unverified accounts that he dismissed as easily as UFO sightings. There were some common threads, but no clear evidence that it wasn't just propaganda, a way for the police to keep the citizens in line. After several minutes of futile searching, he pushed the palette away in disgust.

"Nothing?"

"No one is talking about Seers." Russo touched his chin, picked at an invisible pimple. "What kind of magic does that?"

"Which? The seeing through veneers or convincing people they don't exist?"

"Either," he replied, shrugging. "Shit, both!" He turned to Jalay with wide eyes. "That means there's something they're not teaching us! Some other magic that makes this veneer bullshit look simple."

Jalay raised his hand, but Mr. Lee didn't look up. "Mr. Lee, do they teach advanced magic in college?"

"Ha," he replied, "you think you're going to college."

"What about me?" asked Russo.

"Maybe if they leave the doors unlocked," said Mr. Lee.

"What if I turned my life around and became a model student?" This made emo girl laugh, to which Russo replied, "Nobody's talking to you."

Mr. Lee sat up straight and folded his hands on the desk. "No, Mr. Chapman, they do not teach advanced magic in college."

"Why not?" asked Jalay and Russo in unison.

"Ms. West?" Mr. Lee raised an eyebrow at emo girl.

She turned halfway around and spoke while staring out the window. "Because there's no such thing as magic." Then, gravely, "There's nothing magical about what we are."

"What about veneers? I can paint a picture on a wall just by thinking about it."

"Yes," said Mr. Lee, "but you don't say any spells, do you? You don't wave a wand. You just do it. It's not magic; it's just a part of what you are."

"The real magic is that we can even think," said the girl, still engaged in her daydream. "That we can speak and listen and smell and touch. And nobody knows how we do it, even after thousands of years. No one understands that magic."

Jalay frowned and looked at Russo. "I'm confused. Is there magic or not?"

"I think," said Russo, pointing an accusatory finger at Mr. Lee, "that all teachers are part of some conspiracy to keep us from realizing the true extent of our powers. Think about it. Those skyscrapers they put up. Every Christmas they change color, change design. Is someone actually climbing out there and reconciling each panel? And if not, who could do such a large area? No!" He crossed his arms in protest. "There has to be more to it."

Mr. Lee chuckled and returned to his palette.

"There's only one problem though," said Russo after a few minutes of silence. "I still remember him. If Seers were such a big secret, why would they let me leave with that information?"

"Because no one's gonna believe someone like you," said Ms. West.

Before Russo could respond, a bell rang out in the hallway.

"You going to next period?" asked Jalay, standing up.

"Dunno. Doesn't seem worth it anymore."

"What does? Come on, maybe one of the shops is still up. I hid a few in good places."

Russo smirked. "What'd you end up posting?"

"Just your standard PB and V."

Jalay's response didn't make any sense, but Russo was too preoccupied with the stoic Eric to care. In the hallway, he made his way through the crowd, looking at all the veneers, all the façades that never faded but rather intensified as time went on. Everyone at Easton Central was beautiful, attractive in their own conformist way. But beneath those veneers, they were normal, as normal as Russo had looked when Eric reconciled his real face onto the EPD tablet. It was a neat trick, but it was also power.

A power that Russo wanted more than anything.

Blinking away the possibilities, Russo settled into his normal gait, pushing aside the sophomores when necessary and sneering at the girls who rolled their eyes at his approach. They would learn soon enough. As soon as he became a Seer, he would show the world what they really looked like under all that pretty wrapping.

SIX
ROSALIA

She waited in the hallway while Deron turned in his test. Although her Pre-Cal class was on the other end of the building, Rosalia wanted to make sure he had been able to answer the questions. It was standard interpretation stuff with no right or wrong answers. And Deron was nothing if not a competent bullshitter.

He was one of the last students to exit the classroom and the smile on his face almost resembled relief.

"How did it go?" she asked, falling into step with him.

Deron laughed maniacally, whether at the question or the answer, she couldn't tell. After the fit passed, he said, "Let's pretend that didn't happen."

"The crazy laughing or the test?"

"Both," he replied, putting his hand on Rosalia's back.

She felt that familiar electricity on her skin at the touch of his fingers. Deron was frugal with his public displays of affection, which made them all the more wonderful. The teachers frowned on such intimacies, the other students jeered at them, but Rosalia felt it was the most natural thing in the world to have that tiny bit of pressure at the small of her back, pushing her along ever so slightly. At the end of the hallway, his hand moved to her elbow, then slipped past her hand.

He disappeared without a goodbye, just an expression on his veneer that Rosalia had decided meant undying love but that could have easily been an upset stomach. As she lost his face in the crowd, another came into view, the sharp lines and angry eyes of Russo Rivera. His presence sucked all the happiness out of her, made the brief stroll with Deron seem like a distant memory. He was walking with his longtime accomplice, Jalay, who was basically a Russo clone without a grasp of portion control.

The little shit actually smiled when he saw her staring.

Russo, on the other hand, was looking away with forced detachment. A confrontation with him would have been fun and likely satisfying, but all it would accomplish would be the revelation that his antics were getting to her. Murder, as practical an idea as it was, would probably result in her incarceration, unless she hired someone else to do it. She sighed, imagined the possibilities. It was too extreme a reaction, killing someone just for making fake pictures of her boyfriend.

Besides, Deron didn't seem to care that much. At least, he never consciously showed it.

There was a substitute teacher in Pre-Cal, which meant Rosalia would have the whole hour to plot her revenge. If Russo wanted to play the shop game, then it was time she responded in kind on Deron's behalf. She spent most of the class running through the gamut of embarrassing pictures on her palette, shying away from the man on animal action and eventually settling on an almost artistic depiction of Russo and Jalay in a mutual tugfest. Her fingers moved deftly, adding various background items like S&M gear and bottles of lubricant. Finally, she added past shops of Deron, a little blurry, to an assortment of photos on the floor.

A giggle off to the left got Rosalia's attention. It was Ilya, sneaking a peek from her desk.

"It's funny," Ilya offered.

"I know," said Rosalia, admiring her work. "Now, to expose it to the masses."

"You could post it in the bathrooms. I just saw one this morning—"

"Yeah, it's been done. I need something epic."

Rosalia saved the photo and closed her eyes, letting her mind drift into an arena where ideas were birthed and destroyed in fits of rapid chaos. She made a mental catalog of every available surface in the school, coupled it with the ease of reconciliation, and ranked it by risk of getting caught. The main hallways were no good; there were cameras on constant watch. A presentation in the cafeteria might work, but it would only get one of the lunch periods. Whatever the solution, it had to hit every student at once.

"You love him, don't you?" asked Ilya. She had a playful look in her eyes.

"How do you figure?"

"Defending his honor." She gestured to the blank palette. "It's very noble. Especially for a high school boyfriend."

"So because we're in high school our relationship doesn't matter?"

Ilya's eyes went wide for a second. "Just saying…"

"What *are* you saying?"

She began playing with the tips of her hair. "It's just the way it is. These relationships don't last. We go off to college, we meet new people, try new things. Doesn't leave a lot of room for the people we reconcile in our lockers."

Rosalia started to respond, but a sudden idea stopped her. "You're a genius," she said, bringing up a new portal on her palette.

The Ukrainian had been right; a locker was a place that every student visited at least once a day. At Easton Central, each locker came equipped with a portal on the front that displayed the student's class schedule, lest they forget. But a central database provided that image, meaning all Rosalia had to do was find a way in, change the schedules to her shop, and bingo, instant saturation. She smiled thinly, already imagining the glorious fallout.

Of course, it was all easier said than done. She already knew that the central server was only accessible via palette as an interactive menu system. To even bring up the menu, she would need a faculty ID card, which most teachers pinned to their shirt or hung around their necks. She wanted to help Deron, but stealing a card from a teacher would be too risky.

"Never mind," she said, dropping her palette onto the desk.

"What's the matter?"

"I need an ID card to get into the server." When Ilya didn't flash recognition, she added, "Only teachers have them."

Ilya nodded and looked away. Tiny lines on her forehead danced, until finally she whispered, "Do subs have cards?"

"Probably..." Rosalia followed Ilya's gaze to the front of the room. There, in the corner of the sub's desk, was an ID card on a lanyard. "But how?"

"Don't worry," said Ilya, reaching for her blouse. She dragged her finger down the seam and popped three of the buttons.

"What are you doing?"

"Come on, bring your palette." Ilya slid off her chair and started towards the front of the room.

Rosalia hesitated, but the smile on Ilya's face was too inviting. She stood and followed, clasping her palette to her chest. When they reached the sub's desk, she circled around to the left while Ilya stood dead center and leaned over at the waist.

"Can you help with this problem?" asked Ilya, sliding her palette across the desk.

From her vantage point, Rosalia could see Ilya's breasts spilling out of her shirt, though it was clear the bra was doing most of the work. The sub barely glanced at the math problem before his gaze fell on the free show in front of him. He stammered out a useless explanation, pausing every time his eyes got lost in Ilya's naturally occurring parabolas.

Rosalia took the opportunity to place her palette on its side on the desk, shielding the ID card from the sub's view. While Ilya flirted, she concentrated on moving the plastic strip to the reader on the front of her palette. With one quick motion, she scanned the card. After a moment, the sub's picture appeared, followed by an *Access Granted* message. Setting the card back on the desk, Rosalia cradled her palette in her arms and cleared her throat.

"Oh," said Ilya, feigning an epiphany, "we were supposed to take the derivative here, right?" The sub looked up at her, annoyed to have his attention diverted.

Rosalia thanked the sub for his help and Ilya took the opportunity to straighten up. Together, they hurried back to their desks.

"Not bad," said Rosalia. "You're kind of a slut when you want to be, huh?"

"When you've got it," she replied, sticking her chest out a little.

With the faculty menu glowing on her palette, Rosalia attacked the system in earnest. All it took was a little thought about the personal pastimes of Principal Ficcone to break in. Once in the database, she reconciled her shop and overwrote every schedule. Even though a knot formed in her stomach, she couldn't help but feel pleased with herself.

"It's child porn, you know that, right?"

Rosalia looked at Ilya, confused.

"Russo and Jalay are still minors," she explained.

After considering that for a moment, Rosalia replied, "Well, that's bad news for a certain substitute teacher, isn't it?" She shook her head. "They really should do background checks on these people."

"Don't you think that's kinda harsh?"

With forced solemnity, she replied, "In every war, there are casualties. Even the noblest of men must be sacrificed for the good of the whole."

"I guess."

"He was leering at you. A man his age ogling a girl like you… It's unseemly."

"So you're saying he deserves whatever he gets?"

"Everyone deserves something."

Ilya snorted. "Deep," she observed.

Rosalia nodded. The clock in the corner of her palette was still ticking, inching closer to the top of the hour. Soon, the bell would ring and students would pour into the hallways. Some of them would end up at their lockers only to find Rosalia's creation staring back at them. Then the laughter would start, growing from a mild chuckle to a thunderous roar. Heads would turn, seek out Russo and Jalay as they walked the halls with undeserved confidence. The pointing. The laughing.

The crumbling of Russo's tough veneer would be magnificent.

"Thanks for your help," said Rosalia, without looking up.

"It was fun," Ilya admitted, her voice pensive. She made a noise like she wanted to say something else, but decided against it. Then, giggling, "He's staring at me."

"No." Rosalia tried to hide her smile. "He's staring at both of us."

Ilya spoke in a Russian accent, "Dirty old man."

"Da," agreed Rosalia.

SEVEN
DERON

"Things going the way they are and the world moving the way it does, it's any wonder we're stuck here trying to understand the big picture when in fact, there is no picture at all, just a veneer, a model of the world the way they want us to see it. Except there is no they, only us; only *we* have the power to change the world and while the life-size models on my walls are aesthetically appealing, they don't really make my bedroom a better place. It's just polish for a reality we can never truly escape."

Deron nodded, pretended to listen. It was the only way to respond when Sebo started babbling in his rapid legato. Only after he had put down the final period was the listener able to extract any meaning from the long string of syllables. He owed his smooth delivery and intimidating verbosity to Dahlstrom Academy, which he attended until the middle of seventh grade when, as he put it, the banality of systematic study became too overwhelming. Most of the time, he spoke like a normal person, but when he wasn't concentrating, he slipped back into the lofty prose as if it were the rule instead of the exception.

"This brings up several good questions," continued Sebo, his tone more suitable for a large crowd than an audience of one. "First, how can we ever trust what our eyes are telling us? They're just biological entities after all, no more equipped to understand the world than a turnip."

At that, Sebo's eyes began to cycle through the primary colors. It was something he had learned to do when he was younger, practicing repeatedly until it was second nature. Deron found it entertaining, especially when they grew stale, usually when Sebo got lost in simultaneous speech and thought.

"Of course, there're some exceptions. Pornographic images, for one, when strewn across all the lockers at once are artificial, but they elicit very real emotional reactions."

"You saw that, huh?"

Sebo pulled out his palette and reconciled the now famous shop with a simple touch of his finger. He tilted it towards Deron. "Impressive work," he said, pointing to the crisscrossing of arms between Russo and Jalay. "You can't even see the shop marks." His face grew serious, darkened just a little around the eyes, which had turned an impassive brown. "Why do I get the feeling you didn't do this?"

"You don't know that." Deron looked away, pretended to be interested in a pair of girls walking towards the far end of the plaza near the street. They were underdressed for the weather, at least as far as short skirts and wind gusts were concerned. When he looked back, Sebo was still staring him down.

"Well, first, you don't have the talent, we both know that. Second, even if you could, you wouldn't."

"You saying my testicles are of insufficient size?" asked Deron, mimicking his friend's speech. He leaned back slightly and turned his head to the sky. The immense clouds reached high like plumes of smoke.

"Something like that." Sebo pointed to the image. "Observe the detail around the penile area."

Deron squirmed and tried to resist looking. When Sebo pushed the palette towards his face, he put up a defensive hand.

"Look how uncomfortable you get just looking at it. No one as homophobic as you would be able to craft the male sex organ so lovingly. What we have here is an artist who is not afraid to visualize the wang." He paused, mulled something over as if selecting from the cafeteria menu. "A real wang-thinker."

"So a—" started Deron.

"Yes! A girl!" Sebo beamed triumphantly. "I figured it out. The artist must be female." He lapsed into a trance for a few seconds, during which his eyes continued to cycle, once taking on a bright pink that made Deron chuckle.

"There's nothing homophobic about being repulsed by the sight of another man's..." Deron waved his hand around uncertainly.

"So you would characterize your condition not as anti-gay but more anti-wang?"

"Yeah."

Sebo huffed. "This from the guy that consistently sucks balls in Destined 4 Death." Something flashed across his veneer, a changing of gears so sudden that Deron didn't even have time to respond. "Did you get that trailer I sent you? They're going to be demoing the new map packs in Paramel this weekend."

"No," said Deron, reaching down for his backpack. He pulled his palette into his lap and thumbed the corner. A second later, his portal filled the screen. Multimedia clips played silently in the lower left; one of them showed the Destined 4 Death Marauder Pack. He selected it and made it fill the screen.

He was only thirty seconds in before the instant messages started popping up, as if the entire school had been waiting for him to sign on so they could congratulate him. Some were from people he knew, other kids that shared his classes, but a lot were from relative strangers, normal students who were just happy to see someone put Russo in his place.

"Unwarranted acclamation is what ruined the first half of the twenty-first century. History shows that people who accept credit while fully aware of their lack of merit eventually get found out and castrated."

Deron shot him a glance.

"So you *are* listening."

"Yeah," said Deron, clearing away the messages. "I'm starting to think Rosalia had something to do with this."

"Agreed. Who else besides her would keep a catalogue of Russo's work? Shop or no shop, they're still naked pictures of you."

"Either way, she's doing exactly what Russo wanted." He sighed and a picture of Rosalia appeared in the corner of his palette. She was smiling at him, her eyes and lips a bright and fiery red. "I thought if I just ignored him long enough, he would stop. I guess I just made it worse."

Sebo clucked his tongue. "Post hoc ergo propter hoc."

"Yeah, helicopter carrot rock to you too."

"It means you can't attribute your actions to his response just because they followed."

"So," said Deron, scratching his cheek, "he's a dick regardless?"

Sebo nodded approvingly. "And we've already established your aversion to dick."

"Now you understand."

"Hold on," said Sebo, putting his hand up. "Let's not get all slap-happy just because you admit your homophobia. We're missing the real issue here and that's that Rosa has engaged the enemy." He mimed taking the handles of a truck-mounted machine gun. "This means retaliation on Russo's part and nobody knows the extent of his dickishness. At the minimum, I see backlash towards Rosa. Worst case? Maybe violence."

"Since when do you care about her?"

"Make no mistake. Every moment you spend hypnotized by Rosa's tits is time we could be spending taking down the Death Monkeys in D4D. That's important to me. War is progress and it's the kind of release I need after suffering the indignity of public education every day."

"That was your choice," Deron pointed out.

"I have tried finding other players," he continued, ignoring the interruption, "but no one even approaches your skill level. You're a killer at heart, no matter what your veneer says."

"Lady-killer maybe," said Deron, chuckling.

"However, as your best friend I understand that over the years I will become a second thought to any girl with a low-cut shirt and a tight ass." He put his hand on his chest and sighed. "I've accepted that. So to keep myself in good spirits, I simply remember that you have a habit of reconciling your girlfriends in semi to fully nude states and that when you ingest a sufficient amount of illegal drugs, you tend to reproduce them subconsciously."

Deron reconciled a blushing effect. "Whatever."

Sebo's sudden laughter made the couple sitting across from them look up. "It was only a month ago," he said, reconciling a memory onto his palette. "I can't believe Rosa never told you."

"Told me what?"

"We were hanging out in your room," he began, the scene appearing under his hand. It showed Deron's bedroom, fuzzy but recognizable. The lights were out and the three of them were huddled around a low flame in the center of the room. An open window provided a breeze that made the light flicker. "Your mom was at some show, so we were smoking out."

"Oh yeah," said Deron, feigning recall. "I remember that night…"

"No you don't. You crashed out early because you're a woman and can't handle your smoke. So Rosa and I are just sitting there making fun of you and then we notice the floor is changing colors, but we can't make out what it is. She starts laughing her ass off and I drag you to the wall and put your hand on it."

Deron closed his eyes and muttered, "Crap."

"Crap is right. Rosa and I are about to lose it, but then you open your eyes and start staring at her like she's your favorite stuffed animal."

"What does that mean?"

Sebo waved the question away. "So I thought there was gonna be a show because you looked like you wanted to do her right then and there."

"And?"

"You pussied out. All you did was draw naked pictures of her on the wall."

"So what? I reconciled the wall. Anyone can—"

"That's the thing with you. You're the only one I know who does it involuntarily. You know why I remember that night so well? Because after you stared at Rosa you turned the whole room into a shrine to her. And it was fast too." Sebo pinched at an imaginary wall in front of them. "Boom, picture here, boom, tits there. And perfect detail too, way beyond your skill level. Of course, when Rosa saw what you were doing, she went to the wall and started reconciling something else. You guys fought it out for a long time."

"Why didn't she just move my hand away?"

Sebo's smile deflated. "I don't know. Maybe that's her competitive nature. She wanted to see if she could out-reconcile you."

"She can," admitted Deron. "No contest."

"Yeah, when you're trying, but when you're messed up, you become something else. I think you've got a mental block of some kind. I mean, I already know you're a killer, but now I think you might actually be an artist too. It's just your brain keeps getting in the way of that."

"It does what it wants to do."

"Yeah," replied Sebo, distracted.

Deron followed Sebo's gaze and saw that Principal Ficcone had popped his head out of the cafeteria door and was surveying the students. When he spotted Deron, he started walking towards them.

They both wiped their palettes clean out of habit.

"Mr. Bishop," said the principal, "I would like a word with you."

"Sure," replied Deron, fully aware that his agreement wasn't required. He stood and slung his backpack over his shoulder.

"Watch that trailer later," said Sebo. "I want to go tomorrow."

"I'll go if I'm not grounded," he replied, looking to the principal.

"That's entirely up to your mother, Mr. Bishop."

Deron fell into step behind Principal Ficcone, unsure of what trouble awaited him.

EIGHT
RUSSO

Ficcone's office smelled like day-old deodorant mixed with burnt coffee. It tried its best to appear like the room of an important man, but Russo knew that every veneer in sight was just trying to mask the truth. The Berber carpet, the reconciled bookshelves, and the accents of purple and silver after the school's colors couldn't hide the room's true purpose. Students sat in one of two chairs in front of a large desk, behind which the principal would sit and hand out sentences like a judge.

Like a court room, thought Russo.

Instead of the city's seal hanging behind the desk, there were floor to ceiling windows that looked out over the plaza in front of the school. Instead of a jury box, there was a fish tank with a solitary Beta in it, swimming back and forth for no reason, stuck in a prison within a prison. Rubbing at his nose, Russo looked over the fake diplomas and certificates on the wall—fake in the sense that there wasn't really a frame or paper, just some good shadow reconciliation to make it look three-dimensional. No matter what the veneers on the wall said, nothing gave Ficcone the right to judge, even though that seemed to be his primary function.

Russo slouched in his chair and tried to take his mind off the impending trial. Unlike the real thing, he wouldn't get to hire a lawyer or be able to present any evidence. When the principal walked through that door, he would simply hand down his sentence, having decided the verdict long ago.

Exhibit A: Escorted to school by uniforms.

If Ficcone wanted to give him shit about being late to school, then he had taken his sweet time coming up with a punishment.

Exhibit B: The shop of Deron and his dog.

Groaning, Russo put his hands to his face and tried to press away the indignation. The sons of bitches were really going to try to pin that on him? It didn't even make sense for Russo to post something like that, not after the constant threats. Ficcone had to be the dumbest motherfucker ever. He probably thought he was doing a good thing by punishing Russo, thought he was helping a troubled kid get back on the right track.

Un-fucking-likely.

The door behind Russo opened, and Ficcone walked in with that waste of space Deron trailing behind him. Though his face was impassive, Russo could see the subtle alarm appear in Deron's eyes when he saw who else was in the office.

"Please have a seat, Mr. Bishop." The principal moved behind his desk and sat down in the cushy, high-backed chair. He sighed as he swiped his hand across the dormant portal in front of him.

Russo looked at Deron out of the corner of his eye, daring the bastard to look over for just one second. "Do it," he commanded mentally, "turn your fucking face so I can put my fist into it."

"Gentlemen, you know why we are here." He had that look on his veneer, that I'm-gonna-fuck-you-sideways-whether-you-cooperate-or-not kind of expression.

Of course, he only looked at Russo like that. When his gaze fell on Deron, suddenly he was all flowers and rainbows. Well, it wouldn't last, not when he found out what Deron had done.

"This is the reason," said the principal, lifting a palette containing the shop of Russo and Jalay standing over the photos of Deron. Someone had censored it with black bars before entering it in the school's database. "I would like to know why you felt the entire student body should be exposed to this filth."

"Don't look at me," sneered Russo. "Ask him!"

"You two have been at each other's throats since you first stepped foot on my campus and I want to know why. This feud has to end."

Russo bit his lip at the sight of Deron smiling. It'd be a lot harder for him to smile if he were missing all of his teeth.

Ficcone sighed and leaned back in his chair. He eyed his charges one at a time. "What am I going to do with you two? It's my job to keep the peace around here, which is why I can't let this go on any longer. From now on, there will be no unauthorized reconciliation outside of normal classroom activities. That goes for the both of you."

"Or what?" asked Russo.

"Excuse me?"

Fuck it—might as well go for broke. "Or what? How are you going to punish Deron when he puts up another picture of me?"

"I didn't make that picture," whined Deron.

"Who did what makes no difference now. And to answer your question, Mr. Rivera, the punishment will become clear to you at the appropriate time. I *will* tell you that this'll be the last time we discuss this issue. From now on, I'll have no choice to include the authorities and your parents."

Deron winced—probably scared of what his mom would do to him, something extreme like take away his video games.

Russo looked down at his hands in his lap. He clenched them into fists and released them slowly. When he looked up, he saw Principal Ficcone shaking his head.

"Sometimes I don't know if you young people understand the gift you've been given." He stood and walked towards the window. With a quick tap of his finger on the glass, the principal reconciled an ornate floral design that spread out in waves and covered the entire window. "To reconcile is to change the world to your liking. You can create beauty or you can bastardize reality." He motioned to the palette on his desk. "Right now, you take this ability for granted. You think you have the right to reconcile anything you want, anywhere you want. But you forget this is a society of people who can do the same thing you can. Reconciliation is a privilege of living here, not a right."

The hell it wasn't. Reconciliation was a part of human evolution, a magic usable by age six, earlier if you could get into Dahlstrom Academy. It could no more be taken away than... His mind jumped back to the morning's events. It was also impossible to see past the veneer, but some jackhole in a fitted suit had done just that and with considerable ease.

"I see that bothers you, Mr. Rivera. You never considered someone could take your ability away? You don't even want to know what they do after that. Do you think Easton has any use for someone who can't reconcile?"

"If it was true—" he replied.

"*Were* true," corrected the principal. "*Is* true." He turned again towards the window. "If you asked someone a hundred years ago whether what we do would ever be possible, they would laugh at you. But here we are, using innate abilities to effect change. Think about what that means for just one minute and you'll realize your petty squabbles aren't worth the effort. We do something now that people couldn't do before. Think of what we'll be able to do as our power grows."

"How do you stop someone from reconciling?"

Ficcone shrugged. "That I don't know, Mr. Bishop. I've never met anyone who couldn't reconcile. No one has."

"Because it's crap," said Russo.

"No," replied the principal, his voice somber. "Those who can't share in the veneer have no place here." His lips moved to say something else, but he changed his mind. "Just trust that you don't want to know what happens to people who keep making pictures—"

"I haven't made a goddamn thing since you told me to stop last year! Check my palette, you won't find anything."

"What about you, Mr. Bishop?"

Deron answered meekly, "I don't have the skills to shop like Russo."

Fucking right you don't.

"So this is no longer about you two, is it? Your quarrel has spread to the masses, become a hobby for the great reconcilers to prove their worth." Anger flashed across his face. "You two sit back and watch the mayhem while I have to explain to parents why their children are being exposed to obscene images. Or to the police why my halls are filled with kiddie porn! You are putting my job in jeopardy and I can't allow that." He squared his eyes at Russo. "So maybe they won't take away your power for this, maybe you just pay a fine or spend some time behind bars, but you're establishing a pattern. It all starts here." He pointed emphatically to the floor.

It was all just posturing, Russo decided, all empty threats meant to keep him in line. But it wasn't enough. The principal might have been the Big Shit when it came to Easton Central High School, but off campus he was just another clueless adult that needed to grow old and die so that the younger people like Russo could take over.

"Detention," proclaimed the principal in his official voice, "both of you, two weeks."

"The hell?!" Russo almost rushed the desk, but only his feet moved, shuffling backwards slightly.

"Language, Mr. Rivera." Then to Deron, "You will serve your detention with the sophomore class. I won't have you two antagonizing each other. Now, that is all, gentlemen. Mrs. Rhodes has your write-ups."

Deron stood and left immediately, but Russo approached the desk.

"What do you want, Russo?"

He leaned over slightly. "If you ever threaten to take my power away—"

"Three weeks detention."

"Fuck this," said Russo. He turned and left the room, ignoring the principal's extension of his sentence to four weeks. It didn't matter; he had no intention of serving it anyway. Ignoring the note in Mrs. Rhodes' outstretched hand, he headed into the hall. To his left, Deron was just turning the corner towards the cafeteria. He ran to catch up with him, but when he made the turn, he saw Deron talking to the lunch monitor at the cafeteria doors. When he looked back, Russo pointed a finger at him.

"We have business," he warned, then turned and stalked angrily back to class.

NINE
ROSALIA

Deron told her about it between classes, but it wasn't until the news got around during last period that Rosalia discovered it was because of her shop that he now had to spend two weeks in detention. He didn't seem angry when last they spoke, just the same kind of blissful indifferent that he had always been on the outside. But then he didn't show up at her locker after school, didn't give her the opportunity to apologize for her lapse in judgment. She even walked by the detention room, saw him sitting alone in the back, but he never looked up.

Rosalia lingered in the hallway, wondering if she should knock on the door or just barge in and deliver her apology by way of a kiss. Ultimately, she settled for an instant message, a simple *sorry* with no punctuation or clichéd emoticons. She waited the requisite few minutes for a response, but nothing came through. He was probably busy copying words out of the dictionary.

By hand, she thought, and shuddered.

Outside, small groups of students were still milling around, sharing one last story before hurrying home to their rooms so they could talk to each other on IM. Rosalia walked through them undisturbed, though at times she did feel their eyes on her back. They were staring at her because of Deron, because of the threats Russo had made, threats that rumors had exaggerated. He was either going to punch Deron, beat him up, or just plain kill him. Nobody knew for sure, but that didn't stop them from adding their own flair as the story passed from student to student.

She passed a line of waiting buses, all of them humming in their idle states. A knock on a window made her look up, and there she saw a concerned Ilya looking down at her. The Ukrainian raised her too-perfect eyebrows as if to ask, "What do we do now?" Rosalia could only manage a weak smile and an undecided shrug in return. What does it matter to her anyway, she wondered. It wasn't as if Deron were *her* boyfriend, her sole reason for existing.

Detention was as much her punishment as his. That hour after school, before their parents got home from work, was theirs to spend together. They would take the long way home, window-shopping at all the boutiques on Parker Avenue, her for the clothes, him for the latest video games. What they did wasn't important;

it had become a ritual, their way of maintaining what little companionship they could afford. They could chat in the evening and throughout the night, see each other briefly between classes, but nothing rivaled the simplicity of just being together, of being walked home by her protector and confidant.

The further Rosalia got from campus, the less the noise of the student rabble affected her. It was quiet in the adjoining neighborhood; the empty driveways meant the worker bees were still away. The houses eventually faded away, replaced by condos with reconciled walls that displayed advertisements stretching ten stories high. Beyond that was Parker Avenue, a long, four-lane thoroughfare that almost bisected the city, growing out from downtown in a vine of commerce. It was a strange break to go from homes to condos to businesses and back again in the space of six blocks, but that was what they called progress.

Rosalia didn't mind the artificial border between home and school. It was, after all, a welcome rest stop, a place to hang out with her friends and feel like a part of downtown without having to suffer the homeless or the crowded streets. Parker was a never-ending Main Street feeding the suburbs, full of restaurants and cafés, dress shops and sim parlors—everything an attention deficit disorder kid needed to get by in the world.

Their favorite place was Café Perrault, a blend of coffee and smoothie shop. The portals on the walls were always alive with some new distraction, programming geared towards the afternoon student crowd. It was the kind of place she could sit with Deron for an hour, ordering perhaps only one drink, without being pestered or told to leave.

"What'll you have?" asked the barista in a sickeningly cheery tone. She had a smile on her veneer so artificial that it looked like her boss had reconciled it for her, one of six variations from the Café Perrault Customer Service Manual.

"Fountain of Youth smoothie," said Rosalia, realizing she had entered Perrault's out of habit and a subconscious desire to avoid going home.

Finding her usual table near the front windows, she sat down and set her bag on Deron's seat. Her palette glowed when she pulled it out of her bag, making her hopeful for a message, but it turned out to be from Ilya.

"Fun game I found," wrote Ilya, with a resource locator following.

The barista reappeared as the game was beginning to load and she slipped a napkin and the tall drink onto the table next to Rosalia's palette.

"Enjoy," she bubbled.

Rosalia smiled politely even though she was aware that everything the barista did was for the sake of business and had nothing to do with being a nice person, inside or out. But that was the way with everyone. She could spend a lifetime trying to guess what was under the veneer of people she passed on the street, but even on her deathbed she wouldn't be one inch closer to the truth. Returning her attention to the palette, she watched the game's menu fill the screen.

It was called Canvas and was evidently some kind of massively multiplayer art game. A small avatar representing Rosalia appeared on the screen, nothing more than a collection of white spheres that begged to be reconciled. Rosalia put in the necessary effort, taking care to sculpt her in-game character into something approaching reality, or at least, veneered reality. Once dressed, the avatar moved out of the small entry room and into a larger gallery. There, the pentagonal shape gave her five expansive walls. She approached one of them, feeling the blankness as a dull ache for color and shape. After staring at it for a moment, a dialogue bubble appeared in the air beside her. Blue letters exploded from a jumble to form a message.

"Reconcile your dream," it said, and then popped out of existence.

How it qualified as a game wasn't exactly clear to Rosalia, but she played along, reconciling an expansive vista from a viewpoint high atop a mountain. Her avatar stood on the precipice of a waterfall, surrounded on both sides by lush overgrowth that encroached on two stone statues. Only their overall shape was discernable, giving the impression of two men standing guard over the water's escape. Where the land fell away, Rosalia brought up distant terrain, alive with animals and birds, their cries and calls filling the gallery with the music of the rain forest.

In the distance, the horizon sizzled under the heat of an orange sun. Above, the clouds cycled through various pastels before settling into a pleasing pattern. Rosalia drew her avatar back to examine the masterpiece. It wasn't her best work, but it had killed half an hour. She sat back, sipped the last of her smoothie, and waited for another prompt.

Again, the bubble appeared next to her and when the letters fell into place, it read, "As you dream, others dream."

Rosalia watched as her avatar's hand came up and touched the wall. The canvas gave way and there was a rippling effect as she moved through her image and ended up in another gallery. This one already had two walls painted and when she examined the one behind her, she found a scene similar to what she had reconciled. The water ran a little faster and the trees were in a different stage of bloom, but overall, they were undeniably alike. All those little choices could have gone another way, she realized. Maybe if she had ordered a Blueberry Swirl, she would have been more inclined to make the statues more visible, as in this version, where the one on the left was clearly a woman and the other a man.

On the very edge of the cliff, Rosalia noticed a young girl with a folded piece of paper in her hand. It felt familiar and after a few seconds, she realized that it was a scene from the story she had read for English. That was why the veneers were so similar; another student at Central had interpreted the words in the same way.

Amused, she turned her attention to the other wall and saw a painting of a sandy beach that featured crystallized grains at the forefront. The rest of the beach expanded beyond it, folding into a horizon, into a starry sky, into galaxies. It made her think of nighttime, of the moon that wasn't shown but that was clearly reflecting light onto the sparkling sand.

So that was the game. Person A drew a picture and through it, could access the pictures of Person B. It made sense as a social process, lending at least some credibility to the idea that people with alike dreams would also be alike. But who among her classmates had drawn this picture? Had she already stepped away to another beach?

Whoever she was, she shared something with Rosalia and that meant reciprocation. Approaching a bare wall, she began reconciling her strongest dream, a nightmare made fresh in her memory at Deron's insistence. The moon stretched from floor to ceiling, sitting regally above a surge of water and a beach that revealed itself as the ocean drew away. A familiar sense of dread crept over her skin as she finished the detail on the moon's surface. Cracks and craters, all with the right shadows, were as real as anything she would ever see in her lifetime.

Now, she wondered, who shares this dream with me?

The avatar stepped up to the wall and put its hand on it, but nothing happened. The image did not ripple as before and there was no way to move forward. Off to the right, the bubble appeared.

"The unique dream uniquely," it said, accompanied by a short melody on a violin.

Great, she thought. Even games knew that she was alone, that some nightmares existed just for her.

"But I knew that already," said Rosalia, surprised she had said it out loud. She wiped her palette clean and brought up her portal again. The time in the corner said it was now four-thirty. Detention would have let out fifteen minutes ago, so Deron should have been on his way home. Turning in her seat, Rosalia put her feet up on the low windowsill and scanned the pedestrian traffic. It didn't take more than ten minutes to get from the school to Parker, and whether he went to her house or straight home to his, he would have to pass right in front of Perrault's.

Her thoughts turned to forgiveness, hoping he wouldn't be too angry to continue their relationship. Plastering the entire school with her shop had been a bad idea and she cursed herself again and again. It wasn't her fight, wasn't her place to be inciting more hostility in what Deron considered a nothing war. He did his best not to let it bother him and she should have respected that.

If he showed up angry, it would be justified.

A flash of something tall and lanky caught her attention outside, but it was just a random teenager kicking a skateboard along the sidewalk. Where is he, she wondered. Part of her started to worry, but she tuned it out.

Believing is seeing, she reminded herself. Just believe that Deron will walk around the corner and he will.

Any minute now.

TEN

DERON

The cramp started in his palm, concentrated around his pinky, but soon it spread to Deron's entire hand, making it ache in protest against the archaic activity. Copying words from a dictionary wasn't just boring; it was a form of physical punishment. He couldn't remember the last time he had actually written something down instead of typing on a virtual keyboard, or easier still, just reconciling the text onto a palette. It was kind of brilliant when he thought about it, giving the students something to remember their detention by. It was much more of a deterrent than the impotent paddles that hung in Principal Ficcone's office.

Just as Deron began to imagine the principal sitting there in his fancy leather chair, the man himself stepped leisurely into the classroom. He nodded to Mr. Lee but didn't say anything. Instead, he scanned the room, locked eyes with Deron, and then beckoned him with a quick turn of his head.

Grateful for the early exit, Deron closed the frayed dictionary and stood up. As he crossed the front of the room, he glanced at the clock. It was already ten past four; five minutes of reprieve was all he got.

In the hallway, Principal Ficcone settled into a slow amble and Deron tried to mirror the nonchalance. "How is your hand?" he asked with practiced sincerity. He tried to evoke informality by clasping his hands behind his back.

"It hurts," admitted Deron. "I'm not used to writing."

"It will get easier. By the end of next week, you'll be a pro."

Deron said nothing in return, didn't feel like thanking him for the hollow attempt at comfort.

The principal coughed and cleared his throat in the way only old people found socially acceptable. "I need to apologize to you, Mr. Bishop."

"For what?

"The photo that was passed around today. You didn't make it." His voice was quiet as if he didn't want anyone else to hear him admit his mistake. "I checked with your teachers and they all agree that you don't have the skill to reconcile something like that."

Deron laughed despite the insult. He never thought being a substandard reconciler would one day get him off the hook.

"Don't beat yourself up about it. A lot of people struggle with the veneer. I didn't realize my full potential until my third year of college. You'll learn to master it soon enough."

"So does this mean I don't have detention tomorrow?"

Principal Ficcone reached out and put a heavy hand on Deron's shoulder. "No, detention still stands. You see, although I accept that you didn't make the shop, I do think you know who did."

Deron searched for a response, but didn't feel confident he could say anything without broadcasting that it was a lie.

The principal removed his hand. "And I don't think you're going to tell me who the true artist is."

"Even if I knew," said Deron, trying to steady his veneer. If it wavered even a little bit, the principal's keen eye would catch it.

"I know," he replied, nodding, "which is why you will continue to serve detention. I will let the matter drop and leave it to you to make the necessary corrections with your conspirator."

"She was just—" He caught himself, but it was too late.

"She?"

They were at the end of the hallway and to the right, the outer doors opened to the back of the school. Deron could see the sidewalk give way to a green lawn. Further on, it dipped to reveal the tops of the bleachers by the football field.

"As I said, I'll leave it to you. I trust we'll have no repeats?"

It wasn't fair, him thinking Deron had wanted any of this. But those were the cards on the table, and it was no use thinking about the ones that had been burned. He shook his head feebly and looked away.

"Then have a pleasant evening, Mr. Bishop." Principal Ficcone walked away, resuming his frantic pace as he rushed about the school tending to the late-afternoon fires.

Rather than follow the man that had just berated him, Deron exited through the double doors and took in a breath of fresh air. It smelled good, not like the stale air-conditioned environment inside the school. Finally free to pursue his life again, he thought of Rosalia. She was probably waiting for him, sending him messages every few minutes, holding a one-sided conversation until he got out of detention. Smiling, he unhooked the plastic clasps on his bag to take out his palette, but a flash of movement in the distance distracted him.

Deron paused, could just make out Sebo's signature jacket. He was sitting on the bleachers on the other side of the field and when he noticed Deron, he waved invitingly. Sebo wasn't one to hang around after school, so if he had waited for Deron to get out of detention, it must have been for something important.

Trudging across the lush lawn, Deron felt his shoes sink into the ground as if it had just been watered. He veered to the left to take the stairs down the small incline and as he did, he saw Sebo jump down behind the bleachers. He was reckless like that, both in reality and in the games they played. Destined 4 Death was always a crapshoot with Sebo; sometimes he liked to play it straight, stay in formation, and coordinate with other players. Other times, he preferred to interpret the term *run and gun* literally and forgo all planning. That was the way most of their nights ended, devolving into mayhem when everyone was tired and ready to quit.

At some point, Deron realized that the guy kneeling on the ground behind the bleachers wasn't Sebo. It was in the shoes; Sebo always wore reconciled throwback Skechers. Though nothing in Easton was constant, Deron had never known him to wear the heavy boots that the person in front of him was sporting. Then there was the general shape: broad shoulders that didn't match up with Deron's memory, hair that peeked out from under a baseball cap, and finally, the design on the back of the jacket. Up close, there was no mistaking the imitation.

Of course, all of this became clear a moment too late. By the time Deron had processed this new information, a blunt object was already moving swiftly through the air.

It made contact with Deron's head just above his right ear and sent tremors through his vision. He watched half of the world sizzle, as if the outlines of every object suddenly had a million volts passing through them. His body leaned dangerously, threatening to fall over. Stumbling, Deron managed to raise his eyes to see Russo standing there, a twisted smile on top of his normal veneer. He held a metal pipe in his hand. It looked dull and out of place in the shimmering world.

"I told you we had business."

Despite the pain, a knot of worry began to tighten in Deron's chest. He knew this wasn't going to be like Destined 4 Death or even the kung fu movies he watched late at night. No part of what was about to happen would be choreographed for the safety of the actors.

It would be brutal and it was going to hurt. A lot.

Deron opened his mouth to respond, but Russo had already closed the distance. Putting his hands up to protect his face, Deron felt the pipe strike his forearms, making them tingle at first and then burn a moment later as the signals reached his brain. It came from the left, from the right, and sometimes glanced off his arms and connected with his head. He leaned backwards, tried to escape the barrage, but couldn't hold his balance. The next moment, he was falling, collapsing onto the worn grass.

His right eye felt funny, as if someone had their thumb pressed to it. There was too much of a blur to even tell which way was up.

The taste of blood distracted Deron long enough to miss the pipe flying through the air; it caught him on the left side of his temple. Stars erupted all around him in little golden explosions, as if reality were just a palette and some first-grader learning to reconcile had suddenly decided that what it needed most were twinkling decorations. He knew the pipe was nearby, even reached out for it, but before his fingers could locate it in the grass, Russo's boot came crashing down on his elbow.

Russo pulled Deron to his feet and shoved him towards the bleachers. The metal scaffolding was rounded but solid—so much of his body had already gone numb that he barely registered the impact. A few feet away, Russo stood alternating from one foot to the other, jacked with adrenaline, concentration in his eyes.

It was time to *rage quit*, as Sebo put it. Had this been a session of D4D, the frustration of losing would have already taken over and he would have jacked out and punched Sebo in the chest for cheating.

Deron groaned, tried to spit out the excess blood but ended up with most of it on his chest and hanging from his chin. Something felt weird in his head, like a fluctuating headache. He couldn't concentrate on anything, not even the fleeting hope of being able to fight. He flashed on Rosalia and her misguided attempt to help him. There was anger there, a desire to punish, but that only made him furious. She loved him more than any girl before her. She wasn't to blame for the beating.

Russo was.

Summoning his last bit of strength, Deron shot forward and began swinging. He felt his fists land a few times, but mostly they caught the wind. Russo moved around them with ease and the smile on his face was so bright that it broke through the blur in his vision. The momentary adrenaline rush waned, and Deron felt the twinge in all his joints. His lungs burned and his lips tasted tears. Closing his eyes for an instant, he retreated to the eternal darkness, only to be pulled back by something bony catching him on his jaw.

All the grass in Easton was engineered to be soft and pleasing to the eye, but nowhere was it more comforting than the patch behind the bleachers at Easton Central. It reached up to support Deron as he fell, cradling him as best it could. He ended up face down in a heap and in a moment of perverse humor, he imagined what the chalk outline would look like when the police discovered the body. Not that they would need to chalk up the grass when they could just reconcile the scene on their palettes, but still.

He shook his head to clear the insanity, to inventory his situation.

Only one eye still worked and he used it to search the horizon for Russo. He found him standing near the bleachers absently brushing the blood away from his shirt.

Be careful with that, thought Deron, I need that blood to live.

It only took Russo a moment to reconcile the stains away. Evidently satisfied with his handiwork, he walked over and stopped a few inches away from Deron's face.

Deron could see his boots plainly, shiny black with thick soles. They probably weighed a few pounds each. Russo said something, but the ringing in his ears drowned it out. It was probably just another threat, something about his superiority—it didn't really matter. All Deron cared about were those boots. They were all he could see. They were immediate. And when one of them disappeared, the insanity revved up. It began talking to the boot, asking it where it was flying away to. Was it not happy there on the grass with Deron? There was nothing better than lying face down in Easton's finest Bermuda.

The mystery of Russo's boot unraveled in a brief and unsatisfying way. After being gone for an eternity and Deron unable to locate it in time and space, he felt it reappear on the back of his neck. His brain registered the sudden pressure of the boot's treads as they pushed unevenly at the base of his skull. They tore a little at first, making the skin redden in instant bruises. But that was all minor compared to the crushing weight that followed.

And just like that, the other boot disappeared too, along with the rest of the world.

Lights scrolled by overhead. It was a common scene from movies and in-game cinematics, a way to show the viewpoint of a victim whose existence had become nothing but waiting for the next light to come up and the last one to sink out of view. They should have put something over his eye, the one that worked, the one he couldn't command to close no matter how hard he tried.

There was nothing worth seeing out there, nothing he wanted to see. But they kept showing him things. Lights, mostly, but then someone turned his head. It was an ancient nurse with bad skin and wrinkles around her eyes.

When his head went the other way, Deron saw a doctor with a mask over his face. He had large eyebrows that ran from one side to the other uninterrupted. He was squinting at Deron, looking for what?

A realization: this was no hospital.

He was in some kind of abandoned building with blank evercrete walls that looked like they hadn't been cleaned in years. Everything was covered in dirt and grime.

The nurse pulled his head again and Deron felt something pop in his neck. He screamed a silent and horrifying scream. He saw the alarm in the nurse's eyes, the red veins that stood out so brightly around her iris.

There were harsh words muffled by the pain.

All at once, it began to fade. The scrolling lights grew dimmer. Something passed through his field of view. It vaguely resembled a palette, except that it was blank. Cold and blank. Like the world. Like existence.

Deron took a labored breath, felt as if his lungs were filled with shards of glass.

They couldn't keep him there, no matter how loudly they yelled at each other, no matter how fast they pushed the gurney. He was going to a place beyond the confines of his mortal body.

He couldn't see it, but he believed it was there.

ELEVEN
ROSALIA

Three weeks.

Three weeks to the day of not being able to see Deron, of curt updates from his mom that merely confirmed he wasn't dead yet. It was time spent sitting in uncomfortable plastic chairs in the hallway, of being hassled by the nurses, and being told that his girlfriend had no legal visitation rights. That's what hurt Rosalia the most, the idea that their relationship meant nothing in the adult world. She cared for him with all her soul, but because they weren't married, because they were minors, she couldn't walk through the door to his room and hold his hand.

So she waited—in the hallway, in her room, and in the private bubble she adopted while at school. There were rumors flying around, about Deron, about the list of suspects, though she knew without asking that it had been Russo. The looks from her classmates varied, but they never spoke to her. Only Ilya dared mention Deron and in desperation, Rosalia found herself spending more time with her new friend.

Three weeks was a long time any way it was counted. The walks home were lonelier, the evenings seemed to drag on a bit longer than usual, and the dreams were not as vibrant as they used to be. Something about the nightly ritual of subconscious reconciliation needed fresh images of Deron, reminders of the feelings she experienced while in his company. So her dreams remained empty, mirroring her life. Ilya tried to convince her that Deron wasn't gone yet, that he was just resting up for his triumphant return.

It was kind of her to say.

The hardest part was seeing Russo in the hallways those first few days and not being able to do anything about it. If he had been his normal asshole self, treated her with the same contempt that he held for everyone else, she might not have suspected him. But there was the way he averted his gaze, subtly avoided coming into contact with her, as if his secret would be revealed just by looking closely at his face. He wasn't being nice to her; he just wasn't going out of his way to be a dick.

It was a text message from Deron that had brought her to the micro-park a few blocks away from her house. This one was aimed at an older crowd and eschewed the normal playscapes for benches set apart at a respectful distance around a large pond. A flat rock at its center was caged by the water, giving the turtles a safe place to sun themselves. At night, it was empty. The pond contained nothing but a reflection of the universe, an alternate world where maybe things like this never happened.

Rosalia had wanted to be there when he got out of the hospital, but Deron was discharged during fifth period, and she didn't find out until well after school when he messaged her asking to meet at Gillock Pond. And although she had been waiting for that moment for three weeks, she was surprised to find herself overcome with apprehension. She tried to push it down, bury it amongst the other unnecessary emotions, but it kept bubbling up. There would be time for apologies later. For now, she just wanted to see him, just wanted to put her arms around him and hold him forever.

He appeared like a ghost in the night, a hazy form moving beyond the manicured hedges. It was the slight limp that gave him away, the kind of awkward locomotion that a free-floating spirit wouldn't have bothered with. Rosalia could only stand and watch him approach. She felt his eyes on her, saw the determination and frustration flash like ripples in his veneer. At ten paces, he stopped.

Rosalia tried to smile, but she felt the tears coming and had to look away into the infinity of the pond. It had been forever, but it still felt too soon to look into his eyes. She listened to his footsteps and then the rustle of his jacket as he sat down on the bench. He was so close, yet he hadn't touched her yet.

"Rosie," he said, his voice as perfect and as soft as ever.

"Deron," she replied, barely getting the second syllable out before her voice cracked. She wanted to turn to him, throw her arms around him, and beg forgiveness. Her body felt rigid, immovable, locked in the hunched-over sadness that had gripped her since she heard the news that Deron was in the ICU at Easton General, that a group of wandering gypsies had beaten him to a pulp and left him for dead on the football field.

"My mom says you tried to come see me in the hospital."

"They wouldn't let me in." It felt good to tell that to someone who would care. "They said 'family only.'"

Silence again, only the insects chirping in the distance. It was barely after eight but the entire city seemed to be asleep. There was something special about the park that dimmed the faraway neons of downtown, muffled the noise to afford its occupants some peace. From her pocket, Rosalia extracted a worn tissue and wiped at her nose. If Deron hadn't picked up on the sadness in her voice, he was sure to know her feelings now.

"The first time I opened my eyes, I couldn't move," he began. There was a drowsy quality to his voice, as if the memories could only be replayed in slow motion.

Rosalia felt her throat tighten.

"But I got better. They put me under a few times and each time I came back better." He reached for her wrist and pulled her into the seat next to him. "I never stopped breathing. I didn't die."

"Almost."

"Doesn't count. I've got a few scars, but nothing a little reconciliation can't fix."

He was right; she couldn't see anything through his veneer. His face was still the same shape, still looked the same as it had for the past few years. The damage was completely obscured, which meant it wasn't real. When he smiled, she almost believed him.

Slipping her wrist from his fingers, Rosalia swallowed hard. It was time to do the thing she had come to do. Her fists balled up, pressing her fingernails into her palms. It shouldn't have been that hard to tell him how she felt. Moreover, it was the right thing to do, but admitting guilt meant admitting she had put her own desires before his when she had no right to do so. How could two words be so difficult?

"Rosie, I—"

"I'm sorry," she interrupted, blurting it out before she could change her mind. It hung in the air for a few moments, answered only by the crickets around the pond.

Finally, Deron said, "You don't have to be."

It was hard to talk when the edges of her lips were plunging involuntarily. "That doesn't mean I'm not. He almost killed you."

"But he didn't."

So it *was* Russo, she thought. "I never would have done it if I thought Russo... He's a psycho, but how could anyone..."

"He has issues," agreed Deron, "but that's not your fault."

"He should be in jail."

"Probably."

In the resulting silence, Rosalia felt her anger boiling over, but in Deron's company, it had no choice but to fade away.

"Hey." He put his hand on her shoulder, gave her a little squeeze. "Do you know what I've been thinking about for the last three weeks?"

She shook her head.

"It wasn't Russo." As he said that, his hand moved to her neck. "I thought of you, of what you must be feeling, if you thought this was your fault. I actually thought that for a minute, too."

Rosalia scrunched her eyes together and turned away.

"But then I realized, there are two ways this makes sense. Either this wasn't your fault and you shouldn't feel bad."

"Or?"

"Or it was indirectly your fault." Before she could recoil in shame, he added, "In which case I forgive you. I know you. I know what you would do and why you would do it."

She couldn't think of anything to say, so she repeated, "I'm sorry." When he put his arm around her, Rosalia knew he truly meant what he was saying. It was what she wanted, but the guilt remained. Deron loved her and would probably forgive anything; couldn't he just once afford a little anger?

They sat together for a long time, not talking, just watching the pond together, the lifeless water that rippled with the occasional breeze. The smell of smoke was in the air, perhaps from a nearby restaurant. It reminded Rosalia of a bonfire and she thought of the beach, or at least, the beach sims she had run with Deron. It was the only way to go without having to deal with the garbage-ridden sand and toxic water.

That was life in Easton; everything enjoyable was just a simulation.

Eventually, the last piece of the veneer dropped into place and Rosalia felt herself speaking casually again. "Sebo misses you."

This got a chuckle from Deron, though he followed it with a groan. "I know. He messaged me like a hundred times. He wants to go to Paramel tomorrow night, but I don't know..."

"You should go," said Rosalia. "You've been cooped up for too long. Did the doctor say you could play video games?"

"Not full contact, but sims should be okay. I'd rather spend time with you though."

"Full contact?"

His teeth glinted in the moonlight. "So long as you're on top."

She nudged him with her elbow. "You pick the time and place and I'll be there."

"Here," he declared. "Now."

"In front of the turtles?"

He leaned in close and Rosalia felt his chin move across her cheek. He was nodding.

"Did they give you any drugs for the pain?"

"Yeah," he replied, "but nothing really hurts anymore. My neck just feels like I slept on it wrong." He rubbed at the base of his skull.

"It's horrible what he did."

"Don't think about it. It'll give you nightmares."

She looked at him and raised an eyebrow.

"No, not me," he assured her. "I don't really remember much of it. I think he got me on the side of my head to start with, so everything was kinda fuzzy after that."

Rosalia shuddered, tried not to imagine someone truly intent on hurting her. She buried her face in his shoulder and took a deep breath. "Feels like you've been gone forever."

"Yeah, I don't even know how I did on the English test."

"You got a C." She chuckled.

"What else have I missed?"

Of all the things, she thought. All the things that have come and gone since he was put out of commission. What news, what art, what music and shops have lived and died in that interim? She tried to think locally, to the immediate, to the things that both of them really needed. It wasn't passionate sex on a bench at Gillock Pond, nor was it simply his arm draped over her shoulder. There had to be something in the middle, a happy place that could make the world melt away, shed its color, and become background for a moment of oblivious contentment.

Forgoing any warning, Rosalia pulled herself up and pressed her lips to his. He resisted at first, but softened as she put her hands on his neck. It felt like she expected—reality with the volume on mute. Everything had been reduced to the pressure on her lips, the heaviness in her cheeks as her eyes threatened to water again.

It was a long way from her lips to her fingertips, but there was a small subroutine running, keeping track of the skin that moved under her fingers. Deron's neck was smooth—no five o'clock shadow like her dad. A large vein pulsed rapidly, increasing in tempo as she applied more pressure. She moved her hands up, cresting the edge of his jaw and flirting with the tips of his ears. It was there that she found the first stitch. She traced it up his head and behind his ear, a good three or four inches long.

She cursed the deceptive veneer.

Of course he wouldn't show her the injuries he'd sustained. He would cover it up, and he had, very convincingly. But while he could trick her eyes, he couldn't change what her fingers felt and as she continued to explore his face, she learned the true extent of his pain. The scars were everywhere: on his ears, forehead, and cheeks. She pulled back, looked into his eyes as she traced over his nose, felt the course texture of a second-skin bandage. He winced when she touched the bone around his eyes and that brief flash of pain was enough to splinter the dam and drown her in a deluge of guilt.

Without another word, Deron pulled her in close and held her tightly. Rosalia's veneer put up a fight, obscuring the tears as best it could. But eventually they got too far away, broke free of her cheek, and landed on Deron's shirt where residual reconciliation made them disappear again.

In her mind, Rosalia saw Deron's face as her fingers had felt it.

"Oh, God," she cried, unsure of how to finish such a prayer.

TWELVE
RUSSO

The Drag on a Saturday night wasn't one of Russo's usual hangouts, but he had walked its lengths several times in the last few weeks. Blending in with the crowd was easy, especially when he could just copy their veneers on a whim, be anyone he wanted for that five-block march through obscurity. The mission he had undertaken called for the utmost security, a constantly shifting veneer, a changing of color and texture so that his presence would go unnoticed. Walking amongst the very people he wished to subjugate was a necessary annoyance; they were, after all, giving him cover as he made his approach to the TNC Bank building.

They were old and young, rich and poor, yet all had the same stench of consumerism on them, coming to The Drag in the evenings to check out the recently erected booths, to see what junk the local artisan community was selling. There were necklaces, rings, and little pieces of stone—all useless, but all haggled over and bought up. Even Russo wasn't immune to the conditioned desire to acquire junk. He passed a table full of multi-colored stones shaped like eggs that caught his attention. Most were vibrant and flashy, but one egg on the corner had an understated veneer of black obsidian with a streak of red running through it. The edges of its crimson lightning bolt sparkled with electricity.

Emerging on the other side of The Drag, Russo ducked along the scaffolding in front of the TNC Bank and slipped inside. They had an expansive atrium along the front of their building, extending six floors up. The first floor opened to elevators and stairs that led up one level to a food court. There, ample seating dotted the outer windows, giving patrons a clear view of the intersection and the buildings on its corners. One of them was a tram station, and the other had the green and white color scheme of Notacorp Investments. The last building, in plain view from where Russo sat down, was the Easton Police Department.

It looked different at night, with large spotlights along its steps that shone up into the dark sky, a beacon to uniforms and criminals alike. Saturdays seemed to be particularly busy; the flow of Easton's oppressed citizens into the jail had already begun. It would continue until around four in the morning, but Russo had no intention of waiting that long again.

He had started observing the police department only a few days after his arrest and subsequent encounter with Agent Eric Tavarez, or as Russo called him, the Seer. His dreams had centered on the man's piercing eyes, seeking an explanation for how a veneer could be undone. The more he thought about it, the more he wanted to understand the Seer, to know where he had learned to harness such an amazing power, and ultimately, to wield that power himself. At one point, he even entertained the idea of committing a misdemeanor so they would arrest him again, just to meet with Eric face to face. Unfortunately, there was no guarantee that he would even get a complete sentence out before they socked him in the gut with a baton.

The only way to learn about the agent was to bump into him outside of his daily job. But so far, Russo had not seen him enter or leave the building once. The possibility of Eric being a machine, some kind of advanced cyborg, began to take shape, as far-fetched as it was.

Russo spun the black egg on the glass table and waited for its energy to dissipate. The individual sparks flew away from it, creating a barrier that encircled the already protected contents. When it came to a stop, Russo picked up the egg and examined it closely. Somewhere beneath the fancy exterior was its original color. But how could he get at that color? Looking around at the chairs and tables and large banners hanging on the tall beams, he wondered what they all looked like on the zero level. Did they even have a true color?

A casual glance backwards revealed a lumbering Jalay coming up the steps to the food court. His veneer resembled a young entrepreneur that had dropped out of college to start his own business. There was black in his hair and on his shoes, making him the very picture of a man who belonged downtown. The only pieces that remained Jalay were his eyes; they were as devious and dim as ever. He stood at the edge of the cafeteria until he spotted Russo by the windows, at which point he moved nimbly through the maze of tables to join him.

"Look who took a shower," said Russo, spinning the egg again.

"My dad made me go to church," he explained. After an unimpressed look from Russo, he added, "There were some girls there. In dresses."

"You must have pissed yourself."

Jalay pulled his chair closer to the table and set his palette on it. As he waited for his sites to load, he asked, "What have *you* been doing all night?"

Russo motioned to the police department with his head. Two cops were struggling with a rowdy drunk who had managed to pull down his pants.

"You see him yet?"

Shaking his head, he replied, "I wonder if it has a room. Or a closet."

"Closet?" Jalay tapped into his desktop, filling the palette with a browser, a notepad, and a little picture frame that shuffled through various genres of pornography.

Snatching up the egg, Russo said conspiratorially, "I think Eric might be a cyborg."

"Where'd you get that?"

"Drag," replied Russo. "This old lady wanted twenty bucks for it."

"That's a bit steep," said Jalay, distracted. His portal was displaying three photo streams at once, images culled from an array of mixed-media blogs. When one of the pictures caught his interest, he dragged his finger upwards, reversed the stream, and enlarged the photo. A young Asian girl appeared, naked, sitting on the floor with her legs tucked under her. She was looking up, somewhere off camera. Jalay dragged the image to a folder on the left, saving it.

Russo looked away, outside again to a small group of uniforms coming out of the building. It was getting close to ten, which was start time for the third shift. He had learned a lot about the way the police force operated over the last three weeks, from when shifts began to what uniforms looked like before they hit the street. There was some kind of auto-reconciliation happening when police boots came into contact with the sidewalks. The group of uniforms making their way down the steps looked like they were off-duty, but their bluish gray clothes suddenly became black after that last step. Then the standard attire took over, making them appear more menacing to the public.

"You weren't in school yesterday," said Jalay. He dragged another Asian into his save folder.

"Fuck school," Russo replied. "If I can learn to do what Eric does, I won't need high school at all."

Jalay chuckled. "Oh, I thought you skipped because of Deron."

"The fuck does that mean?"

"He…" Jalay started but then paused as Russo's face turned serious. "They let him out of the hospital. People say he's probably going to press charges."

"The hell he is!" Russo turned away. "I should have ended him."

"Sure, why not?" asked Jalay, bobbing his head sarcastically. "Let's just murder anyone who gets in your way. Don't be retarded."

Russo's fist shot out and caught Jalay on the shoulder. "I tell *you* what to do, not the other way around."

"Whatever," he replied, rubbing his arm.

Jalay had been acting strange for weeks. He was never around when Russo needed him and even though he had shown up in detention a few times, they couldn't talk. Most likely, the principal had gotten to him, given him one of those signature lectures about hanging out with the wrong element.

The wrong element.

Russo thought about what that meant, tried to see himself as everyone else did: a bully, an asshole, and an attempted murderer.

"So he lived."

"He lived," parroted Jalay. "They say he was in a coma for the first week, but it's not like he's brain damaged." A chuckle. "Well, no worse than before."

"Why didn't he tell the cops when he woke up?"

Jalay shrugged. "Who knows? He hasn't even broken up with Rosalia yet."

"Why would he do that?" Russo squeezed the egg as hard as he could, but it was solid. When he didn't get a response, he looked up and saw Jalay staring back at him.

"Are you serious?"

"Don't look at me like that," warned Russo. "Fucking what?"

"She's the one that shopped that picture of us, the one that sent you into a 'tard frenzy. It was all over the school boards today. You didn't see them?"

"Like I give a shit when the pep rally is."

Jalay's mouth dropped open for a moment, followed by a shimmering of his veneer. Shaking his head, he dimmed his palette and stowed it under his arm.

"Where're you going?"

"Home," he replied, standing up. "I'm not sitting here all night."

As he walked away, Russo felt the stifling pressure of betrayal descend on him. Never would he have thought Jalay capable of walking away from him, certainly not in the middle of a conversation. Angry, he stood and followed his former friend down the steps and through the lobby. He caught up with him on the sidewalk outside and pulled at his thick shoulder.

"What the fuck is your problem?" Russo demanded.

Jalay stared back, his veneer blank, his eyes a bit disinterested.

"You don't walk out on me! You need me!"

"Yeah, like I need someone to beat me half to death when I step on his heel!" Jalay barked the words, as if he had been preparing them for days. "Someone to lose his shit over a fucking *shop*! We've been making fun of Deron for years and not once did he ever do anything to us. That was the game! You took it too far. You always do that."

Russo felt the pain in his teeth spread to his jaw, then his entire face. He was biting down so hard, trying to stem the flow of anger. Every part of his body was primed for a beating, ready to strike out at Jalay and teach him to be more appreciative. There was a lot of history between them, a lot of shared experiences that would cease to mean anything if he laid him out on the sidewalk.

Maybe it was meant to end that way.

Maybe life as he knew it needed to change if he ever wanted to take that next step up. He looked back towards the PD, saw someone exiting the large wooden doors in front, someone he had been expecting for a long time.

"First," said Russo, buttoning the lower part of his jacket, "fuck you."

"Not with your mother's dick," replied Jalay.

"We don't know each other anymore, you hear me?" Russo's voice was calm and steady. "Next time I see you, I treat you like anyone else. So stay out of my fucking way."

Jalay rolled his eyes. "Thanks for not murdering me," he said, turning on his heels. As he walked away, he reconciled his clothes into something more befitting a Saturday night on The Drag. And with that superficial change, Russo lost him in the crowd.

That was okay. He wasn't interested in a talented but mentally deficient reconciler. He wanted the big fish, the gaunt man making his way down the steps of the Easton PD, the one whose veneer changed dramatically as his shoes hit the sidewalk. At that point, he looked just like anyone else. He didn't even seem that tall anymore. Maybe it was all an act, the way uniforms dressed up when they were out on the street, only in reverse. For the Seer, his work was inside the building, so when he arrived, he changed himself into something other-worldly to inspire fear.

Russo smirked, couldn't believe he had been fooled so easily. Agent Tavarez wasn't a cyborg or an alien; he was just a normal guy with a strange veneer. Everything about him was unarguably human, from the way he nodded to strangers, to the slow pace at which he walked.

Human. And easy to follow.

THIRTEEN
DERON

It took half an hour to clear security at the southern gate leading out of Easton. Even though the bus terminal was right across the street, the same uniforms that watched them get on made them get off again after a mere fifteen second trip. They had to stand beside the bus while men in black camouflage searched their belongings, which they had to leave unlocked on their seats. That wasn't a problem this time around; neither Deron nor Sebo were carrying anything explicitly illegal. Deron hadn't even brought a bag, instead relying on his pockets to hold his wallet, music player, and mini-palette. As they stood outside in the cold evening, Deron noticed that Sebo was shivering a little, a natural response that unfortunately made him look nervous.

"If I were any kind of courageous, I would say this is cruel and unusual punishment," said Sebo, his teeth chattering. "Unlawful detainment," he added.

"Good thing you're not," muttered Deron. It was one thing to question the behavior and motives of the police from the safety of his mind, but to make those questions public would invite unnecessary attention.

"Did I tell you about Gemma Reese?"

Deron shook his head, listened as the engine behind him changed pitch.

Sebo crossed his arms and put his chin to his chest. "I don't understand why it has to be so cold."

"It was fine last night," said Deron, thinking back to his meeting with Rosalia at Gillock Pond. He didn't like seeing her so upset, not when their reunion was supposed to be happy.

"Of course it was, because last night I was sitting in my room watching the veneer dry. But the moment we decide to trek to Paramel, it turns arctic."

"It's not that cold."

"Tell that to my balls."

Down the line, a man in a trench coat was examining the passengers, comparing their faces to the palette in his hand.

"So what about Gemma?" asked Deron.

"Quite a story, that," said Sebo, effecting an English accent. He cleared his throat. "Twas a night similar in demeanor to tonight with the exception of not being colder than an Icelandic outhouse. Enter one Gemma Reese and her gaggle of vapid chums, all of whom have imbibed more than their fair share of spirits."

Deron groaned at the act, prompting Sebo to shift voices again.

"Among these chums is the dark-haired vixen Miko Newton. You, ah, remember her from last year, don't you?"

Miko's bountiful chest flashed in Deron's memory, making him nod emphatically.

"As we all know with dames like Miko their brain power is always occupied with the expansion of their, ah, bosoms. I believe it was this deficiency that led her to park her personal conveyance in a tow-away zone. Can you guess what happened when these future ladies of the night returned from their hobnobbing?"

"The car was gone, wasn't it?"

"And assumed stolen, as any Easton resident who had coasted through high school on their veneer and endowments would. She rings the flatfoots and the one that shows up is a real crumb, you know? He starts talking down to her, making her read the tow-away signs, all six barrels."

Laughing, Deron could already imagine where the story was going.

Sebo coughed and rubbed at his throat. He continued in his normal voice, "So Gemma tries to stick up for her friend and loses her shit on the uniform. And then all the girls start crying and the uniform is just standing there laughing at them and looking all smug in his veneer." He blew a plume of hot air as a nonverbal protest against the cold. "Now, before I continue, tell me what you would have done in this situation."

"Nothing," said Deron, selecting the only correct answer.

"Exactly. Absolutely nothing. But evidently Gemma is far more courageous than we. The cop tells her to take it up with the towing company and this was her response I shit you not." He paused for effect. "*Well, just know that karma's a bitch so you better hope your vest works.*"

Deron licked his lips and blew an ominous whistle. In his mind, he saw the uniform's veneer flash red and then the baton come flying out of nowhere. He winced at the familiar violence.

"Now, had that been you or I, we'd be in jail getting backdoored by Drag Rats."

"What happened to her?"

"Absolutely nothing," said Sebo, shrugging. "I guess all you need to beat a rap is a fine pair of tits."

"She threatened to shoot him."

"Right?" His eyes went wide with recollection. "I told her that and you know what she said?"

Deron shook his head.

"*I didn't even have a gun!*"

"She didn't."

"My hand to God's dick!"

"Having a good evening, gentlemen?" The interruption put a quick stop to their laughter. The man in the trench was much taller up close and though he smiled, he didn't look all that friendly. On his right, a uniform stood stoically, just along for the ride and to beat any unruly passengers into submission.

"It's a little cold for our taste," said Sebo. "You don't have to be out here all night, do you?"

There was a flicker at the edge of the man's lips. "Half an hour," he replied, glancing between the palette and Sebo's face. "Then I switch off." He shook his head minutely and shuffled one step over to look at Deron. "Officer Hawkins here, on the other hand, has been toughing it out all night."

"It's not right." Sebo shook his head sympathetically.

The uniform didn't acknowledge the sentiment. His face held steady in a professional but aggressive veneer. It was possible that under his mask he was smiling or fuming, but no one outside would ever know it.

"Don't worry," said the man, "I'm sure he gets hazard pay…" His sentence trailed off as he took in Deron's face. The moment of shock was plainly visible, regardless of how brief it was. "What's your name, son?"

"Deron Bishop."

The man looked away, did some quick tapping on his palette. "I see you were recently released from Easton General. Just yesterday?"

"Yes, sir."

"We're going to Paramel for some run and gun action," Sebo explained. "He's been bed-ridden for three weeks."

"It's a shame you haven't pressed charges against your attacker."

"My head's fuzzy," admitted Deron. "All I remember is Sebo's jacket."

"Did *you* assault him?"

Sebo raised an eyebrow. "Let's see. I've shot him, exploded him, set him on fire, pushed him out a window, decapitated him in front of his teammates, and even questioned his hygiene. But no, ours is not what you would call a physical relationship." He put his hand on Deron's shoulder.

"Alright, boys, keep it in your pants."

Once the man had moved down the line, Sebo said in a low voice, "You see, that's how you handle a uniform."

"That guy's not with the police." Deron kept glancing down the line, watching the tall man go about his business, whatever that was.

"No, but the one that was. Yes sir, no sir. Notice that I didn't threaten to test his bulletproof vest."

"Sebo, that was a haiku," said Deron, absently.

Sebo pursed his lips thoughtfully. "No, no it wasn't." Something clicked behind his amber eyes. "We have just wasted, ten minutes of our lives; what, do you think that means?"

Deron ignored the stilted speech and said, "I wonder who he's looking for."

"Criminals, con artists, synth pushers, people on the lam."

At last, the inquisitor stopped in front of the bus driver and Deron was surprised to see him get the same treatment as everyone else. After a few moments of inspection, the man slipped his palette into his leather jacket and began walking back down the line. He stopped in front of Deron and extended a business card.

"When you remember," he said, his eyes exploring Deron's face again.

Deron took the card with a gracious nod of his head. He eyed it for a moment, saw the man's name was Memo Ruiz, Special Agent for the Consolidated Easton Territory. That put him above the uniforms, above local government. He was part of the agency responsible for keeping Easton safe from whatever dwelled outside its borders. They were the ones who built the walls, trained the guns, and set up the roadblocks.

Slipping the card into his back pocket, Deron tried to ignore the stares from the other passengers as they filed back onto the bus. He knew from rumor that agents didn't have much interaction with the locals and evidently, they didn't hand out their cards to just anyone.

"Are we not going to discuss the absurdity of what just happened?" asked Sebo as he unraveled the earbuds from his music player.

"We could just ignore it," replied Deron.

The engine revved up to a soothing electrical hum. Under the bus, hydraulics hissed as they lifted the chassis into its travel configuration.

"How did he know you were in the hospital?" In his hands, Sebo's music player came to life. Its display was a miniature palette that he could use to browse through his songs or select playlists. When idle, it showed a photo stream of album art and stills from music videos.

"He's an agent. Maybe he has access to medical records."

Sebo chuckled. "What I wouldn't give for ten minutes alone with his palette."

Deron nodded in agreement and slipped his own earbuds into place. He selected a playlist of old ambient cuts that went along with anything, especially the recent feeling that life was just a movie and with the right soundtrack, anything, even a mundane bus ride, could take on higher meaning. A soft pulsating beat filled his ears, something low on the clef, joined later by a casual tapping of a cymbal. As the bus rolled through the gate and into the outland, the music swelled, creating the perfect traveling music.

The land beyond Easton wasn't much to look at; it was mostly undeveloped, owned by the government for future expansion of the city-states. Ostensibly, people couldn't live there or even visit. The bus would not make any stops between Easton and Paramel and if it did, the militarized SUV trailing them would ensure no one disembarked. Locking down a good reason for the quarantine wasn't easy, not when the info on the network disagreed with the info in the textbooks. The official story was that of governmental providence, but the conspiracies told stories of nuclear fallout, of wars that began and ended long before Deron was born.

A small display in the lower right-hand corner of the window showed their speed, estimated arrival time, and the current time. It was dark out, with the moon barely visible through the clouds. It reminded him of Rosalia and he thought about what she was doing at that moment, how she was coping with being abandoned so easily. She had told him not to think on it, that he needed to spend time with Sebo and blow off some steam in Paramel. That was all well and good, but Deron wanted to be back in his room or back at Gillock pond—either way, with Rosalia nearby.

Deron looked over at his friend who had shut his eyes and was nodding to a syncopated beat. They would have a blast in the run and gun tonight, he was sure of that. And even if Sebo spent the entire time babbling in his run-on sentences, at least it wouldn't be time spent alone. He suddenly remembered the new map pack for Destined 4 Death that Sebo had been talking about three weeks ago. That was a long time in the gaming scene. Depending on who they played, it might not be the cakewalk they were expecting.

For the first time in a while, Deron thought of violence and felt anticipation.

FOURTEEN
ILYA

The tram rocked lazily as it adjusted to the flow of traffic heading down Parker Avenue. Ilya found it fascinating that such a bulky vehicle could drive itself through crowded streets without running anybody over. More than that, it stopped only when there were passengers to pick up or when somebody wanted off. It should have taken a human to figure that out, but somehow the software in the tram did it with infallible accuracy. Most riders took no notice, and Ilya thought that the absence of a real driver made them less inclined to fool around when getting off or on. Distrust of the onboard sensors resulted in people finding their seats quickly, lest the tram start moving without them. It made for a marvel of automated efficiency, but there were still some things that the tram's artificial driver couldn't detect.

Graffiti, for one, like the crude veneer someone had reconciled on the partition in front of her. It was arguably obscene, though so poor in composition as to be laughable. It was likely the work of a pre-teen, a kid going through the public reconciliation phase that was pretty much a rite of passage for Easton residents. Ilya thought about undoing the work, but there was a connotation of civil disobedience in the wildly exaggerated breasts of the stick figure and she figured it would be wrong to silence nonviolent protest. She let it remain, but not without her mark.

Touching the corner of the partition, Ilya reconciled a shaded fold with a three-dimensional effect that made it look like the backing was coming loose. Behind it, she colored in a blue-white background and then an angel with a smile that showed its appreciation if not outright endorsement. It looked out of place, but the juxtaposition made the image stronger—the fighters and the spectators together in one place.

Sitting back in her seat, Ilya turned her attention to the passing shops and restaurants with their internal lights playing off the glow of the sidewalks, an effect that grew more intense as the sunlight faded. It was nearing eight, which on a Saturday night meant lots of customers for the parlors and cafés sprinkled amongst the locally owned businesses. Perrault's was lit up for the weekend crowd; Ilya recognized a few faces from school sitting at the small tables that bled out onto the sidewalk, sipping their faux coffees and vitamin-enhanced smoothies. It was the kind of thing her grandmother would scoff at, that Babushka would call an idle existence. Avoiding that kind of behavior came naturally to Ilya, the byproduct of some ill-defined prejudice locked away in her DNA.

A trio of newly teen girls got on when the tram stopped at Trinity; they shared a two-person bench a few rows back from Ilya. Their conversation was what she expected: shallow obsessions and useless gossip, nothing geared towards real problems. It was just like the graffiti, meaningful only in a certain light, only to the person that created it. That was a better time, thought Ilya, before reality brought gifts like loneliness, attraction, and mortality. Once recognized, those issues seemed to dominate her daily thoughts.

That was why, when the instant message popped up on her palette an hour prior, she gladly accepted the invitation to a night out. With dinner done and no plans for the night, Ilya had already changed into comfortable clothes and settled in her grandmother's rocking chair with a palette in her lap. Going out would have been something different, a borderline cliché, but the idea of forsaking something for its conformity seemed in itself too conformist.

That it was okay to be different never even occurred to Ilya. It was an accepted fact that didn't require debate, internally or externally. Choosing to get dressed and hop on the tram was just as valid an option as remaining in the rocking chair, reading for a couple of hours, and then turning in before the clock struck ten. The more time she spent watching the world scroll by outside the tram, the more confident she became in her choice. There was so much to see in Easton, so many pretty veneers going about their lives in a world that celebrated ostentatious artificiality. It was a strange paradox, like rats in a well-decorated maze.

Parker Avenue split right after Browning Road, as if the Tsugumi Galleria had always existed and the road forced to go around it. The shopping center was a squat three-story building that, thanks to an animated veneer, made a fitting cap for a street dedicated to commerce. It was there that residents could find the legacy chain stores, the once-great giants that the city had forced into small pens to keep them from overtaking local businesses. At least Victoria's Secret still had a varied collection.

There were two stops on each side of the mall and when the tram paused at the second one, Ilya disembarked.

It had grown colder throughout the day and with the sun finally gone, she was starting to feel the chill in her bones. Her shirt, though long-sleeved, felt thin against the constant breeze, and the loose bottoms of her jeans fluttered constantly as she made the short walk to the entrance. The double-doors parted for her automatically and once she passed the second set, a blast of warmer air enveloped her. The activity inside, the noise and the sparkling veneers, distracted her and for a moment, she forgot why she had come. There was so much going on, so much liveliness compared to the laid-back aura of Café Perrault.

The smell of pastry reminded her of the instant message.

Fountain in front of the Cinnabon.

Ilya caught the scent on the air and followed it to the left. Merging into the crowd, she listened to the many voices around her, all talking at once about nothing.

Her date was sitting alone on the edge of the fountain, spaced evenly between a couple eating pretzels and a man reading a palette. Thinking herself unobserved, her face had a blank look on it, one that could approach sadness if the right screws were turned. The ponytail that she wore at school was down; one side of her hair hung by her cheek while the other disappeared behind her shoulder. Unlike Ilya, she had been smart enough to bring a jacket, one of those white half-trenches with wood-colored buttons on the pockets. It would have made a good picture with the water falling in the background. Ilya concentrated on the details, resolved to reconcile it later when she got a chance.

"Been waiting long?" Ilya asked, her apology hidden in her playful tone.

Rosalia looked up and flashed a new veneer, this one with vibrant eyes and a smile to match. "Just a few minutes." Her gaze wandered to the left. "I was thinking about getting a cinnamon bun."

"They smell good." The aroma grew more intense the longer Ilya stared at the flashy advertising above their storefront. "Have you eaten?"

"No. Didn't really have an appetite today. You?"

"My grandmother made *kapustnyak*."

"What's that?" asked Rosalia, scrunching her eyebrows.

Ilya shook her head slightly, surveyed the other eateries in the food court. "I'm not sure. Maybe one day you'll come try it." Her lips spread in a smile.

"I'm in the mood for Mexican."

"Nachos," said Ilya in agreement. "I love nachos." She waited for Rosalia to stand and then together they navigated the distracted throngs. "I tried to make them for my family once. Babushka said, 'What is this? Chips and cheese? This is meal?!'" She adopted a thick accent for the quote, garnering a small laugh from Rosalia.

"All Mexican food is like, three or four things."

"Italian food too," offered Ilya. "Sauce and noodles. They think just because they make the pasta into a corkscrew or a bowtie that it's a different meal."

"Yeah," replied Rosalia, chuckling.

The El Chico restaurant was on the edge of the food court in the gray area between food and retail. It was late so they didn't have to wait long before the hostess showed them to one of the high tables by the windows. They had a view of Parker, of the cars and trams zipping by, and of the neighborhoods beyond with their lines of streetlamps snaking into the darkness. Ilya made small talk as Rosalia stared at the twinkling veneers, her face alive with their muted reflections. Only after the waiter had brought their food did Ilya dare bring up Deron.

"Where is he tonight?" Ilya asked, reaching for the salt shaker.

Rosalia stared at her food as if her appetite had suddenly disappeared. "In Paramel with Sebo."

"What's in Paramel?"

She laughed in response. "Sex, drugs, violence." Looking up, she added, "No, he's going to play video games."

"You wish he was here, don't you?"

"Why do you say that?" Her eyes darted away as she took a long drink. "I've seen that face before, in a book." Ilya touched the amber glass of the table and reconciled the cover. She flipped it around so Rosalia could see it.

"*Show Me Love*," she read, "*erotica by Claire Beaudoin.*"

"I found it on my mom's palette when I was thirteen."

"A little young, don't you think?"

Ilya shrugged as she coaxed a jalapeño onto a chip with her fingernail. "You have to learn about sex eventually. What would you prefer, a beautiful story about people making *passionate* love, or a diagram of a penis in health class?"

"That's how I learned," said Rosalia.

"Either way, Deron should be spending time with his woman instead of his man."

"No, I told him to go. He deserves some release."

Ilya smiled knowingly.

"He'd like that," Rosalia admitted. "At least this way he can go out and have some fun instead of being with me and remembering…"

The pall that followed made Ilya shiver. "Russo is an asshole." It was all she could think to say.

"I just don't understand Deron," continued Rosalia, her head dipping. "I always thought he was a little disconnected from the world, but not like this. There's carefree and there's careless. If he's gonna do something, he's not telling me." A pause while the waiter refilled her glass. "We met last night. I was ready, you know, to *comfort* him, but he didn't bite. We kissed, but that was it."

"Maybe he wasn't in the mood?"

Rosalia scoffed. "Have you ever known a boy that wasn't in the mood?" She looked away, watched the people walking by. "It might have been the pain. Or the drugs."

"Da," said Ilya. She wanted to comfort Rosalia, say the right things to make her happy again, but even she could see the subtle rejection coming from Deron.

Maybe he was doing it out of some romantic necessity, pushing her away so he wouldn't have to look into the face of betrayal. It was a scene straight out of *Show Me Love* with the broad-chested Salvio and his cheating lover, Dominique. Ilya smiled, recalling a passionate scene.

"What's so funny?"

"Well, I was just thinking…" She gnashed her teeth. "You haven't given him the ultimate gift yet."

Rosalia blushed and tried to hide it with her veneer.

"Just saying it could help."

"Sure," replied Rosalia. "I almost got you killed so let's fuck?"

Ilya spread her hands. "If he can get it up on his meds…"

"You mean if he still wants me." Rosalia stabbed absently at her food.

"Come on, who wouldn't want you? And you're right, all boys think about sex all the time, so that works in our favor." She looked Rosalia up and down. "Though, we do need to find something more enticing than that shirt."

"What?" Rosalia looked down at her dark blue tee with its understated floral design. "Deron loves this shirt."

"It's nice, but it doesn't show off your body enough." Then, in epiphany, "We should do some shopping!"

There was hesitation in Rosalia's eyes. "I guess we could go to the Gap."

"Yeah, no," said Ilya. "I was thinking something more Secret."

FIFTEEN
SEBO

When it came to overwhelming the senses, American Reality had their veneers down to a manipulative science. Their storefront was, in essence, just an extension of the virtual worlds contained within, so it fit that the displays gave people a taste of what they could expect if they had the guts to walk inside and slap down thirty bucks. A novice player could lose their mind just standing on the sidewalk, staring at the screens and the replays of explosions and aliens and grisly dismemberments that would rival the most realistic of snuff films. And even if they closed their eyes, the smells would still be there: fresh blood pooling around their feet, the acrid smoke from a signal flare, and even the oily aroma of a Signet, a half-lizard, half-infant concoction found in the later levels of Destined 4 Death. It was a devastating display of sensory overload, which was encouragement enough for some to let go of the real world and embrace the nightmare.

"You don't mind, do you?" asked Sebo, as he laced up his game boots. The ready room in the bowels of American Reality smelled like disinfectant, a deliberate choice to match its Spartan motif, complete with blank walls and a light overhead that flickered like an old-style bulb. It was atmosphere, a bland cracker to clear the palette for the feast to come.

Deron shrugged in response and fiddled with the harness on his chest.

He *did* mind. Sebo could usually read Deron's true emotions, even if his veneer suggested otherwise. All he had to do was watch his body language, examine the way his shoulders slumped, the way his hands moved slowly, lacking enthusiasm. Sebo frowned inwardly. He wanted to tell him that this was for his own good, but it felt too soon to bring up the business of Russo Rivera.

Sebo had made the decision while staring at a Destined 4 Death display in the lobby. It was a full-wall veneer that enumerated the new features and bug fixes. The advertising was characteristically slick, and every image that ran in high resolution only made Sebo want to play more. There were so many ways to die, so many ways to kill. The preview made it look like it could rival the military-grade simulations, those recruit-only games that had a reputation for being so visceral as to cause mental breakdowns in one out of every ten players.

Though every inch of Sebo was dying to get in there and kill some Signets, he knew that D4D wasn't what Deron needed at the moment. The accounts of his altercation varied, but anything that would put a person in the hospital for three weeks had to have been brutal. The line that sealed the deal came in the rules of the expansion pack, red text that said *hand-to-hand combat only*. Ultimately, Sebo chose the more docile Swarm Survivor.

"Your game is ready, gentlemen," said a sultry voice from the ceiling.

Sebo stood up and checked his harness. The small electrodes fitted throughout the straps and plates would provide feedback during the game in the form of electric shocks. They weren't powerful enough to scar, but they wouldn't exactly be pleasant.

"This will be fun," Sebo assured his friend as they walked to the entry door on the far side of the room.

Deron's veneer flashed a smile; it froze in place unnaturally.

There was an eerie green glow in the next room caused by the dimmed portal on the wall to the left. Within it was the stuttering image of a slick-haired suit; he was adjusting his collar and talking to someone off camera.

"This is going to be a slaughter," he said, pushing a thin red tie into his jacket. "I don't know how they get people to sign up for this suicide mission."

Sebo chuckled, started to feel better about the production values of a game that had less than a third of the budget of Destined 4 Death.

"What?" asked the suit. He leaned his ear off screen and then flashed recognition. The previous smirk turned into a cordial smile as he faced the camera. "Welcome employees three-five-sixteen and three-five-seventeen. Congratulations on your recent promotion to border security! I trust you found all your equipment?"

"What the balls is this?" asked Deron.

"Great! You'll find that Graypoint Security has only the best weapons and armor to keep you safe." He gestured to the armory rack on the adjacent wall. "Well, I'm sure you're eager to start your shifts. Today's assignment is the southern echelon, codename Monaco, which shouldn't be too much trouble even for you two. Turret emplacements are ready to fire and the first wave is on radar and will be arriving soon. Prepare yourselves."

"I don't know if I like this blended reality stuff," said Deron. He pulled a rifle from the rack and handed it to Sebo. "All this running around is gonna feel like exercise."

Sebo grinned. "Do you think those aliens care that you've been confined to a bed for the last three weeks? Do you think they'll give a dingle about your extenuating circumstances when they're eating your liver?!"

"Don't get me wrong, I want to kill." He curled his fingers into a fist in the space between them. "But I wanted some full sensory Death. This is just a rich man's tower defense."

"Oh I see," said Sebo, checking the ammunition count on his gun. "You're concerned that your near-death experience will prevent you from picking up a new game. Well, if his eminence feels this game is below his regal stature, then he can just stand back and do his nails while I dominate this course on my own."

"It's gonna take more than rhetoric to beat this game." By the hesitation in his voice, it was obvious he was uncertain about his word choice. Then he smiled, let Sebo know he was teasing.

That was the whole point of coming to Paramel—to allow Deron to let loose and enjoy himself. He had been unnaturally quiet on the ride over, staring out the window as if the outland held anything worth looking at. And on the walk through the Mains, the central hub-street of Paramel, he had kept his head down, even when there was underdressed scenery to take in.

A humming in the command room culminated in the illumination of the Monaco echelon. The window that separated them from the playing field flashed, and an overlay appeared along with a small arrow pointing to a blur in the distance. To the left, a large green triangle pulsed. Underneath it was the word *PLAY*.

"Before we do battle," crooned Sebo, bowing his head ceremoniously, "let us pray for the souls of our enemies. They know not the sins they have committed, having occupied this planet before we arrived, having resisted our attempts to convert them to the Lord. Oh Godless heathens, we give thanks for your efforts, for your determination to provide us with a glorious death. We fight you in the spirit of all men and insects that have fallen before us. May our battle be long, hard, and throbbing!"

Deron smacked the *PLAY* button with his gloved fist.

Sebo changed characters quickly, "Look at me, soldier! You remember this: we do not stop. No matter how much blood, no matter how much pain, *we do not stop!*"

Before they could even exit the command room, the suit appeared once more on the wall, looking more disheveled than before.

"What the hell am I paying you two idiots for?!" he boomed. "The cannon on level five is down and you two are just standing around! Get your asses out there and fix it!"

The door to the battlefield slid open and Sebo and Deron rushed out in formation. Somewhere in the back of his mind, Sebo knew that they were in the expansive warehouse behind American Reality, that everything they saw was just a veneer on movable partitions. Years of immersion had given him the ability to ignore what he knew to be the truth, to simply enjoy the fantasy for all it was worth.

A distant crunching sound alerted Sebo to the imminent arrival of their insect enemies. Once that crackling wormed its way into his eardrums, he forgot all about the simulation and lost himself in the game. Instead of the slightly padded floor of a warehouse, he saw dirt, dry in most places except for the occasional blood splatter—evidence of previous attacks. The partitions were high evercrete walls topped with razor wire to keep the insects from crawling over. After all, the alien creatures were just like any other biological enemy, easy enough to destroy once enough of their cells had lost contact with each other.

The path through the Monaco echelon was a serpentine pattern that created five levels of defense, each with their own set of guns, mostly consisting of cannons. The third level had a flame thrower that hummed ominously as they ran past it.

"Exercise," commented Deron, his breathing already labored.

The chittering grew louder as they turned the corner onto the fifth level, which opened up onto an expanse of dead land, really just a veneer on the back wall of the warehouse. Sebo could see the first wave, a flowing mass of little gloopy animals that looked like over-inflated frogs with elongated arms and legs. The crackling sound they made didn't match their appearance.

"Cover me," barked Sebo, crossing the exposed entrance to examine the outer gun. Its light blinked yellow and the panel on the front showed the outline of a glove with the word *REPAIR* under it. Sebo put his hand to the display and watched the progress meter increment.

"Bango! Bango! Ba-boom!" yelled Deron, squeezing off several rounds from his rifle. In the distance, a tiny insect exploded in a golden firework.

Without warning, the cannon above Sebo's head discharged all four barrels at once, creating a deafening boom in the maze. He fell back, dazed, and tripped over his own feet. Before he could get his bearings, the guns fired again, eliciting a chorus of death wails from the incoming wave. A second later, Deron was by his side, thrusting Sebo's gun back into his hands and yanking on his harness.

"Goddammit soldier, on your feet! It was your dumbfuck idea to come to this shithole planet and I'll be damned if I'm gonna *die* on it!" There was sweat peeking out from under his battle-scarred veneer. Deron looked up quickly, trained his gun, and fired. The sudden kickback put him off balance.

Sebo rolled out from under the line of fire and scrambled to his feet. He pointed his gun in the general direction of the threat and squeezed the trigger. One hundred forty-seven virtual bullets later, his gun clicked empty.

"Magazine!" He looked over at Deron, who stared back at him with wide eyes. "You forgot the ammo?!"

They made a frantic dash back to the command room as the second and third waves appeared on the horizon. The barrels of the outer gun rotated back, angled upwards unnaturally, trying to find an effective trajectory. Its rounds were much too large for the blob-frogs, which meant a good number of them were making it through. It wasn't until the flamethrower started spewing a mix of napalm and accelerant that they really started to squeal.

Back in the relative safety of the command room, Sebo pulled the extra magazines from the rack while Deron examined the status board.

"Level three is breached."

"I'll get a visual," said Sebo, choosing the icon from a row at the bottom of the window. It filled the screen and showed the view from within the four barrels of the cannon. Larger baddies had shown up, oddly shaped masses that looked like they might tip over at any second. It reminded Sebo of a spider, but one whose legs grew from the underside of its body so that it resembled a detached hand running along the ground.

Deron replaced the magazine in his rifle, smacked it until it clicked.

"Guys, I have some bad news." The suit appeared again, a covered phone in his hand. "I just got a call from MachTech. They say we haven't paid maintenance on some of our guns, so…" He cleared his throat. "They're taking the guidance chips offline on most of our echelons. I'm on the phone with corporate trying to get a purchase order, but I think accounting has left for the day so I don't know when we'll be able to get the guns working again." He shook his head, out of things to say. "Good luck."

As soon as the image faded, two alarms appeared on the status screen.

"Gun three is down," yelled Sebo. "Guidance is offline. I'll have to aim it manually." He jabbed at the screen, brought up the camera view, and switched the gun into manual control. A holographic yoke grew out of the display and when Sebo wrapped his hands around it, he found he could move the targeting reticle. A quick twitch of his index finger fired a triplet of shots into the hand-blobs. He caught one in what looked like its shoulder and smirked as it flew backwards into a wall.

"Four is down too," said Deron, a strange grin growing on his face. He looked at Sebo and said with mock drama, "Someone's gonna have to go out there!" Without waiting for a response, he yelled something unintelligible and raced out of the room.

Sebo watched him sprint down the first two levels but lost him after the third. It was tough shooting the gun and keeping track of Deron on the cameras. Most of the cannons were firing blindly, but he could hear the tinny sound of a rifle in the distance. At first, the reports came in controlled bursts, giving the impression that Deron was doing well, methodically exterminating the infestation. But the string of bullets got progressively longer, until finally he was firing at full throttle, pausing to reload, and then firing again. And in the corner, gun four still showed down.

"Contamination imminent," said that sultry voice from above.

Sebo made a face at the ceiling. "Shut up, bitch!"

The suit flickered in. "Hold them back! They've made it into level two! I'm instituting quarantine restrictions until you clear them out!"

Locks clicked in the outer door and Sebo abandoned his gun to try to open it. It didn't budge. He cursed himself for leaving Deron out there all alone, but there was nothing he could do now.

Fight to the finish. Embrace victory or accept defeat.

Those were the rules of every game.

Back on the guns, Sebo focused on taking out the larger of the insects using an amputation strategy to slow them down, made the others crawl over their carcasses. The dirt had long ago turned into mud; it kicked up in brown drops with every bullet that missed its mark.

Something was off; some instrument in the back wasn't playing up to its full potential. The screams were there and the cannons were blasting. He could even hear the sizzle of blob flesh as the flamethrower spewed fiery death into level three. But again, it was incomplete. Then it hit him. Deron's rifle—he couldn't hear it anymore.

Sebo checked the cameras, but his comrade had disappeared.

SIXTEEN
ROSALIA

The mood in the mall had shifted by the time Rosalia and Ilya rejoined it outside the El Chico restaurant. Gone were the adults with their early bedtimes. Gone were the tweens with their neon clothes and inane babble. All that remained was an in-between crowd of teenagers and college students, the kind of people the mall at night was made for. Soon enough, the bright lights would dim, giving a softer atmosphere to the expansive retail space. The benches along the inner track of the mall would fill up with groups of friends or couples out on dates. Rosalia looked over at her companion for the evening, Ilya, whose eyes jumped from one passerby to the next like a queen surveying her subjects.

Only a few weeks ago, Ilya had been like a stranger who lived on the periphery of Rosalia's world in more ways than one. She had been blessed with natural beauty, and any decent reconciler would have known just from looking at her that she had no need of a veneer. Now, after getting to know her better, Rosalia saw more than just the blessings of genetics. Now, she saw a friendly face, a little smile to make her feel better, someone she could trust with a few preliminary secrets. She tried to ignore the little voice inside telling her that she was just lonely, that Deron's extended stay in the hospital had been just the excuse she needed to go out and make new friends.

If anything, Ilya was a great listener. She had a habit of keeping quiet at the right times, smiling and nodding as Rosalia droned on and on. Sometimes her eyes wandered, as if she weren't listening, only to follow up with a question that got at the heart of whatever Rosalia was trying to say. The first couple of weeks had been like that—deeply invasive interrogations that got beneath the veneer. But now, she had settled down, accepted the fact that Rosalia was just a private person and no amount of digging would uncover more than she was willing to share.

They stopped at the Tropical Smoothie Café in the food court as they made their way to the north end of the mall. Ilya chose a blue concoction that must have been sour based on the way she crinkled her nose when she drank it. Rosalia got her standard: a blend of strawberries, bananas, and pineapple. It didn't taste as good as The Fountain of Youth at Perrault's, but it sufficed. She sipped it up quickly, creating a momentary brain freeze in her forehead.

"Too much of a good thing," Ilya commented. She was walking close to Rosalia such that their shoulders occasionally brushed together.

"I should have tried something new," she replied, taking another sip.

"I always order the Blue Rain when Travis is working."

"You know him?"

"We dated. Briefly. I wasn't impressed."

The glimpse into Ilya's past focused Rosalia's attention. "Didn't he graduate last year? So he was a senior and you were a sophomore?"

Ilya sipped loudly and nodded.

"That's kind of…"

"Yeah, but his parents had just given him a car, so it made sense. I didn't ride a tram for weeks." There was a forced glee to her voice that didn't match her body language. Looking straight ahead, it appeared Ilya was trying to avoid eye contact. "Anyway, he was always trying to put the moves on me."

"Is that why you broke up?"

A scoff. "We broke up because I found out he was seeing Gemma Reese on the side." Waving her hand dismissively, she added, "God, she'd spread her legs for a friendly smile."

Rosalia wanted to laugh, but the idea of Ilya being cheated on played on her empathy. "That was you?" There was too much cheerfulness in her delivery. "Sorry, I just remember it being some girl."

"I was new," said Ilya, shrugging. "The only regret I have is the wasted time. You and I could have been going shopping every weekend."

Rosalia felt a squeeze on her arm as Ilya collapsed the space between them. It wasn't like walking with Deron, who would hold her hand but still maintain a respectful distance. Ilya didn't seem to know or care about personal boundaries. She did as she pleased, despite the pious looks from the people they passed.

"Can I tell you something honestly?" asked Rosalia, looking away.

"Sure."

"I didn't think you were into boys." When she heard a giggle in response, she looked back to find Ilya smiling brightly.

"You think I'm a lesbian?" She let her hand drop from her arm. "Is that why… You thought I was coming onto you?" The delight in her eyes was obvious.

Rosalia blushed and waved her hands frantically. "No, of course not. I just hadn't seen you with anyone this year and…"

Ilya bit her lip and beamed mischievously. "Well, you *are* attractive, I'll give you that. But anyone can see you're in love with Deron." A hint of sadness flitted across her eyes. "You have a Fool's Love. Very deep and very dangerous. But that's the best we can hope for right now." Then, resolutely, "We'll get over the pain."

"A *fool's* love? What's that supposed to mean?"

"That's what my grandmother calls it." She slipped into an exaggerated accent. "Teenagers love like lemming jumping into pit, with all their heart and no idea how to get out." She paused, returned to her normal voice. "Then it rains, fills the pit with water, and all the lemmings drown. That or your boyfriend asks you to have a threesome and you refuse and he goes out and bangs the first available nailable he can find."

They reached Victoria's Secret and found a gaggle of fidgety boys sitting on the benches making lewd gestures at the underdressed mannequins in the display window. Rosalia ignored them, held her question until they were within the sound-proof glass doors and examining a table full of spring underwear.

"So Blue Rain holds some kind of significance for you two?"

"Oh," said Ilya, noticing her drink again. "No, I thought you knew. It has vodka in it. And curaçao and pineapple, I think. They're really good when it's all frozen together."

Rosalia suddenly understood the weird faces Ilya had made while sipping her drink. "And he just spikes your smoothie whenever you want him to?"

"That sounds dirty." She put down her cup and picked up a professionally reconciled pair of panties. Holding them to her body, she shook her head in disgust. "I'm getting big." Then, looking up, "I think he's still holding out for that threesome."

"Ew! With Gemma?"

Ilya shrugged. "With anyone with tits and a south mouth."

"You should have told me. I could use some alcohol."

"You drink?" She folded the underwear carelessly and tossed it back onto the pile. "I never would have taken you for a vice girl."

"I do," explained Rosalia. "It's just harder for me to get." With a haughty voice, she added, "I never denied sex to a blender jockey at Tropical Smoothie."

Ilya allowed for a pause. "We could go back if you really want a drink."

"No. I'd probably start laughing if I saw Travis again."

Nodding, Ilya wandered towards a nearby rack. She pulled out a sheer shirt and held it up for inspection. "Why would anyone buy this?" she wondered aloud. "Why not just veneer your skin?"

"Would *you* go to school wearing just a veneer?"

"I don't like reconciling my body," said Ilya, her voice brimming with proud conviction. She replaced the shirt and pulled another one. "I've heard stories of people that reconcile themselves so much that they forget what they used to look like." Facing Rosalia, she declared, "This is the body God gave me. It doesn't need a veneer."

She had a point, Rosalia admitted. Ilya's earlier comment about getting big was more self-deprecation than anything else. She was one of the lucky few who could rely on the less-veneer-is-more style, a theory most girls abandoned the moment they realized they could change their entire appearance with mere thought. With the exception of their physical shapes, everyone looked exactly how they wanted, with clear skin and sparkly eyes and clothes that were always unique. Nobody seemed to care that none of it was real. Instead, there was backlash against girls like Ilya, those who refused or didn't desire to reconcile themselves into perfection. It all stemmed from envy, of course, envy of a natural beauty that even the best veneers struggled to duplicate.

Ilya had been talking for several seconds before Rosalia latched back onto the conversation.

"And if you really want to make an impression, we'll need something truly wicked. Grandmother says there is nothing in the world that rivals American decadence."

She had forgotten about Deron, but the prospect of a romantic night with him drifted into her mind and made her smile.

Ilya held up a red full-body piece that was dangerously short on fabric in key areas. As Rosalia approached, she changed her mind. "No, we need something memorable, but not trashy. We don't want him to think you were thinking too much about sex. But you can't be unprepared either."

"He's seen me in my underwear before." She pointed to a simple ensemble on the opposite rack. "And his favorite color is blue."

"Trust me, he'll see the fabric, but he won't really be looking at it if you know what I mean." Ilya pulled another hanger from the rack and held it up to Rosalia's body. "If only I had your boobs." She shook her head. "The bottom is revealing. Are you prepared to wear something like this?"

Rosalia smiled, her mind lost to daydream. "I think it's Deron we have to worry about. I can't wait to see his face when he sees me in this."

"He'll think he's died and gone to heaven."

Rosalia's face blanked with a flicker of her veneer. It took a moment to recover, but she managed to force the words out. "Yeah. He'll love it." Turning away, she pretended to browse the rack behind her.

"I'm stupid," said Ilya. "I shouldn't be allowed to talk."

"It's fine," she assured her.

"You'd forgotten about it." Her voice was soft, almost a whisper. "That's what I was hoping for."

"I can put it out of my mind if I want to." Rosalia turned the lingerie over in her hands. "I just hope Deron can too." A pause. "Maybe we *should* go see Travis again."

They walked together to the cash register. Ilya wanted to pay, saying she felt bad about bring up Deron's accident. Rosalia declined, thinking it would have been too strange to be on the bed with Deron, him running his fingers over her blue panties, saying how nice they were. And she'd have to tell him they were a gift from her new girlfriend.

"We don't need Travis if you want something relaxing," said Ilya, as they made their way out of the store. One of the kids on the bench gave them a thumbs-up sign.

"Do any of your ex-boyfriends deal?"

"Your point being?"

Rosalia laughed, felt the memory of Deron's scarred face recede in her memory. It was fading out, but not quickly enough and certainly not permanently.

"Can we go back to your place? My parents aren't very…" Ilya trailed off, as if her knowledge of English had suddenly failed her. "Understanding," she said at last, nodding as if agreeing with herself.

"Sure," said Rosalia. "Do you want to stay over tonight?"

A thin eyebrow climbed her forehead seductively. "You really *do* want to get high, don't you?" When Rosalia began to laugh, she put her arm around her back and said in someone else's voice, "That's cool, baby. I've got what you need."

SEVENTEEN
DERON

The smell of seared alien flesh permeated the air.

Deron wished his costume had included some kind of mask that would filter out the offending odor. It worsened the further he got from the command room, becoming unbearable at the third level. There, the ground writhed with crispy remains, parts that were still jittering, pushed around by little bubbles of air popping through the top layer of congealed blood. Beyond the gulf of sludge, the incoming swarm was relentless even as the mounted guns tore through their ranks. Deron fired his weapon, discretely at first, until finally the bullets were flowing of their own accord, spilling out into the battlefield in random trajectories.

They barely made a dent.

"Contamination imminent!" announced a voice from the heavens.

The ground gave a frightening shake in response and Deron watched as the dirt began to sift through previously unseen grates. The revealed metal glowed dully, highlighting a strip of green down the center of the giant red grid. Without thinking, Deron shuffled to the middle of the path, made sure his boots were well within the line. A second later, spikes shot up from the ground, pointed towards the enemy. Squeals went up from around the corner; a good number of aliens had just impaled themselves on the automatic defenses. He moved forward cautiously and put a few finishing shots into the baddies that were simply hung up.

On level four, he found a large number of critters walking through the spikes. Though they were small enough to avoid being impaled, they did lose some time moving around the obstacles. Most were dutifully following the green strip, lining up in an orderly fashion to meet their deaths.

Deron trained his gun and put down suppressing fire until he noticed an empty patch in the grid. About halfway down the level, the green broke off to the right and led to the wall. There, he found a glowing portal with the word *PURGE* flashing on it. It sounded like a good idea, even though he had no idea what it would do. The chittering from the crowd rose to a fevered pitch as he moved his hand towards the portal, as if they could sense what was about to happen.

The sound of petrol igniting echoed from the other side of the wall, filling level five with enough heat to melt just about anything. The light from the flames flickered unnaturally on the ceiling; the glass simultaneously reflected the carnage and showed the infinite night sky. It looked like the entire universe was burning. Deron shook away the moment of wonder and hurried to the end of level four. Peeking around the partition, he saw that the flames had spread through the enemy like they were kindling. Holding his nose with one hand, Deron moved forward.

It was carnage unlike anything he had ever seen; piles of bodies reached to his knees, throbbing masses of limbs and pinchers and other strange appendages. They looked dangerous and he was suddenly thankful that the outer guns were still working. Turning in place, he retreated to the 4A gun and put his glove to the repair portal. The progress meter filled slowly, but Deron kept his head moving, always looking for the next alien to come around the corner.

Most of the guns had gone silent except for the flame thrower on level three; he could still hear the popping and hissing of the few stragglers that had made it past him. From his vantage point, he could barely see the barrels of the outer gun rotating slowly, searching for a target. With things winding down, Deron couldn't help but feel victorious.

Out of nowhere, a tiny electrical shock exploded on his shin guard, simulating a bite from the critter that had latched onto him. Deron kicked wildly, stumbling away from the cannon, watching helplessly as the progress meter fell back to zero. With his other boot, he pressed down on his shin, his steel toes moving through the oatmeal lump of a creature. After the third try, it came off, skittered away, and assumed attack posture again. Deron emptied his clip into the dirt and luckily, a few bullets hit their mark. Adrenaline pumped through his veins and the familiar sensation made him smile. He hadn't had this much fun since the first few runs of Destined 4 Death. The sim games were like drugs in that way—indescribable highs and diminishing returns.

Off in the distance, Deron heard a growl that rattled his bones. He crept over the pool of dead bodies, keeping close to the wall. At the edge, he stuck his head out and saw the barren landscape, saw the stars setting in the distance, and saw the large plant-like alien bearing down on him. The outer gun only got off three shots before it was upon him, crashing through the wall with a sickening boom.

Deron stumbled, unsure of where anything was anymore. He groped blindly for something to support him while simultaneously pointing his gun at the level boss. His aim was imprecise with one hand; it shook as more sparks zapped at his legs. Somehow he had missed the floodwaters gathering at his feet. The input stream was overwhelming, but he laughed out of frustration, remembering that it was all a game, knowing he would have the upper hand the next time around. He screamed his battle cry and swung around to face the enemy. Above him, the boss prepared for its main attack. It swung a thorny whip dangerously close to Deron's face, making him recoil.

Off-balance, he fell backwards and struck his head on the barrier.

"Son of a bitch!" he yelled as the tendrils of pain erupted from his neck. Something angular had caught him in the same place Russo's boot had, giving him a sharp reminder of his last memory before the coma. There wasn't supposed to be real pain in the game, but that was the risk with the blended reality types. Gravity was gravity, simulation or not. Deron opened his eyes expecting to see the fly trap descending on him. Instead, there was only a drab gray roof crisscrossed by various pipes and wire bundles. Loudspeakers dotted the scaffolding every few feet, pointing in all directions. The night sky was gone, taking that somehow comforting infinity with it.

We do not stop. Sebo's words echoed, but the urgency was lost on him.

Deron sat up and took in the colorless environment. Instead of blood-splattered walls, all he saw were particle board barriers with white tape on their seams. The ground consisted of firm padding that rose and fell to give the impression of uneven terrain. After a moment of staring at the empty corridor, Deron became aware of the sound of aliens crawling along the floor and of guns firing in a controlled rhythm. All around him, the ambient noises ramped up, but there was nothing to look at, no alien marvels to behold. According to the squeals, the enemy was eating him alive. He stood despite the shocks radiating throughout his harness; their tiny zaps were nothing compared to the throbbing in his head. Using the wall for balance, Deron staggered to the end of the maze.

Where there had once been an alien landscape, there was now a wall, worn in places where previous players had tried to run through it, but otherwise just an everyday wall. Deron walked its length beyond the outer barrier until he came to a door. Its outline was recessed and barely visible. There was, however, a tiny indentation at waist level. Deron pulled it and found that the door slid into the wall. Inside, he found a darkened room and a thin man sitting at a desk. He was moving his hands over the plastic surface like a pianist over an imaginary keyboard.

"Holy shit!" said the man, finally noticing Deron. He ripped the headphones from his ears and stood up. "You scared the shit out of me." Then, he seemed to remember himself. "You're not supposed to be back here. How'd you even *get* back here?"

"The game glitched," said Deron. "The sound's still on but all the veneers are turned off. It looks…" A wave of warmth floated up through his body, tingling his extremities. The game-runner blurred out and then back in.

"The game's fine," he replied, sitting down again. He pointed to the blank wall above his desk as if there was something to see.

"But..." Deron reconsidered his question.

"I'm ending the level. You guys lost anyway."

The prospect of defeat wasn't fair; the game obviously had some problems. Now their names would go up on the boards as *Did Not Finish*. Grumbling his protest, Deron followed the man back through the maze, past the particle board and cannons made of foam. As they walked, it looked like the game was trying to recover; bits of veneer flashed here and there. By the time they reached the first level, most of it had come back.

"Where the fuck have you been?" asked Sebo as Deron entered the command room.

"Stupid game glitched," he replied.

"It did?" Sebo looked at the displays on the window. "I didn't see anything."

Deron still felt woozy and for a moment he lost his balance. His quick grab of the wall made Sebo's eyes widen.

"What happened to you?"

"I fell," he explained. Then, rubbing his neck, he added, "I hit my head."

The color drained from Sebo's veneer. "Do you need—?"

"No, I'm fine." The lie didn't help the pain in his head, but it was better than going back to the hospital. Without waiting for more questions, he exited into the ready room and sat down on the bench. The electrodes on his harness were still warm between his fingers as he dismantled it; they had gotten a good workout.

Sebo sat down across from him, his veneer cycling through various levels of concern. "You sure you're alright?"

Deron shrugged. "My neck hurts, but not as bad as last time."

"Last time," said Sebo. He groaned as he undid the snaps on his vest. "You know we owe him, right?"

"Owe who?"

"Russo." Sebo dragged out the syllables.

"And what do we owe him?"

"A fucking beating," he replied, throwing his harness into a bin in the corner. He stood, agitated. "You know, when I was at Dahlstrom, they taught us some basic self-defense. If you'd have had that kind of training, Russo wouldn't have gotten away with it."

Deron forced a laugh. "What the hell kind of school was that?"

"The kind where they don't let in people like Russo."

"Well," said Deron, standing up, "it's too late now."

Sebo followed him out of the ready room and into the lobby. "It's never too late, man. I know you're all Zen about Russo, but he needs to have the shit kicked out of him for once in his life. We need to teach that fucker a lesson."

A boisterous group of teenagers coming out of the Destined 4 Death room cut their conversation short. They were displaying the post-game euphoria that only full sensory immersion could provide. Swarm Survivor was good for its genre, but nothing beat virtual. Deron rolled his eyes at Sebo. For all the shit he was giving him about getting back at Russo, it had been his idea to play the safer game.

Safer, thought Deron, touching his neck. There was too much pain for a complete sentence.

At the front counter, an overweight man in a shiny purple suit looked from Sebo to Deron and back. "I don't tolerate threats to my staff." Beside him, the game-runner looked nervously at the floor.

"Who made a threat?" asked Sebo.

"You said you owed Lionel a beating. That's a threat where I come from."

Sebo smiled and cycled his eyes. "You are quite mistaken, kind sir. My friend and I were simply having a private discussion on the merits of retribution—a discussion, I might add, that does not concern you or this Lionel you speak of."

"Just give me your fucking tickets and get out of my parlor."

Deron tossed his tab onto the counter and nudged Sebo to do the same.

The fat man scanned the tabs into his palette. "Lionel says one of you fell and hit your head."

"Yeah," said Deron.

"Well, if you're even thinking about suing us I'd remind you to remember the waiver you—"

Sebo feigned rebuke. "We wouldn't dream of it, your corpulence." He thumbed the portal on the counter to pay the bill and then pushed Deron along until they were outside. "That guy was a dick," he said, once they were safely out of earshot. "They think just because someone signs a wavier that they don't have any responsibility to help them. That's the true American reality." He rubbed his arms with his hands for several seconds before asking, "How did you fall?"

Deron smirked and reconciled a flickering clock on his sleeve. It was getting close to eleven; the last bus back to Easton would leave at half-past. "I was startled."

"Pardon me?"

"I said I was startled," he repeated, kicking at the litter on the sidewalk.

"Oh," said Sebo, as if he had never considered the possibility. Then, in a very serious voice, "Was your character a woman?"

"This from the guy who locked himself in the command room where it was safe. I tangled with a twelve-foot plant!"

"And he kicked your ass." Sebo crossed his arms.

Deron chuckled, surveyed the street for a place to eat. "Yeah, but I tangled with it. I did that shit."

"And then the game glitched?"

"Damn right it did." The memory of the gray maze flashed in his head. Everything had looked so strange without color, but it wasn't a completely unfamiliar scene. Somewhere in his memory there were blank walls and empty palettes, but he couldn't place it.

A sick part of him extended the absence of veneers to the entire world, creating a place where the sun was just a gray circle hanging in a gray sky, barely visible without any veneers to give off light.

Blinded by the darkness, thought Deron.

EIGHTEEN
RUSSO

A light mist had begun to fall by the time Agent Tavarez paused at the corner of Brazos and Eleventh Street. Russo had tailed him all the way from The Drag, at first blending in with the crowd and then keeping to the alleys and recessed windows as the population thinned out. Soon it was just Russo and Eric walking the streets, the night becoming more ominous as the veneers diminished. There was no expectation of midnight revelers this far out from downtown, so decorations were limited to the tops of buildings, beacons for condominiums and extended stay hotels that could be seen at a distance. Closer to street level, the only glow was from the running lights on the sidewalks and even those seemed to recede at the agent's approach.

Tavarez stood motionless at the edge of the sidewalk. If he knew he was being followed, he wasn't letting on.

Russo watched from a doorway, taking the opportunity to stretch his feet in his boots. While they were great for making an impression on Deron's neck, he'd have chosen something more comfortable if he had known he'd be walking downtown Easton for an hour. At the same time, he wished for a jacket or long sleeves. His lack of preparation opened a pit in his stomach. For all the time he had put into staking out the PD, he hadn't really planned for the confrontation that would follow.

The stone egg in his pocket was the closest thing he had to a weapon.

After a few minutes, the agent crushed out a cigarette that Russo hadn't even seen him light. Then without looking for traffic, he crossed against the flashing red hand to the other side of Eleventh Street.

Russo looked up and saw that he was heading into the Brazos Place condominiums, a luxury high-rise that went up maybe thirty floors. Most of the windows were dark, their sills lit from below by ambient veneers. Only the ground level looked alive, though the only person Russo could see was a bored cashier behind the counter of a small eatery in the building's corner. An etching program was running on its windows, filling them with swirling lines that grew from the bottom and then shimmered into nothing. Russo watched the agent through this pulsating curtain as he ordered a late dinner.

When the cashier turned to make his meal, Tavarez drifted to the windows to survey the intersection. The way he crossed his hands behind his back gave Russo the impression of a man standing guard.

"We're all criminals, aren't we?" asked Russo. He had moved closer while the agent's back was turned and from his new hiding place he could see the look of determination on Eric's face. He was scouting for prey.

It was common for uniforms to look for the worst in people. To them, everyone had the capacity to break the law. Easton was populated by millions of time bombs, each one ready to go off in a blast of civil disobedience at a moment's notice. The only option was a pre-emptive strike. It was as easy as picking out a random citizen and busting them for minding their own business.

But Tavarez wasn't a uniform, and he wasn't EPD. So why the night watch act?

The cashier dropped a paper sack onto the counter and called the agent over. Tavarez collected his dinner and headed back towards the foyer, disappearing behind the large outer doors of the building.

Russo took a deep breath, counted to twenty, and then darted across the street. The doors opened inward as he approached and revealed a lobby with a rustic design full of brands and silhouetted livestock. A marble veneer covered the floor, providing a light background to the black B within a star that someone had reconciled in the middle of the room. Russo looked past the decorations to the slight shoe prints of a man who had just come in off the damp streets. The first line veered left into the cafe; the other came from that direction and went forward through two saloon-style doors. A portal off to the right said *Elevators*.

Pushing through, Russo found himself in an octagonal lobby with two elevators on each side. A circular couch occupied the middle of the room, providing respite to an older man who sat absorbed in his palette. He said nothing as Russo moved to the elevators to examine the building directory. The list of names was long, but not one of them was Eric Tavarez. He cursed as the directory auto-scrolled back to the top.

"Are you looking for someone?" asked the man on the couch. His voice was soft and cordial, tinged with a rare southern accent. When he looked up, Russo saw that his eyes had a white film over them.

"Did you see a guy come through here?"

"Lots of people come through here," he replied, scrolling to the next page on his palette. "What did he look like?"

"He's an agent, about this tall." Russo put out his hand.

"An *agent*? In my building?"

"Yeah. I saw him come in here." He swiped at the directory again and set it scrolling.

The old man took a quick look around the room. "I didn't see anyone."

"Well, then it's a regular fucking mystery isn't it?" asked Russo, waving his hands in the air. He felt the urge to punch the portal, but there was no glass to shatter into a million satisfying pieces.

"Oh, I love a mystery, though I admit it takes me longer to figure them out these days. Maybe I could help you?"

"Whatever," said Russo. He reconciled a portal next to the directory and did some basic math. Thirty floors with six apartments each. How much time would it take to knock on all those doors? And that was assuming the agent even lived in one of them. He could have given Russo the slip out the back.

"Let's see. A man goes into a room. A boy follows him. When the boy gets there, the man is gone."

Russo sneered at being referred to as a boy.

"If you follow a man into a room and the man is no longer in the room, logic suggests that the man has left the room. Now, the man could have exited through one of the four elevators, which all go to the same floors, so there's no real difference between them. Or he could have gone out the back door towards the gym. Except that the gym is closed."

"Will you shut the hell up?"

"The real mystery comes from the addition of a third party, namely myself, who has been seated at this couch for the better part of an hour and has witnessed the comings and goings of six individuals, but none within the last half hour."

Russo wondered why the directory wasn't like the faculty directory at school that had pictures accompanying the names.

"The problem with logic puzzles is that to properly deduce a solution, you must be in full possession of the facts. If no solution can be derived, you should go back and examine your theorems and see if any of them can be challenged."

Behind him, Russo heard the rustling of a paper bag. He turned slowly to see the old man pull a sandwich from it.

"You cannot trust what you see," he said, preaching. "In fact, you should not trust any of your senses at all. You followed a man into a room. When you entered, there was a man, but not the man you were following. You assumed this because when you looked at the man, he appeared differently. But even someone of your age knows how easily veneers can be applied." The white film slipped from his eyes. "And removed."

The whole veneer dropped and then it was Agent Eric Tavarez sitting on the couch enjoying a sandwich, his eyes delighting in the lesson he was teaching Russo.

"Why are you following me, Russo Rivera?"

Russo hesitated, crossed his arms reflexively to build his defenses. He was once again staring into those piercing eyes, feeling like he was being torn open. "How do you know my name?"

"I remember your case. Trespassing, right?"

"Something like that."

"I was expecting to see you again now that Deron Bishop has recovered, though admittedly, not at my residence."

Russo swallowed hard.

"Oh," said Eric, smiling, "news to you? Well, you can take solace in the rote procedure of the Easton bureaucracy. They won't bring charges against you on rumor alone."

"I..."

"Of course you didn't. Stick to that until your trial. Now, I would say that you've come to exact revenge for me identifying you, except if I recall, you got off light for your misdemeanor. So, that said, why are you here?"

Although Eric's attitude grated on him, Russo understood exactly where it was coming from. The agent operated from a position of power, a position he gained by having knowledge that Russo didn't. Where he had learned the power was irrelevant; taking it from Eric would be Russo's shortest path.

"I want to see like you."

"I'm not sure I follow," said the agent, his voice full of deceit.

"You see me, don't you? It doesn't matter what I reconcile, you see the real me."

"That would be a useful magic to have," admitted Eric. He stood abruptly. "I can *see* why you'd be so anxious. If I were in your shoes, I would be curious too."

"I want you to teach it to me."

Eric laughed, approached the elevator, and hit the call button. "Even if there were anything to teach, I doubt you would have the discipline to learn it. You tracked me through a crowd, which I admit is impressive. But your soul," he said, motioning to Russo's chest, "is just not evolved enough for that kind of power. And I don't need any magic to see that."

"Just tell me how!"

From within the elevator, Eric shrugged. "Apply yourself. Graduate high school and college. Stop trespassing and assaulting people. In short, be exactly like you aren't. Maybe in ten years or so, after you prove yourself a good beat cop, I'll consider taking you on my team." He raised a warning finger as the doors closed. "But you need to be spotless from here on out."

Ten years, thought Russo.

Fuck that.

Above the elevator doors, a dormant portal began displaying numbers, incrementing before finally stopping on twelve.

Big condos in a small footprint, only six apartments per floor.

Russo smirked, waited the requisite five minutes, and pressed the call button.

NINETEEN
SEBO

It was only a few minutes before the cold drove Sebo and Deron back to Paramel Terminus. The flashy graphics of the Chinese eateries on the south end of town would just have to wait until next time. It wasn't such a terrible fate; the transit station was home to many convenience shops and food kiosks that could whip up an eighty percent approximation of whatever meal they desired. The concessions comprised a neat row on one side of the holding pen where Sebo sat with one leg crossed over the other and arms folded in an attempt to warm his body. His eyes were on the large portal above the security gates showing the arrival and departure of various trains and buses. One line was for Easton, with a departure time of eleven-thirty.

On one side of the veneer, Sebo was happy to be out of a cold that had turned frigid while they were playing Swarm Survivor. On the other, it felt like a waste to come all the way to Paramel and not spend every moment of it in a sim parlor or at one of the many adult-themed sensory shops. There was one store in particular that he enjoyed, a place called Natural Designs that sold full-wall veneers that at the right angle looked three-dimensional. The illusion made the viewer think that the room extended further into the wall and the extra area just so happened to contain a young woman suffering from Agora- and Vestiphobia. She would sit at her desk or watch television or sometimes even just stand in front of the wall as if there were an invisible mirror between her and the viewer. But like all great advances in pornography, it cost over four grand, leaving Sebo with no option but to wait until it went on sale.

Browsing the local shops was also a great way to avoid The Shakes. It kept the body moving and the eye processing data, activity that was important if he wanted to stave off the inevitable backlash against the drop in sensory input. Whether it was blended reality or full immersion, simulations had a way of over-stimulating the brain, feeding it so much data so quickly that when it stopped, it caused involuntary panic in the player. Sebo could already feel his fingers twitching under his arms and the more they shook, the harder he pressed down on them. Food would have helped, but a quick glance showed the lines were already too long. The discomfort would have passed by the time he got back to his seat.

Deron didn't seem to have any problems with sensory withdrawal, though he had lapsed into a pensive mood again. He was holding a slice of pizza and studying it as if it were a work of art instead of a greasy amalgamation of dough and synthetic cheese. Or maybe that was how Deron dealt with the aftereffects, by withdrawing from the world, closing up shop for a short time while he mourned the loss of data. Sebo watched him for a few minutes until the spell finally broke and Deron took a bite of his slice. He chewed thoughtfully.

"Is it good?" asked Sebo.

"It's not Kung Pao chicken," said Deron, taking another bite. He used his napkin to wipe the sides of his mouth. "But what is?" he mused.

"I suppose it would be the intersection of two sets: chicken and the Kung Pao preparation style. Just like how pizza is the intersection of pepperoni, cheese, tomato—"

"And ovens."

Sebo nodded. "And ovens, yeah." He pulled his hand out and examined it; the tips still trembled, so he shoved it under his armpit again. "It makes me wonder if simulations are ultimately bad for the human brain."

"Huh?"

"The Shakes," said Sebo, squeezing his arm. "What is it that makes simulations more intense than the video games we play on our portals? And why don't we play those anymore? Do you remember Carnage?"

Deron scrunched his eyes in recollection. "Is that the one where you run over people for points?"

"That was one option. But what was so engaging about the game was that its race track was in an open world. You could race, you could run over pedestrians, or you could spend the whole time knocking out your opponents." Cartoony explosions of rocket-propelled grenades striking other drivers flashed in his head.

"Which did you do?"

"Neither," replied Sebo, thinking of the time he had spent in that virtual world and the lack of any meaningful progress. "What I enjoyed most was putting on some music and just driving for hours, you know, exploring."

"Sounds boring." Deron took another bite, again chewing it with gusto.

"You would think so, but I liked it. I'm not sure how to describe it, but it was just me, sitting at my desk, driving a little car around in my portal. There was a whole world for me to explore and that's all." He paused, remembered the nights, the music, and the empty energy drinks piling up on his desk. Touring the unknown land made him feel like an explorer, a pioneer, but it came with loneliness, a suffocating isolation. He shuddered involuntarily.

"I used to play Arms Race," said Deron, looking up.

Sebo followed his gaze, examined the shifting veneer on the ceiling of the station. It had three sections, each with a vaulted inner rectangle that held the dizzying array of reconciled images. Above the entrance and kiosks, flashy advertisements exalted the latest advances in fast food technology and directed tourists to the sim parlors and boutiques within walking distance. Directly overhead, a serene collection of borderless portals showed clips from movies and television shows and even bits of gameplay, anything to distract the waiting crowd below. Above the gate to Easton, Sebo could just make out the almost full moon icon and a temperature that read somewhere in the fifties.

"I liked how at the beginning, you started off weak," continued Deron, reminiscing. "You had to gather resources to build up an army and research new weapons. But the enemy kept attacking and it felt like you'd just keep doing it over and over." He swallowed, cleared his throat. "But then you reach critical mass. You have enough resources to build an army and suddenly you don't care how much is coming in, because no matter how much you spend, you can't spend it all. Then the tables turn. You invade and conquer the map. And that's the way it always goes. At some point, you just overwhelm your enemy."

Sebo smiled to himself. "Are you building an arsenal of resources?"

"I'm amassing wealth."

"To what end?"

"Annihilation?"

"Of what enemy?"

Deron turned his head and grinned. "All of them."

A polite nod was all that Sebo could muster. One of the public service announcements that ran in homeroom replayed in his head, the one about troubled teens and their potential for mass murder. Deron didn't seem capable of killing though. It was only in video games that he unleashed his violent side and even then, his ferocity paled in comparison to what Sebo could summon. For that matter, Deron didn't have any enemies save one and any kind of retaliatory strike against Russo would be well-warranted.

"It's dark in here," said Deron, after a while. He put the grease-stained pizza box on the seat next to him and wiped his mouth.

"No it's not," replied Sebo, acutely aware of the ubiquity of veneers, how their light stung from every angle. If anything, it was too much, too overpowering for a night that was winding down. He glanced at the portal over the gates. The departure time for Easton had begun to flash. "Come on," he said, standing up. "Or you won't get a window seat."

Security in Paramel was as stringent as that in Easton, but at least they had the good sense to pat them down before they got on the bus. Once Sebo and

Deron had made it through the gauntlet of metal detectors and beeping wands, they found two seats near the back of the bus and sat down, Deron next to the window. The veneered glass showed an advertisement for a new condo development just off the main thoroughfare. Sebo shook his head and reached for the window, reconciling the ad into a dull gray that was comforting in its simplicity.

"Advertisements are the bane of my existence," Sebo said, growling. "When I become mayor of Easton, the first thing I'm going to do is outlaw most advertising. Everything will have to be static text, one or two photos of whatever you're shilling, but that's it. No voiceovers, no ambient aromas, nothing. It's assault is what it is."

"She's kind of cute," said Deron, stubbing his finger on the window.

Sebo's response got stuck in his throat as the bus started to hum. He tried to look where Deron was pointing, but only saw the gray anti-veneer. As the bus rolled forward, he watched his friend's head turn to the left. "What are you looking at?"

"The girl on the other bus. She reminds me of Rosalia, except her chin was bigger." He touched his own face. "Is that right?"

"Is *what* right?"

"Is that the right way to describe her?"

"Who are we talking about?"

Deron didn't seem to register the frustration in Sebo's voice. "I've heard people say that chins are sharper."

Sebo sighed and sat back in his chair. The button on his armrest let him recline, but not enough to get comfortable. He closed his eyes and tried to ignore the ramblings coming from the seat next to him. Deron never knew when to quit, but that was what made him interesting. There was not just wonder in the world, but in people as well. Sebo didn't know which he would come to understand first, or if such breakthroughs were even possible.

"There's nothing to see out there," said Deron. He was sitting at attention, with one hand on the window, peering out. "Where are all the roads?"

"It's nighttime. This precludes you from seeing anything."

"But we could see them when we were coming in," he protested.

"No," said Sebo, "that was on the other side of the road. You were facing the other direction. You see?" That seemed to shut him up for a minute.

"That's just not right. I didn't know it was so empty."

Sebo muttered something under his breath and reached for the window again. He reconciled a cartoon picture of a rabbit under a watercolor sky. Two eggs in the foreground sparkled blue and white. "There, look at that for a while."

After a few minutes, Deron said, "I see something."

"It's called a rabbit."

"Rabbits don't glow like that. But it's very…" He paused, searched for the word. "It's almost like low resolution. Blurry, I guess?"

That didn't make any sense. The image he had reconciled was perfect down to the last pixel.

"It's so far away," continued Deron.

"What are you talking about?" demanded Sebo. He sat up and gestured to the window. "It's right there: a rabbit, eggs, and the sun. The veneer looks fine."

Deron narrowed his eyes suspiciously.

"Fine, whatever you say." Sebo settled into his seat again and crossed his arms. "This blindness act isn't very amusing."

"You're the one who's blind," mumbled Deron, barely audible over the noise of the road passing beneath them.

TWENTY
ILYA

The street name for the drug was Mellow, so-called because of its ability to pacify even the most hyper or anxious user. It didn't come on immediately; there was a period when the world seemed to sparkle, when everything was funny, and love in all its forms was reciprocal. That lasted about half an hour, most of which Ilya and Rosalia spent riding the tram back from the Tsugumi Galleria. It wasn't that it was far away, just that there were so many stops, so many people still getting on and off as Saturday crossed into Sunday. They kept climbing aboard and casting veiled glances at the two giggling girls sitting in the back.

Ilya loved the feeling that Mellow brought on, the way it took even the toughest puzzles and reduced them to an afterthought. Even though she was still cognizant of reality, she found that it no longer mattered to her. The tram would get them where they needed to go, so there was nothing to do but sit back and enjoy the ride. Beside her, Rosalia slumped in the seat with her head on Ilya's shoulder, laughing every now and then at a funny shape that passed by.

The commerce sector's fancy light shows gave way to residential neighborhoods as they turned off Parker Avenue. The streets were mostly empty, but the convenience stores on the corners were still bright and welcoming of the late-night shopper. Surrounding those beacons was the soft glow of amber streetlights set just close enough to afford no shadows between them.

At the end of Rosalia's street, the tram came to a stop and Ilya had to put considerable effort into navigating the rows and stairs to the sidewalk before it took off again. She watched her friend barely escape the last step before the warning bell tinkled and the electric engine revved up. They both found it hilarious, the idea of Rosalia hanging by the ankle as the tram sped down the street. Ilya smiled when Rosalia put her arm around her shoulder to steady herself. Walking had become quite a chore, but together they managed to make it halfway down the street to her house without falling over once.

Fortunately, her parents were asleep when they entered. It wasn't until they were opening the door to Rosalia's room that her step-mother—or as Rosalia called her, Lynn The Evil Bitch—poked her head out from the master bedroom and inquired about the late hour. Ilya didn't listen to the whole exchange; she was lost in the veneer on Rosalia's door.

There was water that sparkled at different angles, not moving but alive in some way. It contrasted with the darkness behind it, a deep black that extended into the distance where the tiniest flame silhouetted two figures. They seemed content at having found each other in the reconciled emptiness. One figure was likely Rosalia and it didn't take much effort to deduce who the other was.

Rosalia's bedroom lit up as they entered. It was the first time Ilya had been in her room and her first thought was how messy everything was. The bed was just a mattress on the floor and Rosalia's desk looked like a drafting table with the legs cut off. Her possessions formed a small mountain in the middle of the room, leaving a border along the walls so that a person could sit or stand next to them. It took a moment for the portals to buzz in, but when they did, Ilya understood the design choice.

Rosalia was still standing by the door with her hand on the wall, smiling and looking intently at Ilya. She blushed under the attention. It didn't matter what appeared, Ilya would act like it was the most amazing thing she had ever seen. The words were already forming when the first image shimmered into view, a placid lake ending in a waterfall in the distance. The shadows gave it depth, made it appear like the room was floating on the water, perhaps even fated to fall over the edge. The statues on either shore were regal and imposing; they held out their hands in warning to all who approached. Beyond, she saw the canopy of a forest, imagined the trees moving in the breeze. Ilya put her hands to her mouth.

"I did this in Canvas," said Rosalia, looking up to reconcile the ceiling. The default lights softened until the room was lit by the reconciled landscape on the wall. She moved to a bean bag in the center of the room and plopped down, her Victoria's Secret bag crumpling in a heap next to her.

"It's fun, right?" asked Ilya, moving closer to the painting. "You're supposed to be able to find people who dream like you." She was fully aware that none of her dreams remotely matched what was on the wall.

Rosalia giggled, put her legs out in front of her, and tried to reach for her toes. "I found someone who painted something like that, but they haven't played in a while."

"Have you done more?" Ilya turned, caught sight of Rosalia in her stretch. "What are you doing?"

"I need my toes."

"Your shoes are still on," she replied.

"Oh," said Rosalia, bending her legs and pulling her feet closer. She began untying the shoelaces. Once her feet were free, she rolled off the bean bag and crawled along the floor and over her bed to another wall. Speaking into her pillow, she said, "I did this one the same day, but no one else has." She sounded disappointed.

Ilya joined her on the mattress, sitting on the edge with her legs folded to the side. She watched as the moon formed, part of it reconciled on the window, breaking up the masterpiece. The proximity of the heavenly body made her heart beat faster, frightened by the possibility that it might strike the Earth. Ilya shuddered and looked with new appreciation on Rosalia, on the unassuming girl who had entered Mellow's second stage. Just enough energy would drain from her body to make her languid but not unconscious.

With a huff, Rosalia rolled onto her back and stared at the ceiling. There were words on her lips, which parted and closed purposefully, but she said nothing. Instead, her hand found its way to the wall again and suddenly all four began to shimmer with photo streams. The little rectangles fell from the crease in the ceiling, tumbling end over end through the waterfall or in front of the moon. They landed in piles along the floor like blocks, some of them upside down, some of them backwards, until finally they slid through the floor and out of view.

"I never knew," said Ilya, leaning back on her elbows. It was hard to tell which images were photos and which were pure reconciliations; Rosalia's skill enabled her to create either interchangeably. There were so many virtual destinations, places of pure fantasy that existed only in a young girl's mind and as two-dimensional representations on her wall.

"Yeah. I draw a lot." Rosalia's speech was beginning to slur as she dragged herself back to the bean bag. She found a comfortable position and put her head back.

It was then that Ilya realized the ceiling was a reconciled portal, not just a veneer that needed to be touched to be changed. Rosalia was running some kind of program that dropped pictures like rain from clouds. They came out of the distance, fell with simulated physics, and landed on the artificial barrier of the ceiling. Ilya joined Rosalia at the bean bag, carved out her own little space, and rested her head near her shoulder.

Together, they watched the downpour.

Ilya saw the sum total of Rosalia's existence expressed in hundreds of thousands of pictures, from things that actually happened, like a junior high dance, to things Rosalia had only dreamt, like a school on the edge of a cliff with its playground hanging precariously over the edge.

"Beautiful." It was all Ilya dared to say because deep down she knew that pictures were just pictures and while enticing, they were only tiny encapsulations of the beauty within the artist.

It was fortunate that Rosalia had such a command of reconciliation, that it allowed her to translate the beauty inside so that everyone else could share in it.

Such talent languished in the ugly, even in Ilya herself. She thought about what was inside her, a mix of unrequited emotions and generational prejudices. There was nothing remotely beautiful except for the love she so desperately wanted to give away.

A bluish-white picture caught Ilya's eye as it fell in the corner of the room. It looked like an elongated light bulb at first, but as she turned to get a better look, she realized that it was an x-ray. Raising her wobbly hand, she pointed to it.

"What's that?"

Rosalia mumbled, tried to look where Ilya was pointing. "Bitches wouldn't let me into Deron's room," she said. "I had to sit outside. The doctors were looking at his x-rays in the wall. I reconciled…" She drifted off for what felt like minutes. "Onto my palette." A thin smile. "I was born."

"Born?" Ilya turned back to Rosalia.

"Bored," she corrected, repeating the word a few times as if to verify it. "I reconcile everything I see." She spread her hands in demonstration.

"Do you ever make mistakes?"

Rosalia huffed, blew a raspberry. When she finally spoke, the words came so quickly and so close together that Ilya had trouble understanding. "I reconcile what I *see*. I don't even think about it. I could close my eyes and reconcile you and get every detail in your face from your eyebrows to your pupils to your lips to your teeth and chin and…" She ran out of body parts and trailed off.

Ilya tried to ignore the warmth filling her cheeks. "So that x-ray is exactly what the doctors were looking at?"

"Sure." She rolled onto her side; her breath smelled vaguely of strawberries. "Why?"

The question hung in the air for a long time during which Rosalia's eyes darted back and forth over the features of Ilya's face. They were mere inches from each other and for a moment, it appeared that Rosalia's inhibitions would succumb to the Mellow and she'd close the distance with a kiss. Ilya reached out and placed her hand on Rosalia's cheek and then slid it to the back of her neck. Her fingers moved tentatively, seeking out the hollow under the base of her skull, pressing firmly, trying to feel something: a lump, a scar, anything. Then, something hard pushed back against her finger, making her heart jump. She looked quickly to the ceiling again.

"Are you sure that's *Deron's* x-ray?"

Rosalia looked up. "Yes. I remember reconciling it."

"Are you sure it's not yours?"

She laughed the way she had on the tram; the questions weren't really reaching her anymore. "My head isn't shaped like an egg."

Ilya continued to prod, at one point feeling what she thought was a tiny scar. She ran her finger over it several times. "Do you see that little square on Deron's neck?"

"Yeah," said Rosalia, as if noticing it for the first time. "What is that?"

Whether from the Mellow or just the situation, Ilya struggled to get the next words out. There was apprehension on Rosalia's veneer, reconciled concern for her lover's welfare. Ilya could see the gears turning, could see her trying to imagine the different explanations for why this bright white speck appeared in Deron's neck. It could have been something from the attack, a metal plate inserted to patch a crack in his vertebrae. And those were all reasonable explanations, to some extent, but only because she was missing a vital piece of the puzzle.

Ilya removed her hand, hesitated before touching her own neck. "I don't know what it is," she said. Then, with just a hint of alarm, "But you've got one in your neck... and so do I."

TWENTY-ONE
DERON

Deron was sitting at the small table in the dining nook, looking through the sliding door to the patio where two red-chested birds had stopped to survey their breakfast. They were vibrant, so out of place on the gray railing and against the equally gray backdrop of the patio walls. The only other color in sight was green, the tips of trees peeking over the wall. He couldn't see the sky, couldn't confirm whether it had lost its color too. One thing was for sure—reality was broken.

He had spent most of Sunday in his room staring at the walls, touching them gently, trying to coerce them into changing. Thinking back to elementary school, he employed the old maxims, tried to remember what teachers had told him about reconciling. A lifetime of instant access to information on the network made him reach for his palette, but he quickly realized it would be as useful as an audio recording that taught the deaf how to hear. If he couldn't reconcile a veneer, then he couldn't use a portal. The reach of the veneer went far beyond his imagination. It covered everything, from walls to bed sheets, from magazines to chairs. His room used to have color; now it just looked like a reconciled picture that someone had shopped to grayscale.

It wasn't until Monday morning when his alarm went off that Deron realized the veneer wasn't really gone; it was his perception that was flawed. There was sound emanating from the wall, but there were no numbers indicating time, no portal providing a black background to the red digits. He had to psyche himself up to reach out for it, to hit the snooze as he had a thousand mornings before. There was something ominous about the bland drywall, a possibility that it might suck the pale pink from his fingertips.

The alarm cut off the second he touched the wall, giving credence to his perception theory. He tried to follow it to its logical conclusion but kept dead-ending in blindness. The idea would have made sense had there been a physical clock in a dark room, but this...

Nothing added up. First, the alarm had sounded, which meant software was running in a portal somewhere. Second, when he touched the wall where the portal should have been, he activated the mute function. If he had closed his eyes while doing this, the events would not have seemed that extraordinary. So what did that all mean?

The question so consumed Deron that he began his morning routine without even noticing it. He put on a pair of pants and an undershirt and headed into the hallway. It was dark without the glow of the baseboards, but he had walked the path from his room to the stairs often enough to find his way without running into anything. The sight of the kitchen, usually filled top to bottom with colors that *popped*, as his mom put it, made him cringe. The description he had been avoiding since his initial discovery wormed its way into his head.

Dead. Everything looked dead.

It wasn't until he sat down at the table and looked outside, watched the first rays of light come up, and saw the birds with their brightly colored feathers and yellow beaks. He didn't know their names, didn't really care. All that mattered was that there was still color in the world.

"What're you all smiles about this morning?"

Oh yeah, thought Deron, remembering the other problem still plaguing him. It had to do with the strange woman roaming his house, an ersatz version of his mom that sounded the same, smelled the same, even told the same boring stories, but looked nothing like the woman who had raised him. This woman looked years older, had wrinkles at the corners of her eyes, splotches on her cheeks and neck. The skin on her arms and legs was pale, marked by blue veins that turned a sickly purple in places. Whoever she was, she thought herself Deron's mother. So far, his plan had been to simply play along, wait for the right moment to confront that issue.

"Do you want breakfast?"

"No," replied Deron, watching the birds fly away.

She seemed to know where everything was, had knowledge that his real mom couldn't pass on in a single day. He tried to imagine the exchange, the information dump of so many collected years in the house. Most disturbing was the way she prepared her morning coffee, pulling blank containers from the cabinets as if she somehow knew their contents. It all added to a mystery Deron didn't fully understand yet. Some things had color while others did not. The coffee can was gray, the scooper too, but when she dumped the grounds into the coffee maker, they were dark brown. Water looked like water, as did the milk when she poured it into a serving cup.

"You don't have to go to school if you don't want to." She spoke with her back to him. Through the sheer robe, Deron could see too much.

He cleared his throat. "I'll think about it."

The woman poured herself a cup of coffee as soon as it was ready and took a seat opposite Deron. She sipped silently, staring at him with the same eyes but a different face. Finally, she asked, "Can you fix your veneer? I don't like this all-black look. It makes you look like a hoodlum."

Deron tried to remember how many times he had touched his face without realizing it. Sunday morning had been a mad dash to reconcile something, anything. It was possible that in the process he had ruined his veneer. There was no way to check, no real mirrors in the house that weren't just portals with reflective software. It was all spurious: the mirror, the process of reflection, and even the image that came back.

He stood and walked around the table, careful to keep his gaze on his mom's face. Kneeling down beside her, he asked, "Can you fix it for me? I'm having… trouble."

Her face twitched, contorted in a way that somewhat resembled concern. It was then that he noticed the brown in her eyes was actually colorful, a gradient between amber and brown, nothing even remotely gray. She placed a finger on his cheek, blinked slowly. "There," she said. "Good as new."

There was no sensation. His face and body had just changed appearance dramatically, yet he felt no warmth, no coolness—nothing. More confused than ever, Deron left the kitchen, left Ania staring blankly after him. He walked the darkened stairs, crossed the loft to his room, and shut the door. It was brighter now that the sun had come up and his first response was to reconcile the windows to blot out the daylight. He couldn't, of course, but as he stood there staring at the unyielding glass, his mind drifted back to Saturday night.

To the bus, to the windows.

The ride back from Paramel had been uneventful save for a landscape that looked nothing like it had on the way over. The first mile from the gate was a wasteland, but in the miles between, it was different. For one, it wasn't as empty as previously shown, didn't have that nuclear fallout aura that made it seem so forbidding. What Deron saw under the glare of the moon looked inviting. There were trees, brush, and a wilderness of unexplored land, full of overgrown grass and small animals darting through it. The abrupt change in content had made no sense then, but now, looking through the windows that couldn't hold back the sun, he realized it had all been a smokescreen.

Someone had reconciled the windows on the bus to show passing scenery that fit in with the government's storyline. It was the same with the windows in Swarm Survivor, just an overlay of veneer, a painting on a painting. He should have made the connection then, but the headache and the injury and…

"Fuck all," he whispered.

Any semblance of control over the world was simply an illusion. The magic that let him change an object's color was the same magic that veneered windows, only someone with a lot more skill had done those. Who could be trusted with such complete control over the world?

Deron gasped, felt the air start to leak out of the room. There was something else going on, something beyond schools and police and government. Something controlled the veneer at the deepest level, kept everyone in line with what amounted to lies.

Lies as unreal as the woman claiming to be his mom.

Deron considered the possibility that his imposter theory was just a way to deal with the truth about a mother who was barely recognizable anymore. No longer was she the picture of regal beauty that her veneer made her out to be. Underneath, she was still human, but that ancient kind that showed their age in their skin. It pained him for many reasons, for the face of a woman closer to fifty than forty, for the knowledge that the process would never stop. She would keep decaying, little by little, until she was dead.

Worst of all was the ignorance. Had she ever looked at her true image in a portal? Had anyone in the world for that matter? Was everyone just lying to themselves, letting death sneak up on them, suffering a heart attack with the face of a college graduate or a stroke at what looked like a professional thirty?

There was a tickle in his nose and Deron dropped out of the cloud long enough to realize his eyes had started to water. He stared at his lap, at the previously black jeans. A moment went by when he thought of nothing but Rosalia's face only to see it consumed by a vortex of questions that blotted out all input.

A million miles away, he heard the door open.

"I'm leaving for work now," said Ania, said the middle-aged woman with streaks of gray in her hair.

"Okay," said Deron, standing and walking to the window. He took in the selectively colored world outside.

"I'll call the school and tell them you won't be in today." She paused as if she wanted to say something else. "Don't watch too much TV," she said finally, her voice uneven.

"Don't worry," replied Deron to the closing door. "I can't."

TWENTY-TWO
ROSALIA

Rosalia was already imagining the discussion in her head when she stepped onto campus. Her route from home brought her into the parking lot, but over the last few weeks, she'd developed a habit of circling around to the courtyard at the front of the school to sit with Ilya. She got to school by bus and since it usually dropped her off early, Rosalia would often find her sitting on the evercrete wall that surrounded the plaza.

Ilya explained that school didn't really start until eight o'clock, so even though they had the option of going inside, she preferred to spend as much of her life outside Easton Central's walls as possible. Today was no different, except that instead of having her head buried in her palette, she was actively scanning her surroundings, probably in anticipation of Rosalia, of the impending conversation.

It would start with a question that expressed her struggles with understanding men, the entire gender in general, and Deron, specifically. And if she knew anything about Ilya, her attentive confidant would reply with some old-world wisdom probably passed down from her grandmother, which would make sense in a logical or mystical kind of way but wouldn't apply to her current situation.

More than anything, Rosalia wanted to know what Deron was thinking when he did certain things or how to predict what he would do if she said certain words, made certain advances. There was no ancient insight for that, just conjecture, no better than Ilya's or asking a random person on the street. The only way to test her theories would be to try them out on her boyfriend, and the wrong move could lead to disaster.

Rosalia shrugged when Ilya asked her why Deron had stood her up Sunday night. It seemed like the right response—a mix of ignorance and apathy, a nonverbal statement when no words would do it justice. Of course, she wanted details, as anyone who was living vicariously through her friend would. Sparing no mundane moment, Rosalia recounted the day, starting from Ilya's departure Sunday morning. She had spent the day reconciling her outfits, trying to find the right colors to compliment the undergarments she had purchased. Around noon, she started sending instant messages to Deron. The fact that he didn't respond didn't bother her until dinner had come and gone. The romantic evening she imagined in her head was shattered, but even then, she was optimistic. After checking her veneer for the thousandth time, she set out for Deron's house.

The next part made Ilya frown, out of concern, empathy, something. Rosalia described the evening, the chill in the air, the breeze blowing down the street, and the feel of her clothes as they moved across her body. She didn't have the right words to say it was sensual without sounding dirty, so she went straight into the approach to Deron's door.

His bedroom window was dark, along with the rest of the house. She knocked on the door and waited. His mom answered, flustering Rosalia. Ania didn't actively dislike her; she was just leery of any girl that could get her little boy into trouble. Rosalia asked for Deron and Ania disappeared without inviting her in. She could only watch through the frosted glass as a shadow trudged up the stairs.

Ilya asked why Ania didn't just let her go up or at least let her wait inside. Again, Rosalia shrugged, tried to explain the complicated relationship between them, but her words came out disjointed. Waving the topic away, she continued the story at the point where Ania came back downstairs and told her that Deron wasn't feeling well, that he needed to get some rest. Rosalia asked to go up and when rebuked, even begged. His mom simply wouldn't budge.

All the dreams, the fantasies of a special night with Deron, were engulfed in a blue flame and crumbled into a heap. And from those ashes rose more questions, most important of which being why he didn't want to see her.

"Have you talked to Sebo?" asked Ilya.

"No, why?"

"I've seen the way Deron looks at you. I don't think he'd pass up a chance to see you unless he had good reason. Or someone had convinced him not to."

"Sebo's not that kind of guy."

Ilya ignored her and tried to change the subject. "Well, so you didn't get to give him your cherry. At least we had some fun on Saturday, right?"

"Yeah," she replied, recalling the feel of Mellow in her veins.

"And Deron's out of the hospital, so he should be back in school today."

"You think?" Rosalia had been sending him messages since yesterday and he hadn't responded to any of them. Even if he were laid up in his bed, it would take minimal effort to reconcile a portal on the wall and send back a note saying he was alive.

"This is why we should question Sebo. He was the last one to see him, right?"

It sounded so ominous, as if she could have said, "He was the last one to see him *alive*, right?" But that would have meant Ania had his body stashed upstairs or already disposed of, weighed down with rocks at the bottom of Gillock Pond. She shook her head, dismissed the crazy theories. Ilya was right; before she went off thinking the worst, she should at least consult with Sebo. Maybe something happened in Paramel. He could have gotten into another fight. There were all sorts of people walking the streets there: punks, synth-addicts, and runaways that had nothing to barter except their bodies. Rosalia shuddered, flashing on a picture of Deron with one of those girls, her torn jeans aimed skyward as he ploughed her in an alley. It would have been Sebo's idea, of course.

Ilya remained silent for a while and when Rosalia looked over, she found her averting her gaze politely. She was wearing her hair up today, matching Rosalia's. It exposed her long neck and evoked images of Saturday night, of a discovery they hadn't talked about since.

"Did you find out anything about our necks?" she asked, happy to see Ilya reengage the conversation.

"Nothing for sure. Some sites say they're biological monitors, other people say they're tracking chips so the government can keep tabs on us."

"But everyone knows about them? How did we not—"

"I didn't know I would bleed from my vagina until the sixth grade," she replied, without missing a beat. "It's like hearing aids or braces. No one teaches us about those, but people still have them."

"Yeah, but people chose to get those things. They don't wake up one morning and find something embedded in their necks. I don't remember ever having anything put in, which means they must have done it when we were little." A horrible thought occurred to her. "Who cuts open babies?"

"We put chips in pets," offered Ilya, though she didn't sound sure of her supporting evidence.

"Yeah, so we can find their owners if they get lost. I know where I live." Rosalia sighed. There was no use arguing; she needed to speak with someone knowledgeable.

Add it to the pile, she thought. Add it to the millions of other things she had to do to get the world back on track. Getting an audience with Nurse Hendricks would be the easiest, but would a school nurse know enough? There was also Mr. Randall, the biology teacher. Maybe he knew why humans needed to have implants in their necks.

"What are we doing in P.E. today?" asked Ilya.

Inside, Rosalia recoiled, amazed at how easily Ilya moved between topics of grave importance to those that meant nothing to anyone except the lacrosse coach. It didn't matter one bit what they did to meet their daily physical education requirement. They could run ten miles, take a fitness test, or play volleyball. Either way, it wouldn't change the fact that...

Groaning, Rosalia put her face in her hands, tried to take a deep breath through her palms. A moment later, she felt Ilya's hand on her back.

"Are you okay?"

"I don't know. Before… before it happened, I told Deron that I was going to kill Russo. But I made that shop instead. I should have gone with my original plan."

Ilya's fingers stroked her gently. "We could still do that."

"We?" Rosalia stole a look sideways.

The way her face changed made Rosalia see her in another light. Up until that moment, Ilya had always seemed harmless, a girl whose words and actions often didn't match the intensity in her eyes. But did that make her a killer?

Not waiting for an answer, Rosalia added, "I was joking."

"Then so was I," replied Ilya. Her voice was cheerful, but Rosalia read disappointment in the way she removed her hand, tracing her fingertips before withdrawing completely. "At least killing Russo would solve one of your problems. Then no one would have to see you sad anymore."

"I thought I was hiding it," she said, adjusting her veneer.

"Some things are more than just appearance. When you—"

"No," Rosalia interrupted. "We can't just murder someone." It was absurd, the idea of actually taking someone's life, even a person as vile as Russo.

"We *can*. The question is do we want to."

In another life, thought Rosalia. It would only work in another world where she wasn't the sum of seventeen years of civilized development, but rather some reconciled version of herself, one free from morals and consequence. That only happened in movies, in video games. This was real life.

"There has to be something in the middle," said Rosalia, glancing at the clock above the front doors. It was getting close to eight and Principal Ficcone was already staring down the stragglers in the courtyard. "Some way we can score one back for Deron without more backlash."

"I have some ideas."

"Ilya," she said, the name still sounding foreign on her tongue, "can you promise me something?" She extended her pinky, slightly curved. "Promise me you won't kill Russo."

Ilya took her entire hand, cupping it gently. "I promise not to kill Russo until you tell me it's alright."

"Thank you." Rosalia stood and slung her backpack over her shoulder. She was about to take a step when she realized Ilya hadn't moved, was still sitting there with a grin on her face. "What?"

"It's too funny," Ilya replied. Standing, she looked Rosalia up and down before saying, "You think I'm a lesbian and now a killer. You don't know me very well, do you?"   The ringing of the first bell saved Rosalia from having to reply.

TWENTY-THREE
JALAY

The smell of reheated fish product pervaded the air as Jalay stood at the cafeteria doors that led out to the plaza. Sebo was out there, sitting on the low wall with a palette in his hand and a smug veneer on his face. Jalay tried to think of what he would say to him, how he could convince him that he was no longer his enemy, but the words wouldn't come. He went through dozens of false starts in his head before taking a sharp breath to calm himself. It was just Sebo, friend to the pansy Deron; there was no reason to be afraid of him. Bolstered by the momentary confidence, Jalay barged through the cafeteria doors, crossed the plaza, and sat down next to his enemy by association.

"Those who have knowledge do not predict. Those who predict do not have knowledge," said Sebo, without looking up from his palette. "Lao Tzu said that, six hundred years before Christ."

"Jesus," said Jalay.

There was no amusement in Sebo's veneer. "It means that you shouldn't try to predict the future because by its very nature, it's unpredictable. And when you hear a quote like that, you start to ask yourself, do I live that way? Do I avoid making bold predictions about the future because I know that I can never be certain what will happen? I thought yes." He ran his hand down his palette, cleared away what looked like a trailer for a video game. "Until now, that is."

Jalay squeezed one hand in the other, convinced that the words were some kind of weapon meant to confuse him. Russo had played the stupidity card with him all the time, making Jalay out to be some kind of retard, but it wasn't true. He could understand a lot, even the ramblings of a pretentious student.

"If someone would have asked me just five minutes ago whether Russo's boyfriend would be joining me for lunch, I would have laughed in their monkey faces. I would have told them with one hundred percent certainty that no such thing would or *could* ever happen." He scratched his cheek. "Yet here we are. So tell me, my bovine friend, when Russo is pounding you from behind, do you ever look over your shoulder and catch eyes with him? And if so, do you honor him by keeping eye contact while he rams you?"

"No," admitted Jalay, refusing to reconcile the image in his head. "Russo isn't caring like Deron." He made his eyes go wistful. "What's it like to have such a gentle lover?"

That got a smile that morphed into a smirk. "Fair enough. So what's your deal? Are you supposed to distract me long enough so Russo can sneak up and pipe me like he did Deron?"

"So you know it was him?"

Sebo laughed. "Seriously? The entire student body knows it was Russo. If the uniforms weren't so fucking incompetent—"

"They can't do anything anyway," said Jalay, pulling his palette from his bag. "They don't have any witnesses. Without witnesses..." he began, but thought the better of trying to explain how courts worked to Sebo.

"There were no witnesses. And if there were, no one at this school has the fortitude to come forward. Not that I blame them."

"We don't need *real* witnesses." Jalay reconciled a portal and brought up a folder of images. "I worked on these yesterday." He enlarged a picture of the football field. There was a shadowy figure on the left, barely recognizable as Deron. He was walking towards the bleachers where another figure sat. "Notice the low angles, the blur at extreme distances, the slight glare from the sun."

"Who reconciled this?"

"I did."

Sebo's face flashed an angry veneer. "You saw it happen?! Why haven't you said anything?"

Jalay groaned. "I didn't see it. No one did." He minimized the image and brought up another one. "But it doesn't matter. *I* reconciled this, all of these. I've been making shops of Deron for years and hanging out with Russo for even longer. I'm the only one who can reconcile what might have happened."

"These are fake?"

"Yes," replied Jalay. "I did five different angles. Two of them actually show the fight taking place." He scrolled through the pictures, found one of Russo standing over a fallen and bloodied Deron.

Sebo cringed.

"That's why I had to tell you first," he continued. "When I start posting these on all the boards, I didn't want you to think they were real."

"I don't get you, Jolly. What's your angle on this? Why would Russo tell you to incriminate him?"

"Fuck Russo." Jalay cleared out the palette and for a moment, couldn't think of anything else to say. In the lull, he reconciled idly, bringing a random collection of color and shape to his portal, a piece of art that meant nothing but seemed to express how he felt. "I like to reconcile," he muttered. "Some people are good at math or piano, but all I can do is draw."

"No," said Sebo, trying to correct him. "What you do is play lackey to a psychopath who has no qualms about dragging someone to the blood-slicked precipice of death and just leaving them there. When you think about it, you two are a classic pairing: the brute and the buffoon. And historically, the buffoon doesn't realize it's too late until he's turned on or killed. So this whole pretext of you having a lover's quarrel with Russo just comes off a little dubious. People like you... People like you and Russo just can't be trusted."

"You don't need to do anything yet."

Sebo raised his hand. "Don't even bother. The day I help you is the day..." Again, he fell silent, looked away. "I can't conceive a situation in which I would ever help you. You've humiliated Deron for years. You've *tormented* him. What kind of person are you anyway? How do you get off reconciling all that gay shit? Honestly, you must have gotten hard a few times right? Nobody reconciles naked guys for that long and doesn't start getting some kind of perverted sexual joy out of it. So come on, fess up now, no judgments."

Jalay couldn't find the strength to laugh. His stomach was starting to complain about lunch and the fishy aroma that had been so stifling before now seemed enticing in his memory. Only after downing five or six square fillets would he be ready to argue his sexual orientation with Sebo. Still, there was a way that didn't require him to go toe to toe with the Dahlstrom dropout.

The portal under his hand came back to life, filling the screen with folders that shrunk the more their numbers grew. It settled into a yellow field with little black dots, held for a moment, and then exploded into a slideshow of various folder icons, each with three representative pictures of its contents.

"I don't think I've shared this with anyone, ever," said Jalay, holding the palette at an angle.

Sebo leaned in and clucked his tongue. "I think you may have an unhealthy obsession with pornography." Suddenly, his finger shot out, tapped one of the folders as it scrolled by. It expanded into the forefront and a caption faded in. "You have stuff from Natural Designs?"

"These are just the stills," replied Jalay, browsing into the folder and pulling up the profile pages of the most recent girls, a newly eighteen model by the name of Jordan.

"Do you have their Roommate software?"

Jalay managed a weak smile, could almost smell the desperation coming off Sebo. Old allegiances died easily in the face of free jackware.

"I do," he replied at last, amused by the sudden excitement on Sebo's face. Then, mocking Sebo's style, he asked, "Is that something you would be interested in?"

"Something in which I would be interested," replied Sebo, who then put his hand over his heart. "If you let me copy that program, I swear I will never question your sexuality again. Not in public for the amusement of the student body, nor in private with Deron and Rosa. Furthermore, if a third party were to ever question your sexuality, I will make a passive effort to refute such accusations, but only to the extent that my standing relationships allow. Do we have a gentlemen's agreement?" He removed his hand from his chest and held it out.

Jalay looked around; there were a few curious faces in the crowd. "I'd rather not shake," he said. "But it's a deal."

"Well that's just balls," declared Sebo. He brought up his instant messenger on his palette. "What's your handle?"

"Jalay, with six L's." When Sebo's message popped up on his screen, he dragged Jordan's Roommate files onto the chat window. Together, they watched the transfer bar grow.

"This doesn't make us friends."

Jalay nodded in reply. "Of course not. I'm not friends with queers."

"Coming from a stolid heterosexual like you, I completely understand."

When the file finished, Jalay noticed that Sebo deleted him from his contact list. It was such an insignificant act, but it reminded him that nothing had really changed. Trading some porn at lunch wasn't going to undo years of antagonism. It would take a grand gesture, something like putting Russo behind bars, to even start down the road to earning their trust.

He *needed* to befriend Sebo because he *needed* to befriend Deron. Once he had those two on his side, Rosalia would have to give him a chance. She might resist, which was understandable after the hell he had put her boyfriend through, but eventually she would come around. A couple of years from now, they would all be sitting around some bar, talking about their classes and how boring their professors were. Then Deron would have to piss and Sebo would go with him to hold it and they would be alone.

Jalay flashed on the fantasy, felt the awkward pall as Rosalia realized she was sitting with a man who was once her enemy. She wouldn't know what to say, wouldn't need to say anything. He would just put his hand on the table, start reconciling it, changing the wood into water, bordered on the sides by lush banks of grass, ending in a waterfall. And if she didn't recognize the scene, he would wipe it clean and replace it with the terrifying moon. That would get her attention.

She'd look at him in wonder and ask, "How do you know about that?"

And he'd say nothing, would simply wipe the table clean once more and show a beach with sparkling sand leading off into the distance. The stars beyond it. The galaxies. She would understand.

"When are you going to post the shops?"

Jalay barely heard the question, but he still managed to answer. "Soon, now that you know. If you want, you can tell Rosalia to make a few of her own." Even as he said the words, he realized how it sounded. "You don't have to though. Or at least wait until mine." Not that it mattered. His own work would be enough to stir up some activity. If Rosalia chose to join in the fun, so be it.

Finding the conversation exhausted, Jalay stood and looked towards the cafeteria. The serving line had dwindled to nothing; he still had time to eat some lunch.

"Leaving so soon?" asked Sebo.

"I'm hungry."

"Can you bring me back a burrito?"

Jalay shook his head, checked his palette to make sure it was blank. "Not coming back."

TWENTY-FOUR
DERON

The closer it got to noon, the more Deron's leg shook at the notion of abandoning the safety of his home for the uncertainty of the city. It was the memory of her face that made him even consider it, her face that blossomed in his mind and beat back the fear.

Rosalia had the lunch period after his, which meant there was a fair chance she would be sitting outside enjoying the fresh air between twelve and twelve forty-five. That was the window and though it was as discrete as anything else, he couldn't be certain when it started and ended. There were no clocks in the house that weren't just numbers in a portal on a veneer. The only other indicators were the shadows outside, the grid that the patio wall made as the sun rose behind it, one that gradually shrank until it barely pulled away. That meant the sun was more or less overhead, that it was noon.

It was time to brave the wilderness.

Deron remembered Easton as a relatively safe city, but that was when he could still interact with the veneer. Now, it lacked basic information. It went far beyond color, a fact he became aware of as he watched his mom combine ingredients from similar cans in the cupboard. What was to stop her from pouring drain cleaner into her coffee? From that one example, he extrapolated the walk to school. Even though he wouldn't need them, all of the street signs might be blank. And if those were gone, what else? How much of the world was just a veneer and how much of it was real?

Sitting on the stairs with his chin in his hand, Deron tried to visualize himself opening the front door. Rosalia was out there, maybe on her way to the cafeteria to collect her lunch. She'd stand in line with the rest of the sighted and ask for the light ranch, the skim milk, and the other healthy alternatives to the city-mandated lunches. Maybe that Ilya girl would be tagging along behind her.

Flashing on a foggy veneer, he saw Rosalia standing in the distance, looking at him, her eyes gleaming. And then Ilya emerged from the haze and took Rosalia by the hand, pulling her away, pulling her back into the land of color, of veneers and reconciliation, where boys could only see the beauty that girls created for themselves instead of the truth that hid beneath, the plainness or maybe even the ugliness. It wasn't a pleasant idea to think that the girl he loved could be something less than perfect under her decorations. All he had to do was look at his mom to see what could happen eventually. Would he even recognize her? Would he recognize anybody?

It didn't matter; he was fucked no matter what he did. They would categorize him as handicapped and treat him with special gloves until he died and the burden of his well-being was lifted from those who were paid to maintain it. He'd be an affliction to his mom and even Rosalia. No woman would want his company now that he couldn't function in the real world.

Deron took a deep breath, sought solace in the simple act. His concerns were valid, but none of them needed immediate resolution. The trick was to break everything down into easily digestible fragments. All he needed to do was take that first step.

"Fuck it," he said.

He was talking to the world in general: to the railing he used to pull himself up, to the floor he walked across, and to the friction of his shoes against the tile that propelled him forward. The front door swung open and Deron put a hand to his brow to shield his eyes from the sun.

Truth: the grass was not as green and luxurious as the veneer had made it out to be. Brown patches dotted the pale green lawn, the dead grass both natural and wrong at the same time. The sidewalk that took him from the front door to the street was cracked and stained, so unlike the previous sandstone veneer. When he reached the street, Deron turned and glanced back at the house, saw the same drab box he had seen when he returned home Saturday night. It didn't look any better in the daylight, but at least now he understood its lack of color.

Deron felt the warmth of the sun on his neck and arms despite the chill in the air. He stuck his hands in his pockets and walked slowly down the street, checking out the houses as if he had just moved into the neighborhood. At the intersection, he looked up and saw that the street signs lacked any writing. After crossing the unnamed street, he turned left.

It would all be okay if he could stay at Gillock Pond. The realization hit him as soon as he saw the micro-park still alive and vibrant. Nature's colorful display melted away the anxiety. The smell, the sounds, and yes, even the sight of the pond, it all made him think that maybe everything could work out. The turtles, for instance, the ones sunning on the rocks, had no awareness of the veneer at all. Yet they lived their lives, swimming and sunning and breeding until they finally died. Every living thing was driving that long highway towards death; the veneer was just the decoration, the ceaseless billboards along the side of the road that briefly made an impression and then receded.

Although he wanted nothing more than to stay, Deron couldn't ignore his sole motivation for leaving the house. There was still a chance Rosalia was out there and while that chance existed, he had to try to see her, tell her what had happened. It couldn't have been easy for her to come all the way to his house only for his mom to turn her away. It sure wasn't easy for Deron.

Again, the fog crept in, carrying with it the conversation they would have. She'd be happy to see him, maybe throw her arms around his neck in unrestrained joy. They'd kiss and look into each other's eyes.

His smile faded when he thought about her eyes, her *real* eyes. Not the green she wore to entice him, not the blue she used to brighten his day, and certainly not the red, the passionate crimson that spoke of her attraction, the only indication of the lustful thoughts going on behind the scenes. They would never burn for him like that again. And even if they did, he wouldn't be able to see it. He paused, stymied by the weight of the underlying truth. He was on the other side of some invisible barrier, occupying the same space, maybe, but existing in a completely different world.

Deron turned the realization over in his head and was surprised when he looked up and found himself already on Parker Avenue. He was standing at the light where it met with Treaty Oak or, more exactly, at what used to be the light.

So much of Easton's transit system depended on the veneer, not only to distinguish one car from the other but also to direct traffic and let pedestrians know when it was safe to cross the street. Hanging above the roads on thin wires were blank rectangles that lacked their yellow framing and colored circles. The cars on Treaty were moving, so that must have meant the light was green, but Deron saw nothing.

Despite waiting for several minutes trying to pick out a pattern in the madness, Deron still managed to get a few honks from the passing cars. Evidently he had stepped out into the crosswalk at the wrong time and had to sprint to the curb as a tram came barreling down the inside lane. The noise attracted attention from the midday shoppers who all looked like paper dolls in their off-white clothes. The exceptions were the two men standing in front of a parking meter— they didn't need their signature black and blue for Deron to know they were uniforms.

Before they could react, Deron slipped into the thin alley between Jilly Beans and a Get Ripped gym. He knew what was supposed to be happening on the walls as he passed them; the presence-sensing advertisements would have followed him all the way to the other side if he could have only seen them. He tried to imagine what they would have looked like, what they'd be selling at this time of day. There were always a few fast food ads, whatever new hamburger McDonald's was trying to pass off as innovation. Someone would be hawking new cars and reminding even buyers with bad credit that they could afford a shiny gray hunk of fiberglass. Public service ads were rare, but he found one on the evercrete towards the end of the alley.

Deron stopped, blinked a few times. It was actually there on the wall in color he could see. He approached the sign, put his hand up to verify its existence. Some of the red marking got on his finger when he touched it.

So it wasn't a veneer; someone had actually written on the wall.

YOU ARE NOT BLIND.

It was vindication, but from what source? Deron hadn't considered the possibility that his was not a unique affliction. If there were others…

Beneath the block letters, he found smaller text.

Fifth & Navasota.

Deron looked away towards the school, to a distant destination that seemed to recede even further. Rosalia was there. He needed to see her.

But these words. This address. How could he ignore them?

TWENTY-FIVE
ROSALIA

There had been a moment at lunch when something on the wind drew her eyes to the north, past the faculty parking lot with its aging cars and lone scooter, past the neighborhoods and mini-malls—past all of the empty places that were nothing more than obstacles, asphalt and evercrete that separated her from Deron. She had looked into the distance, seen nothing, but felt his mouth at her ear, felt him saying her name in one smooth whisper, drawing out each syllable. Then the wind had come up, rustled the trees enough to drown out the cry in the darkness, and when the sound abated, nothing remained. Not the voice. Not the swaying leaves.

Perhaps not even Deron.

Now, sitting in the waiting room of the nurse's office, Rosalia stared blankly at the empty chairs around her. It wasn't a very welcoming room, not with its bright orange color scheme and strongly worded posters reconciled on the wall. She tried to take her mind off her discomfort by reading them carefully, repeating in her head the necessity of protected sexual intercourse. It was sound advice, but its presentation was too cartoony for its intended audience.

She was halfway through the benefits of regular flossing when Nurse Hendricks appeared from the examination room. Her veneer was spotless, as always, with a pressed uniform and a cute hat on her perfectly arranged hair. The smile on her face looked permanently tacked on, but it grew when she saw her patient.

"Ms. Collier," she said, approaching the counter. "It's been a while." With a quick movement, she spun the sign-in sheet around in its portal and frowned. "You forgot to sign in."

"Sorry," said Rosalia, standing up. She shuffled from foot to foot, wondering if running out of the room screaming at the top of her lungs would be considered rude.

"No worries. I can put you down." Her rosy fingertip traced across the portal, leaving behind Rosalia's name. "What is the nature of your visit today?" she asked, mock-professionally.

"Just… questions." Rosalia raised her eyebrows a little, looked around again at the empty waiting room.

"General health concerns it is." With a satisfied smile, she beckoned to Rosalia. "Come on, sweetie. Let's go have a chat."

Unlike the waiting area, the examination room was decorated for its purpose, with solid white walls and gleaming metal cabinets. A large exam table dominated the center of the room, a wide strip of paper running its length. As Rosalia sat down on it, she noticed the facing wall was shimmering, as if the entire surface were a portal instead of a simple veneer.

"Let's do a quick checkup first," said Nurse Hendricks, approaching the wall. When she touched it, the mirage dissolved into an image of an office. Seated at a desk was another woman wearing a white lab coat adorned with the Easton General Hospital emblem. A moment passed before she realized they were watching her.

"Lucy," said the woman. She stood leisurely and came towards the wall as if she expected to shake her colleague's hand. "How are things at Central? Any Westlake flu going on around there?"

"No," laughed Nurse Hendricks. "Not on my watch."

"And who do we have here?"

Evidently, this woman could see them as easily as they saw her.

"Ms. Collier, this is Dr. Blake."

"Hello, dear," said the doctor, her voice growing softer.

Before Rosalia could answer, Nurse Hendricks spoke, "Just a little woman to woman chat today, nothing I can't handle."

"That's fine," she replied, nodding approvingly. "So, just the vitals then?"

"Yes, Doctor." The nurse pulled a stethoscope from the wall and approached Rosalia. She slipped one end under Rosalia's shirt without warning and placed it against her chest. "Alright, Ms. Collier, let's have three good breaths."

As she concentrated on breathing, Rosalia noticed that boxes of data were appearing on the wall. All sorts of metrics spilled into the portal, displaying figures that represented her heart rate, oxygen levels, and average blood pressure over time. After the last breath, Nurse Hendricks turned around and examined the data with the doctor.

"To be young," said Dr. Blake. "If only I had your blood pressure." She touched a finger to the wall and her signature appeared at the bottom of the report, followed by the date. "Everything looks fine to me. I'll leave the rest to you, Lucy."

"Thank you," replied Nurse Hendricks.

The far side faded out under the chart. After signing her own name, the nurse minimized the charts to the left, where they disappeared amongst the thousand other scribbles on the wall.

"Well," she said, "now that that's out of the way. What can I help you with today?"

Rosalia thought about telling her the whole story, how the night had begun at the mall with Ilya, turned to dinner, to shopping, to drugs. Then she thought about the sleepover, about describing the way Ilya had put her hand on her neck before she knew why. In that hazy moment of indeterminate motives, she had considered the possibility that—

"Sweetie?"

"Oh, sorry." It took a moment to come out of the fog. "I… my friend and I had a question. We both have something in our necks. Here." She pointed to where her skull met her spine. "If you press on it, you can feel something under the skin." She had to dip her head to show the nurse, but upon looking up, she found her smiling kindly, the way an adult would look at a child who had just dropped her ice cream cone.

"There shouldn't be anything in your neck except your Guardian chip," said Nurse Hendricks. She walked around the table and put her fingers on Rosalia's neck. "And I doubt you would have both suffered a hemorrhage at the same time."

"A what chip?"

Ignoring the question, she followed up with, "Why didn't you just ask your parents about this?"

"I don't know," replied Rosalia, thinking of how Lynn would have simply dismissed her.

"Well, I don't blame you for being curious. I've always thought they should teach this stuff before senior year."

"What is it?"

The nurse must have detected the trepidation in her voice. "Don't worry, it's perfectly harmless. Actually, the name pretty much says it all. Guardians are what monitor our internal systems and keep us healthy. Think of it like an around-the-clock physician that lives in your neck. Twenty-four hours a day, she's checking your blood pressure and examining your neuro-electrical responses for any kind of anomaly. That's how we got your vitals on the wall, by querying your chip." She dropped her hands and walked around the exam table again. "Do you want to see it?"

"The chip?"

"I have an imager here," she replied, motioning to the cabinets with her head. "I can take a picture and show you what it looks like." Her face grew serious. "It's the only way to make sure there hasn't been any damage." Without waiting for a response, she crossed the room and pulled a small box from the cabinet. From inside, she withdrew a thin sheet of what looked like plastic. After removing the paper tabs, she brought it to Rosalia. "Turn a little for me, okay?"

Rosalia felt the cool film on her neck and the warmer fingers of the nurse smoothing it out. A fuzzy picture appeared on the wall, but the colors were a little off, as if someone had simply guessed what each value should be.

"Just needs a little adjusting, I think," said Nurse Hendricks. She placed her hand on the wall and made the image sharper.

It looked like a small square, though Rosalia had trouble picking out the surrounding tissue, couldn't find a reference point to judge its scale. It was devoid of all markings and only after the nurse pushed through the image was Rosalia able to see the pins on the opposite side. Her stomach heaved involuntarily; the idea of a piece of metal tearing into her spinal cord didn't sit right with her.

"Quite beautiful, isn't it? And just about the size of your pinky nail. This is the most important piece of technology that you will ever own. Things your grandparents had to worry about—heart attacks, stroke, even asthma—will never concern you. It protects you—"

"Like a guardian angel," said Rosalia, scooting off the exam table. She moved closer at the wall, still amazed and disgusted to be looking inside herself.

"So now you know. And you can go tell your *friend*."

"I thought it was supposed to be a secret."

Nurse Hendricks shook her head. "Just because things aren't common knowledge doesn't mean they're a secret. This is just part of growing up. There are things that are mysteries until the day they're revealed. That's life." She moved closer and put her hand on Rosalia's shoulder.

Nodding, Rosalia returned her attention to the wall. She wanted to thank the nurse for her time, but a strange pattern on the image caught her eye. It looked like little letters on the edge of the chip.

"We can zoom in if you'd like," offered Nurse Hendricks.

"Please."

The picture grew on the wall, but whatever occupied the corner remained illegible.

Stubbing her finger against the portal, Rosalia asked, "Can you make this clearer?"

"Huh," said the nurse. "I never noticed that before. Yeah, I think I can do something." Her eyebrows furrowed in concentration. "You know, most people think that nurses only have to know bio stuff, but there's more to it. You also have to be an expert in reconciliation. Manipulating scans and x-rays and real-time imagers; that's where the real work is. There, that's the best I can do."

They stared at the picture, each trying to sound out the barely legible word.

Finally, as if sensing competition, the nurse blurted out, "Vinestead!"

"Vinestead," repeated Rosalia, picking the copyright symbol out of the jumble. "Never heard of them."

TWENTY-SIX
RUSSO

So much blood.

Just the sight of it pooling in the bathroom sink was enough to make Russo's stomach turn. He'd seen blood before—there was more than enough flying around when he kicked the shit out of Deron—but this was different. This was *his* blood collecting around the drain.

Above the sink, a portal reflected Russo's image back to him, providing no indication that he was even injured. His veneer still sported the all-back camouflage, making him blend in with the shadows. He could see his features, but none of the wounds that he knew to be there were visible. Little red drops fell from his chin, appearing suddenly just beyond his skin.

There was the issue of seeing the truth beneath the veneer, something he assumed doctors could do since they were the ones treating reconciled bodies on a daily basis. Or is it something else, he wondered, bringing his fingers to his face. He moved them gingerly over his lips, over his wet nose, and to his left side where an impressive mound had formed next to his eye. It felt like a large blister that had cracked at the top, the skin stretched so tightly that it had no choice but to bleed. Russo couldn't see under his own veneer, but he could bring the cuts and bruises to the next level. With another pass, he traced along his face and as his fingers moved, they left behind color: reds, purples, and blacks. Within seconds, the consequences of his violent nature became apparent.

Russo found a box of assorted bandages in the cabinet beneath the sink and dumped them out on the counter. His left arm was trashed; the only skill it retained was the ability to feel pain, crying out every time he tried to move it. Doing everything one-handed was a challenge, but he managed to fill the sink with paper pull-tabs.

Looking at himself in the portal, he laughed at how ridiculous he looked with all the white strips on his face. The mild convulsions sent a spasm down his back, crumbling his entire body in place. It was as if an invisible hand had closed its fingers around his spine and squeezed in anger. Just when he thought he would lose it completely, the sensation subsided and he found he had only fallen a few inches, saved by his good hand on the counter. It would be days before he would be able to move freely, a fate he accepted willingly. After all, he wasn't Deron; a little fight with a bigger opponent wasn't enough to send him to the hospital.

Satisfied with his work, Russo returned to the living room where he sat down on the cushy couch and crossed one leg over the other. His palette glowed on a throw pillow next to him, flashing text and images as it scoured the network for information about Seers. The term itself appeared several times, but not in the context he needed. A lack of results made him nervous; it meant either he was crazy or the conspiracy went deeper than he realized. Eric could have been withholding the truth, not just to be a dick, but because his life depended on it. That kind of information couldn't get out into the world. If people knew…

A short trill got his attention, made him pull the palette into his lap to investigate. Someone had sent him an archive of images with a note that read *thought you should see these*. Examining them one by one, Russo felt the numbness of his arm spread to his entire body. Someone had rewritten history in the form of obviously fabricated veneers. The idea that anyone had seen him settle his score with Deron was laughable, yet there it was, with a crappy grain filter to make it seem more authentic.

"Fucking Rosalia." He tossed the palette aside and stood up. At the window, he looked out over Easton, at all of the veneers that were no more real than the bullshit on his palette. The propaganda would work, of course. People had given up their right to question what they saw. Believing was seeing, but it worked just as well the other way around. So maybe it wasn't enough to get the uniforms to do anything about it, but it would get people talking. He punched the wall next to the window and received a painful reminder about the state of his injuries.

When was Rosalia going to learn not to mess with him, that any attempt to hurt him would be met with such a disproportional response that even Russo would have trouble explaining it? Deron had learned that lesson well; now it was time to teach Rosalia. Maybe a few weeks in a coma would do her some good. At that, he laughed, again felt the pain, again scowled in discomfort. He hung his head in frustration. The truth of it was that he needed to put his old life behind him. Focus on the goal, he told himself.

"Something bothering you?" slurred a voice from the corner of the room.

Russo pointed angrily without looking up. "I don't want to hear a fucking word from you unless it's about veneers."

"Veneers are the byproduct of reconciliation, a decorative façade that can be applied to any surface that can be accessed physically."

He had broken his nose, Russo reminded himself. That's why he couldn't gag him, since every time he tried to breathe through his nose he either started choking or blew out a bloody snot bubble.

It was a shame; silence would have helped him think.

"I remember when I was your age, Russo. I wrecked my dad's car. So he—"

Crossing the room quickly, Russo jumped into the man's lap, leading with his knee. Ignoring the spray of blood, he grabbed his captive with one hand and pulled his head forward.

"Listen to me," he growled. "The more you talk, the closer you get to bleeding out. Is that what you want? Should I just do you now? Are you too fucking stupid to save your own life?"

He broke off, crossed the room to the serving bar that separated the living room from the kitchen. An assortment of knives had been laid out, all part of an intimidation attempt that hadn't produced any results. The whole night had been like that, Russo realized. Beating Agent Tavarez to a pulp had only made it possible to subdue him. Getting information out of him remained a challenge.

Russo took a deep breath. "Maybe I've made a mistake," he said, using his good arm to lift the other onto the counter. He fingered the handle of a carving knife.

"You think?"

"We all make mistakes," Russo continued. "That uniform made a mistake taking me in just for hanging around a building no one was using. You made a mistake by identifying me without pretending to use some kind of device. Do you realize all of this could have been avoided with a camera and a slick veneer? Just hold it up when you do whatever you do and people won't suspect. Then, you let me leave with that information. You let me follow you home. Which leads us to now."

Russo turned with a flourish and tried to spread his arms. In his right hand, the carving knife dangled menacingly.

"And what was *your* mistake?" asked the agent. "Stalking? Assault? Attempted murder?"

"I haven't *attempted* anything yet," interrupted Russo. He was tired of hearing his crimes read back to him. The list was far longer than Eric knew and nothing he had done in the last twenty-four hours even made it into the top ten of his evil deeds. Killing would be a first, but the agent didn't need to know that. Russo let the tension build before saying, "This is where you beg for your life."

The fucker actually laughed. "I'm not begging shit from you."

Behind his veneer, Russo smiled. From the moment he first met Agent Eric Tavarez, to the conversation in the lobby, to the violent struggle in his doorway, he had never heard the man curse. It was part of his programming, that politically correct way of talking, trying to make himself seem impartial and above emotion. But now he was breaking down, becoming sloppy and desperate. The smile bubbled up. He was becoming human.

"Hello, Eric," said Russo. There was recognition in the man's face; he knew he was slipping. "I don't know if you've been following along, but I'm trying to get some information out of you. You can see through veneers. I want you to teach me that magic."

"Magic," repeated Eric, chuckling again. "You fucking idiot."

Russo approached his victim and spoke in a child's voice. "Oh yes, I'm the idiot. Just a dumb motherfucker with a knife in my hand. And you're just a glorified uniform with a death wish. I guess that's why I'm giving you one last chance to tell me your secrets. But I'm so stupid that the only thing I can think now is that the magic isn't with *you*. I think it's in your eyes." He leaned over, his face near Eric's. "Are those special eyes?"

"Only to me," said Eric, his voice shaky. Finally, he was afraid.

"Only to you? Well, you know what's special to me? Magic. So how about you give me the magic and I let you keep your eyes?"

"If you kill me, you'll never find out."

Retreating, Russo raised an eyebrow. "Is that so? So I won't find your contact list on your phone? Your portal won't have any info about who you work with? Their names? Where they live?"

"I should have put you down."

"Yes, you should have." He pointed the knife at Eric's face. "Last chance."

Eric's head dipped and he spoke into his chest. "You're headed somewhere that you're not gonna like, Russo. And it's not gonna be anyone's fault but your own. You will have cheated your way to a place that you can't come back from." Looking up, his eyes barely open, he added, "If you make it there, don't forget I tried to save you."

"I don't want salvation!" yelled Russo, switching his grip on the knife. "I want your fucking sight!"

The veneer over Eric's eyes held only for a moment; there was simply too much blood to contain.

TWENTY-SEVEN
DERON

Fifth and Navasota met at the southeast corner of One-Zero plaza, an expansive memorial site comprised of decorative gardens and a single, dominating spire in the center. Its silver veneer simulated the reflected light of the sun at any angle. Flanking it were two conic sails that appeared to billow even when the wind was calm. It was along the base of the memorial that Deron found the next set of markings, another in a series of addresses for him to pursue. Some were within walking distance; others required the use of the trams, like the one that had brought him all the way south to Vargas and Freight Lane, just a mile away from the outer wall of Easton.

Now, staring at a hastily scrawled arrow pointing out of the city, Deron considered the possibility that he was walking into a trap. It was Principal Ficcone's vague warning that gave him pause, made him wonder why the police would pursue someone who couldn't see the veneer. The better plan would have been to set up some kind of automated system, like a series of addresses, to draw the blind in, bring them all to one location so they could be rounded up. Hunters of the blind would be crafty in their methods. Those without sight must be detained before they could spread their disease to others.

Deron sighed, followed the viral hypothesis to its illogical conclusion.

He replaced the fantasy with what he already knew: the injury, the Swarm Survivor arena, and the slow degradation of the veneer. Paramel Terminus had been so dim that he could barely see anything. Then on the way home, visions of a strange landscape, reality itself dissolving. A flash of a dingy hallway emerged from his memory and blinked out. A hospital, he thought, nurses with ugly faces, walls with nothing on them.

Deron cursed under his breath. He had seen it, weeks ago, seen the truth and not even known it. It was injury to the brain that caused it, that somehow shut down the evolutionary ability to reconcile visual data onto any surface. They could say what they wanted about magic, but here was real proof that it was biological. There were systems in his body responsible for all the major senses and the one that controlled his reconciliation was broken.

Around him, the foreign veneers of factories and warehouse made him feel lost, as if he had been dropped in another city or another time where reconciliation was a pipe dream, a power wished for as often as invisibility or immortality. He thought about his ancestors, about how they saw the world before veneers. It wouldn't have looked like this; the buildings were only the color of off-white evercrete because there was no reason for them not to be. It was probably cheaper to crank out the undecorated parts and let the customer update it with the right design.

Truth: Deron was not blind. Rather, he could finally see. He could see as humans had for hundreds of thousands of years, without reconciliation, without what they called *magic*. But why was it so dangerous? What was it about a man with true vision that worried them so? And who was *them*? Deron shook his head, tried to clear away the confusion and the conspiracy theories. It was all too much. Focus on the messages, he told himself.

Deron checked the arrow again; it was still pointing to the outer wall. Though a mile was nothing compared to how far he had already travelled, he couldn't ignore the sinking sun and the rising hunger in his stomach. Freight Lane went all the way to the edge, cutting through the outer tract of Easton, a ring of the city dedicated to small factories and light industrial. Here, the people simply ignored him and went about their work with forced detachment.

Fortunately, the outskirts were home to a fleet of mobile eateries, little carts that followed lunch bells and quitting times. There were already several in a parking lot across the street, taking up position around half a dozen worn picnic tables. Deron tried to imagine what their signage looked like, how flashy their advertising would have been. Not that it mattered; a hot dog stand needed no signs when there was a mild breeze.

It was a large tortilla hanging from a cart that drew him across the road. The woman smiled at his approach; given the empty tables, it seemed she had been waiting eagerly for her first customer. He ordered an oversized burrito and had the woman fill it with beans, rice, and barbacoa. The anticipation was marred by a tense moment when she held out a palette, wanting payment. Though he couldn't see the scanner in the portal, he pressed his finger and didn't take another breath until it beeped approvingly.

Deron chose one of the sturdier-looking tables and sat down to peel the paper wrapper from his burrito. As he savored the first bite, he couldn't help but glance once again towards the wall. The idea of approaching it in broad daylight made his leg shake uncontrollably. No one touched the wall; it was one of the rules. Don't mess with it and the double-barreled sentry guns on the watchtowers wouldn't mess with you. He chuckled. It was just like Swarm Survivor, except *he* was the fleshy blob trying to get *out*.

The burrito went down easy, devoured in a matter of minutes. By then, more people had shown up looking haggard and hungry. They filled in the tables around him, each bringing the smell of dinner and nine hours of physical labor. Only when there were no more seats did they join him at his table. There was no acknowledgement of his presence and no one even looked in his direction until a wide-jawed hulk sat down, glanced at Deron, and asked, "Another one?"

The men took turns sizing Deron up and shaking their heads. They seemed to know something he didn't.

"Another what?" he asked, his voice squeaky.

"It looks like you're done," said the jaw. "Why don't you move along so someone else can sit down and eat? What you're looking for is down that way." He pointed to the outer wall, but only Deron followed his finger.

"How do you know—?"

"Kid, I'm asking politely." He took a bite of his sandwich. "It gets ugly after that."

Although no one else at the table seemed to be behind the threat, Deron knew he couldn't take on the jaw alone. He stood and walked away, avoiding the glances from the other diners. They knew he didn't belong there and the more he thought about it, the more he realized he might not belong in Easton at all.

Deron almost missed the next message as he made his way down Freight Lane. It had been placed at an angle along the rise of a loading dock. Its arrow pointed to an empty field or the wall beyond it, but he couldn't see anything interesting about either. The sick feeling returned; it could have all been a trick, a wild goose chase to poke the eyes of those who were already blind. But who would go through all that trouble?

It could have been anyone, he realized. Anyone could have done it blindly, magic or no magic, just by marking up buildings as they walked to nowhere. It made him wonder if anyone else had ever been dumb enough to follow them.

"Another one," he said aloud.

That's what the jaw had meant. Deron wasn't the first.

TWENTY-EIGHT
SEBO

Easton's veneers were adjusting to the low light when Sebo set out from Deron's house. They changed minutely, their intensity ramping up to visible but not overwhelming. Downtown was the exception; even at a distance, it burned as brightly as its daytime counterpart. Signage and decorations at the very tips of the skyscrapers blotted out the stars.

The plan had been to meet up with Rosa and her friend, Ilya, at Perrault's around eight, but a dinner that ran late had delayed Sebo's trip to check on Deron. Now, burdened by the weight of bad news, he paced himself, already convinced of how Rosa would react. She had gone all day thinking Deron was ignoring her and now she had to find out he was missing, likely by choice.

Sebo cringed, thought about the faces she might make and how ill-equipped he was to comfort her. At least Ilya would be around, give her a shoulder to cry on if she needed it.

Amber running lights at the edges of the sidewalk began to glow brighter the closer he got to Parker Avenue. That the rest of the world seemed so normal, so unaware of the turmoil happening in the lives of a few students, left Sebo amazed. Not that they *needed* to care, but it made him wonder about the reverse, about how many other crises were taking place in Easton, other stories of violence and despair that he would never know about. Maybe someone else in the city right then felt the way he did, had a friend who by all accounts had gone out of his mind and simply slipped away beneath the veneer.

Slipping beneath the veneer, thought Sebo, smiling. It sounded romantic: becoming one with the artificial world, seeing what other people couldn't see, hiding in plain sight.

Now there was a frontier to explore.

Parker Avenue was teeming with its typical weeknight bustle. The citizens of Easton walked the street dutifully, tired after a long day on the job, but out and about just the same. Walk around, meet some people, have some food, and do some shopping. Long ago, someone had broken society down into a set of basic habits and used that knowledge in the planning of Easton, the closest thing to a utopia in recorded history, a place where every desire could be satisfied except for a select few and most of those were just down the road in Paramel.

Rosa and Ilya were already at Perrault's when Sebo arrived. Seated on the same side of a booth near the back where the light was dimmer, their mouths moved simultaneously, as if conversing synchronously. Sebo bypassed the expectant gaze of the barista at the counter and headed for the booth. Ilya saw him first; she nudged Rosa to look up. He gave an ambiguous apology for his tardiness as he slid onto the empty bench. In the middle of the table, someone had reconciled a portal and within it, an image of a gunmetal gray chip, shiny and expensive-looking.

"Thanks for coming," said Rosa, her previous levity fading.

She was good at reading veneers. If his face betrayed the bad news, she would surely see it.

"Anything, for a lady," replied Sebo. The sentiment was not quite true. There were some women for whom he would do anything, but their beauty started more at Ilya's level than Rosa's. The only reason he sat across from her now was because of Deron and that tenuous connection was always under constant strain. "Is this all of us?"

"All who care," said Rosa, through a sudden frown.

At that, Sebo cast a quick glance at Ilya.

"Friends have all things in common," she explained.

"Sure," said Sebo, shrugging. There was something off about Ilya, beyond the fact that her parents had given her a boy's name.

A pall followed during which Elijah engaged in people watching while Rosa stared at Sebo with increasing agitation. She had her fingers snaked tightly around a tall glass of pink smoothie. Her concern shone through her veneer as easily as the blue shadows that surrounded her eyes. The façade she had created for herself couldn't hold back what she was feeling inside and Sebo imagined those emotions boiling in the space between Rosa and her veneer, extruded from the skin but not yet past the outer boundary.

Trapped, compressed, and yearning to break free.

"So what did Deron say?" she asked, the question spilling out of her in a jumble of syllables. Then, in a quieter voice, "Is he mad at me?"

"That remains a mystery." Sebo shifted uneasily in his seat, thinking briefly about ordering a drink so he would have something to do with his hands. "I didn't actually get to speak with him."

"I thought you said you were gonna check on him? Why—?" She stopped abruptly and looked away. Her lips came together tightly, damming whatever angry words she had for him.

"I did go to his house," Sebo pointed out, trying to keep his voice level. He recounted his time starting from the outset, leaving his house after dinner to make the short trek to Deron's place. He had been optimistic then, almost confident that Deron would welcome him and explain away his absence from school with tales of fatigue and pain medication. But then he knocked at the door and his normally stout mother opened it with such a piteous look on her veneer that Sebo thought for moment that perhaps Deron had passed on, that the injury sustained in Paramel had somehow caused internal bleeding in his brain. He'd read about that happening before, a slow bleed that filled the skull, compressing the brain until it was no longer viable.

Sebo recalled the face Ania had made when she delivered the news and his veneer shifted subconsciously as he passed it on to Rosa. It was a look that conveyed sympathy before the person even knew they deserved it.

In the stilted conversation that followed, Ania quizzed him on the sequence of events in Paramel. Sebo did his best to answer her questions, but his mind had suffered such a jolt that he couldn't concentrate. When the news that Deron had fallen during the game slipped out and produced a look of horror on Ania's face, Sebo realized just how distracted he was. He became more selective with his words after that, tried not to volunteer information that might make Ania think he was complicit in hurting her son.

Deron was gone, she told him, by the time she got home from work. She had called the house a few times during the day, but he never answered. So when she returned and found the house quiet, she knew almost immediately. There was no note, just walls with smeared veneers, as if someone had touched them and thought of nothing. No signs of struggle, no forced entry; he had simply gotten up and walked off. But to where, she wondered, and Sebo had no answer. They stood together on the porch, thinking, Sebo unsure of what to say or where to start. Ania had already informed the police, so his face was on their radar, but they wouldn't actively pursue him until he had been missing for a day. And even then, the odds of finding him—

"Are pretty good," interrupted Ilya. "The city is only so big, right? And he can't get out without going through security, where they'll pick him up anyway." She turned to Rosa. "They'll find him."

"That's assuming he went for a walk and just hasn't come back. What if he's hurt or in danger? What if he fell in a ditch and no one's noticed him?" Rosa had more hypotheticals, but she chose to express them as short halting breaths, punctuated by a whimper. Finally, she asked, "How does this happen?"

Sebo thought back, to the shops, to Russo, and everything in between. If causality ruled the universe, then he was obligated to share what he knew. Without his knowledge, Rosa would have no chance of imagining the future.

He cleared his throat and reconciled his own portal on the table. "First, we have the fight." A shop that Jalay had produced appeared. With each event, he made a little circle containing another image. "Then, Deron goes into the hospital. Coma, stitches. Lots of trauma. Fast forward, he said you two met the day he got out. Did he seem any different?"

"No," said Rosa.

"Then for argument's sake, let's say he was fine. Next day, we're at Paramel." A slight hesitation, enough to elicit a raised eyebrow from Ilya. "In the heat of the game, Deron takes a fall. He hits his head and then—"

"He hit his head?" Rosa's eyes widened.

"Yeah, but—"

"He could have had a concussion!" She crossed her arms tightly. "Why didn't you tell me?"

Sebo shrugged. "I thought it was nothing. Deron's always a little off the tram after we finish a run and gun. He had some pizza and made all the nonsensical ramblings like he always does." The night's conversation came back to him, scrutinized for the first time. "Things like how dark the terminus was when it really wasn't. Then on the bus, he kept looking out the window."

"What was out there?" asked Ilya.

"Nothing. I put a veneer on the glass, but he acted like it wasn't there. I thought he was just being Deron."

"Concussion," repeated Rosa. "He hurt his head and you let him go home like nothing was wrong."

He considered a counter-argument about how Deron was a big boy and could take care of himself, but that would have just led to more squabbling, more accusations that didn't help anything. They needed a plan, a discrete goal and a means to attain it.

"Look," he said, "maybe I messed up and maybe I didn't, but what's done is done. We need to worry about what we do now."

"You go look for him!" shot back Rosa. Her veneer took on a stormy sheen. "You get on the trams and ride the whole fucking city if you have to."

She didn't have to yell, but even Sebo could appreciate the effect it would have on her emotional state if she could blow off some steam, heap some blame onto his plate. Pleasing Rosa was not his job and Deron's appreciation of his efforts wouldn't repay the time lost sitting in Perrault's arguing with a distressed woman. Riding the trams seemed like a good enough compromise, a passive search that wouldn't take much effort on his part. He could put in a few hours, pick up again after school tomorrow.

"I can ride too," said Ilya, raising her hand. "I don't have anything better to do. Maybe you take south and I take north?"

Sebo eyed her suspiciously. Sometimes it was difficult to see past the veneers, to believe anything beyond what the reconciler invented. Other times, it was just a nice pair of tits being suffocated by a tight shirt that kept him from knowing the person within.

"Alright," he said, sliding out of the booth. "Then there's no point sitting on our cocks anymore." He put his hands in his pockets. "I'll see you at school tomorrow."

Rosa didn't look up, just kept staring at her drink. Out of the corner of her mouth, she said, "Message me if you find him. Before the cops, before his mom. You message *me*." Her voice broke then, and Ilya put her hand on her back.

"I'm going stay with her for a bit," announced Ilya. "Maybe we'll cross paths later?"

"One can only hope," replied Sebo, turning on the spot. As he walked out into the cold night, he glanced back through the glass doors, but Ilya wasn't looking after him, wasn't watching to see if he'd try to steal another glimpse of her artificial beauty.

"Friends have all things in common," he repeated and then shook his head.

There was something so familiar about those words.

TWENTY-NINE
ROSALIA

Ilya insisted on walking her home, but thankfully she did it in silence. Rosalia was feeling the beginnings of remorse, for not being stronger, for yelling at Sebo. He was only trying to help, even if it was his mistake that had gotten them into this mess. At least he was doing his part. And Ilya, offering to ride the trams, was more than she had expected from someone only indirectly connected to Deron. Except that she wasn't on the tram yet, was instead wasting her time making sure Rosalia got home safe, as if anyone between Perrault's and her front door would dare attack her. If Ilya didn't want to look for Deron, she shouldn't have offered.

"Do you want me to stay a while?"

There was kindness in her face, but all Rosalia wanted was to be left alone. "I'll be fine. I'm just gonna lie down."

"Good," said Ilya. "You get some rest. I'll message you later."

"Thanks," said Rosalia, her word almost cut off by an abrupt hug.

Ilya said goodnight and sauntered down the walkway. At the street, she gave another little wave before setting off at a quick pace for the tram stop at the end of the block.

Rosalia waited until she was completely out of sight before opening the door and stepping inside.

It was quiet and dark in the foyer, but she could hear her dad talking in the living room. She slipped into the kitchen and pulled a glass from the cupboard. The fridge made a racket as it crushed the ice, which elicited a greeting from Lynn. In time, she told herself, as she drank slowly from the glass. After all, there was no way to get upstairs without going into the living room where her dad would look at her and if he were any kind of father, would see the pain in her eyes and the flutter in her veneer. He might even have the answers this time, as he often did, but something prideful in Rosalia made her want to solve this one by herself.

When the glass was empty, she refilled it and then grabbed a small bag of chips from the pantry. The lights dimmed as she exited and with a sigh, she made her entrance into the living room. Her dad was sitting on the loveseat and watching the portal above the fireplace. Next to him, Lynn sat with her hand on his leg, looking quite content in her mother's rightful place. It wasn't so much that she hated Lynn, but the way her father doted on her, the way he ignored her mother's legacy by consorting with some random woman he had met at work, made her feel an anger and betrayal she couldn't ignore. She misplaced it on purpose, directed it at the woman who had come in and tried to fill a void no one could ever hope to fill.

She was nothing like mom and she never would be.

"It's late," observed her father, without looking away from the television.

"I know," said Rosalia, stopping behind the sofa.

"It's a school night," he continued. "Do I need to have a talk with Deron?"

She laughed to stifle a whimper. "Yes, please. You should go over and talk to him right now. And if he's not home, you should drive around the city until you find him." Her voice broke. "And I don't care if you threaten him or tell him he can never see me again, just so long as you find him and let me…" Trailing off, she averted her eyes when he looked up. Even Lynn was staring at her now.

"Rose, what's the matter?"

"Nothing," she replied, concentrating on her veneer. The tears welled at the corners of her eyes, but she reconciled them away as they came.

"Did you and Deron have a fight?" asked Lynn.

Contempt took over, allowed Rosalia to steady herself. "No, *Lynn*, we didn't have a fight." Her tone evoked a frown from her dad and she pulled back for his sake. "It's nothing," she explained. "Same old bullshit."

He must have seen something in her veneer because instead of yelling at her, he just sat there, speechless, an aborted warning on his lips. Rosalia took the opportunity to cross to the stairs and as she climbed, she heard concerned whispers trailing after her.

Her bedroom door lit up at her approach, showing off the mural she had reconciled there a few weeks ago. Its design consisted of water that fell in thin lines, obscuring the detail behind it: a darkened cave, sparkling stones, and a fire in the distance where two shadows sat together, huddled next to it and each other for warmth.

It was time for a new image.

Grasping the glass and chips with one hand, she used the other to reconcile the old scene away and replaced it with a field at night, silhouettes of tall grass under a black sky. No one walked in the field, no shadows held hands on the horizon. There were no stars, no moon, nothing to light the way of anyone foolish enough to venture in. It was a lonely place, somewhere she would go if she only could.

Safe in her bedroom, Rosalia reached for the virtual keyboard on her desk and turned on some music. The first track was from her regular playlist, something too upbeat for the hour and circumstances. She swiped at her music library, winding back the clock to the Classical era, to songs that still managed to evoke emotions and soothe the heart even after so long. Something obscure began to play, a sonata perhaps, on the high end of the piano. She couldn't place the name, but the melody felt familiar, took her mind off the world just enough to let her slip out of her clothes without realizing it.

Rosalia stood next to the wall, staring at the lush jungle veneer, trying to remember what she had been feeling when she made that. She puzzled the lapse in memory as she brought up a portal and expanded it to fill the entire wall. Its liquid contents began to shimmer, trying to anticipate her next command before defaulting to her start page. The icons shrunk to a manageable size at her insistence, revealing an empty inbox. Nothing was new; all she had were static icons that only came to life when she put her hand near them.

The network awaited her, that vast ocean of information that in a million years she could never swim across. But the idea of worldwide calamities, misguided social networking, and omnipresent pornography didn't sound appealing. She almost gave up when she saw her bed off to the side, its covers turned back in anticipation. Then, an icon shook in place and a little exclamation point appeared above it.

Updates.

Shrugging, Rosalia tapped the icon and let Canvas expand into the portal. Her home room appeared, with four of the walls still holding their original designs. She looked at the waterfall and thought of the room beyond it, the one with the moon nightmare. With its pale light obscured, it wasn't as menacing, not as important when compared to losing Deron. She thought of him, but not without acknowledging the need to put him out of her head. Reconciliation would distract her. Changing the last blank wall of her gallery to something magnificent would make Deron's face go away, if only for a little while.

Rosalia put her hand on the wall and took a deep breath. In the darkness behind her eyes, she waited for something to emerge from her clouded mind. Images flew, but none substantial enough to waste time on. Retracing her steps, she thought about everything she had seen, tested the ideas to see if they were worthy of reconciliation. After a few minutes, she gave up, but when she opened her eyes, the wall had already changed.

It was blown-up reproduction of her Guardian chip, down to the last detail, just as she had seen it on Nurse Hendricks' wall. The tissue around it was pinker than she remembered and now there were little veins crisscrossing within it, little pulses of blood that appeared blurry from their motion. A smirk crept onto her face as she realized she *had* been thinking about the chip. In the game, her avatar backed away from the wall and watched as the sparkling curtain fell over the image, assimilating it into the public collective and comparing it with the thousands or millions of other players. She let a minute pass before walking her avatar to the wall and through it.

The other gallery was dark, lit from the center by a red orb embedded in the ceiling. Only one other wall was reconciled and its contents didn't make any sense. A series of three images stared back at her, all containing a chip similar to her Guardian except that these had tendrils extending both up and down. They were small, almost invisible; the artist had used contrasting blue on black to highlight them. The upper lines extended in an oblong pattern, which she recognized as the shape of a brain. The lower tendrils descended in a solid stalk before breaking away to form a small clump.

A heart and a spine.

The labels beneath the images suddenly made sense. *2, 13, 21*; they were ages. What she was looking at was the growth of a human and its internal wiring growing right along with it. The Guardian chip reached further into the body than she had thought. It seemed to require an entire network of wire to probe every last piece of it.

"A whole new system," she said aloud, comparing what she was seeing to the established circulatory, respiratory, and central nervous systems. A shiver went up her spine and she wondered whether the wires shivered too. For a moment, all she could think about were the metal vines in her body, intimately entwined with her spinal cord, poking and prodding their way into the depths of her brain. It was too much.

She imagined herself biological, all natural, but she was actually a mix, a half-breed of woman and circuitry.

What that meant for her soul, she wasn't sure.

A familiar concerto started, rescuing her from the spiraling breakdown. Logic crept back into her reality and reminded her that she was seeing an image inside a game. Whoever had reconciled it had seen a Guardian chip, but there was no proof that what they painted on the second wall even existed. Rosalia had seen no wires in the nurse's office and never in her life had she even heard the possibility advanced.

If anything, she had overreacted, panicked not because of the veneer's content but because of her emotional state, the fatigue that threatened her ability to stand.

She almost smiled at her own foolishness. But even that moment was short-lived as she realized she could verify the story by touching the wall. If she moved through it, then someone else in Canvas had seen the same thing. Or, her rational side pointed out, had imagined the same thing. Cautiously, she approached the wall.

Her heart sank as her avatar passed cleanly through it.

Another room, another wiring diagram, and a slightly different angle of the Guardian chip. On the fourth wall, set apart by the drawing of a nude woman swimming, was a cityscape that resembled downtown Easton. In the center was a dull building that seemed out of place with all the finely veneered skyscrapers around it. It was the kind of structure people wouldn't give a second glance to, yet there it was, focal point of a crude but ambitious cityscape. As her avatar approached the wall, a small bubble popped into being next to her, informing her that annotations were available. She pressed the *show* button and watched as a single word in rounded red letters appeared above the building.

"Vinestead," she read. "I've heard of you."

THIRTY
RUSSO

The tremors started after the first incision and didn't stop until long after the soul of Agent Eric Tavarez had been sucked into the fiery void. Since then, the sun had set, bringing darkness to the apartment. Russo didn't even have the strength to reconcile some mood lighting. Instead, he sat unmoving at the half-table in the dining nook and watched Easton's veneers through a thin window. He forced himself to catalogue the view, to count the windows on the facing building.

It was something to do while he waited for the trembling in his fingers to pass. The rest of his body had relaxed, but his hands had done most of the work, remembered too well what had happened.

So things had gone a little overboard.

Out of the corner of his eye, Russo could see Eric's limp body still tied to the chair. It was just a mass now, covered in a blanket he had found on the couch. Seeing a man bloodied and beaten was nothing new, but Russo couldn't stand the sight of the agent's empty eye sockets. Just thinking about them was enough to make him convulse, make his throat tighten in protest.

He thought of the dark pits swallowing up the light and shivered.

"Yep," he whispered. "Right off the side of the ship."

There were twenty-eight windows that he could see from his vantage point. Of those, only seventeen were lit from the inside. Some had people in them, those strange types that could walk around their apartments with unreconciled windows, uncaring of what they were doing or who was watching them. Russo counted them too, broke them into demographics of age, race, and estimated income. He did everything he could to avoid looking at the thing on the table.

He had seen diagrams before, three-dimensional models that could be rotated in space, but never in his life had he seen a human eyeball detached from the human. Free from its casing, the iris seemed to stare back at him, even when he closed his eyes and thought of something else.

At least there weren't two. Eric had put up such a fight during the first extraction that his right eye ended up getting torn to pieces. The second eye was easier, came out cleaner, but even then Russo's enthusiasm had waned. When it finally popped out, he threw it on the table and hurried to the bathroom to wash his hands.

It was more than blood that caked his fingers. He scrubbed as hard as he could, all the while watching his enjoyment disappear into the drain.

In the distance, someone was whispering, "What the fuck?"

The only explanation he had for his actions was that it wasn't him, the same way he hadn't really been in control with Deron. What started as a harmless ass-kicking had culminated in a neck stomp. It put Deron in a coma, but Russo knew he could have severed his spinal column and paralyzed him forever. Maybe if he had pushed a little harder, added just a fraction of force, Deron would be dead, just like Eric.

Russo imagined the power inside him, the ambition and fortitude obscured by his veneer for too long. The idea of murdering someone and removing their eyes was only abhorrent to him because that was what they had drilled into him behind the barred windows of Glenmore Elementary. In reality, it was justifiable if the rewards were great, if it allowed him to fulfill his destiny.

He looked away from the window and stared at the eyeball. Bringing forth his power would mean more blood and sinew. Eric had given up his life to protect something and he was just the first rung. The people higher on the ladder would likely do the same if he ever got to them, if they didn't kill him the second he started sniffing around.

It was ten-thirty according to the glowing numbers on the wall, but already Russo felt a fatigue unlike anything before. Every time his eyelids closed, he struggled to get them open again, until finally he was looking at the world through his eyelashes. They bent the light and made the apartment look ethereal, made the buildings outside look like the vague echoes he imagined would populate the afterlife. It was the world Eric lived in now, full of indeterminate shapes and diffused light. There were bright points, like the tips of skyscrapers or the glistening of the eyeball that extended out along the optic nerve—

Something caught his eye. It was faint, but if he turned Eric's eyeball the right way, he could see a metallic glint. With numb fingers, Russo stripped away the extraneous veins and tissue until the specimen stood naked. Some kind of silver sheathing was on the nerve extending away from the eyeball.

"Magic fucking eyes," said Russo, looking over at Eric and smiling. "You son of a bitch, I knew it!" He put his hand to his face, felt the bruises along his upper cheek. "That must have hurt like hell to put in. How did they even do that?" His stomach heaved as he flashed on the possibility of popping out the eyeball, attaching the sleeve, and fitting it back into the socket.

"Oh fuck," he cried. If it took special implants to see past the veneer, then it wasn't something he could just *take* from someone. He would need a doctor to perform the operation and an accomplice to keep the doctor in line while he was under. Unless they did it without anesthesia, he thought, and then shuddered again.

Russo groaned, cursed himself for having dismissed Jalay so easily; that kind of blind obedience was hard to come by. But there would be no need for apologies if he offered Jalay the same power. Even his simple mind would comprehend the advantages of seeing through the veneer.

Standing on shaky legs, Russo crossed the living room and entered Eric's bedroom. In the almost twenty-four hours he had been in the man's apartment, he hadn't yet set foot in the master suite. There had been no reason to before, but now he needed more information, more details about the man whose life he had taken.

Like the rest of the apartment, Eric's room had that professionally reconciled feel meant to convey independence and a refined taste. Everything was in its place, from the slippers along the footboard to the shirts hanging in the open wardrobe. The sheets on the queen-size bed were folded back on one side and the pillows were stacked two deep against the headboard. Across from the bed was a dresser and on the wall above it, a dormant portal. He tested it with a quick swipe, but it came back with an *access denied* message and shut off.

So maybe he couldn't get into Eric's portal, but they hadn't reached a truly paperless society yet. There had to be something. Opening the small door to the right of the bed, he reconciled some light on the walls and found a closet with shelves full of books and folders.

Russo sat down on the floor and began pulling items. There were some textbooks, old collections of faded paper with cracked bindings, but nothing about law enforcement or being an agent. He guessed those were secret, reconciled only on approved portals and only within the walls of the precinct. He found a couple of old photo albums on disposable palettes but lacked the strength to turn all of their virtual pages.

The jackpot came at the bottom of the shelf in a faded leather binder that looked like it hadn't been touched in years. Inside was a certificate of graduation from the Easton Police Academy, dated long before Russo was born. So what had happened in the interval, he wondered. Did Eric gain his sight after joining up, maybe when he advanced to a special team? There had to be some record of a procedure; nobody got their eyes popped out and put back in without something in writing.

Frustrated, he flung the binder out of the closet where it hit the bed and cracked open. Its contents spilled out, but in addition to the certificate and a personal note from his instructor, a third piece of paper fluttered to the floor. Russo pulled himself over the pile of useless antiques to get his hand on it.

It was another certificate, but instead of the Easton PD seal, this simply had a large V within a circle in the corner, raised and dated before the police academy diploma. In the center was his name, *Eric Tavarez,* and below that, *License #21928.* The only other markings were in the lower right-hand corner, two illegible signatures on a line. But below them, finely printed, were two names.

Paul Barre, Instructor.

Victoria Dahlstrom, Vinestead Services - Easton.

Whatever the license signified, Eric had attained it before his time at the police academy. And if this was Victoria Dahlstrom of Dahlstrom Academy, then it went back even further. At least Russo had heard of the exclusive school. Vinestead Services, on the other hand, was new to him.

There was so little to go on that Russo frowned. It took all of his remaining energy to get up off the floor and stumble back into the living room where Eric was still waiting patiently.

"Is this it?" he yelled. "A license? To do what? To kill? To see? Someone has to give you permission? Do you realize how fucked up that is?" He collapsed onto the sofa and put his feet up on the coffee table. Scooping up his palette, he altered his search from Seers to Vinestead Services. When nothing came back in the first few seconds, he set the palette aside and leaned his head back.

"Another dead end," he said. Another wild goose chase for something the network wanted to tell him didn't exist.

By the time the first hits started appearing on the screen, Russo had succumbed to his fatigue.

THIRTY-ONE
DERON

Deron wasn't sure when he had dozed off, only that after the sun had gone down, he had retreated to the one place where he could still see the veneer. It was wonderful there, feeling more like reality than the waking nightmare he found himself in. In his dreams, the veneer was absolute and reliable—everything he touched bent to his will and remained even if he took his eyes off of it. Colors held fast, didn't fade out like the blue from the sky when the sun set. They stayed because that's what he believed they should do.

The dream itself was nothing more than a loose arrangement of recollected memories, visions of Sebo in Swarm Survivor or Rosalia batting her eyes at the edge of Gillock Pond. He moved through the various scenes with confident detachment and didn't worry when the moment froze on the image of Easton's skyline as depicted by a hundred different reconcilers over the years. All the signs were there, all the fancy decorations that made downtown such a vivid and beautiful place.

The dream came to an end, but the image held despite being at a different angle. He straightened up, grimaced at the cramp in his neck, and looked towards downtown. Faintly, very faintly, he could see the glowing signs at the tops of the spires. Some of the windows glowed, but when he looked directly at them, their brightness faded.

Deron stood and walked a few steps from the loading dock. All around him, the veneer fluctuated, its color fading in and out depending on how hard he focused or by the angle at which he held his head.

A growing optimism led him to the side of the building where he put his hand on the wall and concentrated on the letters of his name. When they didn't appear, he closed his eyes and tried harder. Looking again, he still couldn't see any characters, but under his hand, the drab metal showed flashes of its former color scheme. It came and went, following his hand as he moved it around. The minor progress supported his theory that his body was trying to repair the damage in his brain. That meant one day he might be able to reconcile again.

Deron turned his attention to the field, to the final destination specified by the hidden markings. He considered the latest development, wondered if he should even follow the trail anymore. After all, it was for people who couldn't see, or could see, depending on how he looked at it. He could head home and hopefully reconcile a portal to let Rosalia know that everything was going to be okay.

Up until that moment, Deron had considered his inability to see the veneer as a defect. But now that he was improving, he saw it in a new light. If he healed completely, he wouldn't be able to see the world beneath anymore. And as for the trail, he knew where it ended, but there could have been more to it that required Undersight.

"Undersight," he said aloud, finally putting a name to his affliction.

While he pondered the new word and what its entry would look like when the next generation of kids had to copy it from the dictionary, he caught sight of something flickering in the field, beckoning him. As he trudged through the high grass, he kept searching for that little flash of light. All around, the grass and weeds grew unchecked, making his pursuit difficult. Just as he was about to turn back, he saw it, a brief flash like a speck of magnesium exploding on a stalk of grass. But that was impossible, since…

Deron chuckled as the reconciled patch of grass faded away into nothing. He had almost waited too long; if his sight had returned in full force, there would have been no way to discern the metal grate sitting flush against the ground. There were no visible handles, but he could slip his fingers between the bars and get a slight grip. He lifted and found that the grate was some kind of prefab material made to look like metal. Setting the lightweight cover aside, he peered into the hole.

The darkness swallowed up any features or objects besides the rungs that led down. The thought of descending into the total black made him hesitate. In a world of veneers, he had been used to seeing everything without effort. This wasn't the same as being cursed with Undersight; this was total blindness.

Groaning, Deron dipped one leg into the hole and placed it on the second rung. His other leg followed and before he could change his mind, he was climbing methodically downward. When just his head was visible, he reached over and pulled the prefab grate into place again. With each step, the world above receded until only a small section of sky was visible through the bars.

The bottom came quicker than he expected and when he looked around, he found a tunnel extending away from the ladder. Though dark, there was a discernable light at the end—nothing bright, but enough to follow. He walked hurriedly, grimacing at the thought of runoff from the industrial park. Deron kept his arms close and his head ducked to avoid contact with the walls.

As the light got closer, Deron noticed he was breathing faster. Something about the enclosed space was sparking a biological response, making his muscles ache with apprehension. He had to concentrate to bring them in line, but the thought of taking deep breaths didn't seem right in the tunnel. There were probably bugs flying around, little gnats or flies that he could suck in through his nose. The thought made him clam up and pull his shirt up to his eyes as a barrier. In the distance, he saw open land and broke into a run.

The first thing Deron noticed about the new environment was the clear horizon. Spinning in place, he gazed at the outside walls of Easton. The tunnel had taken him underneath and now he was in the open.

Panic set in and he stumbled.

No one goes outside the walls. And even if they could, they shouldn't.

There are bad things out there, he thought, recalling the warnings of childhood. Things like plants that would poison you just for looking at them or animals that would rip a human to shreds for fun and sustenance. The three F's of the outland were Flora, Fauna, and Fallout. Even if he could survive the local hazards, there was still the radiation. He could never outrun or outwit that. It was just there, sucking the life out of him, maybe even now.

Get out, he thought. If you can't see, get out of my city.

The trail had led him out of Easton and towards his death. There was nothing for him to do out here, no path that wouldn't lead to radiation poisoning.

Deron dipped his head. He kicked idly at a rock and watched it tumble along the dirt a few feet before coming to rest next to an arrangement of pebbles that looked suspiciously like an arrow. Examining it closely, he found it was pointing away from the wall, maybe thirty degrees to the left. There were no glinting clues to guide him—just a bent line that promised nothing.

After a glance backwards, he began to walk.

Deron tried to enjoy the freedom of being outside, of seeing a horizon with no razor wire, and of breathing crisp air that hadn't passed through any factories or restaurants. His mind wandered as the quarter mile turned into a half, then a full. Units of measurement passed without acknowledgement and the only way he could gauge his progress was by how small Easton got and how much effort it took to draw another breath. He fought through it, pushed himself to keep going and not give up. But eventually his body failed him enough to make him pause and rest against a pile of rubble that looked like evercrete but seemed immovable.

All night, the horizon had remained static, full of silhouettes of small plants and discarded junk. It reminded him of a veneer in the way its invariance betrayed its realism.

Then, one of the silhouettes moved, making his heart beat out a tempo so intense that it actually pained him. Deron narrowed his eyes, tried to bring the distant image closer. There was no denying the shadow moving under the moonlight. It was a smallish figure with a walking stick in one hand and some kind of disc in the other. It moved slowly as if it had no particular destination in mind. Still, it was coming towards Deron, towards a confrontation he might not survive.

There were stories about raiding parties and ambushed travelers taking the road to Paramel or Sonora. Whether they were true or not didn't really matter; the moral was always the same.

Never trust an outlander.

At a hundred yards, the figure's body language changed. Its hand went up in the sign of a greeting, but Deron remained suspicious. He didn't move, relied on the shadows of the rubble to keep him hidden.

"Hey," called a boy's voice over the diminishing gulf. He sounded excited and soon enough his smile became visible. "Finally!"

At close range, Deron became more optimistic that he could hold his own in a fair fight. His opponent was shorter but a little stockier. Even though his heart was about to explode, he still had the option of running away.

"Can you see?" asked the boy.

"Of course I can see," replied Deron, clenching his hands into fists. He thought about how vicious Russo had looked during their last meeting and tried to channel the same aggressive posture.

"I'm Valentin. What's your name?"

"Deron."

"You gonna hit me, Deron?"

"Depends." He felt foolish trying to sound tough. "What are you doing out here?"

Valentin's smile shifted but remained friendly. "I'm here for you, for anyone that's free of the veneer." He put his hands on his waist and looked back the way Deron had come. "This is like, my tenth time coming out here. I was beginning to think I'd never get one."

"One what?" Deron took a step backwards, unsure what to make of Valentin's subtle claim.

"A defector. A fugitive." Valentin scratched his chin. "Outcast?"

"I left on my own," said Deron, proudly.

"Sweet."

"Yeah," he replied, nodding at the unfamiliar expression. "Do you live out here?"

"Not here," said Valentin, looking around in disgust. "You'll see." He extended his arm in invitation.

Deron took one last look at the dot of a city. "Do you come out here every night?"

"No," he explained. "We have shifts. It's a long way, but you only have to do it every few weeks, so it's not bad. Just have to stock up." He gestured to his backpack. "It's like going for a long walk. You're just the icing."

All Deron could do was nod.

"You thirsty?" Valentin handed over the disc. "I've got my own flask. I only get to drink this if I don't find anyone. My dad says it has extra vitamins and stuff in there, but you can't taste 'em."

"It's good," said Deron, after a quick swig. The texture was different than what came from the faucet at home.

"So what's new in Easton?"

"You've been there?"

"No," replied Valentin, visibly saddened by the admission. "I was born in Dos Presas." His accent slipped for a second as he pronounced the name with a Spanish flair. "My dad says even if I get in, I wouldn't be able to see anything."

"You don't have the magic," said Deron.

At that, his new guide smiled and changed the subject. "We should go. It's a long walk back home and it's not gonna get any warmer until the sun comes up."

Deron shrugged, felt himself caught up in the torrent that flowed under Valentin's feet. So many pieces of the puzzle had just fallen into his lap and he hadn't had a moment to arrange them properly.

The trail led outside. There were people outside, people that came back looking for others with Undersight. Then what?

Though Valentin was leading him somewhere, he hadn't said anything about what they would do when they got there. There were no possibilities that jibed with what they had taught him about the outland. Valentin was young, but he had survived the radiation so far. And it hadn't made his dad sterile.

So many lies, he thought.

"So," asked Valentin, after a long silence, "tell me about yourself. Do you have a girlfriend?"

"Yeah," said Deron. "Her name's Rosalia."

"What does she look like?"

Something caught in Deron's throat. "I don't know."

THIRTY-TWO
SEBO

Principal Ficcone pulled Sebo out of the crowd as soon as he stepped through the front doors of Easton Central. His curt *come with me* didn't suggest a good mood.

Sebo was surprised by the early morning ambush, but his lingering grogginess kept him from puzzling out the impetus. Instead, he simply followed the principal away from the flow of students towards his office. His secretary opened the door for them as they approached and that's when Sebo saw the two uniforms waiting inside. He shot a look at Principal Ficcone, but the man's veneer was impassive. Ushering him into the room, he instructed Sebo to sit down.

Settling into the leather chair, Sebo wanted to ask what was going on, but the principal left the room abruptly and the two uniforms didn't seem inclined to speak with him. Every question hung in the air unanswered, met with a stern look and a warning to sit quietly. After a few minutes, he gave up trying to get information out of them and switched to listing all of the possible reasons why the cops would want to talk to him, or worse, arrest him. His mind cycled through his recent transgressions, arranging them in descending severity, but nothing came close to breaking any important laws. Then, like a smack to the face, he flashed on the answer.

Deron.

Worst-case scenarios began to play through his head, aggravated by the silence coming from the uniforms. If they knew something, they weren't telling. Unlike Sebo, they had the resources to mount a proper manhunt, to do much more than ride the trams until two in the morning looking for someone who wasn't there. All night, he had circled the lower half of Easton, watching the crowds get progressively smaller, watching his optimism dwindle in the reconciled twilight.

By the end of the night, all he had to show for his efforts was an ache in his back and a desire to sleep until July. Then, when he did rest, he found himself again on the hunt, spying Deron from the tram but losing him on the double-take.

After Sebo turned his attention inward, the uniforms drifted to the window and started mumbling about the attractive girls passing through the front plaza.

As far as they were concerned, guarding Sebo was secondary to ogling the young flesh on display outside.

"Did you hear about Barber?" asked the larger of the two. His hand seemed glued to his Blackjack, the hefty black baton hanging from his belt.

"Who?" The other officer was slightly shorter than his counterpart, but his muscles bulged distinctly under his uniform.

"You 'member that rookie we met at Poe's weekend before last, when we busted up that party?"

Muscles laughed. "That little five-foot-nothing chump? What about him?"

"Censured. Six weeks as a desk jockey."

"Sheeeit, what'd he do, slap the chief?"

"No," laughed Blackjack. "He was doing traffic duty at Rio Vista, you know, on the north side?"

"Did he slap a fifth grader?"

Blackjack put up his hand. "Just listen. Barber's working traffic, right? And he sees this group of kids walking to school and one of 'em has this box in his hand." He mimed the object. "And when Barber looks at the kid, he hides the thing behind his back all suspicious-like."

Muscles nodded.

"Barber says to the kid, 'What you got there?' and the kid, being the genius that he is, says he has a bomb."

"Fuck all," said Muscles, crossing his arms.

"Naw, it wasn't a *real* bomb. Turns out this kid made it out of rubber bands and one of those little ring boxes—I don't fuckin' know. But Barber's a fuckin' idiot, so he gets all up in this kid's face and tells him to open the box."

"So…"

Blackjack lowered his voice. "So the kid starts opening the top and Barber leans in and then the little fucker yells, 'Boom!'"

"And *then* he slapped him?"

"No, fucking Barber draws his sidearm and points it at the kid and yells, 'Bang!'"

"He got censured for that?"

"Yeah, well, the kid shit his pants." He shrugged. "So his parents wrote a letter."

"Is that true?" asked Sebo.

"Nobody's talking to you," reminded Blackjack.

"He should have shot him in the face," said Muscles, looking out the window again. He stubbed his finger against the glass. "Dig on those," he said. "I'd punch your mother for a shot at—"

Fortunately, the door behind Sebo swung open, saving him from a degenerating conversation that would have explored the limits of indecency among the ranks of the Easton PD. He turned in his chair, expecting to see one of his classmates joining him, but instead saw Principal Ficcone accompanying a well-dressed man with a familiar face.

"This is Mr. Kahani," said the principal.

"We've met," said the man. He crossed the room and extended his hand. "Agent Ruiz. How are you today, son?"

"Confused," replied Sebo. He cast a glance at the uniforms by the window.

Agent Ruiz took the hint and sighed. "Officers, can you please wait outside? I'd like to have a chat with Mr. Kahani."

They grumbled in response, but complied. As they passed Principal Ficcone, he shuffled awkwardly in place.

"Mr. Ficcone, please, a little privacy?"

"Sure, sure," he replied, appearing flustered for the first time in Sebo's memory.

When they were alone, Agent Ruiz reconciled a friendly veneer, "Please relax, Sebo. You're not in any trouble." He walked around the principal's desk and sat down in the high-backed chair.

"And Deron?"

The agent's eyebrows jumped a micrometer. He pulled a palette from his jacket and reconciled a portal on it. "Aside from the fact that your friend is missing, no, he is not in any trouble that we know of. According to his mother, he left his house sometime yesterday and hasn't been seen since. Has he tried to contact you?"

Sebo shook his head. "No. Rosa and I—"

"Rosa," said the agent, consulting his palette. "Rosalia Collier. Deron's mother indicates she is his current love interest." There was something detached about the way he said *love interest*, as if it were a habit of the proletariat, a group of which he was no longer a part.

"Yeah."

"And how would you characterize their relationship?"

Sebo had never really examined it before; he shrugged to fill the moment. Although it was clear why Deron liked Rosa—she had tits, after all—it wasn't obvious why she liked him in return. "Well," he said, after collecting his thoughts, "I suppose it's a normal relationship. They—"

"Are they sexually active?"

Sebo blinked slowly, tapping out *that's none of your business* with his eyelids.

Agent Ruiz smiled. "Forgive me. I'm just trying to get a clear picture of Deron's life. Strong hormonal and emotional factors, especially in young men, can often make them behave erratically. If Deron and this Rosa had a falling out or if they argued about sex, for example, then that helps define a psychological profile which, sometimes, can provide clues to a person's intentions."

"You think Deron killed himself because they broke up?" It was laughable, but coming from such an official source, Sebo couldn't bring himself to smile.

"No, no," said the agent, waving the suggestion away. "Our current focus is on whether Deron is still in the city. He doesn't show up on any of our systems: presence-sense, security posts, you name it. Can you think of any reason why he might want to go on vacation?"

Sebo shook his head, lost in thought.

Agent Ruiz sat back in his chair and tried to effect a more casual attitude. "Last Saturday, you two were going to Paramel, right?"

"Yeah," replied Sebo, wondering if the agent could sense his omissions.

"And did you meet anyone there? Perhaps…" He paused, making a show of it. "Russo Rivera?"

Sebo narrowed his eyes at the mention of the name. "Why would we meet with him? He practically—"

"Practically what? Practically killed Deron? Say what you will about the police force, but the people I work for actually do some investigating. Approximately three weeks ago, Deron was involved in an altercation with this Russo, was he not?"

"I don't know." He spoke the words quickly to avoid being interrupted again.

With a sigh, the agent changed his tone yet again. "Look, Sebo. I'm trying to help Deron. I know he hasn't identified Russo as his attacker yet and I know you think you're protecting him by lying to me. But what you don't realize is that Russo's been missing a lot of school lately. In my business, we call this putting two and two together. Deron is missing. Russo is truant. Two boys unaccounted for with a history of violence between them. You see how it all reconciles?"

Deron would never do that, thought Sebo. Not even in his diminished mental state would he try to confront Russo on his own.

"Of course, this is only one of many theories we're pursuing, and I admit it doesn't fit with some of the things we know. But after I talk to your classmates, I should have a better picture to work with. In the meantime, I guess I'll just keep watching the streets." He paused, scrolled through a few screens on his palette. After reconciling some notes, he stood and walked to the window. The last bell had long ago rung, and the previously crowded plaza was now deserted. The two uniforms were outside, leaning against their cruiser and laughing about something probably inappropriate.

"Question," said Sebo.

Agent Ruiz nodded without looking back.

"Why are agents involved in this? Shouldn't the police department be handling missing persons?"

The agent chuckled in response. "Look at those two cavemen out there. Would you want *them* in charge of bringing your friend home safe?" He turned and put his hands behind his back. "In all honesty, I volunteered my assistance because I recognized your friend's face from the other night. You two seem like good kids."

Maybe it was cynicism, maybe it was simple distrust of authority figures, but a small part of Sebo doubted the agent's sincerity.

"My card," said Agent Ruiz, crossing the distance and offering a small, veneered rectangle. "If you hear from Deron or think of anything else that might be useful in this investigation, I would appreciate a call."

"Okay," he replied, unsure. He slipped the card into his pocket without examining it.

"Well, I suppose that is all for now. Thank you for your time, Sebo." He feigned a bow and retreated to the doors.

Sebo leaned forward and put his elbows on his knees. He held his breath as he asked, "Are you going to arrest Russo for what he did?"

"Naturally," replied the agent.

"He'll resist."

Agent Ruiz scoffed. "I'm sure he'll come quietly. They always do."

"No," said Sebo, looking up and locking eyes. "You're not hearing me. He *will* resist arrest."

Recognition flashed on the agent's veneer, and he chuckled. "No promises, kid."

THIRTY-THREE
DERON

The sun was up and blazing by the time Deron rolled out of the unfamiliar bed and walked to the window. His entire body felt weak, not just from the lack of sleep but for the distance he had walked the night before. It was still dark when they made it back to town and Valentin had urged him to get as much rest as possible. The Path from Easton, as he put it, had broken stronger men than Deron. But even though the bed was somewhat comfortable, he couldn't ignore the questions running through his mind or the ache of his calves as he tried to peer out through the dirty glass.

While waiting for his eyes to adjust, Deron looked around the room and saw things as they should have been—in color. There were toys and trinkets on the desk and on the shelves, charred pieces of plastic and wood that looked ancient in the dusty light. There was nothing quite like it in Easton, not when the veneer could obscure the very suggestion of age, on objects as well as people. Deron thought of his mother, of the lines he had seen the morning before, and wondered if she even knew they were there, plotting and growing beneath her veneer.

A knock at the door made Deron take a step back. It was a louder sound than Valentin could have made and that meant someone else wanted to talk to him. His mind raced; he had taken Valentin at his word that he was out looking for refugees from Easton. But what if he had made it all up? What if this little town with a name Deron couldn't translate wasn't open to newcomers? They lived in the outland without access to modern amenities. Maybe they didn't need another mouth to feed.

The knock came again, softer this time.

A gritty voice called, "Are you up yet?"

Deron opened the door and found a tall man blotting out the sunlight.

"Good morning," he said. "My son tells me you come from Easton."

Deron nodded in response.

"My name is Timo." He extended his hand. "And you?"

The man's grip was rough and strong. "Deron Bishop."

"What say we get some breakfast, Deron?"

"Alright," he replied, slipping into the shoes he had left by the door. He followed Timo out into the sunlight and immediately felt his skin begin to sizzle.

"This is the center of Dos Presas," said Timo, motioning to a large open patch of dirt surrounded by grass. "See how all the buildings form a circle around us? They go out in all directions, with shops, a cafeteria, and a clinic. Houses form the second and third rings." He turned to Deron. "We have about six hundred people the last time we counted. Some come and go, but most live here full-time." He gestured with his hand into the distance. "Beyond the homes are farms and beyond those, the river borders."

Timo led him to a grouping of picnic tables on the edge of the circle. They reminded Deron of the parking lot dining room in Easton except these were not uniform, as if they had all been built from scratch.

"Mornin', Deron!" Valentin looked different in the daylight, much less menacing than his silhouette suggested. He had been sitting at the table but got up and approached with a smile when he saw Deron.

Timo interrupted the greeting. "Go fetch our friend some breakfast. Tell Carrie it's for a new arrival."

Valentin nodded obediently and set off towards a building whose sign read *Cafeteria*. It was a good thing there were signs since everything had that same log cabin kind of feel to it. Deron was sure these people had heard of evercrete, but most likely they didn't have the knowledge or resources to make it. He sure didn't.

"Have a seat, Deron," said Timo, indicating one of the tables. He sat down on the opposite bench, put his elbows on the table, and folded his hands. For a moment, he said nothing, just let his eyes drift off as he tried to think of how to begin the speech that Deron felt coming.

"Easton," he said at last. "I hear that place is becoming more and more like Sonora every day. But I guess that's what they do. Gotta keep that iron fist tight, right?"

Deron shrugged, unsure what Timo was referring to.

"You're lucky you got away when you did. I left Sonora after the lockdown. You don't even want to know how I got out of there."

"Did you lose your magic too?"

Timo chuckled, eyed Deron playfully. "Yeah, I lost my magic. I stopped reconciling when I was twenty-three, some kind of ocular chip failure."

"Did you walk from Sonora?"

"Yeah. One hundred and fifty miles. Now that sucked."

Deron laughed and felt the ache in his abs and stomach. He caught sight of Valentin coming out of the cafeteria carrying a plate in one hand and shooing the flies away with the other. He had a grin on his face as if he could sense Deron's hunger at a distance. With a flourish, he set the plate on the table.

"Bacon, eggs, and diced potatoes. Carrie says hi too."

"Thanks," he replied, picking up the fork. The first bite tasted a little off, but as he chewed, he sensed the familiar flavors. "It's good," he concluded.

"Go tell Carrie he says it's good. That woman feeds on praise."

Again, Valentin nodded without saying anything. It was a father-son dynamic that Deron was unfamiliar with. He had always questioned his dad, always talked back and disobeyed at random. Even after he left to chase after other women, the problems didn't cease. The only reason they didn't fight as much now was because he travelled all the time.

"So how did it happen?" asked Timo. "For you, I mean."

Deron thought of the scars on his face and neck, the lingering reminders of Russo's anger that the veneer had been hiding.

"I got in a fight," he replied. "I was in the hospital for a while."

"Is that what did it?"

"Did what?"

"Is that what opened your eyes to all this?"

"Oh," said Deron, thinking back. "I don't remember being able to see after that. It was only…" An alien blob flashed in his mind. "I hit my head a couple days ago and haven't been able to reconcile since."

"Hmm. It must have been a controller failure. I'm guessing you didn't tell anyone?"

Deron shook his head.

Timo's face went solemn, a transition smoother than anything reconciliation could provide. "I understand the fear. We all share a common experience here, Deron. All that uncertainty, thinking the world's come to an end. But it's not the end. People do live without the veneer."

"But not in the cities?"

"No," said Timo. "People like us are dangerous there, not only to ourselves but to the system. When you've been around people long enough, you begin to see just how much you were missing before."

Deron stared at his food. He thought of his mom, of Rosalia and Sebo. Timo was right; he hadn't realized how much he missed them.

"You've had a rough go," said Timo, folding his hands on the table. "Dos Presas is a safe place. We're surrounded on three sides by a river that forks around us. East of us, the two dams create another border. The only way in or out is by one of two bridges or by boat. You could try to swim across, but I'd be surprised if you made it. Point is, we've been living here for decades without any trouble and we intend to keep it that way. We have laws just like anywhere else. Kill another man, damage property, or put the town at risk, and we'll drop you on the road back to Easton faster than you can say reconciliation."

The word made Deron think about home. "Do you guys have any tech?"

Timo flashed a smile. "That's Abernathy's department. He gets all the electronics we salvage, though they're not much use to us out here. Lot of it requires reconciliation and as you know, that skill's in short supply in this town."

Deron nodded in agreement even as the soft blue color crept out from under his hand. It followed his gaze and settled under his plate, making the stained tin suddenly pearly white. Surprised by the sudden change, he looked up to see if Timo had noticed.

"Good eats, huh?" he asked.

"Just like mom makes," replied Deron.

Timo looked away. "I left my parents and a sister in Sonora. You?"

"My mom. And dad, but he's never there anyway."

"I can't tell you how to decide, but I can say it'll be difficult. Leaving your mother…"

"Have you ever gone back to see them?"

"No." His eyes became stern. "The veneer is no friend of ours anymore."

"But what if our magic comes back?" Deron looked at the fork in his hand as it sparkled gold for half a second.

Again, a hearty laugh from Timo. "Maybe we should save the tour for later. I think you need to meet Abernathy."

"Why?" asked Deron, biting a piece of bacon.

"Because there's no such thing as magic."

THIRTY-FOUR
ROSALIA

It wasn't possible to reconcile a fever, but Rosalia had no trouble changing the hue of her skin to appear flush. After that, all she needed was a reddening of the eyes to convince her dad that she was too sick to attend school. There was something in the way he looked at her when he agreed, some hint that he knew she was lying but that it was okay.

After he and Lynn left for work, Rosalia reconciled herself a pink t-shirt and blue jeans and left the house to catch the tram. It was waiting for her at the end of the street, and she managed to step on before it took off towards Parker Avenue. There, rush hour was clogging the streets with pedestrians. They were all older than her, but in their distraction, took no notice of the sullen-faced girl sitting alone in the back row of the tram. They all had their own lives to lead with their own problems and excuses. She almost wanted one of them to ask her why she wasn't in school. It would have been just the thing to set her off, make her yell and scream and wave her hands around like a lunatic.

It was no business of theirs whether she went to school or not. They didn't know what was going on in the world; they just kept getting on and off the tram like the little lemmings they were.

As the tram moved further southwest, the number of passengers and stops began to dwindle, until finally it was just Rosalia and a frail man with a vintage veneer but a body that had been ravaged by too many years on Earth. He was hunched over, making Rosalia wonder if she too would reach a point where her body would be on the verge of collapsing like a termite-ridden house with a fresh coat of paint. Before she could worry too much about it, the tram came to a stop at Walsh Street. Rosalia disembarked and waved to the waiting Ilya.

She was seated at a table outside a faux French restaurant, looking quite trendy in her tight ponytail daniel oversized sunglasses. If it hadn't been for her signature half-smile, Rosalia might not have recognized her at all. To everyone else, she probably looked like one of those trophy-wife sophisticates out for a morning latte before heading uptown to do some shopping. The way she sat, the way she held herself with impeccable posture and one leg crossed over the other, sold the illusion even more. Rosalia wanted to comment about trying too hard to look like an adult but the widening smile on Ilya's face distracted her.

"Look at you," said Ilya, her eyes hidden behind veneered lenses. "Cutting school like a rebel."

Rosalia nodded and pulled the opposite chair around so she could sit closer. "Thanks for coming," she said. It felt as if she had been thanking her constantly; the words were starting to lose their meaning.

"Beautiful day." Ilya tilted her head back, exposing her smooth neck. "When I die and go to heaven, I'm going to spend half of eternity in their best French café." A chuckle rippled through her neck. "My grandmother says there is not one coffee shop left in all of Ukraine."

"That's sounds a little—"

"Well, Babushka also says laughing on Sunday was punishable by firing squad." Her face scrunched up in thought. "Her mind is starting to go."

Another thing to look forward to, thought Rosalia. "How did," she said, before stalling out, embarrassed to be changing the subject so selfishly.

"No luck," replied Ilya, looking away to a passing group of young businessmen. "I rode until ten, but nothing. Sorry."

Rosalia dismissed the apology with a wave of her hand. "It was one night. Thanks for doing that."

"I'm happy to help," she said, smiling again. In the pause that followed, Ilya offered her drink, but the slight breeze had already brought the pungent smell of cappuccino to Rosalia's nose.

"I was thinking of going to see Deron's mom today," she announced.

Ilya replied with a weak shrug. "Do you think she'll even let you in the door?"

"I don't care. I have to know if she knows something. I'm tired of being out of the loop. I'm tired of being alone." Rosalia hesitated, surprised by her own admission. The words had come out of nowhere, had not existed in any intelligible form until the moment they were spoken. If they were true, then her problems were just little islands in a sea of solitude. Without those, she would have nothing.

It was easy to see the emotion cycle onto Ilya's face. She took her sunglasses off before saying, "You're not alone."

Rosalia nodded. "I found something interesting last night, in Canvas."

"I'm still waiting for one of my veneers to match up with yours, but so far, all I get are young girls."

"There seem to be a lot of people who like to reconcile Guardian chips."

Ilya shuddered. "Don't remind me about that thing. One day when I'm drunk enough, I'm going to cut it out." She paused. "Or maybe I'll just hire someone to do it."

"I bet you could find instructions on the network. *Warning, may result in death.*"

"But there's no way I'm living with a little computer inside me. I don't care if it's for my own good." She blew the steam from her cup. "So who are these chip people?"

"No clue. But it's like there's this whole group trying to figure this out."

"Where?" asked Ilya. "Here in Easton?"

Rosalia nodded. "You're right. It has to be bigger than just us. How could one city come up with technology like this?"

"Then it's whether it's the whole country or the whole world."

"No," she countered, "it probably costs a ton to implant a chip in a baby." She visualized herself as an infant, watched as the needle pushed into her skin. Without realizing it, she began to reconcile the image on the table.

Ilya gasped. "That's horrible!" She slapped the table and wiped the offending picture away.

"You think that's gross? Check these out." Color spread from Rosalia's fingers in a quick swirl of grays and reds, filling up the pock marks in the plastic.

The chip took form first, then the metal tendrils that rose and fell to encase the brain and strengthen the spinal cord. Somehow having it out in the open, out where someone else could witness the horror, made it that much more visceral. Looking up, she saw shock on Ilya's face, a kind of restrained terror that made her regret reconciling the picture. Rosalia moved to clear the image away, but a sudden hand on her wrist stopped her.

"Is that real?" asked Ilya, shaking.

"Real as in someone reconciled it. But whether that's in our body or not, I don't know. I didn't see anything in the picture Nurse Hendricks gave me."

"This can't be right."

"I'm sure it isn't," said Rosalia, feeling unnatural in the role of comforter. "Probably just someone imagining what life might be like in a few decades. Technology is always getting better…"

Ilya slipped her sunglasses on and looked away.

"What's wrong?" asked Rosalia.

"I don't know," she admitted. "I just hate these points of no return, these little moments in our lives that we can't come back from. Not like skipping school or shoplifting, but like you and Deron. One day when this is all behind us, you'll get all hot and bothered and end up going to bed with him. And that will be it. Innocence gone forever." She paused, sniffled. "And now we find out there are chips in our necks and maybe more?"

"It's not that bad," she offered. "It's not like the chips are controlling us or something."

A quiet scoff. "This is the one thing you and I disagree on."

Rosalia realized that Ilya was sharing one of her worries. She, the unflappable Ukrainian, was scared to death about a little circuitry in her body.

"Do you really want it out?" Rosalia asked.

"Yes, but I know that's not possible. The point of no return was before I could even comprehend. I didn't have a choice. I don't know any life except one with a chip."

Nodding, Rosalia leaned over the table and began reconciling a cityscape. She remembered the Vinestead building well, had encountered it several times while moving through the walls in Canvas. Though, she did note that it was always the same angle, same distance from the subject, as if one person's memory had been reproduced several times. It made her giddy to think how people would react to seeing it from a different viewpoint.

Close up. Even inside.

"I've seen that before," said Ilya, noticing the new picture. She touched her sunglasses briefly and reconciled clear lenses. "It's," she said, then looked up at Rosalia. "Why do I know that building?"

Rosalia gestured with her head, "Because it's right across the street."

THIRTY-FIVE
RUSSO

Russo tried to think of a word to describe Easton Central as he stood observing it from behind the bleachers. He had never given it much thought before, but now with the idea raised, he couldn't think of a simple definition. Something about the school's veneer had changed. Or had it?

Maybe it was just that he was questioning it now.

He realized he had been doing it all day, looking at things, seeing their reconciled façades, but not really accepting what his eyes were telling him. Just having the knowledge that something else was under there, waiting to be discovered, had changed his whole perspective. Looking over the school, he noticed how small it had become, noticed that when he stripped away all the fancy colors, it was just a building.

At least, that was the theory. To confirm it, he would have to see under the veneer. The desire that had been percolating since his first encounter with Eric had come to a full boil; every moment that he spent just standing around only made him more anxious. Russo tried to calm himself, tried to explain to the impatient child inside that he had to wait for the right moment, that from the bleachers he would be able to hear the bell ring and then he could slip into the school unnoticed and find Jalay at his locker. He would win back his partner in crime.

It'd be easy.

"I'm sorry," he said, testing his sincere voice. Trying again, he softened his delivery and accented different syllables.

When his eyes drifted, he noticed students on the far field, running around and screaming in their shrill voices. The girls were playing lacrosse, and from the look of it, not too successfully. Most of them seemed timid, afraid to get in the way of the ball even with their protective gear in place, those massive helmets that obscured gender except for the tell-tale hair flowing out from behind them. The strange dance continued until the whistle blew and the uncoordinated gaggle of bitches came running back to the main building.

Pushing off from the bleachers, Russo shook his head at their feeble attempts at sports and started towards the back doors of the school.

The bell rang just as the doors closed behind him and the hall filled with students. The things they talked about were so inconsequential, yet within the banality was a discernable difference between freshmen and sophomores, juniors and seniors. That there would be so much change from year to year surprised Russo, made him wonder who his new peer group was now that he had elevated himself to a new level.

Turning the corner into the main ring of the building, he grinned at the confused faces of the juniors he passed. Conversations came to a halt, changed to whispers about the return of Russo. He could have masked his appearance before coming in, made himself out to be a generic student, but that was for the old Russo, the one that cared about rules.

He found Jalay with his face buried in his locker. Russo nudged another student out of the way and moved close enough to make his voice heard over the crowd.

"Hello, my friend," he said, reconciling a smile onto his face.

Jalay paused, betrayed recognition. "I thought you didn't know me."

"Why wouldn't I know my oldest comrade?"

"Because that's what you said, remember? What are you even doing here?"

"I go to school here," explained Russo.

Jalay scoffed. "Like shit you do. If Ficcone sees you he'll expel you."

"Well, until then…" The fingers on Russo's right hand twitched, while the others failed to respond.

"Yeah, until then. So what do you want?"

Interesting question, thought Russo. If Jalay knew what he truly wanted, would he even agree to help? "To apologize," he said, turning away slightly to see if anyone had heard him. "I…" One, two, he counted, giving it the right amount of hesitation. "I thought about what you said, about Deron. I overreacted."

"No kidding."

"Wait," said Russo, putting up his hand, "I get it, alright? I was just so angry. He insulted us."

Jalay shook his head dismissively. "You kicked the shit out of Deron over a shop. How would you have felt if *he* snapped, if *he* brought a gun to school and shot us in the face for all the shit we've done to him over the years?"

"But that's the difference! People like you and me, we have the balls to fight back. We crush those who insult us and make them never want to do it again. We have that power—"

"What *power?* You're stronger than him, but can you stop a bullet?"

This time, Russo sneered. "Deron's too much of a pussy for that."

"So because he's a pussy, it's alright to push him until he snaps? You're the one who's going to make him into a killer."

A smile bubbled up onto Russo's veneer. He had spent so much time lost in introspection, wondering what it meant to be a new Russo, that he hadn't even considered that without him, Jalay had changed as well. Here was a boy who a week ago wouldn't have dared disagree with his better. He just did the shops, did whatever shit work Russo told him to do. But this was a new Jalay. His veneer looked the same, but he had augmented it in some way. It was there in his eyes.

Defiance.

"Do it," said Jalay, his jaw clenched.

"Do what?"

"Hit me. I know you want to. That's you how control people, isn't it? Just intimidate and attack until people do your bidding. Well that shit isn't going to work on me anymore."

Russo raised an eyebrow, noticed the stares from the students around him. They had all stopped to view the spectacle unfolding in the hallway. Over their heads, he could see the concerned eyes of a teacher a few doors down, who upon seeing Russo, turned and reconciled a portal on the wall. Time was running out.

"Old friend," said Russo, putting a hand on Jalay that he immediately pushed away. "I am sorry." He paused for the audible gasp from the audience. "I'm sorry you're so utterly fucked in the head that you can't see a good opportunity when it's dropped at your fucking feet. You could've heard me out, held your fucking tongue for sixty goddamn seconds while I laid out how you and I were going to rule this city."

Jalay crossed his arms.

"You!" Russo pointed at a boy standing nearby. "You remember this moment." His finger swept the crowd. "When it happens, when you all hear about it, I want each and every one of you to track down this dumb motherfucker right here and remind him of this moment. Tell him I gave him a chance. And he said *no!*"

"Go fuck your mother, Russo," said Jalay.

It started with a tremor in his right hand, then a series of explosions up and down his arm. The numbness came on strong, making him feel as if he couldn't control his body at all. Except that his hand was moving, the muscles contracting with enough force to raise it up, shoot it out, and grasp Jalay on the side of the head. Then, contractions in his foot, a bracing against the floor as his hip jutted out to put more lateral force into the movement.

His body moved without instruction, applying pressure with his hand and driving Jalay's head into the metal frame of the locker. The impact sent a painful series of vibrations up his arm that faded into a throbbing tingle. He had pulled something, but his discomfort would be minimal compared to Jalay's. Subconsciously, Russo had known the locker was still open and not wanting to force his head into empty space, had tried to pull it forward so that it would smash into the one next to it. A miscalculation had put the side of Jalay's face into the midpoint, into the angular edge that was just sharp enough to split his face wide open.

Jalay fell in a heap at Russo's feet, dazed.

"Rivera!" The voice boomed over the stunned congregation.

Russo turned along with everyone else and viewed the three men standing at the end of the hallway. There was Principal Ficcone sporting his customary scowl. Flanking him were two generic uniforms, one with his arms crossed and the other with a twitchy hand on his sidearm. Together, they didn't seem all that imposing, not with the exit only a short sprint down the hall in the opposite direction. They wouldn't be able to catch him, not with the current traffic jam.

"You stop right there!" The principal motioned to the uniforms.

"No," replied Russo, raising his voice to the same ridiculous timbre, "*you* stop! Come any closer and I start cutting!"

At the sight of the knife, the mob erupted into panic. It worked in his favor as those in front of him surged towards the uniforms while the rest made off the other way. Looking down at Jalay, he pointed the knife. "I gave you a chance," he said, before bolting down the hallway.

There were screams from all directions as the students scattered in front of him, some seeking refuge in classrooms. All at once, the veneers in the hallway changed, with the ceiling morphing into a threatening red that undulated in waves. Decorations faded into the distance and were replaced by beige backgrounds with the word *LOCKDOWN* reconciled in large black letters. An alarm ramped up, sounding from above. Russo smiled, amused at the chaos he had created. It was good to inject a little excitement into their lives. They'd talk about him for a long time, talk about where they were when Russo went on a rampage.

Russo's Rampage, he titled it, and then laughed. They hadn't seen anything yet.

Turning the corner, Russo saw the windows on the outside doors gleaming. He barreled towards them, legs now under his control and pumping as hard as they could. Although his adrenaline surged, his mind was able to break his escape into a series of easily achievable tasks. Get to the door, get outside, turn left, and head towards the street. Lose them in the neighborhood. It was as good a plan as any.

The outer doors banged into the walls as he pushed through them.

"Where you running off to?"

The voice came out of nowhere so suddenly that Russo stumbled and almost took a header into the grass. Regaining his balance, he slowed and turned to face his interrogator. There was something about the way the man dressed, the way he looked at Russo, that seemed so familiar.

"Do I know you?" asked Russo, between breaths.

"My name is Ruiz and no, you don't. But the important thing is that I know you. And that I know what you're after."

There it was, thought Russo. Even at a distance, he could tell the man's eyes weren't normal. "How many of you are there?"

"Enough," Ruiz replied, lifting his palette and showing it to Russo. "Do you recognize this person?"

Russo smirked at the image of a bruised Deron. "What about him?"

"We have reason to believe you are responsible for his stay in the hospital."

His face scrunched in disbelief. "What is wrong with you people? You use your magic to solve little bullshits like this?"

"Okay," said the agent, reconciling a new image on the palette. "How about him?"

Russo bolted, kicking up the grass as he went. The entire world receded as he put all of his concentration and effort into the picking up and putting down of his feet. Flying across the lawn, he jumped down the five steps leading towards the bleachers, cut through the lacrosse field, and finally made his way off school grounds. He crossed more streets than he could count, turning down alleys and cutting through backyards, until his lungs broke down and refused to continue their frenetic pace. Crumbling to his knees beside a shed in someone's backyard, he struggled to find his breath.

Feeling dizzy, Russo put his hand on the shed to steady himself. Under his open palm, the veneer shimmered, sparked by something in his subconscious, something his magic mistook for a command.

He couldn't look away from the newly reconciled wall, couldn't escape the agent's reconciled image or the piercing eyes of the late Eric Tavarez.

THIRTY-SIX
DERON

Abernathy's shop wasn't so much a store as a shrine to dead tech. Deron couldn't name half of the objects on the warped shelves that stretched from one side of the room to the other, breaking only to allow passage into the back of the shop where Timo was chatting with the proprietor. Timo had joked that Abernathy was old, but not as old as the relics he collected. Now, standing in front of the shelves, staring decades into the past, Deron couldn't disagree.

He had never seen anything like it, not in the history books or even in the museum in downtown Easton that he visited in sixth grade. There were things on the shelves that seemed to predate reconciliation, like televisions and clocks and some kind of telephone with a built-in display. Looking closely, he saw that all the gadgets were suffering from age, wilting like flowers in the hot sun. Though they retained their basic shape, he could tell just by looking that they no longer functioned. Next to the phones, he found a bin full of little slips of gray metal. Deron extracted one of the slivers and felt the poke of the interface pins on his thumb.

"He's a curious one, isn't he?" asked someone from behind.

"Sorry," said Deron, tossing the tab back into the bin.

The voice belonged to an old man whose face had been corrupted by age. Somehow, the frail mouth still worked enough to speak.

"No matter how many times it happens, I'll never get over the astonishment on the faces of the newly gray." He winked at Timo. "Well met, young Bishop. Morten Abernathy, Tech Support." He grinned at his last statement, exposing a pitted smile.

"Hi," replied Deron, shaking the man's frail hand.

His furry eyebrows danced. "I see you've discovered slivers." Reaching over Deron's shoulder, he pulled out one of the shinier ones. "I bartered these from a scavenger on his way to the northern border. Argentinean, no, Brazilian. You ever been to Brazil, Deron? It's like going back in time, technologically speaking. The scav said they had only gotten the veneer, what, five years before he got there?"

Timo shrugged in confirmation.

"You know what reconciliation can do to a country," said Abernathy, gesturing to the wall of discarded technology. "All of a sudden, nobody wants a sliver anymore. So, glut." He coughed into his elbow and for a second appeared as if he couldn't stop.

"What does it do?" asked Deron.

"Information delivery, same as anything else. Society was obsessed with information long before I was born, if you can believe that. This little thing went like this here." He raised his arm and set the sliver down softly on his wrist. "It goes into your skin," he explained.

"In your world," put in Timo, "it would be like reconciling a portal on your body."

"Quite obsolete when the veneer came along, but in its day all the kids had them. We had portals, they had slivers. Same purpose."

Deron examined his own arm and wondered why anyone would want to embed something in their skin. Just the idea of those pins sticking into his muscles made him shiver.

"Ha!" said Abernathy. "Look at him! As if a little endotech's such a bad thing."

Timo smiled. "Cut the kid some slack. He just got back to Kansas yesterday."

"And you haven't told him yet?"

"Told me what?" asked Deron, flustered.

"Don't worry," said Timo, putting up his hand. "I promised you some information; that's why I brought you to Abernathy. He's going to explain your magic."

"Magic!" The old man stifled a chortle. He pointed an accusatory finger at Timo and said, "And they have the sack to call them schools! A place you go to learn, to discover the secrets of the universe." Muttering as he walked away, he suddenly stopped and tossed the sliver to Deron. "Put that away, son. You and I need to have a talk."

Deron replaced the sliver in the bin and shot a questioning look at Timo.

"He's sensitive," he explained. "After everything you learn today, keep in mind you're still young. Abernathy spent half a century in Floren before going gray. Imagine spending your whole life believing in something like the veneer and then one day finding out it's all been a lie. That's all the veneer is, Deron. A giant lie that everyone believes."

"Are you two bajingos coming or what?" yelled Abernathy from the back.

Timo shrugged and led Deron behind the counter to a workbench where Abernathy was searching through a list with his finger. Finally, he stopped and tapped the page.

"Row twenty-six, column fourteen." He shuffled towards a grid of cubby holes on the back wall. "You'd think after all these years of initiating newcomers I'd just keep one of these on my desk." Then, to Timo, "Less this year than the year before. And before and before." There was a sing-song quality to his voice. Suddenly, he belted in operatic fashion, "Every year, every year, less eyes to shed a tear. We can never free them all, save for those that hear our call."

Timo groaned, audible only to Deron.

Abernathy resumed his normal voice. "No one sings anymore. When I was young, we sang all the time about this and that. My Jessica loved to hear me sing. If I recall…" His speech dwindled as he found the item he was looking for. He made his way down the ladder and then handed a small box to Deron. "Open it."

Inside, Deron found a sheet of plastic with a speck in the middle of it.

"Impressive, isn't it?" asked Abernathy, grinning.

"What is it?"

The glee drained from the old man's face. "Sweet Christopher Pike, son, how old are you?"

"Seventeen?"

Abernathy flashed consternation. "Is that a question? Do they not teach you how to tell your own age?"

"Easy," interrupted Timo. He put his big hand on the man's shoulder and looked him in the eyes. "Remember what it's like, yeah?"

The fire dimmed but Deron could see it wasn't gone completely.

"Sorry," sighed Abernathy. "I get old sometimes. Seventeen was… sixty years ago." His eyes drifted. "Things were different then. They taught us about our Guardian chips. That there's what you have in your neck. That's your magic."

Reflexively, Deron reached for his throat but soon felt a warm finger on the back of his neck.

"Back here," said Timo, tapping a spot just below the end of Deron's skull.

"The Guardian chip," explained Abernathy, walking away, "is the regulator of modern man's entire life. Its first function was to allow people to interface with virtuality."

Deron thought back to Destined 4 Death, suddenly unsure of how simply wearing a mask on his face could produce such vivid experiences.

"Over the years, other features were added, some good, some bad. Then one day, they went too far." The old man rolled something tall out of the corner, draped in a black sheet. Chuckling, he began recounting. "They said that the greatest threat to mankind would be the invention of artificial intelligence." Stealing a glance at Timo, he added, "So much for mankind, right?"

Timo smirked but said nothing.

"Great minds! Great minds said he or she or it would emerge one day and enslave all of humanity with its superior intelligence. Luckily, that hasn't happened yet. And why would it? Why do Project A when there is so much more money in Project B?"

"What's Project B?" interrupted Deron.

"I was coming to—" Abernathy took a few quick breaths. "They called it augmented reality. That's when you overlay virtual graphics or text on a physical surface. What you call magic is actually a function of your Guardian chip interfacing with your brain, your eyes, and the central network. Remember the sliver?"

"Just show him already," said Timo.

"This is you," said Abernathy, pulling the sheet and revealing a human skeleton. "Well, a plastic you," he clarified. Slowly, he turned the model around until Deron could see the back of it. "The chip lives here." He pointed to a cluster of wires at the base of the skull. "The tendrils extend throughout the body as far south as the ankles, though at that point they are too small to see. We have intrusion into the heart between these two ribs, mirrored on the other side of the spinal column to accommodate the lungs. And your brain…"

His words became muffled as Deron looked down and reconciled a see-through version of his arm, complete with wires running its length. Shutting his eyes against the veneer, he suddenly felt out of breath.

"Subtle," said Timo, putting his hand on Deron's back. He guided him to a nearby chair.

"The truth is never subtle," argued Abernathy. "It is shocking and bold and there is nothing anyone can do but accept it." He turned his attention to Deron. "You should be thankful, young Bishop. You are stronger, faster, and healthier than your ancestors, an improved model of your father, of his father, and so on. Did you know the first chips used to be called Georgia chips?"

There was too much uncertainty in his stomach to risk responding.

"After the old state, you see? Georgia was abbreviated GA. And GA stood for Guardian Angel. But at some point, we lost the Angel and got this instead." He looked around his shop. "And old version of reality. No longer supported."

Timo cleared his throat. "This is all we have left, Deron. This is our reality now. It was good enough for our ancestors; it should be good enough for us."

Deron nodded, tried to think of some kind of response that would express the turmoil in his head. He was flawed, he realized, since the beginning. All those years his teachers had told him that it was his magic that was failing, that he didn't believe in it enough, but the real culprit had been faulty hardware. They made him believe he was different, somehow deficient in his abilities. Disbelief turned to regret and regret to anger; they had all tricked him, lied to him. And they would keep doing it to generation after generation, making innocent kids feel small, making them doubt their worth.

"I'm not deficient," whispered Deron.

"None of us are," replied Timo. "Our eyes are open. They're the ones living in a false world. So none of us can reconcile… is that such a bad thing?" He extended his hand to help Deron up.

As soon as his fingers touched Timo, the veneer popped into being and overtook the man's arm. In less than a second, Deron had reconciled a completely new appearance for Timo, with clothes that showed no tatters and a face that obscured all scars. It was so unexpected that Deron jumped back, breaking the bond. The veneer remained for a moment before fading in a dull echo.

"What's the matter?"

"I… I reconciled you!" he stammered.

"You can still do it?" asked Abernathy, rejoining the conversation.

Deron couldn't hold back the smile. "I guess I'm only damaged, not broken. I think it's coming back."

"Residual veneer," said the old man. "It will go away if you don't try to use it."

"But what if I want to? What if I want to reconcile again?"

"Why?" shouted Abernathy. "So you can go back to the dream world?"

"Yes," said Deron, standing on his own. He looked to Timo again, but there was little expression on his face.

Abernathy made an indeterminate gesture and stalked to the back door. "Throw this one back, Timo. He's not ready to wake up yet." He slammed the door and was gone.

"Come on," said Timo. As they walked out, he grumbled, "I don't know one person who has learned the truth and wanted to go back."

Stopping outside the door, Deron replied, "But you also never knew anyone who could still reconcile."

"Reconciliation is a lie!"

"I know," said Deron, calmly, "but I believe in it."

Timo shook his head and walked away without further comment.

THIRTY-SEVEN
JALAY

"Sometimes, children just snap," said Principal Ficcone. "You remember what it was like when the hormones started kicking in? Thirteen and full of… full of it, anyway, and nowhere to put it. Then you throw in all these damn video games and synthetic drugs and it's no wonder we lose a few here and there. Most of 'em are good kids, but there's always one little square peg to deal with every year, one little monster that spoils it for everyone else. From the day Russo walked through my doors, I knew he was going to be trouble."

They were sitting in the principal's office after a brief stopover with Nurse Hendricks. She had fixed up Jalay's face, but didn't give him anything to stop the pounding in his head. A short gash above his eye had needed a couple of stitches, but with the help of a remote doctor, she was able to sew him up. Now they were just waiting for his dad to come take him home. Evidently, having his face slammed into a locker meant a half-day.

"He doesn't know his place," said the other man, a hint of authority in his voice. "I'm younger than you, but even when I was coming up, we knew exactly where we stood."

"I blame the parents. If fathers would only beat their sons, we wouldn't have any of the trouble we have today." When the stranger shifted in his chair, Ficcone asked, "How were you disciplined?"

The man's chuckle sounded forced. "With a belt gripped by an iron fist. And he beat us for everything. Forgetting to clean my room, laughing at the dinner table. And that was just second grade."

"This Rivera kid needs a beating," said Principal Ficcone, motioning to the set of paddles on his wall. "We're not allowed to use those, but if I could…"

"Are you sure we should be talking about this in front of your student?"

The principal scoffed noisily. "Hey, Chapman, do you think your friend deserves a beating?"

Jalay nodded.

"That's a nasty bump you've got there," said the man, rising from his chair. He approached slowly and sat down on the bench next to Jalay. Offering his hand, he said, "I'm Ruiz. Your name is Jalay, correct?"

Again a nod, again a throbbing pain in his face.

"I was hoping to talk to you today about Russo Rivera and Deron Bishop, but I understand you will be leaving early. Are you up for a quick chat now?"

"What's there to talk about?" he asked. "Russo attacked me. You should arrest him." Each word stung his jaw, making his sentences brief and labored. "Are you even looking for him?"

"One hundred percent yes," Ruiz assured him. "We would like to talk to Russo about his possible involvement in Deron's disappearance."

"What? When did that happen?" Jalay reconciled the image in his mind: an angry Russo, a cowering Deron, and a second and final conflict. Russo had probably killed him. Killed him and stuffed his body in a dumpster downtown. Anything was possible now.

"Just yesterday," said Ruiz, "but we've been observing him for a few days now. There's not much that goes on in this city without us knowing about it."

"Are you a cop?"

"Not quite. My organization…" He paused, searched for the right word. "We augment your local police force."

Jalay stared back blankly.

"You can trust him," said Principal Ficcone. He stood and walked to the window where he surveyed the empty street in front of the school. "Agents have been in Easton since the beginning. Think of them like the FBI or CIA, if that helps."

"Is this because Russo was hanging out at the po—" He stopped short, uneasy with the growing interest on the agent's face.

Agent Ruiz put his hand on the wall and reconciled a large portal. He brought up various pictures in a slow procession, some of them mug shots, others obvious surveillance footage. "Rivera, Chapman, Bishop, Kahani, Collier, and Yushchenko," he said, pointing to each picture individually. "You know these people?"

"Know them? I'm one of them."

"Right. What about him?" The last blank filled with the image of an older man who had tags on his collar not unlike the agent's.

"Who's he?"

"An agent. Like Deron, he was unaccounted for." There was anger in his voice, professionally subdued. "*Unlike* Deron, Agent Tavarez has been found." Suddenly, he turned to Principal Ficcone. "Do you have any objection to me telling him?"

A shrug. The principal broke from the window and approached with his arms folded. "What do you say, Chapman? Do you want to be a big boy and live in the real world? Or has Agent Ruiz already impressed upon you the seriousness of the situation?"

What was serious was that Russo had attacked two students. One of them went to the hospital and the other couldn't think straight due to the spike of hot death boring into his brain.

"Jalay," said the agent, his voice steady, "Agent Tavarez is dead."

A name called out from his memory. "Eric?"

The agent's eyebrows furrowed. "Yes, Agent Eric Tavarez. You *do* know him?"

"No. I mean, Russo told me about him. It was a few weeks back. He got busted for trespassing and when they took him in, he said a guy named Eric ID'd him." He circled his face with his hand. "Like, the *real* him."

"What do you mean?" asked Principal Ficcone.

"Russo said Eric saw through his veneer." He pointed to the mug shot on the wall. "That's what Russo really looks like, but it's not a veneer he wears."

The principal took a second look and after a moment, it clicked for him. "I'll be damned, he's right." It sounded like it pained him to admit such a thing. "That boy always wore the same thing to school and this isn't it." He turned to the agent. "How did you get that picture?"

"Reconciled during his booking, I imagine," said Agent Ruiz.

"But how did Eric see under his veneer?"

"I'm sure he didn't." The agent looked squarely at Jalay. "An agent seeing under someone's veneer is a good story, right? Because if that happened, Russo never caved, right? More than likely, he was scared enough to do as he was told. I know his type. He may act tough, but people like him crumble when they're cornered." A shrug. "Everyone does."

No, thought Jalay. That was the old Russo, before he became a slave to his obsession. If he had made the whole thing up, he wouldn't have stalked the agent for three weeks. Someone was lying about something. That he was leaning towards Russo as the voice of reason made Jalay queasy.

The agent coughed. "You disagree?"

Jalay reached out mentally for his veneer, checking to make sure it was in place. To anyone observing him, his expression would have been blank, a little apathetic. Underneath, there was conflict in his eyes, but no one should have been able to see that.

"You know, I'm coming to you man to man because I thought this would be easier for you. This isn't a courtroom; anything you say will not be repeated outside of this room."

Jalay parted his lips slightly and drew in as much air as he could. When his lungs were about to burst, he brought his teeth together and began to press. The pain was excruciating, but he kept the pressure on. Without moving his face, he flexed every muscle in his head. Soon his whole face would turn bright red. Principal Ficcone wouldn't see it, not through the veneer. But if the agent reacted in any way…

Agent Ruiz stood and walked a few paces away. "Maybe you didn't hear me. A man is dead!" His voice pitched rapidly. "Does that mean anything to you? I have it on good authority that Russo was stalking Agent Tavarez and that he spent every night last week at the TNC Bank, waiting." He took a deep breath as he looked away. "I also know he wasn't alone."

By now, Jalay could feel the throbbing in his entire face. He must have looked strange sitting there completely rigid, his head slowly turning into a red balloon. To his credit, the agent seemed unaffected, though there was a glance here and there that suggested some insight.

"Answer the agent," urged Principal Ficcone.

The eyes on Jalay's veneer jumped to the principal, but underneath, he kept his gaze on the agent.

"Here's what I think happened. You and Russo waited at the TNC Bank until Agent Tavarez left the police department across the street. At that time, the two of you followed him home, entered his apartment under false pretenses, and then proceeded to murder him and desecrate his body."

"Please!" said the principal.

"No!" Agent Ruiz' voice rose again, speaking to some hidden power. "You were there, weren't you, Jalay? You and Russo cut the eyes out of agent together!"

Jalay wasn't even listening anymore, not with the pain buzzing in his ears. It was a battle of wills and after suffering for so long under Russo's heel, he wasn't about to submit to an agent with a loud voice. It could have been true, the bits and pieces that Jalay caught. There was something about a body, about his involvement in a murder, but it was probably just an act. The agent was trying to rattle him, make him abandon his silly test. Another idea flashed in his head. If the agent was upset because he saw the rage in Jalay's face, then…

Turning wasn't an option, but there was enough residual memory to recall Eric's face. Without breaking the tension, he reconciled the fallen agent's appearance onto his own. There was no reaction from the agent, but Principal Ficcone completely lost his shit.

"Chapman!" He stomped his foot, sent a tremor through the floor.

Quickly dropping the veneer, Jalay let go of the breath he had been straining to hold. It was all there in the agent's face, that look of shock at the principal's sudden outburst.

"I think that is enough for today," said Principal Ficcone.

Again, hesitation, brief but there. "Fine," said Agent Ruiz. He looked quickly between the principal and Jalay.

They had gone past the point of civil conversation, but the agent made no attempt to leave. After a few uncomfortable seconds, Principal Ficcone became impatient.

"I'm afraid you will have to bring him in for questioning under official channels," he announced. Then to Jalay, "Come on, we'll wait for your father outside."

Jalay smiled warmly at the agent as he followed Principal Ficcone out of the office; his veneer didn't react at all.

In the relative seclusion of the hallway, the principal grabbed Jalay roughly by the arm. "What the hell is wrong with you? You don't reconcile the faces of the dead, *especially* not one of them!"

"Agent Ruiz didn't seem to mind," answered Jalay.

"Because he, unlike you, has self-control. Now you've insulted an agent. *Two* agents! If you learn one thing in my school, Jalay, it's that you don't *fuck* with agents!"

Jalay felt himself drawn in by the principal's harsh language. Leaning closer, he whispered, "You saw how upset he got just talking about Eric. Do you really think he'd keep his cool if a punk like me reconciled his coworker's face?"

The fury drained from Ficcone's face as recognition took hold.

"It wasn't self-control," said Jalay, staring down the hall as if Agent Ruiz were hiding around the corner. "He wasn't offended by my veneer because that lying son of a bitch didn't see it."

THIRTY-EIGHT
ROSALIA

There was a cruiser parked on the street in front of Deron's house, complete with a fresh-from-the-academy uniform leaning against it, every fiber of his being trying not to succumb to the boredom of his assignment. He didn't seem all too interested in the world around him until Rosalia started coming down the street, at which point his head turned at the welcome distraction. His eyes looked her up and down and even though she stared back, he wouldn't turn away.

So brash, she thought, so unapologetic in his lewdness. He probably wasn't always like that. He might have even been polite and respectful at some point. It was the badge that changed all that. All veneers were masks, but for most people it meant they could hide who they really were. For a majority of the Easton police force, it meant they could finally be themselves.

If Ilya had been there—and for a moment she wished she were—she might not have been so forgiving of the man's lustful stare. Ilya would have stripped off her shirt and bra and shoved her chest in his face and screamed, "There! Is that better?!"

The thought made Rosalia smile, but she did so inwardly, under her veneer. She hid her feelings automatically now, felt it was the best way to avoid questions. The only time she let them shine through was around Ilya, not so much because she liked and trusted her, but because there had to be someone in the world that she could open up to besides Deron.

It was different with Ilya, though Rosalia wasn't sure why.

She seemed to take everything in stride; the Vinestead building was a perfect example. Rosalia had dragged her away from school and into downtown only to sit across the street from an abandoned building and discuss nothing but the nightmarish visions of other Canvas players. A strange feeling had come over her when they crossed the street and approached the doors, that perhaps it was all a lost cause. And as they stood there reading the poorly reconciled notice on the nameplate, she couldn't help but apologize to Ilya for wasting her time. As expected, Ilya tried to reassure her that it was okay, that she would rather spend the day away from school with her than be stuck listening to Mr. Quan recite the laws of physics.

The uniform didn't say anything until Rosalia turned up the path towards Deron's front door. And even then he had to clear his throat first, as if he had been salivating over her.

"Can I help you, young lady?"

Rosalia barely paused to mutter, "No."

"Are you an acquaintance of Mrs. Bishop?"

Stopping halfway up the sidewalk, she turned in place. "*Ms.* Bishop. And I'm sure that's none of your damn business." There it was, thought Rosalia. The quickest way to turn off that sexual fire was to question their domain.

"*Everything* is my business," he proclaimed, subconsciously touching his belt, as if having a dick were some kind of sanction. "Ms. Bishop is not receiving any visitors at the moment."

"It's okay," said a voice from behind her.

Rosalia turned and saw Ania standing in the doorway; her body language contradicted the polished veneer she wore.

"Come in, Rosalia," she continued, beckoning.

Casting a triumphant glance at the uniform, Rosalia followed Ania into the house. For a moment, she stood dumbfounded in the foyer. Although she had only been to Deron's house a few times, she had never seen it so spotless. She looked at his mom with wide eyes.

"I clean when I'm nervous," she explained. "I made some tea. Would you like some?"

"Please," replied Rosalia, though she wasn't a bit thirsty.

In the kitchen, the virginal motif continued. The counters were bare and their black marble veneers had been reconciled to a radiant sheen. On the stove was a solitary teapot; steam was just barely visible rising from its spout.

"Tea is good for the soul," said Ania.

Rosalia had never spoken with Deron's mom for any appreciable time, so she wasn't sure if she was just making conversation or not. She had always seen her as a protective mother, unwilling to let another woman tear the last piece of her family away. Rosalia could relate to the fear of abandonment, but she didn't know how to bring it up, how to expose how similar the two women were.

"Why aren't you at school?" She placed a cup on the table in the dining nook and motioned for Rosalia to sit.

"I wanted to see you," she replied. "I know how I feel about Deron being missing, but I can't imagine what it's like for you."

"No, you can't." Her gaze fell on the patio doors.

Rosalia didn't know what to say, how to continue after that. Though Ania had been right, it only took those three words to trivialize Rosalia's relationship with Deron to an insignificant speck.

"I miss him too," she said, mostly to herself. "We went looking for him last night, me and Sebo. Ilya too."

"Are they also cutting class today?"

"I don't know. Sebo is his best friend, but I don't think he loves Deron like we do." Her confidence faltered as Ania narrowed her eyes. Whatever questions she had about the validity of Rosalia's love went unspoken. "I can't concentrate on school right now," she added.

"You need to," said Ania in her parenting voice. "You can't skip out on your education for your boyfriend. For all you know, you would have broken up over the summer anyway."

"Maybe," she admitted. Ania was being cold, but a little placation might turn her around. "But we're not there yet. I'm not stupid. I know it might not last forever. Just… while I have him, you know? I just want to do my part." Her eyes drifted during her slow delivery and when she looked back, she saw Ania looking at her. Whether there were tears or even the slightest emotion behind that veneer, she couldn't tell, but at least the woman was acknowledging her presence.

"The police think he left Easton."

"How do they know?" asked Rosalia.

"I don't know," replied Ania, shaking her head. "Nothing they said makes sense. Why would he leave the city?"

The question went unanswered, and a pall followed. Feeling the conversation slipping away, Rosalia stopped actively reconciling camouflage for her true emotions. She focused on thoughts of Deron, things that wouldn't normally make her cry but in that instance seemed to evoke powerful emotions. Streaks appeared on her cheeks and droplets formed under her chin. Wiping them away wasn't an option; she wanted them to drop one by one onto the table. Staring into the untouched cup of tea, Rosalia wondered if her display had made any kind of dent in Ania's armor.

At long last, Ania spoke. "Every mother believes her child will listen to her. If I could only talk to him, tell him to come home, I know he would. I believe he would." She sniffled, her nose barely registering the movement. "As a son grows up, he loses touch with his mother, stops relying on me. Now he relies on you." A bitter but restrained sob. "He's mine, Rosalia. *My* child. But he looks to you for guidance. Because he loves you. I can see it in him. If anyone is going to bring him back, it'll be you."

Rosalia looked up to make sure the words had come from Ania.

"He'll come back for you."

"I don't understand…"

"He'll contact you when he's ready. And when he does, you need to do everything you can to get him to come home. You tell him how much you miss him, how much I miss him, and you *make* him come back."

Ania got up and retrieved a box of tissues from the other room. She slid it onto the table and said, "Fix your veneer, honey." Then she gasped and turned away again. "You and Deron are a lot alike."

"What do you mean?"

"Yesterday," she began, sounding as if she were smiling, "his veneer was all over the place. And out there." She pointed to the hallway. "There were smudges all over the wall, handprints and footprints reconciled here and there."

"Sometimes he reconciles without realizing it," offered Rosalia.

"I know. But not like this. This was too random, like he was reconciling blind."

Rosalia cringed at the sudden pain in her stomach, feeling as if Ania had just delivered a crushing body blow. Two synapses snapped together; it was more than just a concussion, but how much more?

No, thought Rosalia, as she stood up. Her legs felt numb, but it was clear she had to get out of there before she spilled her idea to Ania. His mom would laugh her out of the house, right past the smug uniform, and out of the neighborhood. The only people she could tell, the only people who would believe her, were Ilya and Sebo.

"I have to go now," she blurted out, her voice loud in her ears.

Ania didn't protest, as if she had been waiting for the opportunity to resume her solitude. She escorted Rosalia to the door, but said nothing as she closed it behind her.

Although Rosalia wanted nothing more than to break down, she resolved to hold it together. The uniform was still there, but she brushed by him without a word, keeping her eyes open for a private surface to reconcile. It didn't have to be big, just enough to load a portal and send a message to Ilya and Sebo. Finally, she found a van parked on the street and pressed her hand to it.

Her portal blossomed and when she brought up her instant messenger, she was surprised to find a message from Sebo.

"You missed it," he had written. "Russo came by the school and slammed the shit out of Jalay's face!"

She knew she should be happy about that and a smirk did try to worm its way onto her veneer, but her lips wouldn't follow the direction. Not even the suffering of her enemy could cheer her up.

THIRTY-NINE
SEBO

After the final bell, Sebo stepped into the harsh light of the outside world, happy that school was over but confused by the lingering mood of the day. It occurred to Sebo as he collected his personal effects from his locker that he had barely spoken to anyone and most of his interaction had been through instant messages that went unanswered. That his closed social network could be so easily shattered didn't really surprise him, but it didn't make it easier to bear. It consisted of so few people that when one fell out, the others tumbled with them.

From the plaza in front of the school, he glimpsed Ilya getting onto a bus. She was wearing a long-sleeved t-shirt that was just white enough to discern the pink bra underneath. Even in cold weather, she found a way to show off her body. Not that Sebo didn't appreciate it, but that kind of behavior seemed better suited to pre-programmed Roommates than a junior with understated tits. For a moment, he debated going over to talk to her, but she had been scarce all day. At least she could have sought him out between classes, explained why Rosa wasn't in school. For that matter, Rosa could have sent a message or two.

He laughed to himself, thinking there was no one left in Easton who was amenable to talking to him.

Jalay would have at least made for interesting conversation, but even he had abandoned the school at the first sign of face-smashing. Recalling the details of the story, Sebo basked in the justice of it all. It served Jalay right. He couldn't just spend all of junior high and most of high school being the scrotum to the boy who in the *Encyclopedia of Cock* held both the first and second listings. That the punishment had come from said cock just made it all the more satisfying.

Sebo began the long walk home, during which he perused his mental list of Destined 4 Death friends and wondered if any of them were worth hanging out with in real life. There were all types among them: the fighters, the bosses, the inept, and even the slightly retarded. But few played with the simultaneous indifference and intensity that Deron brought to the game. People who could have fun but still win were rare.

It was then he realized it would never be the same. He could make new friends at school, find people to hang out with, but in the gaming world where it mattered, he was destined for desolation. All he had to look forward to were unsatisfying sessions with random players, most of whom couldn't aim a reticle to save their lives. And nowhere else was that skill more important than when the Nazis were raining down their Stielhandgranates and filling the trenches with fear and guts.

Smiling at a distant memory, Sebo thought of World War II, of an era when men sometimes fought with their bare hands, where death meant death and not simply launching another drone. He had the sudden urge to go back there.

The most likely place to find a new WWII shooter was at Entertainments by Pilar, a small boutique in an ill-placed micro-mall one street over from Parker Avenue. Some time ago, an enterprising homeowner had razed his own creation and decided to rent the land out to small businesses. And when he said small, he meant it. Every shop in the barely five-thousand square foot mall could only accommodate three or four people at a time. As a result, the vendors were often those who had little to no physical inventory.

Pilar's was a monument to stimulus overload and stepping into it was like experiencing the revelation that all in the universe was good and nothing would ever get in the way of a righteous frag. She had beads hanging in the entryway; beyond them was a room lit only by the scintillating graphics on the three walls. There were usually a variety of trailers playing, depending on the crowd and the time of day. On alternate Tuesdays, she used a whole wall to show off in-game footage of the latest mindfuck murder simulator to hit the market.

"Haven't seen you in a while," said Pilar, greeting him from behind her half-counter, one of only two pieces of furniture in the room. She had the friendliest and darkest veneer of anyone Sebo knew, with black being a central color and glints of silver at various locations around her lips and eyes. Tall but not towering, she had an elongated frame that looked somewhat alien. While the trailers might have done eighty percent of the selling, it was clear that her themed veneer and ample cleavage did the rest. "I was beginning to think you'd stopped gaming."

Sebo smirked, tried to imagine what immense tragedy would have to befall him to make him ever give up the game. "I've been… preoccupied," he began, the words tingling as they rolled off his tongue. "There have been, let's say, certain events outside of my control that have prevented me from visiting as often as I would like."

Pilar snickered a little. "Is that so? Then why did I see your handle pop up on the Swarm Survivor board the other day?"

"That," he replied, approaching the far wall to examine a breakout of an enemy model, "was my attempt to reacquaint my friend with the gaming world."

"Going by your score, you didn't have much luck."

"Not. Much." He heard her slip off the stool and turned in time to glimpse her skirt as it slid back into place. Biting his lip, he waited.

She joined him at the wall and folded her hands. "One Man Army," she said, nodding towards the video. Reaching out and touching it, she reconciled the in-game footage away and brought up the polished trailer.

Sebo basked in Pilar's perfume as he watched the gold text float in the darkness. After a quick cut, a ruined city came into view and then the camera zoomed in on a lone soldier running through the rubble. He ducked the incoming fire, the blue beams that streaked across the gray landscape. Gentle fades displayed the many arenas, including jungles and underwater science labs. It all seemed like a retread until the hero took a critical shot to the abdomen and collapsed to the ground. As the enemy soldiers emerged from their hiding places, the hero reached for a device on his belt. A flash of light filled the screen and suddenly he was somewhere else, blinking away the brightness. Above him, several figures came into view and after a few seconds, Sebo realized they were all the same person.

"Looks like we need a partner," said one of the men.

"Fuck it, why not two?" asked another in the same voice.

"One will be fine for now."

Out of the shadows, another copy of the hero stepped forward and touched his belt. After a brilliant flash, he appeared a few feet away from himself, back at the start of the mission.

"I guess I don't make it very far?" asked the hero.

"This time you will," assured his counterpart.

"Now it gets interesting," said Pilar, the smile on her veneer sparkling.

Sebo watched as the sequence repeated, this time with two protagonists, then again with three, four, and so on. After a while, there were twenty instances on the screen.

"It doesn't really play out like that," Pilar explained. "You play one series, through the venues, but at any given time you're either alone or with a random number of yourself. The Director decides how much backup you should get, depending on how well you're playing. So, if you are twenty minutes in and find yourself with an army of ten, then you should probably go back to Scrabble."

"How's the veneer integration?" he asked, chuckling.

"Standard. You can reconcile the hero to look like you and the game will replicate it with its damage engine. It's all procedural textures anyway. You want to try it out?"

He shrugged in response, put out his hand, and reconciled a portal on top of the trailer. Inside, he brought up the shop that Rosa had done of Russo and Jalay with the naughty bits blacked out. He ignored Pilar's raised eyebrow and stepped back. "I want these two as enemies."

Pilar reconciled the trailer away and brought the game up on the wall. She moved deftly through the configuration screens. When the game asked her for the enemy models, she studied Sebo's source material and then recreated it flawlessly on the blank avatars. "Someone's messaging you."

Sebo looked back and saw a flashing icon on his portal. He brought it to the front, a message from Rosa. It read simply, "Great." It took a moment to recall his earlier message about Jalay. As he was pondering her curt response, another came in.

"Are you going to ride the trams today?" it inquired.

"As opposed to walking?" asked Pilar.

"To look for our friend," explained Sebo. He thought of another evening wasted on the uncomfortable plastic seats of the tram.

"If you left a portal running at home, I can have this pre-loaded by the time you get there."

Sebo nodded, not really paying attention.

"Unless you have to get going," she teased.

"Demo first," he announced. "I don't try until I buy."

"You got that backwards," replied Pilar. She had moved to another screen and was carefully reconciling Sebo's veneer. For realism, she added some pre-existing battle scars.

"I'm riding now," he reconciled into the instant message window. "I'll keep looking. Why weren't you in school today?"

"Checking something out," Rosa replied, ending her sentence with a string of frustrating ellipses. He started to ask for more details, but she wrote, "Got to go. Message me if you find him."

The little indicator in the corner of the window changed from green to gray; she had gone offline.

"This is ready to go," said Pilar. "If you buy before you leave today, I'll give you a Preferred Customer discount."

"And what's that worth?"

"Ten percent off," she replied, a thin smile on her face.

"You drive a hard bargain."

"I just want to get this done before you run off and look for your friend." She looked around the otherwise empty store. "Business has been a little tight this month."

"I have no idea what you're talking about. I am a man beset by free time and I demand something to fill it! And since girls evidently find me repulsive, I will just have to make do with this game."

Pilar crossed her arms under her breasts. Nodding to the door, she asked, "What about your friend?"

Sebo shrugged and look at the pretty pictures on the wall. An avatar wearing his veneer was slowly spinning on a pedestal. It had a slightly urgent look on its face, as if it were ready for action.

Clearing his throat, Sebo replied, "Don't worry about him." Then, to himself, "He'll still be lost tomorrow."

FORTY
DERON

As the sun began to set, Deron wondered how much of the trip back he would spend in total darkness. Maybe they did it that way for a reason, set out towards Easton under the cover of night to hide from something or someone. He hadn't noticed anyone following them on the way to Dos Presas, no drones patrolling the skies or hovering ominously overhead like any Friday or Saturday night in Easton. Their fear seemed to be misplaced; nobody really cared that they had escaped. They had left and only a handful of people had even noticed.

Deron kicked at the dirt under his shoes and thought about the people who would have cared about his departure. He hadn't even been outside the city more than twenty-four hours, but already he could feel the impassible chasm opening between himself and the friends he'd left behind. What he had learned, what he had seen, was more than the sum of a night's steps. There was a world outside of Easton's rules where people didn't focus on the appearance of things but rather on their content. Not once during his many introductions did anyone comment on his scars. And though no one in Dos Presas could have passed for a supermodel, he had found a few of the girls attractive. It was the difference between Destined 4 Death and a real fight with Russo. It wasn't just violence that could be more visceral.

The more the sun dipped, the more restless he became until finally he walked out onto the wide bridge. In the center, he stopped in front of a small gap and saw that the two sides were barely connected. The rails butted up against each other, but the planks operated independently. At the very edge, he noticed that his side dipped slightly. Poor construction, he thought, or a way to break down the bridge quickly should the worst happen. That would be unfortunate for anyone on it as the river looked treacherous. Timo had mentioned that it flowed through a large pipe at the bottom of the dam, making the surface seem calm but the depths an inescapable death.

Deron was leaning over the side of the bridge and looking at his wavering reflection in the water when Valentin arrived, his face scrunched in confusion.

"That's it then," he said, forgoing a greeting.

"Sorry?" asked Deron.

"You should be." He flashed disappointment, but it receded. "You know I don't get credit for you unless you stay? Dad was going to take me on my first raid because I got you but now…" He scoffed. "Why would you even want to go back to that place? They don't want people like us there."

Deron looked at the water again, at the shadowy forms of fish swimming deep below the surface. "A few people want me there. More than want me here, for sure."

"We all want you here," said Valentin, his voice pitchy. "New people keep this place going. Didn't you see all those girls at lunch?" He moved closer so he could speak softer. "They're always excited when a new guy shows up. I mean, they really don't have many options."

"I *have* a girlfriend. And family and friends." He let out a sharp breath. "I have to at least let them know I'm okay."

Valentin shook his head dismissively. "They won't let you anywhere near them. The second you step a toe inside those walls, they'll pick you up. You think you're the first person to try to go back? My dad says there's been dozens, people like you who didn't accept their fate and ran back home to mommy."

The rail of the bridge was smooth; someone had put a lot of time into sanding it down. Deron traced his finger along the darkened veins, unknowingly drawing a small portal. Its edges sizzled in their attempt to be black and wood-colored at the same time. Inside, his start page appeared, but only the colors and shapes. All the text was missing; in its place was just black noise. With a little effort, he could reconcile anything into those boxes. He could make an instant message window pop up, make it from Rosalia about how much she missed him.

None of it would be real though. It had not made any sense until the conversation with Abernathy. The portal had to connect to the network and he, or rather his chip, was too far away to transfer data. He wondered how close he would have to get before he could send and receive again.

"Can you see this?" Deron asked, motioning with his hand.

"The rail?"

"No, the portal. My start page."

"What are you talking about?" Valentin took a step back and crossed his arms.

"Back home, we could reconcile a portal wherever we wanted. And in the portal, you had a connection to an infinite network of information. You could play games, find books, talk to people. It was endless."

"You can reconcile?" His eyes widened.

"Sometimes," replied Deron, looking at his portal again. He brushed away the content boxes and replaced them with a picture of Rosalia. "Abernathy thinks I'm a freak." He chuckled. "And your dad wasn't too happy about it either."

"How did—?"

"But it's no good out here. I can't connect. You said people have wanted to go back before. Did any of them just want to say goodbye?"

Valentin's face shifted as if he had never considered the idea.

"Yeah," said Deron. "I don't know if I'm coming back or not. I never felt right in Easton, but my mom is going to worry about me."

"You haven't seen how great this place can be," countered Valentin. "Nobody pays attention to Abernathy anyway."

Deron laughed, glanced again at the veneer of Rosalia. He dragged his finger across her face and made the model spin. He had made up his mind; whether he could convince Valentin of his certainty didn't make any difference.

"Val!" Timo's voice carried over the quiet evening. Without a goodbye, the boy broke off and walked hurriedly to his father. Their voices were sharp but hushed and at one point it looked like Valentin wanted to come back to the bridge, but Timo pointed away ardently. The son obeyed but not without offering a half-hearted wave.

It wasn't going to be pretty, but if Timo wanted to argue about it more, then Deron was ready. It didn't matter that the man had brought someone with him as backup. They both walked slowly towards the bridge, Timo with his eyes locked on Deron, the other looking around, disinterested.

"Deron," said Timo. "This is Skinner. It's his night to walk the path to Easton. He'll take you back."

"Thanks," replied Deron, shaking the thin man's hand.

"He's going that way anyway," he continued. Then, to Skinner, "You go and look for a newcomer but don't stay any longer than normal. And if *he* goes into the city, you book it the hell out of there. They're going to light that place up when they take him."

Deron protested, "They're not gonna—"

"See that they don't!" Even Timo looked surprised at his own anger. He took a step back, echoing a move Valentin must have learned from him.

Skinner didn't seem to be listening to the conversation and he started moving towards the opposite bank.

"I might come back," offered Deron. "I don't know yet."

Timo's face lost its fire. "We need you. But not until you need us. So go do whatever it is you think will make you feel better. We'll be here to put you back together once you realize how asleep everyone else is."

Deron nodded and extended his hand.

With a reluctant sigh, Timo shook it. "You be safe, boy. We can't come rescue you if you get caught."

"I get it," he replied. "Thanks."

Skinner started to whistle.

"Good luck, Deron." Timo hesitated another moment and then walked away.

"Don't mind him," said Skinner, after Deron had caught up. "He loves with anger instead of…"

"Love?" asked Deron.

"That's a word," agreed the thin man.

By the time the moon came out, they had been walking for almost an hour. The sound of the spillway was distant and it took a bit of squinting to see the lights of the town.

"So what's the plan?"

A good question, thought Deron. It would be late when they reached Easton, much too late to show up at Rosalia's doorstep. He'd have to wait until morning or if he could reconcile a portal, send her a message and arrange a meeting. Maybe she'd skip school to see him.

Skinner cleared his throat when he didn't get an answer. He then asked, "What's her name?"

"Rosalia," answered Deron, automatically.

"How does she look?"

That question again. Why was everyone so focused on appearances?

Deron thought about her face. "Her nose is small, but she has a wide smile with a lot of teeth. Her eyebrows—"

"What about her body?" Skinner mimed breasts with his hands.

Deron laughed uncomfortably. "You're old enough to be her grandfather."

"Poppycocks," he replied. "I'm not yet sixty."

"No wife?"

"We don't get many women walking out of the city. Five men to every one of them. And not all of them are lookers, either. Why would they be?" His voice changed slightly. "You seen your woman? For real, I mean."

"Without her veneer?"

Skinner nodded.

"Not yet."

He whistled a low note. "Wish I could stay around for that! See if that don't shrivel your pickle!"

Skinner had a crude point. Deron had never seen what Rosalia really looked like. Could it be so different from what he knew and loved? And in the reverse, would she still look on him fondly when he got her beyond the reach of the network?

If she came at all. If that was the plan.

"Don't worry about my… pickle," said Deron.

"Never do," said Skinner. "Only *whores* worry."

Chuckling, he asked, "What do whores have to worry about?"

Skinner looked at him sideways. "What *don't* they have to worry about?"

Another good point, thought Deron.

FORTY-ONE
ILYA

It started suddenly, out of nowhere. One minute Rosalia was content to sit on the floor and push colors around her palette. The next, she was sobbing openly and falling into Ilya's arms. There was no time to question why; Ilya simply put her arms around her and squeezed.

Ilya had spent the rest of her afternoon riding the trams, ending up back at school in time to see the crowd disperse. Most of the kids were talking about Russo's visit and by eavesdropping, she was able to get the totality of the story. Slightly amused but nonetheless appalled at the violence, she hopped on her bus and rode it home. There, after a brief interrogation by her grandmother, she retreated to her room to await her parents. Someone at school had called them and when they got home, there were harsh words from both sides.

She showed up at Rosalia's door after dark without invitation. Her stepmother, Lynn, greeted her with suspicion, but let her inside. She said that Rosalia was up in her room but showed no interest in escorting her. Ilya shrugged it off, took the steps slowly, and then knocked on Rosalia's door. When a voice inside told her to go away, she opened it a crack and whispered a greeting.

"Oh," Rosalia had said, returning to her wall where she was reconciling a pastiche of neon arcs littered with random images.

Ilya could pick out the individual themes, scenes from their lives or buildings that she recognized. They were all things that shouldn't have gone together but somehow worked as an amalgamation. With Rosalia preoccupied, Ilya got comfortable on the bean bag chair. There was a bottle of water, almost empty, next to the plush pink bag. Beside it was a small pill bottle, a common pain reliever for headaches. When she inquired about it, Rosalia replied with a simple nod of her head, as if the pain were too intense to speak.

"There are other ways to cure a headache," Ilya suggested. She leaned back and fished a small case from her pocket. Holding it up for inspection, she asked, "Want to Mellow out?"

Rosalia dropped to her knees and crawled across the floor like an apprehensive cat. She reached out for her prize and after collecting it, collapsed onto the bean bag next to Ilya. She seemed detached from the world as she tapped out two pills into her palm, as if the normal dose wouldn't do the job tonight. The plastic water bottle crackled between her fingers when she downed the pills, followed by her satisfied sigh. She fell again with her head near Ilya's chest and had to lean back to get her eyes on her.

"No problem," said Ilya, after Rosalia had offered her thanks. She reached out and put a hand on her friend's head, smoothed away the stray hairs of a ponytail that had come undone. When she handed back the case, Ilya tapped a pill out onto her chest and took a swig of Rosalia's water to get it down. Together, they waited quietly for the drug to come on, content to stare at the walls.

In the mutual haze that followed, Rosalia moved closer and put her head on Ilya's stomach.

It felt nice to have her so close, with her arm draped across her waist, almost natural. She wasn't sure how much time went by, but eventually the walls started to dance and soon after Rosalia was sitting up and reaching for her palette.

Then she was crying, despite the drug that should have been dulling her senses. To overcome such a strong chemical barrier, the pain would have to have been so deep and so absolute that nothing in the world could heal it. Ilya didn't know how much her embrace helped, if it did anything at all. Maybe behind those closed eyes Rosalia was thinking about Deron, imagining his arms wrapped around her. It would have been clearer had she said his name. Instead, she sobbed with so much force that it shook her body. Ilya had to reach out and reconcile a portal on the floor so she could bring up some music to drown out the sound. She didn't want Rosalia's parents coming to her rescue.

No one was going to comfort her except Ilya.

She made a soothing noise and clung tightly to Rosalia's shoulder near her neck. It was then that she noticed the palette on the floor with its shapes that somewhat resembled Deron looking spiffy in a fuzzy tuxedo. Standing next to him was a streak of white that looked only vaguely human. Maybe Rosalia, maybe someone else, but it was clear she had been trying to reconcile their wedding. Rosalia probably wasn't used to not being able to reconcile anything her heart desired. That she couldn't bring it to life meant she couldn't see it in her head. She, of infinite imagination and hope, could not envision a scenario that ended with the two of them together.

The fuzzy walls broke down even further as the drug reached its second stage. Suddenly, every sound in the room was a million miles away and Ilya had to look down to make sure Rosalia was still there, still crying.

"You need to take your mind off the pain," Ilya thought she said, though it was anyone's guess whether the words actually came out. Even so, she watched as Rosalia put her hand to the floor and dimmed the bright walls down to nothing.

Then, the wall in front of them returned, bathed in a blue light like a film obscuring something bright behind it. "Pretty moon," whispered Ilya.

"I hate it," slurred Rosalia.

Ilya countered with her own veneer, wiping out the moon and replacing it with a vista from a high hill that overlooked an empty prairie of tall grass and wild animals. The sky was a pleasant blue despite the dim light.

"No," said Rosalia, grabbing Ilya's hand from the floor and pulling it close to her face. She held it captive while she brought the moon back.

It made the room dark, but Ilya had lost all interest in mere reconciliations. A wave of confusion had washed over the moment, most of it focused on Ilya's hand trapped by Rosalia's cheek, the backs of her fingers touching damp but warm skin. It had to be a sign, she thought, an indication that maybe somewhere deep down Rosalia actually did like her, did desire contact despite—

"What do I do?"

Ilya tried to visualize Rosalia's muffled words.

"What do I do if he doesn't come back?"

"You've been together a while," offered Ilya, each syllable weighing heavily on her tongue. Her argument faltered before it even came out. Instead, she asked, "What do you want to hear?"

Rosalia looked up and withdrew slightly. She had a hurt look on her already sullen face. Sitting up, she wiped away her tears. "Tell me it'll be okay." There was desperation in her voice; it made Ilya flinch.

"What is okay?" Philosophical questions were an unavoidable side effect of Mellow. "Will you ever be happy again? Of course you will." Ilya sat up and the change in orientation brought a somber feeling with it. "The time you've known him seems large compared to the rest of your life. But when you're older, this piece with Deron in it will get small, until one day it's not so significant."

"He'll always be *significant*," replied Rosalia, stumbling over the words.

"I know," said Ilya, reaching for her shoulder.

They hugged and when Rosalia's face hit her shoulder, she started crying again. Evidently, Ilya's words had had no effect. That or they convinced her that Deron wasn't coming back and that one day she would forget him altogether.

"The Mellow isn't working," said Rosalia.

"Here," replied Ilya, reaching into her pocket again. Though there were only a few pills remaining in the pink case, she didn't think twice about tapping another tab into her palm.

Rosalia stared at it for a moment before snatching it up like a piece of candy and downing it dry. When the pill finally made it past her throat, she turned her head to look at the moon again. The scene shifted under her command, shrinking the perspective until an empty beach appeared at the bottom of the wall. There, the waves were churning, thrown into chaos by the intruding heavenly body.

It was easy to see the transformation take place on Rosalia's veneer. Little sparkles appeared on her exposed skin, small sections of reconciliation being undone. Concentration wasn't required to maintain an appearance; most everything was simply set and forget. While Mellow appeared to dull the facilities, it actually caused increased activity in the brain. Synapses that rarely fired found themselves processing commands that made no sense. Some of the garbage data worked its way into the reconciliation ability, causing the sort of veneer white noise now overtaking Rosalia's body.

On the wall, the ocean swelled, pushing the water up the beach and destroying the forgotten sandcastles. It gave the impression of impending action, something grand and calamitous. Rosalia reacted by reaching out for Ilya's hand and once grasped, she flashed fear. Her veneer struggled to hold the emotion, but Ilya was able to sense it before it was lost below the noise again.

The third dose hit her quickly, sucking all of her energy inward, concentrating it in a knot, and then blinking it out of existence. She closed her eyes and her body began to sway minutely, as if the muscles were half a second behind the warning that she was falling.

"This is the moment," whispered Ilya, unsurprised by the lack of response to her words. She had been waiting for it all night, the point at which Rosalia would no longer be able to form memories, when Mellow had become enough of a barrier to dull reality into a pleasant humming sound backed up by the classical music playing in the room.

Ilya licked her lips, barely pushing out her tongue. She leaned forward, holding her breath, until she made contact. It was just enough physical stimulation to make Rosalia open her eyes, but she did so lazily, without shock or cognizance. There was a brief moment of anxiety as Ilya wondered whether anything was getting past the drug, but then Rosalia's lips engaged, pushed back with enthusiasm. Succumbing to her own Mellow haze, Ilya let herself slip into the dark world, closing her eyes to focus her attention on the other senses. She felt a hand on her cheek, a soft touch that moved to her jawbone, then around to her hair. Fingers fell into place between the bumps on the back of her neck as a thumb pressed gently against her throat.

They were soft, so soft, but the moment her lips slipped past Rosalia's to catch her breath, Ilya felt herself losing her grasp on the sensation. She remembered that the recorders were offline, that only bits and pieces were being saved, and that everything else was just crumbling off the edge of her memory. After only three breaths, the memory of the exquisite texture was gone. Still, the experience itself was the important part; the memories would just have to wait until next time.

Rosalia was still swaying and it only took the slightest pressure on her hip to urge her towards the bean bag. They fell together, landing in a satisfying clump with their arms intertwined. Before Ilya could move again, Rosalia was upon her, seeking out her mouth and latching on impetuously. It was the first sign of affection from a girl who had previously never displayed any interest beyond platonic friendship.

Ilya reached out for the loose ends of Rosalia's shirt; she was wearing it casually, buttoned enough to hide her bra but still expose her belly button. Exploring the smooth skin with her knuckles, Ilya traced lines up and down until she could bear the constriction no longer. With shaky fingers, she undid the buttons on Rosalia's shirt in a slow march towards her neck. An agreeable sigh on her cheek emboldened Ilya enough to push back the garment and expose a plain white bra with a little bow in the center. Behind it, a clasp glinted in the artificial moonlight, beckoning her to unbuckle it.

With a quick turn of her fingers, Ilya was able to open the final curtain and push it to the side. Then in degrees immeasurable, she began a series of descending kisses that traced from Rosalia's mouth to the center of her chest. There, she caught sight of the moon on the wall again. The scene had become more chaotic, with towering waves that pushed against an invisible barrier at the shore. Something was building out in the darkness, something that would drown them all if it got the chance.

There was still fear in Rosalia's eyes when Ilya looked back. Without anything to stand between her and the moon, she had reverted to her natural state, the instinctual terror of seeing her nightmare reconciled on the wall.

"Are you okay?" asked Ilya, climbing her body once more.

The words barely registered, but Rosalia did lock eyes. She was too Mellow to respond verbally, but some undercurrent of emotion made her reach out for Ilya's face and pull her closer.

The moon did not exist so long as the lovers kissed.

Ilya smiled at her sudden poetry while her fingers sought out the clasps on Rosalia's jeans. One by one the locks came free, each one marked by an encouraging squeeze on her neck.

The blur became too much, even for Ilya. Her heart pounded as she slipped her hand beneath Rosalia's underwear, expecting the drug to suddenly wear off and her oblivious lover to come to her senses. Instead, Rosalia reached down and pushed her jeans over her hips. With Ilya's help and a lot of kicking, she was able to deposit them on the floor by her feet.

For a brief moment, the two girls stared at each other and Ilya thought she saw recognition behind those eyes, that or true desire. But then Rosalia shivered and took a sharp breath through her nose. When it passed, she smiled, parted her lips slightly.

It all ran together: the breathing, the cheerful moans at her ear, and the quickening movement in Rosalia's hips as they bucked against Ilya's hand. The exact motion of her fingers was a mystery, but based on the response, she was doing everything right. There came a point when Rosalia could no longer focus on moving her lips and instead was content to hold the awkward embrace cheek to cheek.

So beautiful was the sound of Rosalia on the precipice of ecstasy. But somewhere deep inside, Ilya was saddened by the knowledge that Rosalia would only ever consider it a lustful dream, if even that much. It would never be clear to her what had happened between them until one day when they could be together without the Mellow. She would feel at home, safe in the familiarity of Ilya's embrace, unsure why it felt so right.

The point of no return came suddenly and Rosalia's breath quickened to a fervent pace. At the same time, Ilya became aware of an uncoordinated hand tugging at the bottom of her shirt. It slipped underneath and founds its place on her breast just as Rosalia climaxed. A long moan through gritted teeth erupted in the room and to Ilya it sounded like a great wave cresting and crashing onto a beach. It went on forever, only subsiding when she removed her hand and traced a glistening line up Rosalia's stomach.

Ilya rolled onto her back, amused by the numbness in her arm. Although she wanted to look at Rosalia, wanted to watch her come down off her high, the energy just wasn't there. Everything began to drift away and she felt reality slipping through her fingers.

And still she wanted more time: enough to enjoy Rosalia's body fully, enough to reach that elusive orgasm of her own.

Eventually, her body stopped listening to her trifling desires and shut out all external input. Ilya drifted in and out of sleep, awaking sometime later to find Rosalia breathing softly beside her.

The room was as she remembered it, clearer now that the drug had moved on. Moonlight shone from the wall, but when she turned to look at it, she noticed something askew in its design. It was in the center of a crater, a rectangular cutout with a flashing window. Ilya moved her hand to the floor and expanded the box until she could read its text. The sender's name made her heart skip a beat.

Ilya sighed and shook her head at Deron's pathetic efforts to reunite with the girlfriend he had ostensibly given up on. Rosalia was hers now; that much was evident from the way she slept under a blanket of satisfaction. Ilya could only imagine what Rosalia would think when she woke up and found her pants in a heap on the floor and her shirt and bra undone. It'd be far more emotional than any message from Deron.

She had to sit up to get Rosalia's bra clasped; there was just too much of her to handle with one hand. The shirt she buttoned slowly, reconciling each inch of flesh in her mind before covering it up. For a moment, she stared at Rosalia's pants, but decided against trying to get them back on. It would be too much movement, too much opportunity for Rosalia to wake up and discover someone dressing her.

Ilya resumed her position next to Rosalia and shut her eyes. This she would remember, even if she wouldn't be able to talk about it for a while. All she could do was hope that one day Rosalia would come around. Until then, it was just an exercise in patience—that and keeping Deron at a distance.

With a single tap on the floor, she reconciled the box away, leaving no trace of Deron's message on the moon's barren surface.

In the quiet moments, Russo was plagued by a lingering sense of dread, by the thought that maybe he wasn't working towards his goal with the necessary speed and determination. He'd concocted an excuse for each step, an explanation why something was required before he could take the next leap. He had to reconcile with Jalay because someone had to hold a gun to the surgeon's head while they operated on Russo's eyes. Now, with that prospect gone and the realization that he had no one to rely on, he was stuck between a paralyzing frustration and a resolution to get things done. All of this ate at him, turned his dreams into nonsensical sequences of pursuit and persecution. He tossed and turned all night, waking long enough to catch his breath before delving back into the nightmare.

The J. Perion Tower was ill-suited for a sleepover. Even though construction had resumed and some furniture now dotted the barren offices, Russo found it difficult to sleep in the high-backed chairs. Instead, he chose one of the longer desks, reclined flat on his back, and stared at the dark ceiling, wondering what kind of stiff-shirted asshole would someday occupy the office, reconciling throwaway memos and filing injunctions and whatever else those corporate types did. Picturing them, seeing them move and interact, was an easy way to take his mind off of his current problems. But that was his conscious mind trying to protect him from the pain. When he slept, his subconscious took over, and it had no qualms about broaching the sensitive subjects.

In the dream, the gift of sight was a tangible object, a glowing red orb that floated in a dark construct. Russo saw it, reached out for it, only to have it move away just beyond his grasp. Again, he moved, again denied. Without a landscape, there was no concept of speed, but Russo felt himself moving quickly, trying to latch on. He made progress, got close a few times, but was ultimately stopped dead by the imposing shadow of Agent...

What was his name again?

The longer the chase went on, the more despondent and angry he became. Finally, with one last summoning of energy, Russo shot forward and touched the orb.

Only, it wasn't solid. It wasn't anything, just motes in the air.

With the orb's dust disturbed, Russo faced the possibility of living with the knowledge of a power without the means to attain it. The prospect was so grim, so horrifying, that it shocked him out of his shallow sleep.

Russo opened his eyes and for a bewildered moment thought himself still dreaming. The voice he heard was slightly digitized, but that could have just been his ears adjusting to reality.

"Good morning, Mr. Rivera," said the deep voice.

The name popped into his head: Agent Ruiz. A flight reflex shuddered through his body, but a night spent on the hard desk had left him unprepared for sudden action. Russo let out a deep breath to signify his resignation. He wasn't going to put up a fight.

"For a while there, I thought you were some kind of intelligent. You managed to tail an agent, overpower him, and remove his eyes. That kind of skill and fortitude is something your generation typically lacks. But then you go and return to the scene of a crime and make me think this has all been about a little case of trespassing. I'm afraid I don't understand your motives."

"What do you want?" mumbled Russo, closing his eyes.

"Why did you kill Agent Tavarez?"

"Who said I did?"

Sounds of a struggle filled the room, followed by a desperate voice that yelled, "I want your fucking sight!" The scene replayed on the back of Russo's eyelids. In recollection, there was more blood, more bits and pieces hanging from the knife. It made him shiver.

"What did you mean about his sight?"

Russo folded his hands on his stomach, sensing an incoming body blow. "He saw through my veneer," he explained. "I wanted that power."

The agent moved around the room. "He didn't have the means to give it to you. It can only be activated with the proper paperwork and years of training. To even get into the program, you'd have to display a pattern of high aptitude. And you're too old for Dahlstrom Academy at this point."

Russo laughed, felt the twinge in his spine as his body adjusted. "Like I need that shit. I already figured it out."

"Is that so?"

"Yep," said Russo, taking another deep breath. If he could keep Ruiz talking for just a little while longer, he might be able to make a break for it. "He had something on the back of his eyes, something metal. It let him see through veneers. And if seeing through veneers isn't magic…"

There was silence in the room. Beyond its walls, cars were moving in the streets and trams were announcing their stations. The world was getting on with the day, leaving Russo behind.

Ruiz cleared his throat. "Did you know people were reconciling as early as the nineteen-hundreds? A man named Fleischer invented a process called rotoscoping that allowed people to trace over live-action movies, basically creating a veneer. That was even before computers. Then later, they digitized the process and over time the technology improved until we have our modern equivalent. It's technological evolution, the only kind we have left."

"People think they can change the world," countered Russo. "But it's just a smokescreen. You give everybody the illusion of privacy and you get to see right through it." Angered, he sat up to confront Ruiz. "You sons of bitches…" His words lost their strength as he took in the empty room. A tipped chair still held the door to the office closed.

"Over here," said Ruiz.

When Russo turned, he found a portal on the wall near the window. In it, he saw the agent smiling back.

"Where are you?"

"At the office. Enjoying some coffee." A steaming cup entered the frame briefly. "This job demands a lot of my time."

Russo slipped off the desk and walked over to the wall. As he reached out to touch the portal, it slid to the left, rounded the corner, and came to rest near the window.

"How?" asked Russo.

This time, Ruiz laughed. "Why does it surprise you that I can reconcile remotely?"

Russo's body went numb. "I just…"

"Never considered it," finished Ruiz. "Of course you didn't. Why would you? Why would anyone living in this city even imagine the possibility? Young people think it's magic. Older people think it's just an innate ability. But me? The people I work for? We know the truth."

The knowledge that they had been lying to him his entire life made Russo frown. He reconciled an empty veneer to cover it.

"Why the long face, Mr. Rivera?"

"Stop it!" he yelled, turning away from the portal only to find it reproduced on the opposite wall. No matter which direction he turned, the agent's smirking face was there. "Fuck!"

Russo ran out of the room and down the hallway, flanked on all sides by the agent. Even the floor changed so that his frantic steps fell on Ruiz' eyes. In his haste, he found himself in a large conference room at the end of the hallway with a large rectangular window that gave him a view of South Easton.

"There's nowhere I can't follow you."

It was true. Russo saw it plainly as the nearby skyscrapers lost their luster and became a fragmented image of Agent Ruiz. His smug smile was four blocks wide. He turned around, unable to stomach the bastardized world. Moving to the table, he slapped his hand down and tried to reconcile a portal, but the agent's face appeared instead. It raised an eyebrow at him.

"We can do this all day," said Ruiz.

"What do you want from me?" asked Russo, backing away. He felt short of breath, as if his lungs were collapsing.

"I don't know yet." He shifted in his chair. "Like I said, I'm not sure what to think about you. You have an interesting set of skills. With a lot of training, you could make something of yourself."

"So what? You want to hire me?" It was a scenario that suddenly begged for consideration, but Russo resisted.

Ruiz grumbled something unintelligible. "I'm not convinced you're right for the job. My boss wants me to bring you in on charges."

"Then why don't you?"

He shrugged in reply. "Tavarez is dead because he got sloppy. And right now the number of people that know about him is limited. I can cover that up no problem. What I can't make disappear is this." The walls of the conference room shimmered and then displayed various shops of Russo standing over a fallen Deron.

To think it would all come back to that little shithead. "What the fuck do you care about him?" demanded Russo.

"Personally? Not much. But this whole situation shows a lack of restraint on your part. It makes me wonder what kind of monster you'll become if you ever learned a fraction of what I know."

So fucking superior, thought Russo, so confident in his own power that he doesn't even realize how ridiculous he looks. What kind of game was this guy playing? Why didn't he just come and get him?

"You know where I am, don't you?"

"Obviously."

Russo walked calmly to the door and stepped into the hall, followed by the agent's floating head. "And there are no pigs here yet."

"I haven't called for them. Would you like me to?"

Ignoring the question, Russo walked to the stairwell door and opened it. It was quiet. "You know what I think?" he asked, starting down the steps. "I think you *can't* bring me in." At a landing, he faced the portal. "You don't have the power. Or the balls."

That wiped the smile off his face.

"Power," he repeated. "We all have power. Power to think and reason and feel. And to *see*."

Russo stumbled backwards as the portal disappeared. Normally, it wouldn't have been so traumatic, but when it faded out, it took the entire wall with it. The stairwell flickered to evercrete; the red stripe that had been guiding him down was gone, along with all other colors. Breaking out onto a random floor, Russo looked down the empty hallway, expecting to see the wood-panel veneers lining the sides. Instead, there was nothing, just blankness, emptiness. He returned to the stairs and started spiraling down again.

"Where are you going? Isn't this what you wanted? To see under the veneer?"

"Fuck you!" he screamed, taking the steps two at a time.

"Look at you," said the voice from everywhere, "scampering around like a lost child. You're no man, Rivera. You're just a punk. A punk with no power and no future."

"I'll show you how much power I have! The next time I see you, I'm going to cut out your fucking heart!" His shoes pounded the evercrete, still needed three more flights before the ground floor.

"The next time you *see* me?" asked the agent. "Well, I guess I can take care of that right now."

Russo thought about pausing, had heard the words and wondered if he should slow down a little. Maybe the agent was waiting for him outside. Maybe he was running into a trap. Before he could stop himself, he was out of the stairwell and running into the main lobby. The glass doors were glowing in the morning sun. Beyond them, he saw no one. No cops. No agents.

"Mr. Rivera," said Agent Ruiz, calmly. "Say goodbye to the world."

With those words, the bland foyer faded out, as did the gray figures walking by outside. Russo pumped his legs, tried to outrun the cloud, but it was intangible, just a little red orb of concept locked away in his brain, inside him. It was supposed to be a place only he could go, where no one else could ever hope to intrude. But the agent had done it, had reached out from miles away and ripped out Russo's eyes.

As the world went black, he stumbled and fell to the hard floor. It was too deep, he thought. He just wanted to see under the veneer, not under reality itself.

FORTY-THREE
ROSALIA

On the way downstairs, Rosalia tried to shake off the disorientation of having woken up next to Ilya. It took a minute to spin up the memories, to pull the images out of the blur and remember that her friend had come over to console her, to sit with her as she cried, and ultimately, provide her with enough drugs to forget any problem. She remembered that clearly.

A double dose. Two pills instead of one.

Mellow didn't come with a strong hangover, but she could feel it still trying to numb out external input, alternating between acceptance and rejection, sort of the way she was feeling about Deron. There was only so much pain to feel, so much agonizing tape to feed into the projector. Now that the drug was leaving her body, she would either have to take up the fight or lay down her arms. It felt too early to give up on Deron just yet.

In the kitchen, she found Lynn sitting on the other side of the serving bar, a cup of coffee in one hand and a palette glowing in front of her. At the sound of Rosalia's bare feet on the tile, she looked up.

"You're going to be late for school," she said.

The tone may have been casual, but Rosalia was familiar with the many ways Lynn could criticize. That was her role as stepmother, to alienate herself from her husband's children. Over the last few years, she had done a pretty damn good job.

"And since when do we have sleepovers on school nights?"

Rosalia glanced at the time on the stove. "We'll make it." Her mouth felt numb, as did the rest of her face. She wondered if the drug would stay with her all day. It certainly seemed more persistent than the last time.

"*We*," repeated Lynn, "like there's nothing out of the ordinary about a girlfriend staying over during the week. What do her parents think about this?"

Shrugging, Rosalia opened the pantry and fished a packet of instant oatmeal from a box. She shook it to settle the contents and then pulled a bowl from the cabinet. "I don't know, but I bet they're not the overreacting types."

"This is still my house," said Lynn, sipping her coffee noisily.

"No, this is *our* house," she corrected, seeing the image of her formerly complete family in her mind. Her mom was always smiling, even when she was angry, even when she was sad. It was as if the muscles in her face knew no other way to be.

But it wasn't muscle; it was a veneer, a mask to keep her husband and child from seeing the pain underneath, from seeing the sickness that would eventually take her. Rosalia flashed on the last image of her mother and felt anger. Turning to Lynn, she said, "You just occupy space here."

There was no change in the woman's veneer, no ripple of retribution trickling up from below. She simply looked down at her palette and pretended to read one of the news stories. After a moment, she took another sip of her coffee.

Rosalia put her oatmeal in the microwave and started the timer. Then, remembering her guest, she prepared another bowl and pulled a serving tray down from the refrigerator. There's cinnamon around here somewhere, she thought, checking each cabinet for a spice rack.

"It's not lady-like," declared Lynn. "When I was a girl, we respected the rules of the house, whoever's house it was."

"Things change," Rosalia pointed out. The microwave beeped and she swapped out the bowls. "Would you rather I have Deron over? We could have unprotected sex all night. Or would that be too unladylike?"

"At least that would be normal. Then maybe your father wouldn't have to run out of the house so he doesn't have to confront his le—" She stopped short of saying the word, catching her tongue between her teeth.

"His *what?*" The silence that followed was broken only by the beeping of the microwave.

Lynn narrowed her eyes and placed the palette on the counter. There was hesitation in her veneer, a definite struggle to keep her lips and eyes from moving. It must have been easier, Rosalia thought, years ago when people weren't always wearing masks. Then, you could see every movement, every nonverbal slip that gave away what a person was truly thinking.

"His lesbian daughter!" Lynn blurted out. Her mouth hung open, perhaps surprised by its betrayal.

Rosalia put her hands on her hips defiantly. "I am *not* a lesbian!"

"You can deny it all you want. I know what I heard."

"What? Are you out of your goddamn mind?"

Lynn raised a finger. "Don't make this worse by taking the Lord's name in vain!"

The anger inside Rosalia slipped away. It was the mention of God, she realized, the inclusion of religion that pushed the argument into the realm of absurdity. There was no point in arguing if Lynn's objections were based on the concept of sin.

Rosalia opened the microwave and took down the steaming bowl. "You're right," she admitted. "I'm a lesbian." It sounded funny to say, evoked images of her and Ilya in their underwear having a pillow fight, but her veneer held steady. "I've been living a lie for years, but no longer." She turned, stared directly into Lynn's hate-filled eyes. "I love the pussy! I can't get enough of it!"

Lynn's veneer finally shattered, settled into a level of contempt so intense that Rosalia was momentarily taken aback. "I will abide you," she said, "for Michael's sake, but Jesus won't. You remember that."

"Are we done? Can I go have breakfast now?"

"You just get to school on time. I'm not signing any tardy notes."

"Fine," replied Rosalia, picking up the tray. "We're just going to eat some breakfast and then have a quickie in the shower and we'll be on our way. You won't even hear us."

"I heard you last night." Again, the contempt. "*Don't stop, don't stop,*" she mimicked and then crinkled her nose. "Disgusting."

Rosalia had heard enough. She exited the kitchen and started up the stairs, shaking her head at her stepmother's crazy ideas. Lying about hearing noises from her room wasn't like Lynn, but then she always found new ways to be an evil bitch. She had probably spent the whole night putting ideas into her dad's head, turning him against his daughter. Groaning, Rosalia pushed open the door to her bedroom with the tray. She found Ilya seated at the desk, trying to reconcile a wrinkle from her blouse.

"The nice thing," she said, as if they had already been having a conversation, "is that people won't know I'm wearing the same clothes as yesterday." The previously white canvas cycled into turquoise, accented by orange flowers on the left side.

"Except for the smell." Rosalia set the tray down on the desk and offered a bowl to Ilya.

"Do I really smell?" she asked, reaching for her breakfast. As she did, part of her shirt fell to the side, revealing her bare chest. When Ilya noticed the look on Rosalia's face, she motioned to the bra on the desk. "I broke a strap somehow, which sucks, 'cause I loved this bra."

Rosalia nodded and wandered over to the window. "This is going to sound stupid," she began, thinking again of Lynn's accusation.

"What is it?"

"Did we surf the porn wave last night?" Behind her, she heard Ilya choke on her oatmeal.

The coughing slowly changed to laughter. "No," she said at last, "I don't think we did."

"I remember…" Trailing off, Rosalia tried to latch onto the wisps of memory passing through her head. In their inebriated states, they could have reconciled a portal and cruised the network for sex videos without even realizing it. A feeling *was* there, something warm and faintly sexual. The sensation of excitement came back to Rosalia in a sudden flash, weakening her knees.

"That's strange," said Ilya, her face turned away. "But then people do strange things when they're Mellow. Maybe we were talking about you and Deron and you ended up…" She seemed unsure of her words.

Rosalia huffed. Had she reconciled a fantasy of her and Deron for Ilya's entertainment? It would at least explain the noises.

"Why do you ask?"

"Lynn thinks we were having sex."

"You and me?"

Turning around, Rosalia found Ilya with her eyebrows dancing. She nodded in reply. "She thinks we're lesbians."

"Oh, I think I would remember that." She smiled broadly.

"Me too." Another flash, another quiver moving up the inside of her legs.

For a few minutes, they ate in silence. Rosalia was consumed by her own questions, but soon began to wonder about the conflict brewing on Ilya's face. She could only see her from the side, but her head was down and her shoulders slumped uncharacteristically.

"If I were," said Ilya. The rest of the question was lost in her rapidly blinking eyes.

"If you were what?" Rosalia leaned against the windowsill, having had enough of her shaky legs.

Ilya's eyes glimmered red, perhaps from the drug. "If I were a lesbian."

Rosalia started to respond, but she knew that anything she said wouldn't be the right thing. There was too much to put out there all at once: her growing suspicions, her acceptance, and even her questions about mechanics. Most confusing was why Ilya had chosen to hide it. Even when they were joking about it before, it wasn't as if Rosalia had displayed the same kind of abhorrence that Lynn had channeled so easily.

Forgoing words, Rosalia put her bowl down on the windowsill and crossed the room. She didn't even consider the implications of putting her hand on Ilya's shoulder.

"Is it too weird?" inquired Ilya.

"No," Rosalia assured her, "it's not weird at all. I mean, I thought…"

"It's not like I was hitting on you. I wasn't trying to give you the gay."

"Is that a joke?"

Ilya looked up and smiled, showing her sparkling teeth. There was a tear trailing down the left side of her face. Rosalia put her hand to her friend's cheek and reconciled it away.

That was the way of things. The indicators of pain could be hidden, but Ilya would still be able to feel the dampness on her cheek, would still feel the lingering teardrop hanging from her chin.

Rosalia chuckled, thinking back.

"What's so funny?"

"I told Lynn that I love the pussy. Is that something a lesbian would say?"

Ilya smiled politely. "I don't know. I never finished my lesbian training." She shook her head. "But, yeah, if I had a stepmother like yours, I'd probably say that just to mess with her head."

Rosalia wanted to ask her other questions, but it didn't seem like the right time. If they didn't hurry, they would be late for school and would have to spend first period in the tardy room.

"I need to shower," said Rosalia, absently. At her dresser, she pulled out a fresh pair of underwear.

"I promise not to peek," joked Ilya.

Pausing in front of the bathroom door, Rosalia considered the absurdity of it all. In a couple of hours, they'd both be naked in the gym showers anyway, same as they had been doing all year.

"I'd be insulted if you didn't," she replied, stripping off her shirt and tossing it by the dresser. In the bathroom, she grabbed an elastic tie and pulled her hair into a ponytail.

Rosalia studied her reflection in the portal above the sink, going over every inch of her veneer to make sure it was perfect. Over her shoulder, she glimpsed Ilya doing the same.

FORTY-FOUR
DERON

It was a long night waiting for a response that never arrived. Deron passed the time by practicing his reconciliation, mystified by its wavering effectiveness. Sometimes he could send out radiating circles of color. Other times, the rubble around him remained a neutral gray. Sitting back against a slanted slab while watching the stars turn above him, he considered the possibility that his message had not gone through. His portal only seemed to work for a few minutes at a time and after that it became inert if it didn't fade out altogether. There was damage to his chip; he was certain of that. Whether it would hold out long enough to send another message to Rosalia was another question.

As dawn approached and the prospect of hearing from Rosalia dwindled into nothing, Deron faced a tough decision. He could wait outside the walls for another day, hope his portals would stay up and connected to the network. Or he could venture back into the city and risk being seen. There would be questions, and he'd have to be clever, come up with some excuse as to where he'd been. He couldn't tell anyone about Dos Presas except Rosalia. She'd have to know because he wanted her to come back with him. And she'd have to decide quickly; the longer he stayed in Easton, the greater the chance they'd discover him.

In the end, it was the twitching of the sentry guns that made him opt for the drainage pipe. At night, they hung their heads as if ashamed of not being able to see in the dark. But with the sun rising, they were coming online, resuming their hunt for fleshy targets. Deron made a break for the pipe before the sun broke the horizon. He was up and into the field quickly, finding the whole trip less frightening than before. Down the street, he saw a tram dropping off the early morning workers. When they stepped off, he stepped on.

As the tram glided towards the center of the city, Deron realized that he had no destination in mind. The clock at the front of the tram was blank, but it felt early enough for Rosalia to be on her way to school. Showing up there was sure to get him caught. Instead, he decided to catch her on the way home. Until then, he could just ride the tram around the city or hide out at Gillock Pond.

Deron changed lines a few times at random just to keep the scenery changing and to prevent retracing his steps. After a while, the tram slipped into the Newell

District and onto a road with apartments on one side and a two-story strip mall on the other. His dad lived somewhere on this street; Deron remembered looking up the return address on a birthday card once. Sitting up in his seat, he scanned the apartments and spied his dad's down the road. Deron reached up and tapped the stop button over the window, but unlike his alarm clock, nothing happened. He tried again with the same result.

Across the aisle, an older woman raised an eyebrow at him. Her face flashed, appeared youthful for a moment, and then succumbed to the wrinkles once more. Without saying anything, she reached up and touched the stop button, bringing the tram to a halt.

"Thanks," muttered Deron as he disembarked. Looking back, he saw the woman was still staring at him as the tram continued its route.

I can't stay here, he realized. There was just no living half in and half out of the reconciled world.

His dad's name was on the directory at the front of the building, a sectioned portal with *Bishop* reconciled in black and white. Deron didn't see it at first, but touching randomly on the adjoining wall had helped him illuminate the panel. Each time that happened, he got a little more frustrated, a little angrier at the city's dependence on veneers. He pressed the call button, but there was no answer. Taking a step back, he looked up at the third floor window, saw nothing moving behind it. Travelling, he guessed.

"Or maybe he's shacked up with the whore," said Ania's voice in his head.

Deron smirked and tried the door handle. To his surprise, the door was unlocked and there was no one in the small breezeway to challenge him. Climbing the stairs was difficult; he had not eaten anything since the awkward dinner in Dos Presas the night before. On the third floor landing, he wondered if his dad had any food in his fridge or if he were living the true bachelor's life.

"Maybe the whore went grocery shopping," said Deron, surprised to hear his own voice.

Pausing at the front door, he tried to think of what he would say if his dad answered. It would have to be anything except the truth, maybe something about wanting to get out of the house, needing to get away from everything for a while. He'd relate to that.

There was a thumb pad to the left of the door that Deron mistook for a doorbell. When he pressed it, the red glow changed to green. Something clicked within the door and it swung open with a just gentle push.

In the foyer, it became apparent that his father wasn't there, hadn't been there for a while. The kitchen on the left was dirty, with dishes piled up in the sink and a box of assorted pizza crusts on the counter.

The living room was in disarray. If this was what his father had given up for a clean home, then he was crazier than everyone thought. There was nothing enticing about the broken-down sofa or the cracked palettes stacked in a pile on the coffee table. The windows that looked out over the street showed their true grime without their veneer.

A stranger lived here, some indeterminate person without a name whose presence he felt only indirectly. In the bedroom, the queen-size wasn't made up. The comforter was crumpled at the foot of the bed, the sheets had been thrown aside, and the pillows were scattered. If he concentrated, he could almost see that person, his dad, waking up, making the short walk to the bathroom to get ready for work. Then coming back in, going to the dresser.

A garment unlike anything a man would wear made Deron pause. So it was true; there *was* a whore. He picked up the bra between his thumb and index finger—a pretty well-endowed whore at that. For a moment, the bra flashed fire red with yellow flames erupting around the straps. Startled, Deron dropped it onto the dresser where it once more became a bland collection of straps and cloth. It had been one thing to imagine his father running off with some younger woman, but to actually touch the evidence…

Maybe his mom already knew; she always seemed to be on top of things, no matter how far removed. She knew when he failed a test, knew when his homework had gone unfinished. There was even a time when he was very young that she had hired a tutor to help him with his reconciliation. No one had known, not his teachers, not his schoolmates. Looking back, it all seemed a waste. Had they just told him it was technology and not his fault, it would have made things so much easier. He shrugged at his own train of thought, unsure if his then undeveloped mind could have even grasped the concept of reconciliation without attaching some kind of mystical aspect to it.

The apartment wasn't much, he concluded, after taking another look around, but it was infinitely better than the outland rubble. At least here he wouldn't have to worry about sentry guns or dehydration. Deron cleared away a collection of beer cans from the recliner next to the couch and sat down. Finding the arm on the side, he pulled back and extended his feet. It was as comfortable as he had been in days and after a restless night, a nap would go a long way into making the hours fly by. Closing his eyes, he tried to sleep, but his mind was running too quickly and despite his best efforts, his body kept shaking itself awake.

It was there in his mind, reconciled clearly as an accusatory statement that spoke both to his dad's indifference and his own tacit acceptance. There were so many questions circling his head: how to fight a bully, how to defuse a confrontation without ending up in the hospital, and how a father could go so long without seeing his own son. Each time he thought about it, he opened his eyes, looked to the side, and realized again that his dad wasn't there. He had come to his home, sat in his chair, and the man still couldn't be bothered to put in an appearance. The anger surged, made him twist in the suddenly uncomfortable recliner.

Deron squeezed his eyes shut and tried to calm his nerves. It wasn't fair to come to this place and see what was hiding behind the image he had reconciled of his dad. It went beyond a simple veneer, something even his mom couldn't tear down. But now he could see past it and it was too much to take in. All he wanted to do was reconcile it away, put up a barrier that nothing could penetrate.

It felt like Easton was crushing down on him, showing him a world that he no longer wanted to be a part of. The only way out was back to Dos Presas where there were no cheating husbands, no ruthless bullies, and no veneers to make people think everything was okay when it really wasn't.

He made a sound somewhere between a cry and a grunt. Only when he took a deep breath and opened his eyes did he find his salvation in the glowing veneer of the apartment.

Everything was still messy, but there were photos and art on the walls. Gone were the smudges and the barren quality of another life abandoned. It was back; the world was back.

Wasting no time, Deron searched for his own face amongst the pictures and found one next to the bedroom door. There, his dad would have seen it every time he went to his room, every time he went to sleep.

Every night, the picture would remind him of his son.

It was a bit comforting, just enough to settle his heart rate. As it did, an inkling of recognition crept up. Something was happening, some correlation that he couldn't quite put his finger on. It was there though, as clear as the fading of his picture. The better he felt, the more translucent it became, until finally he was calm and the gray returned.

FORTY-FIVE
JALAY

The clouds started rolling in shortly before lunch. Jalay watched them build while listening to Mrs. Ratner lecture about the second civil war, a subject that was bloody and violent but uninteresting. He had heard the story before, in previous History classes, about the rise of the corporate giants, the squeezing out of the government, and the eventual collapse. It didn't matter to him how many people died or how the survivors eventually rebuilt. What mattered was that it was all in the past, in an era that no longer concerned the living. The only thing that concerned Jalay was the wall of clouds creeping in from the north.

They were sinister with their dark blue centers and fiery white tips. Growing tall in the infinite sky, they blotted out the sun and cast a shadow on the frail city, causing a panic in the trembling citizens below. Without thinking about it, he reconciled the horizon onto his palette. It was the same image, a perfect reproduction, but it didn't match the intensity of what he saw outside. Out there was power, raw and dangerous. On his palette, it was just an echo of that power, a snapshot of potential that would go unrealized.

Just like me, he thought, if his teachers were to be believed.

When the bell rang, Jalay filed into the hallway with the rest of the class and headed for his locker. He only spent a moment there, just enough time to toss in the History reader and to shed his jacket. The dent in the locker begged for attention, but Jalay ignored it. There was no point in reliving that moment, except for the vengeance it would demand, vengeance that would likely remain as the image of the storm, static and impotent.

The cafeteria was doubling as a sauna when Jalay walked in. He noticed Principal Ficcone standing on the other side of the dining area talking to a janitor. When they caught eyes, the principal turned his back and began gesturing to the walls. He was probably complaining about the humidity in the school, but he should have just admitted he was starting to sweat under his fancy suit and even though he could reconcile away the stains, he couldn't do anything about the smell.

A reflexive breath brought the tantalizing aroma of cafeteria pizza deep into Jalay's lungs, evoking a smile. There was something about the rectangular slices served at Easton Central, something that made them superior to what he could order from The Hut or buy from the grocer's. Its contents were completely unknown, but Jalay believed it to be recycled rubber that someone had reconciled to look like dough, cheese, and sausage. Despite its consistency, it was one of the few reasons he came to school and the best meal that they served, good enough to go back for seconds or thirds. Approaching the serving line with his mouth already watering, Jalay forgot about the impending doom outside.

He tried to ignore the poorly concealed disgust on the cashier's face as he reconciled his signature on the payment palette. Her reaction made him steel his veneer, try to contain the child-like glee welling up inside of him. The fact that he had to eat alone in a sauna no longer mattered. Unless, of course, Sebo would be open to company.

Chased inside by the threat of rain, Deron's best friend had found himself an empty table near the back of the cafeteria. There was no food in front of him, nothing except a small carton of milk, unopened. Jalay walked towards his table as if he were going to pass by.

"How's the face?" asked Sebo.

Jalay paused, took the cheap shot as invitation to sit down. He slid his tray onto the table and plopped down on the plastic seat. "It stopped hurting five minutes ago," he joked.

"I think a heartfelt 'I told you so' would be applicable here. But," he said, pausing and looking out the window. Whatever he saw out there in the growing gloom was hard for him to ignore. His eyes came back a moment later. "I've had a whole day to point my finger and laugh. I owed you that much."

The truth stung, but Jalay was able to soothe it with a large bite of pizza.

"Pizza," Sebo reflected, "the cornerstone of any well-balanced diet. I don't suppose you have any vegetables to go with that?"

"Tomato," replied Jalay, pointing to the vaguely red sauce oozing out from under the impenetrable sheet of cheese. "Tomato is a vegetable."

"Technically—"

"How's Jordan?"

Sebo's face went blank for a moment before flashing disappointment.

"She a good roommate?" he added.

"Oh, the Roommate." His eyebrows furrowed. "I couldn't get her installed. I tried to apply the crack but it kept crashing on me. Are you sure the copy you gave me works?"

"It works," Jalay assured him, his gaze drifting into fond memories. "I have her and Felicity on two walls like this." He put his hands up side by side in demonstration. "Sometimes it sounds like they're talking to each other."

"And it is my understanding that they are both naked, correct?" asked Sebo.

Jalay nodded peacefully.

"Then who cares what they're saying?" Sebo lifted his palette and brought up his contact list. "Jalay with seven L's?"

"Six," he corrected.

"Six, why not?" Finally looking up, he asked, "Is Felicity the one with the massive…" He held his hands out in front of his chest. When Jalay nodded again, he smiled wide. "Can you transfer her? I'm going to make them have a jumping jack contest."

Always play to a man's vulnerabilities, thought Jalay, as he pulled his palette bag onto his lap. He knew why his own collection of nude women was massive and varied, but the motive for Sebo to be such a porn addict was still a mystery. There was rumor that he was quite the FPS player, which taken together showed an unhealthy obsession with sex and violence. So maybe the boy with the strange way of talking wasn't so perfect after all. Everyone, it seemed, had a little bit of darkness in them.

When he loaded his start page, Jalay was surprised to find an instant message not just from Sebo, but some from Russo as well. Only, they contained no text, just a stream of blank images. He closed them out one by one, but as he was dragging Felicity to the transfer window, another image popped up, this one with a streak of white in it.

"Russo's sending me pictures," he said at last, placing the palette on the table. He pushed it closer to Sebo. "But they're empty."

Sebo nodded. "It's a very abstract style of art—minimalism, I believe."

"Or he's lost his mind."

"That's a given. He comes from a broken home, you know."

Jalay raised an eyebrow. "Everyone does."

"Instances of psychosis increase when parents divorce. They did a study a few years back about the development of relationships—"

"These almost look like windows," he interrupted, pointing to a slight pattern in the picture. Then the realization struck him; he didn't care what was in the pictures or what Russo had to say. "Fuck him," he declared, wiping away the message window. When it reappeared a moment later, he put Russo on his block list. Dragging his palette back to safety, Jalay returned his attention to the half-eaten pizza. It still smelled delicious.

Outside, thunder began to rumble in earnest. It probably wouldn't rain, not with Easton's high walls acting like a buffer against the incoming fronts. Cold air could descend on the city, but unless the storms were formidable, the rain would simply pass around it. Most people didn't seem to mind; the city's veneers suffered when coated with water, becoming undefined and lacking discrete borders.

"Any news on your friend?" asked Jalay, after a minute of contemplative eating.

Sebo had busied himself with scrolling through the Felicity stills. "Are you really interested?"

"Agents seem interested."

Looking up, Sebo narrowed his eyes. "He talked to you too?"

"Yeah. I think he hit everyone. Did Rosalia get interviewed?"

"I'm not sure," he admitted. "I haven't talked to her in a while."

"I saw her between classes this morning. She looks sad."

"Ha!" His laugh was just a little too loud. "Now he cares!"

I've always cared, thought Jalay. How many women had he collected in how many folders, each one bearing a resemblance to whatever veneer Rosalia happened to be wearing that day? A hundred? A thousand? Each of them reminded him of her, whether they were on his walls at home or following him in an endless stream as he dragged his fingers along a fence after school.

"More than likely, she's upset that I didn't spend all night riding the trams again."

"Is that what you're doing after school?" asked Jalay. "Because I could come over and help you install Jordan and Felicity. I've done it a few times already. It just takes a certain touch."

He was aware of how hollow his words sounded, how desperate he was for company, for a friend. Worse was that Sebo seemed to take a long time considering the proposal.

"Alright," Sebo agreed. He touched his palette and reconciled his address into the chat window. "We have to do it right after school because I've got a clan meeting tonight."

"Sure, sure," replied Jalay, moving the address to the map generator. Once he had directions, he pulled up his block list only to find forty-eight messages from Russo. Grabbing one out of the garbage, he examined the formless mixture of color, finding no meaning in it.

"What the fuck do you want?" he reconciled hastily. He paused before sending it and downed the last bite of his pizza. Joy filled him up again, gave him the confidence to send the message hurtling into the abyss.

For the remainder of lunch, he kept glancing at his block list nervously, but no further messages came.

FORTY-SIX
RUSSO

Russo sat very still in the expansive lobby, a complete reversal of his first reaction, namely to panic and thrash around blindly, running into walls and furniture. After sustaining a few bruises, he began to realize what was happening to him. It mostly had to do with Agent Ruiz, whose voice he heard beyond the shadows, laughing and taunting. It was all a show for him and Russo was getting tired of it. He found a clear area on the floor, turned his face towards the warmth of the sunlight, and sat down.

The funny thing was that he could still reconcile, albeit on a completely blank construct. With his eyes open just in case, he looked down at the floor, touched it with his hand, and pushed color into it, a nice hardwood grain. As the texture spread, it became uneven, but Russo concentrated harder, forcing the landscape into the infinite distance. Even when he looked away, the veneer remained, making it appear as if he were on a wooden plane with no end. There were walls though, even a receptionist's desk with a chair on his left. He groped for it, found the underside of its arm, and reconciled an off-white veneer to give it shape. He spun it around slowly, painting each surface.

"Impressive," said Ruiz from somewhere in front.

Russo estimated the distance, reconciled a beige wall, and put his last memory of the agent's face on it.

"It usually takes new recruits several days to do what you're doing."

"Shouldn't you be out enjoying life while you can?" asked Russo. Threatening the agent wouldn't win him any points, but there wasn't much more the man could do besides take away all his senses. That the agent could blind him was unsettling, but if new recruits went through it, then it had to be reversible.

"I'm noting a skew towards violence in your record."

Laughing, Russo pulled himself into the chair. An endless plane and one wall, he thought. It needed more. He began pushing the chair around the lobby, touching the walls and translating one sense into the other. It took a while, but eventually the entire room appeared around him. Looking up, he guessed the height of the ceiling, gave it a pocked-grid design he had seen somewhere before. Just as the last piece was falling into place, every veneer in sight began vibrating violently. Despite his protest, the entire world cracked and shattered. All the colorful pieces fell to the ground where they sank through an unseen membrane before falling out of sight.

"There are answers to your questions, Russo. And those answers will give rise to more questions and having this knowledge will weigh heavily on you. It will change how you see the world, how you view history. It will tell you why I let you live instead of putting you to death immediately."

Russo raised his middle finger in the darkness, realized he couldn't see it, and then reconciled color onto his body. It was easier to gesture when his fingers were visible.

"Before we do any real training, we put new recruits in a room and blind them like I blinded you. Do you know why we do that?"

"Because it's the only way you get hard anymore?"

A chuckle. "A fringe benefit," the agent admitted. "But the real reason is because truth is so much more powerful when it is demonstrated. Children hardly blink when you tell them they can reconcile anything they want. It's not until they do it that first time that they realize their true potential. Suddenly the world opens up for them. That's what I did for you. I could tell you the secrets of the Vinestead Veneer, but to simply show you… well, judging by your face."

Russo winced, confused. It was the second time the agent had looked through his veneer. The first time, he thought it was a fluke, a lucky guess. The man wasn't in the same room, yet he could see his true face. That meant he was looking through a portal and seeing something real, both looking at the veneer and under it.

Un-fucking-believable.

Reconciliation was supposed to be a personal experience, shared only indirectly. Someone touched a wall, the other person could see it, but never could the idea pass without some kind of medium. If someone could disable veneers on a whim, if they could take his sight without gouging out his eyes, then it suggested a larger system. One thing was for sure; it really wasn't magic.

"Of course not," said Agent Ruiz. He added a condescending chuckle. "What you and the populace call a magic veneer, we call augmented reality. It's machinery, hardware, and circuitry that makes all of this possible. Do you really think we'd trust control of the veneer to the unwashed masses? You of all people should know how dangerous that is."

What the fuck did that mean? The question slipped onto his face.

"You have incredible arrogance in you, Russo. I noticed it the first time I put my eyes on you. All you need is real justification. And I'm sorry to say that if you've been basing that on reconciliation, or even InSight, then you're going to be disappointed. We've got the same hardware running inside us, Russo. We have the same chips in our necks, the same grow-wire running through our spines. The only difference is our level of access. Bits, Russo, bits in a database make me more powerful than you. I can update your record and give you the same power. Or, I can delete everything about you. Erase you from Easton forever."

"Forever?!" cried Russo. He made a dismissive gesture and turned his back to the agent's voice.

"You should be more appreciative of what I'm offering you. Not many people get the opportunity to become agents, especially those who spend their early years at reform school. Good men have worked themselves to death for this program, men who knew the right way to treat their company. Some argue that doing what is right for your family or God or your country will make you a good person. But to excel as an agent, you have to be willing to do what is best for the company, for Vinestead."

"I don't know who that is. If they control the veneer, why aren't they bigger?"

"Companies change," explained Ruiz. "Sometimes they get big, other times they constrain themselves to save resources. Sometimes a forward-thinking conglomerate just has to step back from the spotlight for a while, whether from government pressure or public outcry, it doesn't matter. You go back to Vinestead's heyday and you'll find people spitting at the mention of their name. But they hold the patents on some fundamental technologies: the veneer, Guardian chips, and even the grow-wire. All of it is Vinestead R&D."

"Turn the lights back on." It was fine to play games, but if the agent was going to stand there and lecture, the least he could do was show himself.

Without a response, the lobby snapped into view. Russo waited for his eyes to adjust and then faced the wall where the agent was looking down at him with amusement.

"Thanks," Russo muttered. Every muscle in his body wanted to reach through the portal and strangle Ruiz to death and yet he was at the man's mercy, forced to play the docile student. It would be prize enough, he concluded, that if at the end of this he could cut the agent's head off slowly. Or another eye-gouging. Not a complete removal, just enough to blind him, let him spend some time fumbling in the darkness. Or better yet, maybe he could get access to the database, turn off all their eyes, and see how they liked it. The possibilities made him smile.

Pushing himself over to the desk, Russo reconciled a portal and brought up his searches for Vinestead. He wanted to show Ruiz the picture of a building he had found, but instead, his instant messenger popped into the forefront with a pending message from Jalay.

What the fuck did *he* want?

"I can take your toy away if you can't pay attention," warned Ruiz.

"Can you make Jalay blind?"

The agent huffed and replied, "Of course I can. Will I? No. You can't just go blinding people for no good reason. We do try to keep a low profile." A pause. "Jalay Chapman," he recited from memory. "I met him yesterday. Squat kid, right?"

"More like fat-ass," said Russo. "Why'd you talk to him?"

"It was part of my search for Deron Bishop."

Russo flashed on the first meeting between him and Agent Ruiz, to the picture he had held up of Deron. At the time, it seemed like a fair question. But based on what he knew now, it no longer seemed necessary. "You know where I am, right? How?"

In the portal, the agent tapped the back of his neck.

"Then—"

"Why don't I go pick up Deron Bishop wherever he is? Because there's something wrong with that boy."

"No shit," agreed Russo.

"With his Guardian chip, I mean. It went off the grid on Sunday. No one noticed until his mother called the locals. By then, there was no trace of him. Until last night."

Russo widened his eyes, prompting for more information.

"He pops up intermittently now, but we can't trust the data because at one point, it showed him outside the walls. And no one goes outside the walls."

"Why not?"

Agent Ruiz sighed. "The signal only reaches so far. If you're not on a networked road, the veneer stops working. Could you imagine what that would do to someone who had depended on it all their lives?"

It sounded like a challenge. "We should do that," said Russo, unable to stop himself. "We should bring the whole damn thing to the ground!"

"And strike two," said Ruiz.

"Shit, don't shake your head at me! You're the one that can't find one little boy even with a tracking chip in his neck. I don't even know why I'm listening to you anymore."

"Because you know the alternative." His voice was surprisingly stern. Something flashed on his veneer, replacing the slight anger with a friendly façade. "Besides, I think Deron would be a great test mission for you. All you have to do is bring him in and your acceptance into the program is assured. Why is that funny?"

Russo considered the question. How about the fact that the people who were supposed to be looking for a missing person cared so little that they would put his classmate on the case? How insignificant did that make Deron? It was almost vindication for the way Russo had treated him over the years.

"Nothing," he replied at last. "I accept your mission." He flourished his best salute.

Yes, he thought to himself, I'll find Deron. But when I do, I'm going to put his chip to rest.

Permanently.

FORTY-SEVEN
ROSALIA

There was magic happening at school, some kind of spell that made the classes drag on without end, that made the clocks take twice as long to change to the next minute. Rosalia tried to keep her eyes off the time, but it was either that or acknowledge the daydreams that had been haunting her since arriving at school. At first, she thought they were just random ideas not unlike the myriad of things going through her head at any given time. But then after lunch, as time slowed even further, she began to reconcile what she could only catch glimpses of in her subconscious. Sitting in the back of the classroom with her palette tilted away from prying eyes, she transformed her fantasies into veneer. The results were confusing at best.

Some of the images were still vague: what appeared to be a leg, slender fingers, and even a lock of hair suspended in mid-air. There was always the chance that her conscious mind was affecting the veneer, an excuse she used when faces started to appear, first hers, then Ilya's. As the colors changed under her finger, the images became more defined, until she was looking at the outline of Ilya on her side, returning an intense gaze, her hand extending into the foreground and out of frame. The bean bag chair under her began to glow, as did the walls behind. Rosalia recognized her room, but the memory of Ilya in that pose wasn't there.

A sexual fantasy, she thought, about Ilya.

Rosalia swiped at her palette, erasing the image and banishing it from her memory. She concentrated on the clock, unable to hear the teacher's voice over the ones in her head that were now questioning things that were better left unanswered. Deron popped into being, a head to toe reproduction suspended in an empty construct. Piece by piece, she stripped him down until he was completely naked. Then, appearing from the left, Rosalia, equally nude, walked into his embrace. Even in the confines of a poorly defined daydream, she could see the love in his eyes, even though she could not match his passion.

Questions: If he didn't excite her, then what did? Where were the butterflies that were supposed to be dancing in her stomach? Why when her mind wandered did she imagine Ilya and not Deron?

"Ssh," she whispered. There would be plenty of time to figure things out, especially with the world slowing down around her. The only time things moved at a normal speed was between classes and even those brief recesses had lost their appeal now that Ilya seemed to show up during each one, smiling as if there were a secret between them. It reminded her of the way she looked—leered?—at her in the shower so many lifetimes ago, that same kind of smile whose intentions she just couldn't be sure of. Then there was her admission, something Rosalia accepted without much surprise at the time. Now, it was beginning to trouble her. Dropping her head to the desk, she lamented the lack of answers.

An eternity later, the spell holding the school hostage finally broke. When the last bell rang out, Rosalia hurried to her locker, intent on taking her things and never returning. It only took a few minutes to make it outside where the world was surprisingly gloomy.

Dark clouds hung overhead and gave Easton an artificial dusk. It wasn't until she started away from campus and heard that voice behind her that she realized she was trying to escape Ilya, avoid the conversations they might have.

"Hey," said Ilya, jogging to catch up. "Where you headed?"

Rosalia nodded towards the parking lot. "Home," she replied, feeling suddenly reticent.

"Oh," said Ilya. She was clutching her palette to her chest and shifting in place. "I was," she began, then stopped, looked around. "Do you want to hang out?"

"I don't know if you should come over again tonight," said Rosalia, looking homeward. There was lightning in the distance. "Lynn was pretty pissed off this morning."

"I didn't mean that. We could go to Perrault's and get some smoothies or something."

Rosalia faced her friend, intrigued by the hopefulness in her voice. Or was it desperation? "Sure," she agreed. "It looks like it's going to rain."

Ilya tilted her head back and took a deep breath. "Not yet, but soon."

They walked side by side, squeezing between cars, their hips touching occasionally as Ilya stopped short to let a car pass by. Rosalia reflected on the innocence of such encounters, how before it had been harmless to put her hand on Ilya, or for Ilya to put her arm around Rosalia. Now, she couldn't stop herself from wondering if each contact meant something more. It was clear that Ilya cared for her as a friend, but it could have been deeper than that. There might have been true attraction there, so deep that if Rosalia had admitted her daydreams, it would probably lead to a wild night of discovering the intricacies of lesbian sex. Rosalia shook her head, cleared away the encroaching mental images.

"What's the matter?" asked Ilya.

A good question, though it had a million answers, all as valid as the next. Rosalia lined them up in rows and columns, threw a mental dart, and chose one at random. "I've barely thought of Deron all day. I haven't called his mom. I haven't talked to Sebo." The guilt overwhelmed her now that the box had been opened. "What does that mean?"

"I could tell you, but you won't like it." Ilya slipped her hand under Rosalia's arm.

"Go ahead."

They stopped at a crosswalk, waited for the guard to let them pass.

"The worst part of losing someone is thinking you'll never get over it." Her voice was mournful, as if Deron's fate had already been decided. "Then one day you think of him a little less and then a little less. You start learning to live without him. But then you feel guilty about it, so the cycle repeats." A squeeze on her arm. "You can't rush it. I'll help you no matter how long it takes."

Rosalia wouldn't get over Deron that easily, certainly not in just a few days. If he were truly gone, it would be years before she could even function normally. At least, that's the future she imagined. He was the only one she wanted to spend time with, the only one she wanted to take her to the movies.

"You would be my friend, right?" she asked.

Ilya scoffed. "I *am* your friend. I've wanted to be your friend for a long time but you were always so busy with Deron." Something flashed on her face. "Sorry, I didn't mean it like that."

"I get it," said Rosalia, finishing the train of thought.

If Deron hadn't gone into the hospital, Ilya would have never stepped in and filled a void. The void never would have existed. How long had Ilya been waiting for such an opportunity? It made Rosalia wonder how many other interesting people went to school at Easton Central and how many of them she had ignored for so long just to spend time with her boyfriend. Besides, it wasn't Deron that was the sure thing. Boyfriends came and went, but having a true friend to commiserate with was invaluable. Ilya was someone she could talk to, share secrets with, and figure things out with. Even just moaning about Deron had made her feel better.

The neighborhoods looked different in the twilight. The veneers were glowing brightly, but behind them, the clouds seemed to absorb all the color. Ahead, the line of businesses on Parker Avenue disagreed on the time of day. Some of them were lit in their nighttime garb, bright neons that drew the eye even at a great distance. Others looked dark, like a shell with a few holes poked in them through which a soft inner light shone.

Increasing rumbles of thunder made them pick up the pace. It felt a little backwards, since Rosalia was in no hurry to get home. She wasn't looking forward to the conversation with her dad, not after her little outburst with Lynn that morning.

"I have to convince my dad I'm not a lesbian," said Rosalia.

"I had to convince my dad that I was," replied Ilya, chuckling.

"You told them? What did they say?"

She shrugged. "Doesn't matter. Mom's always blitzed by noon and dad's got bigger problems." She shook her head. "Babushka thinks it's just a phase I'm going through."

"Is it?"

The smile faded and Ilya withdrew her hand.

Rosalia couldn't help but feel the emptiness of the reverse gesture. Her arm was alone out there now and she was surprised to realize she wanted someone to hold it.

"I just feel what I feel. Like you and Deron. You don't question that you love him. Not because you're unsure but because you accept what you feel. I like who I like. I don't know why people think just because I'm a girl and you're—they're a girl that it's somehow *wrong*. Love is never wrong."

It made sense.

Rosalia looked at the people around her and saw for the first time just a variety of veneers, biological portals that could be reconciled into anything, even to look like a member of the opposite sex. There was nothing to differentiate them except for the shape of their bodies, protrusions from their chest or pants. If everyone looked the same and gender was simply the presence or omission of a body part, did that change the emotional connection? Did that somehow change love?

Rosalia lost herself in speculation as they approached Parker. Then, while waiting at the light to cross out of the neighborhood, she heard a quiet yelp from Ilya. Turning quickly, she watched the Ukrainian's face twist in confusion.

"What is it?"

"De—," she tried to say, but her voice faltered. Instead, she raised a shaky finger and pointed.

The same force that had crippled Ilya overtook Rosalia. Breathing became difficult as she took in the figure leaning against a news kiosk. He was disheveled, his veneer a mess, but it was undoubtedly Deron. Pessimism screamed at her from the periphery, questioning the vision that stood what seemed like only a few feet away. Then those eyes came up, those eyes that in any color or condition she would have recognized as ones that loved her like no other.

He was there.

She turned to Ilya, to ask her to confirm the mirage, only to find her gone. Turning around, she saw her walking away, her head bowed and shaking. The palette she had been holding hung loosely in her hand, swinging as she walked. Rosalia called out to her, twice, but got no response. Ilya never even looked back.

Overhead, thunder rumbled, but Rosalia could still feel the warmth of a single ray of sunshine on her back.

And just like that, Ilya slipped into the realm of unimportance. The only thing that mattered in the world was waiting behind her, standing around nonchalantly as if he hadn't been missing for days.

Be there, she prayed, turning around slowly.

FORTY-EIGHT
DERON

She was beautiful.

Deron almost didn't recognize her at a distance, just one of two random girls standing at the corner of the intersection waiting to cross. But then one of them looked in his direction, a little tall to be Rosalia. Her black hair framed a face full of sudden consternation. The emotional display wasn't one of happiness, wasn't the joy that Deron would have expected from his girlfriend. Instead, she lifted her hand and pointed in his direction.

That's when he focused on the girl standing next to her, a familiar figure with an unfamiliar veneer. Only, it wasn't a veneer; he was seeing the real her, the real Rosalia. All the worry about what was underneath faded away at the sight of this stranger. It was in her eyes, in the way her body resisted the urge to cross the street in front of the fast-moving cars.

Deron wanted nothing more than to reconcile her true appearance. As hard as he tried, he couldn't think of words to describe her that didn't do her a disservice. Still, his mind threw them out, compared her hair to the color of the sun, a color no one could truly know without going blind. Then, once she had crossed the street, broken into an awkward jog, he saw those eyes staring back at him.

His heart pounded; her eyes were blue. And not the dark blue of the clouds overhead or the neon blue of the signs on Parker Avenue, but light blue, like the skies on a cloudless day.

In every imagined reunion, he had seen her at a distance, then she him. She would come running, throw her arms around him, and put him off balance. They would fall to the ground in each other's embrace, laughing, so happy to be together again. But that didn't happen. Rosalia didn't jump into his arms; she slowed a few yards away and took her last steps cautiously. The happiness that had bloomed in her face wilted. Deron watched her eyebrows dip and then suddenly regain their composure. He was at a loss for words, as if the whole affair had occurred without warning.

It was Rosalia that spoke first, licking her lips slightly before saying, "It *is* you." It sounded like an accusation, as if she realized that his return meant he wasn't dead, that he better have a good excuse for going away without explanation. "Where have you…?"

Deron wanted to tell her everything, but revealing the nature of his flight would just cause more problems, more concern on that emotive face of hers. He realized it enchanted him with its simultaneous perfection and imperfection. It was comforting to know that she was pretty under her mask, that her veneers were extensions of something true and not a blatant lie like everything else.

"Say something," she pleaded, her voice cracking.

"I missed you," he replied, opting for the simplest sentence in the queue. There was no better way to say it.

The barrier between them crumbled and Rosalia flowed into the empty space. She slipped her arms around Deron's neck and pulled him closer.

She smelled like flowers.

It was a perfume she wore often and even without sight he would have known it was her just by the scent. Safe in her embrace, Deron thought back over the last few days and regretted all the times he doubted he'd ever see her again.

"You smell," said the voice at his ear, followed by a giggle that evoked a stream of memories. Rosalia pulled back so that he could see she was smiling. When he mirrored the expression, she said, "I should be mad at you."

"Are you?" He tried to grin but thought the better of it.

"Yes." Withdrawing, she crossed her arms in demonstration.

Thunder exploded overhead, so close that it caused both of them to look up. On the air, the smell of rain intensified.

"Can we go somewhere?"

"I was going to Perrault's," she offered.

Deron looked towards Parker Avenue; it would be too noisy in the smoothie shop, too many people. "How about our place?"

That she didn't ask him to clarify made him smile. He took her hand and led her across Parker Avenue, through the mini-strips, and into the fringes of the neighborhoods. She said nothing as they walked, but every time he glanced at her, he found her looking back at him.

"I like it outside," said Deron. "It's more colorful." He had to concentrate to see the veneer and each time he tried, it got a little harder, until finally he couldn't stand the pressure in his head. There was nothing to do but accept the ubiquitous evercrete, the signs with nothing on them, and the blonde hair floating on the gusts of wind beside him. "You're beautiful, you know that?"

Her freckled cheeks blushed slightly.

"I never knew you had blonde hair though." He reached up and pulled a piece of it out of the air. "You should wear this color all the time."

"My hair's not…" she started, trailing off in confusion.

Too soon, Deron thought. Clenching his fists, he pulled his vision back, examined the veneer for a few seconds, and then released. Today, she was wearing a light brown that glowed at the tips.

He remained silent until they reached Gillock Pond and found a covered swing to sit on. Rosalia had a strange look on her face, as if she were waiting for an explanation.

"We," he began, winding the tape back, "we all have these chips in our necks."

"Guardian chips," said Rosalia, nodding.

"You know about them?"

"Yeah," she replied, as if it were common knowledge. "Ilya and I found them in our necks the other night."

"And… you know what they do?"

Her face scrunched up again. "Yes. They keep us healthy."

"Keep us healthy? How does being able to reconcile keep us healthy?"

"What are you talking about?"

The words spilled out, every detail Abernathy had dropped on him. And with each word, Rosalia's face shifted as he had never witnessed before. There were lines around her eyes that only appeared when she narrowed them. Her lips trembled minutely, a subtlety that the veneer had always masked. She stopped him a few times, told him about the pictures she had seen in a game called Canvas. Then about Nurse Hendricks and how she said the Guardian chip was there to protect us. She couldn't believe that someone she respected so much would lie to her.

When Deron stopped talking, Rosalia remained quiet for a long time. Around them, the wind picked up, bringing aromas from the now distant Parker Avenue, mostly restaurants spinning up for the evening rush.

Rosalia touched the side of her face. "You can see what I really look like?"

That was a nice way of putting a positive spin on a handicap. It wasn't that he couldn't see the veneer; it was that he could see past it.

"Yes," he answered, "and you're… You're real."

"Of course I'm real." A sniffle. "Does that mean you can't see anything?" Gesturing to the convenience store on the corner, she asked, "You don't see those signs?"

"Everything's blank," he admitted. "It was scary at first, but I'm used to it now." He pointed up. "Those I can see though." He slowed at the sight of the lightning jumping from cloud to cloud. "It won't be easy."

"What won't?"

"Living like this."

"What do you mean? You need to see a doctor."

"Ha! If anyone found out…" He trailed off, unsure of what they would really do to him, if anything.

"So what, you're gonna spend the rest of your life not being able to see? How will you go to school? Everything is reconciled, Deron."

"Not everything." He turned and put his arm around her shoulder. "You're not reconciled. You have to see what I see." He touched her cheek. "This is unreal."

Rosalia's determination cracked under the compliment. "I thought you said I was real?"

"You're both," he whispered.

The rain began to fall as they kissed.

FORTY-NINE
SEBO

"So, there's like this magic moment between installation and first run that we need to apply the patch. You have to interrupt it right then or no happy juice."

Sebo nodded absently at Jalay's explanations. He understood what the portly hacker was telling him, but the conversation was excruciatingly vapid. Instead, he focused more on the improbability of having Jalay in his room, in his most protected sanctum. He was there, sitting on Sebo's chair next to Sebo's wall installing software on Sebo's portal. How inconceivable it was that a series of events would lead to this moment. Was the universe really so fragile that long-standing rivalries and allegiances could be broken by the absence of one person? Sebo thought back, tried to put the pieces together, but found their simplicity unfulfilling.

"Events of importance are most often the result of trivial causes," declared Sebo, crossing his arms.

"It's not trivial," replied Jalay, pointing at the scrolling text. "There's timing involved, especially in these virtual environments. It's not just going to sit around waiting for you to break it. If you don't time it just right, you have to uninstall and start over again." He chuckled at himself. "It took me six tries to install Jordan. Felicity I got on the first try. Popped her cherry like it was nothing."

What do you know about popping cherries, Sebo wondered. Did there actually exist a woman who would find his bulk attractive or his lame witticisms clever? Like so many other hopeless humans, Jalay was destined to spend his life married to pornography. He'd nominate one woman out of the menagerie of smut and put all of his attention on her. He'd waste away searching for pictures of her, movies, and full interactives. In his mind, a relationship would form, one that he would come to believe in with all the intensity of a man in love. After a while, real girls wouldn't even interest him anymore.

Then, death. Alone and pathetic.

"I heard they're coming out with a new girl next month. Marketa, I think. She's Yugoslavian, like that Ilya chick."

"She's Ukrainian," said Sebo, fidgeting on the bed. Every time Jalay touched the wall, a little shiver of unclean went up his spine.

"Oh." He paused, lost in moronic thought. "Man, how would you like having that girl on your wall? She's got the hottest b-cups I've ever seen."

"Have you ever even seen tits in real life? I mean, do you have any interest whatsoever in flesh and blood women?"

A defeated shrug. "I do like this one girl, but it's complicated."

She not into the one-ton-bag-o-fun, mused Sebo. "What's her name?"

"Yeah, that's all I need," he replied, shaking his head. "There, it's done." He placed his hand outside the portal and pushed the veneer away.

Sebo watched in awe as the portal filled the void, expanding to the corners and then shimmering into a bedroom about the size of his. For what the software cost, he had been expecting a high level of realism, but the three-dimensional effects were years beyond the cutting edge. He tested the focal point adjustments by stepping to the side. The far wall seemed to shift accordingly, keeping the illusion solid.

Jalay stood and took a few proud steps back, finding his place next to Sebo before folding his arms triumphantly. Together, they watched the lights come on, then the door open. And as lifelike and real as any woman, in walked the demure Jordan, pigtails bouncing behind her.

"She'll run by herself," explained Jalay. "If you want her to do something specific, you just reconcile the idea, kinda push her along."

"Sure," said Sebo, dumbfounded. He walked forward, sat down in the chair, and stared intently at the girl sitting on the bed just a few virtual feet away from him. She was dressed in green boy-short panties and a tight undershirt, cut deep enough to show cleavage. The bright white fabric clashed with her tan skin, but Sebo didn't care. The wrapping was inconsequential.

Jordan's body held more detail than any veneer he had ever reconciled, from the tips of her cherry-blonde hair to the reflective gleam of her teeth. Look up, he commanded mentally. Look up and gaze into the eyes of your master. He laughed at himself.

"Mind if I erase this wall?" asked Jalay, from behind.

Sebo waved his hand dismissively, barely listening.

"You've got a lot of pictures of Rosalia. You have a crush on her or something?"

"I hang out with Deron a lot. Deron hangs out with Rosa. Ipso fatso." He glanced back to see Jalay nodding his head.

"She's not bad, is she?"

"The very definition of hot," admitted Sebo, admiring Jordan's long legs as she reached down them to stretch.

"Too bad she's with Deron," continued Jalay.

"What?" He turned in his chair again. "Who are we talking about?"

"Rosalia, she's…"

Sebo scoffed loudly. "She's beyond your skill level."

"I don't know," mumbled Jalay. "If she got to know me… I mean, you and I didn't become friends until we'd talked a couple times."

"Who said we're friends? I don't know what your angle is, Jalay, but I'll figure it out soon enough." It was a thing to do, something on the horizon, but the immediate distraction held his gaze. He spoke absently, rambling, "I haven't really figured out what you want. If you're looking for protection from Russo, you've come to the wrong place. There's just no debt in that direction, if you know what I mean. And if Deron were around, he wouldn't help either. We already saw how his confrontations with Russo work out."

"It wasn't right," said Jalay. "I don't like what Russo did to your friend. You know that…"

"If you say so."

"You should tell Rosalia that too. I had nothing to do with anything. I just wanted to make pictures, like she does."

"What's Rosa got to do with any of this?"

Reaching out, Sebo touched the wall and imagined Jordan doing jumping jacks. She responded by moving to the center of the room and starting her exercises. The smile on her face never wavered and Sebo got the idea that there was nothing he could ask of her that would ever diminish it. Well, maybe a few, but nothing he wanted to reconcile with Jalay still in the room. The fantasies swelled and Sebo had to adjust himself.

"I have the feeling she doesn't like me much," replied Jalay.

It was enough to make Sebo turn away from the show. "Are you serious? I'm not certain she will *ever* stop hating you. You, Russo, you're basically the same person as far as she's concerned. You and I might become acquaintances, but you'll always be an enemy to her."

Jalay stared back with a piteous look on his veneer. Somewhere behind that façade, a lingering hope took its last breath.

"Don't take it so hard. That's been years in the making. Just because you're not with Russo anymore doesn't change what you did, or helped do, to her and Deron. Those were *your* shops, *your* insults."

"Russo came up with most of the ideas—"

"None of that matters." Sebo chuckled at the increasing desperation on Jalay's face. Then, in a flicker of understanding, it all made sense. "Son of a bitch! You like her!"

Jalay turned red, but he must have felt the warmth in his face because his veneer covered it up quickly. Without another word, he abandoned the wall and scurried out of the room. Sebo listened to the footsteps as they echoed in the stairwell. A moment later, the front door opened and from the window, Sebo watched a surprisingly nimble Jalay hurry along the sidewalk. He didn't look back.

"Alright," said Sebo.

It was carelessness that had doomed Jalay. If he didn't want Sebo to know that he had a crush on Rosa, then he should have just laughed it off. But to go running home like a moody schoolgirl was basically an admission of guilt. That was the Jalay he knew, the bumbling simpleton who was too dense to reason through even the simplest of social situations.

Shrugging the awkward moment away, Sebo shut his bedroom door and with an athletic leap, launched himself onto the bed, flipping on his back as he rebounded. With one hand, he started unbuttoning his pants. The other, he placed on the wall, happy to discover he could control Jordon from across the room.

The jumping jacks had taken their toll on the poor girl. Her arms didn't reach as high as before and the frequency had dwindled to a slow tempo. Sweat glistened on every inch of visible skin. Beneath her damp undershirt, Sebo could make out her nipples and he desired to see them fully. He concentrated and sent the instructions down the line. Jordan came to a stop, breathed heavily for a moment, and then peeled her shirt off over her head. It fell with a soundless splat on the floor.

Sebo pawed at the wall and brought up the configuration window. Ambient sounds filled the room as the Roommate software gained access to the audio subsystem. Then, remembering himself, Sebo rolled off the bed and shuffled to his door with his pants around his ankles. He engaged both the doorknob lock and the deadbolt before kicking off his pants and returning to the bed.

He was finally ready for the show.

"Workouts are good for the body," said Jordan in a voice dripping with teenage whimsy. She turned to the side and approached a mirror by her desk. Striking various poses, she admired her reconciled form.

Sebo thought for a moment about the physics involved in having a mirror inside a simulation inside a portal, but was too distracted to follow it to conclusion.

"I could use a shower." Jordan reached for her underwear and slid them down her legs, not reacting in the slightest to Sebo's encouraging whistle.

"My sweet Jesus," he added.

Jordan walked to a door on the back wall of her room and when she passed its threshold, the portal shifted to the interior of a bathroom. A freestanding shower occupied the left side of the space; it had no door or curtain, just pink tile growing out from the corner.

"What a strange shower," she remarked, her tone childlike.

She reached for the dial and when the water began to flow, Sebo thought he could smell it on the air. Stepping into the already steaming deluge, Jordan ran her fingers through her hair and turned her back to the tile to offer anyone who might be watching a better view.

That fuck-monkey Jalay.

For all of his faults, he had given Sebo a marvelous gift. Porn was one thing, but this level of interactivity went beyond the bounds of reason. It was quicksand with a veneer of nudity, a trap that would suck down any horny teenager who dared venture too close. That Jalay was obsessed with pornography was no surprise, but how he endured with this on his wall at home only gave rise to more questions. With Jordan as a roommate, who would ever want to leave their room?

Sebo felt the ache in his cheeks; he had been smiling non-stop for several minutes.

"I love how this shampoo smells."

Jordan's words brought him back to the task in hand. She was lathering up her hair and the suds were sliding down her neck, pooling in the small indentations in her shoulder blades, and then overflowing onto her chest. Sebo followed the bubbles down her smooth stomach to her legs.

"I should probably rinse off," said Jordan, reaching for the removable showerhead. She brought it down and sprayed her chest, sending a sheet of water down her body.

"No, fucking, way," said Sebo.

The showerhead descended and the eyes of his virtual roommate began to sparkle. She leaned against the tile wall, slid down a little to spread her legs.

"I love you," whispered Sebo between breaths.

FIFTY
ILYA

There was shouting coming from the practice field behind the school. The boys were scrimmaging the girls in preparation for the weekend's lacrosse matches. Only a few members of the female team were as tall as the shortest guys, but their speed and agility kept the match close. There appeared to be a no-contact arrangement in effect, but it didn't stop the occasional collision, which then led to verbal arguments, and then to the coaches blowing their whistles, trying to get their teams of hormone-crazed teenagers in line. By all appearances they were playing a game, but Ilya could sense the tension in the air, the desire to shed their protective gear and start a mass orgy right there on the damp grass.

Ilya had found herself a seat on the bleachers on the opposite side of the field, away from the tables adorned with energy drinks, away from the piles of backpacks and spare helmets. At such a distance, it was impossible for any of the players to see that she was not interested in the game, that she had merely chosen a secluded spot in which to reflect quietly.

Ilya sniffled but made no attempt to wipe the occasional tear from her face. They traced lines down her cheeks and she examined each one as its own entity, assigned meaning to it, parceling out her problems in easily enumerated segments. After some time, that well went dry and she was left to wonder why she was crying in the first place.

It was all borrowed time, she realized, a brief suspension of normality that allowed fantasy to take over. With all that had happened, with the fuzzy memories of intimate nights spent with Rosalia, Ilya could almost imagine that it had all been a dream.

But now Deron was back. The dream was over.

Her head dipped and for the first time since walking away from Rosalia, she let out a sob that someone else could have heard had there been anyone sitting next to her. None of the lacrosse players took note of her; the coaches were preoccupied with a girl who had turned her ankle. It was unfair. She had barely hurt herself and people were flocking to her side. Rosalia had ripped a hole in Ilya's heart and no one had come running. No one even knew or cared enough to ask.

"Stop feeling sorry for yourself," she whispered, remembering the speech her grandmother had given her when she got kicked out of Dahlstrom Academy. It was a long, rambling account of her own time as a teenager, with the main theme being that her young mind and young heart weren't strong enough to deal with the world yet.

"Every little thing will be a disaster," her grandmother had said. "You will feel like the sky is coming down on you. It will hurt."

And it does, Ilya thought, crossing her arms around her stomach and leaning forward. It did hurt and it did feel like the world was falling apart.

"Let it hurt," were her grandmother's words.

It was strange advice coming from a woman whose life's pursuit was to protect her family from pain. It was acknowledgement that the world held danger and that sooner or later, it would find Ilya and take hold of her, show her there was no veneer ever reconciled that could hold back the suffering.

A crack of thunder sounded over the school, making the skin on Ilya's arms crawl. As she looked up, a whistle sounded from the field, followed by the coach's instructions for everyone to get inside. That was Coach Baird, always the general to an army that could barely tie its shoes. Ilya wondered what they would do without him, whether practice would ever end and if it did, would they just stand around like robots without a program. As the players made their way back to the school, she noticed a strange face in the crowd.

The man was wearing a dark trench and standing between Coach Baird and Coach Stiles. In his hands, he held a palette, but Ilya couldn't see what was on it. He must have been asking questions because every time his lips moved, the coaches nodded or shook their heads in response. Finally, Coach Baird gestured to the sky and the stranger slipped his palette into his coat. He watched them walk away and as they passed in front of Ilya, his eyes fell on her.

"Thinking of joining the team, Ms. Yushchenko?" asked Coach Stiles as she shuffled past.

Ilya tried to smile politely, but the reaction from the coaches seemed to indicate she had gotten the emotion wrong. They walked on without further comment.

"Excuse me," said a voice from the right.

The stranger was standing at the bottom of the bleachers, a fake smile plastered on his veneer.

"I'm Agent Ruiz," he continued, touching his chest. "I was wondering if I could have a quick word with you."

Agents, thought Ilya. No Dahlstrom graduate ever wanted just a quick word. She made a show of checking the time on the scoreboard. "No, my bus will be here soon."

"I won't take much of your time," said the agent, climbing the bleachers with surprising agility. He sat down a few feet away from Ilya. "I understand you're acquaintances with Rosalia Collier."

"Yes," she answered. "We've been dating for a couple weeks now." Ah, the fantasy. Just saying the words lessened the pain a miniscule amount. If dreams were the only place she could have Rosalia, then so be it.

He didn't flinch, whether from training or a frozen veneer, she wasn't sure. "So she has ended her relationship with Deron Bishop?"

"That loser? Yeah." Screw him, she thought.

"Interesting," muttered the agent. He made a note on his palette. "By any chance have you seen Deron lately?"

So that was what this was about. Deron may have returned and Rosalia may have been reunited with her true love, but the cops evidently knew nothing about it. "Define *lately*."

The agent shrugged. "Last couple of days. Any time after Sunday."

"So you haven't found him yet?" It was Ilya's turn to smile. "If I had known running away was so easy, I would have done it a long time ago."

Agent Ruiz sighed, gave Ilya one of those looks that adults liked to reconcile before they schooled a young person in the ways of the world. Ilya braced for the condescension.

"If you really want to run away, you have to be very careful in how you go about it. I wouldn't even recommend trying it here. Go to Paramel if you can. Their security is lax compared to ours and since you're not a local, they won't be expecting you to be there for a long time. But if you just walk out your front door, like Deron, then it gets a little complicated. I mean, advertisers will pick you up if you get too close to a wall, a record is updated every time you pay for something, and not to mention the security at the gates. It's impossible for someone like you to get through unobserved." He smirked and puffed his chest out a little. "I mean, I could do it…"

"But you haven't found him." Ilya touched her face idly and found that her tears had since dried.

"It's only a matter of time. We've been picking up traces all day. The last one led me here." He nodded thoughtfully, his eyes drifting to the trees beyond the football field. "I think he's very close by."

Of course he was. All the agent had to do was walk down to Parker Avenue and then he'd have the mystery solved.

"She still likes him," said Ilya. "More than me, I think. But if I told you anything, she'd be mad at me."

"That's very considerate, but you're not thinking about the big picture. Whether Rosalia likes him or not is irrelevant. His mother, the woman who gave birth to him, has not seen her son in days. What do you think is worth more? The guilt you would feel for betraying your girlfriend or the anguish of a childless mother?"

It would have solved a lot of problems if Deron's mother had never conceived him in the first place.

The whoosh of hydraulics drew Ilya's attention to the front of the school. A large yellow bus had just pulled up, followed closely by two more. One of them would take her home, take her away from the nightmare and back to the safety of her room. There, she could relax with her pictures of Rosalia and dream of better times. It wasn't much, but it beat sitting on the bleachers answering questions that she didn't want to think about.

Ilya stood abruptly. "I have to go now." When the agent started to protest, she interrupted him. "I love her. I'd never betray her." There was resignation in the lines of his veneer. "But if I were trying to find the only person that stands between me and her, I would start walking in that direction." She pointed towards Parker Avenue. "At some point, I'd probably stop for a smoothie at Perrault's."

The grin that spread on Agent Ruiz' face turned Ilya's stomach. He stood and adjusted his jacket. "You did the right thing. I'll have him back home to his mother in no time."

"What if he doesn't want to go home?"

"He's seventeen," said the agent, his voice turning stern. "He doesn't have a choice." He stepped down the bleachers, jumping over the bottom row to the grass. "*Spasibo za pomoshch*, Ilya." He left the insincere gratitude hanging in the air as he walked away.

Fine, she thought. Go get him. Go take Deron back to his mother. Maybe she'd ground him forever or send him off to some reform school south of the border. At least that way she'd get Rosalia back.

And ultimately, that's all that really mattered.

FIFTY-ONE
DERON

Night fell prematurely on Easton. The reconciled reeds at the bottom of Gillock Pond were illuminated in a soft green glow for anyone that could still see them. A few yards away on a covered chair swing, a pair of inseparable teenagers sat together. The girl had her head on the boy's shoulder and her eyes on the undulating colors dancing in the water. The boy, with his arm wrapped around his prize, had his eyes closed and a peaceful look on his face. They rocked gently back and forth, lost in the simple moment.

At least, that was how Deron imagined it. In his mind, he saw himself the way a passerby would. They were just two kids out for some alone time who had sought shelter under the wide canopy of a swinging chair. The rain was visible only when a bolt of lightning lit up the sky, suspended in the air for that fraction of a second. Otherwise, it was too dark to see much of anything. There were no veneers to light his way, to show him the borders of streets and sidewalks and buildings. Without Rosalia by his side, he probably would have been scared of the overwhelming darkness. But she was there, able and willing to be his candle.

"I don't want to go home," she whispered.

"Then don't," he replied, content to sit on the swing all night if she allowed it.

"We can't stay here." Rosalia rubbed her cheek against his shoulder. "The rain's getting worse."

It wasn't too bad, but the thunder was ceaseless in the distance, speaking to something on the horizon. Placing his hand on the back of her neck, he asked, "Where do you want to go?"

"Somewhere warm," she replied, squeezing him. Her eyes came up and scrutinized his face. "Somewhere we can be alone."

There was something overtly sexual in the way she spoke, some intent in the way her lips pressed together and came apart.

"Just you and me," she added with a smile.

The list of potential places appeared in his mind, the most preferred locale being his room. "I don't know. We can't go to my house."

"Or mine," said Rosalia. "I'm already in enough trouble with Lynn."

"Then…" Deron drew out the silence, gave both of them time to think. When the answer finally popped into his head, he chuckled at the providence. "My dad has an apartment he doesn't use," he suggested.

With a gentle push on his chest, Rosalia sat up. "He's not there?"

"He's never there."

"Take me," she commanded. Her playful eyes showed awareness of the double meaning.

"Okay," was all he could think to say.

Deron tried to shake the awkward feeling as he stood and took Rosalia's hand. They walked through the rain to the intersection, his anxiety worsening with each step. It felt like a bubbling in his stomach that increased every time his thoughts drifted ahead into fantasy. Somehow, he made it onto the tram, managed to sit down without throwing up all over the slick floors.

The ride to his dad's apartment passed slowly and the silence from Rosalia didn't make things easier. He glanced at her a few times; she seemed to be lost in a daydream just like him. Once, she noticed his eyes and smiled, but no words, no discussion of things that needed discussing. Deron started putting together the conversation in his head, tried to figure out how he was going to tell her about Dos Presas, how he could convince her to come away with him. The more he examined the problem, the bigger it became until it had grown into an unmanageable jumble of arguments and loosely connected evidence.

Finally, they were stepping off the tram in his dad's neighborhood.

"You sure he's not home?" asked Rosalia as they approached the apartment complex.

Deron shrugged. "If he is, we'll just find some other place."

She nodded in agreement and slipped her arm inside his. Her clothes were damp, like her hair. It glistened when the lightning struck.

"What?" she asked.

"Nothing. You just look…" Abandoning the compliment, he led Rosalia through building's outer door. They stepped into the humid stairwell and began climbing. Deron felt each step in the small of his back. Whatever demon had settled there, it knew he was getting closer to his apartment, to the blankets he would lay on the living room floor, to…

Deron knocked twice, but nobody answered the door. Beside him, Rosalia let out a relieved sigh.

"We go in?" she asked.

The apartment looked the same; no one had been there in the interim.

Rosalia's hand slipped away from him and he watched her explore the apartment. She approached the couch and looked off to her right in the direction of the bedroom. "Hello?" she called, but got no response. Turning back to Deron, "We're alone." Another look around. "It's not as bad as you made it sound."

"It's better than Gillock Pond," he admitted. Better, too, than the cabins in Dos Presas. The urge to tell her was overwhelming.

"Come sit with me," she instructed, moving around the couch while shedding her jacket. Underneath was a gray t-shirt, damp around the bottom edges where it was exposed to the rain.

Deron followed suit, matched her casual repose on the dusty leather. She wanted him, that much was for sure, but he noted how different her eyes looked now that he could really see them. There used to be a fire, a spark buried in the pupil, visible whenever she got too happy or excited. Now, they were plain, lacking the normal enhancements. She was probably still reconciling the flames, having forgotten that he couldn't see them.

Rosalia reached for his face with her hands, but Deron pulled them out of the air.

"Before..." For some reason, he couldn't finish his sentence. Before we have sex, his brain muttered. Before we make love. Before we fuck. There were lots of ways to say it, but none that his tongue could understand. "I need to tell you something."

She looked hurt by his interruption, but withdrew nonetheless.

Deron explained about his first day, about the markings that caught his attention and ultimately led him to the border of Easton and beyond.

"You left the city?" she asked. "Why would you do that?"

"I don't know. I guess I was hoping there'd be other people like me. I thought maybe they could help me get my power back. That was before I knew about the chips."

"You could have gone to the hospital, maybe they—"

"I did, remember? Don't you think they would have checked for that?"

Rosalia looked away.

"Besides, it's only a problem if I live here in Easton."

That got her attention.

Before she could question him, he said, "There's a town full of people just like me. They don't have veneers at all there. It's... wonderful."

"No," said Rosalia, shaking her head. "That's horrible. You can't stay out there, Deron. You have to stay with *me*."

Deron dropped his head, looked at his hands in his lap. "I don't know if I can. You're right about school. I wouldn't even..." He sighed, looked up. "Dos Presas is the only place I can go."

"But when will I see you?"

"That's just it," he replied, then paused. "I want you to come with me."

Her mouth opened to reply, but whatever she wanted to say was lost to shock. She simply sat there staring at him.

Deron had never considered the possibility that Rosalia might not want to join him. Hadn't he convinced her that veneers were a lie? Hadn't he proved his love by risking his life to come back and get her?

"I thought," he began, but Rosalia interrupted him.

"Reconciliation is the only thing that makes me special," she said.

"Not to me."

"It's important to me. Maybe the most important—"

The world went mute.

Deron stared at her moving lips, but there was nothing to hear. His brain had shut off, unable to deal with the idea that reconciliation could be more important to Rosalia than his love. Who was this girl sitting in front of him? Did he know her at all? Dejected, he turned away, gazed into the darkened bedroom.

After a while, he heard her voice again. "It's okay to cry," she whispered. "I cried too when I thought I lost you."

He was surprised to find tears on his cheeks.

"I thought you were dead."

Deron tried to apologize, but his voice broke.

A minute of silence went by while they listened to the thunder.

"Did I ever tell you about my mom?" Rosalia didn't look up; she wasn't interested in Deron's response. "My dad says she got sick when I was nine, but I never knew anything was wrong until a year later when she went into the hospital. Me and dad stayed with her the whole time."

Deron shivered at the pain in her voice.

"She was brave, you know that? She never let on how much it hurt. My dad used to say she had an unbreakable veneer, that nothing in the world could bring it down. But that was how she wanted him to see her. With me... it was different. She was all smiles until he left. It didn't matter how long he was gone, just to the bathroom or to get some food. When it was just her and me, she..."

He put his hand on her knee.

Rosalia looked up, her eyes devoid of the redness that usually accompanied tears. "She cried. Just... cried and didn't stop until he came back. All I could do was sit there and not understand why my mom was so sad, why she kept breaking down when we were alone. And that's how she went. She died crying." Sniffling, she added, "She died sad."

Death would be a welcome alternative to living without you, thought Deron. If he couldn't take her with him, what good was it to go back?

"But, there was one time when she woke up and said she was sorry. And I asked her why." She placed her hand on his. "She said she was sorry for leaving me." Rosalia tugged his hand and when he didn't respond, she reached for his chin and pulled his face towards hers. "Deron, I'm—"

"No," he said, putting his fingers awkwardly to her lips. "Let's just… talk about it tomorrow."

She shook her head, "I can't—"

"Please," he implored her. "In the morning."

Reluctantly, she took his hand in hers and said, "Okay, in the morning."

"Thank you," he said, drawing her into an embrace. Her wet hair felt cold against his face, but the rest of her was warm and welcoming. Then it slipped out, the words he had often imagined saying but never had the guts. "I love you," he rasped, his lungs barely able to power the words.

"I love *you*," she repeated.

And then her lips were against his and every ache and pain that had plagued his body melted away. It wasn't the way he had imagined it, not with tears drying on his cheeks, not with the world one short night away from destruction. But those worries were in the impossible distance, chased there by the urgency of Rosalia's kisses.

She pushed against him, made him lean back against the arm of the sofa until she was on top of him, her pelvis pressing painfully against his erection. He grabbed at her waist, tried to move her into a better position.

"Let's go to the bedroom," she suggested.

"It's dirty," he replied.

"I don't care." Rosalia slipped off the couch, took Deron's hand, and pulled him to his feet.

FIFTY-TWO
ROSALIA

There was a hidden surface in her mind, one full of veneers, reconciliations of possible ways and places to lose her virginity. Most of them involved Deron, some starred just shadows, but common to them all was a beautiful setting, soft light, and a scent on the air that reminded her of home. Rosalia had been collecting the veneers since the moment she first understood the concept of sex and had rarely considered the possibility that from her list of potentials, she would ultimately select none and instead forge a new option, one that was less than preferable, one that smelled faintly of cigarettes.

Just inside the bedroom door, she stopped to reconcile a new scene on her wall of possibilities, a new veneer that didn't have the grandeur of its predecessors. There wasn't much to it: a dresser, a folded-up treadmill, an opaque window that barely held out the flashes of lightning, and finally, the bed. Rosalia felt one of Ilya's points of no return slip past her like a warm breeze. Whether or not she really wanted it, whether or not she really owed him, it was going to happen right there on the worn sheets.

Deron busied himself with removing the covers from the mattress. He found a comforter in the closet and spread it out on the bed. All of this unfolded with a dreamy quality that made Rosalia question whether any of it was happening at all.

Was this the right place?

Rosalia looked around at the dresser that hadn't been dusted in forever, that only needed a hasty veneer to be presentable. There were clothes scattered on the floor: shirts, pants, and a smattering of black socks. A preview of Deron in the future, she thought. It wasn't difficult to imagine him following in his father's footsteps. If they made it past high school and college to marriage, what then? He'd grow tired of her one day and run off with the first woman at work who would give him a blowjob in the supply closet. She tried to overlay that image on the young boy who was smoothing out the edges of the brown comforter. He *seemed* young, anyway. Maybe it was in his actions, the way he moved with purpose, the way his preparations dripped more with lust than with love.

Above the bed was the sole decoration on the wall, a woman in a meditative yoga pose. Completely naked, her tan skin was vibrant against the black backdrop.

Her face looked completely content; her eyes were closed, unaware or uncaring of the artist who had reconciled her. Rosalia paused to take in what Deron's dad obviously considered the ideal female and wondered if Deron held the same beliefs.

He was sitting on the edge of the bed, staring up at her in anticipation. Deron wasn't going to get up and lift her in his powerful arms and throw her on the bed. Nor would he whisper sweet words to entice her closer. It was unfair, she realized, to hold him to such high standards, to put him on the level of poets—tried and true authors who knew romance like Rosalia knew reconciliation.

It wasn't how it should have been, but what was?

Perfection, Rosalia thought, as she crossed the room to stand in front of Deron's slightly parted legs. Perfection was something that could be reconciled, given enough time and effort. But perfection was just another illusion, a mirage that sat on top of the truth, promising everything and delivering nothing.

His hands grabbed her hips roughly and pulled her close. Off balance, Rosalia put a hand on the wall, reaching over the nightstand with its humidor and lighter. She took the opportunity to dim the automatic lights down to the level she had often seen in her dreams, where Deron was still visible but the discrete curves of her body were not. Without breaking eye contact, she reconciled the nude woman away, banished her to the land of forgotten veneers. There was no need for competition at a time like this.

Rosalia shivered as Deron's fingers slipped under the lip of her shirt and scraped against her stomach. His hands climbed her stomach, encountered her bra, and then drifted to the sides where his fingernails tickled. With a quick motion, she pulled her shirt off over her head. A definite flash of delight sparkled in his eyes and before it could fade, Rosalia reached behind her back and unhooked her bra. With her hands clasped to her chest, she waited, teasing. And just when it looked like he would reach out and force her, she relented, dropping the bra to the floor by her feet.

The reaction on his face made her smile. Deron had seen his share of topless women, even beyond those he had plastered on his walls. But those were all virtual. The difference between reconciliations and reality was miniscule, maybe as small as a single integer, but even Rosalia could see how much space that left. Infinite space. An infinite difference between boobs on a wall and her chest inches from his face.

"What?" she asked, as his hands slipped behind her back. He pulled her to his face, turning his head to the side. Pressing his ear against her stomach, Deron squeezed tightly.

"Nothing," he whispered.

Rosalia wrapped her arms around his head, smoothed out the damp hair that had turned wavy from the humidity. Then he withdrew and she felt his lips on the side of her ribcage, moving forward with restraint and determination. The side of her chest. The left side of her breast. She closed her eyes and enjoyed the sensation.

He was a multi-tasker, that Deron. Even as his mouth covered her chest with kisses, his fingers pulled at the waistband on the back of her jeans. She could feel his fingers venturing downward, his thumbs diving beneath her underwear. Then his hands came forward, rested with clear intent on the buttons of her jeans.

"Are you waiting for permission?" she asked.

"Yes, please," he said, lifting his eyes to her.

Rosalia bent slightly to kiss him. "You have it." Another kiss on his forehead.

Her body lurched as he tugged at her pants, popping the metal clasps in a string of dull staccato notes. He struggled for a moment before Rosalia helped him push her jeans past her hips. Using his shoulders for balance, she wiggled one leg and then the other. Finally, she kicked them to the side.

Deron wasted no time drawing his fingertips up the sides of her legs, over the sudden goose bumps. Then he grabbed her, pulled her down onto the bed. They shared a long kiss, then another, until he retreated and stood up at the edge of the bed looking down at her like a hunter at his prey. She could see his thoughts as they happened, watched each one play out in his eyes.

Rosalia giggled at the way Deron undressed. He was sucking in his nonexistent gut and flexing undeveloped abdominal muscles, trying to impress her. He tossed his shirt away with flair, almost broke into a little striptease. Rosalia watched from the bed, lying back on her elbows with her eyes wide in encouragement. He paused after undoing his zipper as if she weren't already aware of his erection. She made her eyebrows dance, urging him on, to which he responded by shedding his pants and underwear at the same time. He kicked one leg off and then used the other to fling them across the room. Time stopped for a moment as Rosalia took in the boy in front of her.

It would be something to reconcile, the first true image of Deron that she had ever collected. He was revealed, a lanky boy with pale skin and wavy hair hanging over his ears. One day, he would grow into his body, fill out in all the right places, and be the protector that she would need.

"Come here," she commanded, suddenly feeling the need to have him next to her.

He obliged without hesitation, flopping down on his stomach beside her and wrapping his arm around her waist. She rolled onto her side and in the resulting embrace, they kissed.

Rosalia concentrated on his lips, only rejoining reality when he abandoned her mouth for her cheek or neck. It was then that she became aware of his hands, the one that was under her body and caressing her back, the other that was tracing lines on her hip, occasionally tugging at her underwear.

A crash of thunder drew their eyes to the window where a bright blue light was fading behind it. Rosalia took the opportunity to slide out of his arms and off the bed. She walked to the window and put her hand to it, reconciling the frosted veneer away so that she could see the world clearly. With her other hand, she dimmed the walls to nothing, so that the only light in the room came from the glow of the surrounding buildings and the electricity jumping from cloud to cloud.

Turning around, she stood between the window and the bed, aware he could only see her in silhouette. Shifting her hips back and forth a few times, she slid her underwear down her legs. Another flash of lightning illuminated Deron's eyes.

Rosalia began to feel nervous as she climbed back into bed. She had never been completely exposed with Deron before and though she tried to fight it, she couldn't help but feel self-conscious about her body.

Deron had pulled himself up to his knees and Rosalia took a similar position in front of him. Again, he kissed her, his hands appearing at the sides of her face and then receding out of view.

Rosalia let out a sharp sigh as Deron touched her for the first time. The pressure lessened immediately.

"Sorry," he said, whispering to her cheek.

How they must have looked from a distance.

Rosalia tried to imagine it in her head, but Deron's fingers were already marching on the border again.

"Are you waiting for permission?" she asked.

"No," he replied.

"Then what? Don't you want this?"

"I want *you*."

Pulling back, Rosalia put her lips near his. "You have me."

"Forever?" he asked.

For tonight, thought Rosalia.

Instead of answering, she kissed him, forcing his eyes shut once more. Then, with only a gentle push on his shoulder, they collapsed onto the bed.

Rosalia woke to the sound of thunder grumbling in the distance. The storm that had accompanied their lovemaking had moved on, just as the novelty of sex had faded after all was said and done. Beside her, Deron snored like a content baby and it was almost precious enough to smile at. He seemed so happy, both during and in the twilight that followed. The things he had said, the sweet words she thought him incapable of, had shown the depths of his love for her. If it had not been for them, all she would have taken away was the pain of him entering her and the unfulfilled obligations when he finally collapsed on her chest, panting for his life. It was easy to forgive the insensitivity. Having her as he did was the culminating expression of how he felt about her, the logical conclusion of his quest to possess her mind, body, and… and whatever else there was.

Such a fool, she thought, caressing his hair.

Deron thought it would never end, that they would be together until time crumbled and beyond. He refused to believe they were destined for failure, that at some point their relationship would dissolve, whether in five years or five minutes. Rosalia thought she had lost him forever, thought he was dead and gone. It had taken that kind of extreme circumstance to show her that she could exist without him, that the world's veneers would keep on sparkling.

She didn't even take into account the possibility of finding another attractive boy walking around out there, one with a veneer that hid the same sweet and innocent soul underneath. Deron had been a great boyfriend, a perfect boy when she needed one.

But the time of boys had come to an end.

In another year, it would be the time of men. She could afford to lose Deron because by the time she got over his absence, she wouldn't crave that same kind of juvenile spirit that she had adored in him.

"I love you," she whispered, kissing him softly on his back. Then, slowly so as not to wake him, she slipped off the bed and collected her clothes from the floor. Piece by piece, she dressed, all the while too aware that she wasn't crying, that she felt no sadness under her veneer.

Crying would have meant noise and she wanted him to remain asleep. Let him dream, she thought. Let him bask in the residual bliss. There was only pain waiting for him when the sun came up. There would be no Rosalia then, no discussions of leaving the city, no last-ditch effort to convince her that he was right.

Just an empty bed. Just a fading memory.

At the door, she paused, looked at him wrapped awkwardly in the comforter. Rosalia studied it well, capturing every detail should she want to reconcile it later. She'd remember him like this. Happy.

And she'd have to, she realized, because of all the things he would feel when he woke up, happy wouldn't be one of them.

The lights in the room were still down for the night when the wall began to ring. Russo pulled his head out from under his pillow and squinted at the portal glowing brightly beside him. Inside, Agent Ruiz stared back impatiently.

"What time is it?" asked Russo, rolling onto his side. The uncomfortable desk at the J. Perion building had made him appreciate his own bed more and with Ruiz ostensibly on his side, he had nothing to fear from showing his face at home anymore. His parents had said nothing of his absence; he wasn't even sure they had noticed. The first thing he did when he returned the night before was collapse on the double bed, fully clothed.

"It's four-thirty," replied Ruiz. "I let you sleep in."

"Fuck." Russo pulled the pillow over his head again and pressed down.

"This wasn't my idea." The agent sounded somewhat resigned. "But someone shit in my bed this morning so now I have to shit in yours."

The mental picture flashed and Russo almost laughed.

"We need to discuss Jalay Chapman."

Snorting, he replied, "Why?"

"When I questioned him day before yesterday, it seems he got more out of the conversation than I did." Around the portal, more images faded in, filling out Russo's wall. "Someone has been active on a few darknet message boards. We traced it back to this Chapman kid. He believes agents can see through veneers. And he's not afraid to share that theory with anyone who will listen."

"But you *can* see through veneers," said Russo.

"Yes," hissed Ruiz, "but that's hardly common knowledge, is it? Our primary mission is to locate Deron Bishop, but in the meantime, we need Jalay taken care of."

Russo tossed the pillow aside and propped himself up on his elbow. "You mean, like killed?"

The agent shrugged. "How you solve the Jalay situation is up to you. But you need to get it done *today*."

"What about Deron?"

"You didn't make enough progress yesterday. I got within five minutes of putting my hands on him. How close did you get?"

Russo didn't respond; he simply looked down at the wrinkled sheets.

"It's not your fault though."

A smirk. Was the agent actually trying to be reassuring?

"All I had to do was hang around the school for a few hours and the information fell into my lap. Obviously, you couldn't do that."

"I just need more time."

"And you'll get it, but we need to get containment on Jalay before the situation gets out of control. If we don't take care of both of them soon, there's going to be more collateral damage."

The gasping Agent Tavarez made a brief appearance in Russo's head.

"The suits look down on collateral damage," whined Ruiz. "I don't get it myself." A finger came up, pointed directly at Russo. "Learn this well, Rivera. Unless you work for the big V, you're just a sheep in this world. Everyone you've ever known, everyone you've gone to school with, seen out on the street, they're all expendable."

"What about us?"

The finger curled into a tight fist. "We're the control—the shepherds." His veneer shimmered into a grin. "And what do we do when the sheep get out of line?"

"I don't know," replied Russo, yawning.

The agent brought up a flat hand and smashed his fist into it. "We bash them on the fucking head until they rejoin the flock. Or until they're dead."

"I'm not a sheep." He sat up and stretched his arms.

"You were."

Russo narrowed his eyes at the portal on the wall. "Your power used to be a secret, but now I know. Now Jalay knows. You're just lucky he doesn't have any friends or else the news would be all over Easton by now."

Anger flashed on the agent's face. "You're young," he said, his tone not matching his expression. "One day you'll learn that most of your life is spent cleaning up other people's mistakes. And if Tavarez weren't already dead, he'd be at the top of my shit list." He became silent, staring intently.

It took Russo a minute to realize that he had been a loose end. Eric had spilled a secret and Ruiz had come to cover it up. "What would you have done?" he asked.

His eyes turned kind for a moment, the way they did when he spoke to the sheep, but Russo could see just how disingenuous they were. "You already know," he replied.

Death, probably.

"But if I had reached you in time, maybe you wouldn't have blabbed the entire story to your friend." The agent waited for Russo to look up. "Yes," he said, drawing out the word. "You thought I wouldn't find out? You should have read some of Jalay's postings. They're very detailed accounts of how his former friend was arrested and identified by an agent. I don't have to tell you how this sits with the suits."

Russo scooted back on his bed until he could lean against the wall. "What do they care anyway? If people knew agents could see under the veneer, wouldn't they be *more* afraid?"

Ruiz tried to laugh, but the forced levity sounded hollow. "Fearful sheep aren't happy sheep. Besides, we teach them that the world is theirs for the taking, that reconciliation is an evolutionary birthright."

"Isn't—"

"Ha!" barked the agent. "Humans stopped evolving long before reconciliation. Did you really think that being able to change the appearance of an object is an innate ability? Does that even make sense?!"

"No!" he shot back. "That's what I thought because that's what I'd been told. But then I cut the eyes out of an agent and learned the truth!"

"The truth," laughed Ruiz. "You found some wires. That was just a piece of the larger system. How do you think people would react if they found out about that system, if they learned their precious evolutionary skill was just a piece of code on a microchip?" He paused, caught his breath. "It's not really about the veneers," he said, quietly. "Sheep could come to understand the truth, maybe accept it. But when you reveal something like that, go against the official story that we've held for so long, it makes us look like—"

"Liars?"

The smile returned as creepy as ever. "They know we're liars. What they don't know is to what extent. Take the Guardian chip in your neck. Official story is that it's there to protect you, monitor your vitals. But before we shortened the name, it was called the Guardian Angel chip. And it did much, much more." He put up a finger. "One thing," he said. "People believe the chip does *one thing*. They don't question it, but if you tell them the chip's responsible for reconciliation too, then that's two things." He unfurled another finger. "If two, why not three? Why not a thousand?"

"What else does it do?" asked Russo.

The agent made a weird face, as if insulted by the question. "What *doesn't* it do?" Enumerating on his fingers, he said, "Vitals, reconciliation, presence-sense, bio-sec, GPS, interface auditing, InSight..." Trailing off, he let his enthusiasm settle. "We know where every citizen of Easton is at every moment of the day and they have no clue. We have logs, detailed logs, that trace their movements over their entire lifetimes. They can't know. Do you understand? They *can't*."

Nodding, Russo let the revelations wash over him. He'd always known people were stupid, but now he saw them as they truly were, confined to a prison and unable to see the bars because someone had reconciled a pretty picture on them.

After a minute, Ruiz asked, "So are you going or what?"

"Now? Do you have any idea what time it is?"

The agent chuckled. "It doesn't really matter, does it? When you work for Vinestead, your time is their time. And if you don't get out of bed and go take care of the Jalay situation, there won't be any time. For anyone."

"Fine," grumbled Russo, wincing a little from being ordered around so easily. It would take some getting used to, but so far it had been worth it for the intel alone. Lowering his legs to the floor, he sought out his shoes in the dimly lit room. There was a dull pain in his hamstrings, the consequence of too much time spent aimlessly walking the streets the day before. He wouldn't make that mistake again. He knew exactly where Jalay's house was, where he would be headed soon. All he had to do was wait and his prey would come to him.

Agent Ruiz looked away and spoke to someone off screen. "It's not my fucking mess!" he yelled, shaking his fist. "Ah, fuck you!" There was frustration in his face, which he reconciled away when he remembered the portal. "What?" he asked.

"When do I get a gun?"

"Right now, I wouldn't trust you with a butter knife."

"Then how am I supposed to *take care of* Jalay?"

"How did you kill Tavarez?"

If there was bitterness in his voice, Russo couldn't sense it.

"That's what I thought. Like I said, I only care about the results; the method is up to you."

Russo nodded, resigned. Standing up, he looked around at the messy room. "It's not fair," he said, under his breath.

"What's that?"

He turned in place and let a little malice into his voice. "You said I would get to bring Deron in."

"Plans change," explained Ruiz. "You failed. Now *I'm* going to bring him in."

Russo shook his head. "Why even do that? Why do you care about him so much? He's nothing."

"You underestimate him." Ruiz clearly enjoyed having information that Russo did not. "He's more than just a victim of your bullying."

"Fuck that," said Russo, turning away.

"He can see. Did you know that?"

"What do you mean?"

Ruiz smiled broadly. "He can see under veneers. But it's not like InSight; he can't turn it on and off at will. Sometimes people have the unreconciled world thrust upon them. Two things happen after that. Either they wind up at the hospital and get fixed or they find a way out of the city and we never hear from them again. We need to get to Deron before someone else does so we can figure out why this is happening."

"He can see?"

"Does that bother you, Rivera? That he can see and you can't? Well, welcome to the real world. I'm cleaning up Tavarez' mess, but you need to clean up your own."

Russo scrunched up his face, utterly puzzled.

"Yes, *your* mess. You're the one that broke his Guardian chip in the first place."

Thinking back, Russo saw the defeated Deron crumpled on the grass in front of him. He saw his boot lifting towards the sky, then coming down hard on Deron's neck. Who knew that under that tissue was a tiny chip responsible for the one power Russo truly wanted?

"Mind your fucking business!" yelled Ruiz.

Russo turned and saw he was looking off-screen again. "Is every day like that?"

"I'm not saying it's not a fun job, but it's still a job. Be happy you get to go out and do stuff." He lifted a palette from his desk. "You call me when Jalay has been dealt with. I'll send a cleanup crew." The warning finger came up again. "Don't forget that part."

"Yes, boss," said Russo, cringing at the foul taste.

FIFTY-FOUR
DERON

"I changed my mind," whispered Deron. "I don't want you to come."

He thought it would be harder, telling her he'd rather face his new life on his own, would rather make new friends and new loves without being tied down. Perhaps if Rosalia had been lying there when he woke up, naked and on her back with her face turned away, the words would have caught in his throat. But then, if she had been there, he wouldn't have felt this way in the first place.

As much as it hurt to admit, Deron knew he had presented Rosalia with an impossible choice. She could continue to live in a world where her talents made her special or she could follow her boyfriend into the past where people would be able to see her true appearance, where dreams would remain locked in her head as a nontransferable artifact. It made more sense when he thought of the roles reversed, if she had lost her sight and Deron had been forced to choose. He wondered if he would have been as dauntless as he imagined himself to be. A day ago, he would have guessed yes, since that was what he imagined Rosalia would do for him. But now that the truth had come out, it was hard not to see himself as equally cowardly.

It was quiet in his dad's bedroom; only the light rain beating against the window was audible over his own lethargic breathing. Nature had formed its own veneer on the clear glass, using the streaking water to bend the world beyond it. He thought of the city where he had been born and raised. And someday, eventually die there too. Deron nearly had at the hands of a boy whose face he couldn't forget. Russo had evolved into a monster lingering in the shadows. It was in that general direction that he funneled his anger.

Everything ended with Rosalia's decision, but it all went back to Russo.

It was in kindergarten that Deron first met Russo. A couple of weeks into the school year, Ms. Walker had given the class their first reconciliation lesson. They had to sit in a circle on the activity rug while she handed out active toys.

"Change the color," she had told them. "When you finish, you can have free time."

Deron tried to remember the theoretical lessons from earlier in the week, the demonstrations that Ms. Walker had put on showing them how easy it was to change anything just by touching it. Gripping the ball with both hands, he imagined the active toy as blue, but nothing happened. One by one, the other children in the circle got up, showed their reconciled toy to the teacher, and went to the back of the classroom to play. As the only student remaining on the activity rug, Deron tried to concentrate, but all he could hear was the laughter and chatter of his classmates.

Frustrated and on the verge of tears, Deron began to squeeze the ball as hard as he could. Only when his fingers began to throb did the color start to change, a slow bleed of blue from his fingertips. Excited, he stood to show Ms. Walker, but when he turned around, there stood Russo. Without a word, he reached out and touched Deron's ball, pushing back the color until it was gray again. Then he smiled and was gone, leaving Deron with an unfinished project and an approaching teacher with a concerned look on her face. He told her what Russo had done and to his credit, he never turned another object of Deron's gray. Instead, he turned them all red.

If someone had told him then that Russo would one day be responsible for ruining his life, he probably would have believed them. Even at that age, there was something wrong about him, some chaotic force that needed a wide berth.

Deron lingered face-down on the bed, letting the betrayal fill him up.

"Your hand was forced," he told her. "My hand was forced."

Rolling onto his back, he stared at the ceiling and imagined Russo's face. His enemy needed a face because without it, there would be nothing to smash, nothing to spit in, nothing to absorb his anger. "Come on, you son of a bitch," he said. He cursed Russo's name, thought about every injustice the boy had ever done him. The hateful meditation produced Russo's veneer on the pocked ceiling, spanning the entire surface from wall to wall. Deron flinched, tried to erase the unwanted apparition, but the image lingered.

"Fuck you!" he shouted, sitting up in the bed. Rubbing his eyes didn't help; the face stuck fast. Deron tried to imagine everything as black, tried to see that empty place he fled to when he wanted to be alone. Around him, the walls, the furniture, and even the window with its beaded raindrops, bent to his will. All that remained was the looming face that stared down with contempt.

Deron tried to move away, but in the dark he missed the edge of the bed and tumbled to the floor. He closed his eyes, but it was as if he had reconciled Russo's face on the backs of his eyelids. The prospect of staring at those eyes for the rest of his life made his stomach heave.

Standing on trembling legs, he groped around the room, no longer content to hide in his dark place. He raised his eyes to Russo and yelled, "Is this what you want?"

The room exploded in a red hue, drenching the walls in swirling blood. Everything else stayed the same, giving the room a two-tone feel that reminded him of old graphic novels. Stumbling away from the face, Deron found the living room similarly reconciled. It all seemed unreal; no one he knew could reconcile without physically touching an object. It was insane to think that he, a boy who had struggled with reconciliation all his life, would be the first one to develop such a power.

Without any encouragement, the red walls softened to an innocuous pink. Under the rosy coating, Deron could see the outlines of the previous portals, which he brought out one by one, restoring their original contents. His breathing returned to normal in time with the return of reality. Not only did his anger fade, but actual excitement crept into the void it had left. He was really doing it, really changing the veneers again. And he could see them! On the wall across from the couch, he noticed a large rectangular portal. Bringing it out, he tried to activate it, wanted to see some television program—any would do.

But the screen remained blank.

Then, as if someone had pulled the plug, the color began to drain out of every surface. Once again, the veneer blinked out of existence. Deron stood between the kitchen and the living room, waiting for some kind of answer. Finding none, he walked back to the bedroom and found that Russo's face was gone. It was a small consolation.

Deron crossed the room to the window and let his head bang against the cold glass. A sigh caused it to fog up, but when it faded, he saw the city revealed again in the now familiar gray.

"Fuck Easton," he muttered, giving the glass another taste of his forehead. He eyed the common area outside the apartment with its damp sidewalk that led to a gate. The street was mostly empty and across it was the strip mall with its fogged up windows. There was nothing out there, nothing and no one.

Deron smiled. He felt sorry for himself, but at least he wasn't shouldering the blame. The person responsible was out there in the rain, probably doing something terrible to someone who didn't deserve it. He thought of what he'd do if he ever saw Russo again. Clenching his fists, he tried to summon the rage, but all he got was frustration and anxiety. Still, a strange sensation accompanied it, the same he had felt just minutes before. Uncertainly, he reached out with his mind and tried to turn the black iron of the fence to a garish yellow. When it shimmered gold, he grunted.

"No fucking way."

Embracing the feeling, Deron reconciled more colors onto the outside world. He changed the street and the sidewalk and the wet grass. Everything in sight began cycling through a myriad of colors until finally he rested and admired the mess he had created on a single street. It was impressive by itself, but to extend it to the rest of the city would be epic. Just as he was getting giddy about the possibilities, he noticed something out of the corner of his eye.

Parked on the other side of the street was a now multicolored sedan, except that the veneer wasn't holding. Confused, Deron sent out a reinforcing command, turning the car into a hunk of beige that vaguely resembled a peanut. A moment later, the color faded, changed to an ominous black. Looking around, he saw that nothing else was returning to its original state, so then why this one thing?

And then he saw him and realized that it wasn't his own power that was failing, it was just that someone else's was better. The man that got out of the car was dressed in a conspicuous black trench, just like the agent that had questioned him before he went to Paramel. Whether it was the same one, he couldn't tell.

The agent walked to the front of his car and surveyed the virtual damage. From a distance, it looked like he was laughing. Deron almost joined in, happy that someone appreciated what he had accomplished, but then the agent looked directly at him, through the rain and the trees and the glass. In that instant, the man felt too close and Deron backed away.

After gathering his courage, he ventured a quick peek and swallowed hard. The agent was approaching the gate, his eyes glued to the window.

FIFTY-FIVE
JALAY

The Holly Street Hilton parking garage got less crowded the higher Jalay climbed on the circular staircase. By level seven, the only occupants of the numerous reserved parking spaces were shallow puddles that splashed his pants as he scampered through them. Tired and out of breath, he darted behind the first evercrete column he could find, throwing his back against it while trying to convince his body that it could relax for a moment. He knew Russo was right behind him, knew that he had been leisurely following him since their little altercation a few minutes earlier.

Jalay looked around and shook his head. A deserted parking garage was a terrible place to hide.

Before he could feel too bad about his decision, a sharp pain erupted in his left leg—his out of shape muscles were complaining about the amount of work. Thinking himself shot or stabbed, Jalay let his legs buckle and then slid to the ground, landing in a puddle that soaked through his jeans. He grimaced against the pain, pressed his fingers into the muscle to relax it. Remorse took hold, a feeling that maybe he should have participated more in P.E. or at least exercised a little on his own.

The unused adrenaline continued its feedback loop and with each pass it strengthened a tight knot in his back. He arched against it, but the throbbing consumed his entire spine. Even without being there, Russo was inflicting pain on him by making him run, by breaking down his body before the actual fight. With that realization, Jalay decided that he could not keep running from his enemy.

He had to finish it.

"You know what that means, right?" asked a voice inside him that sounded a lot like Jordan.

He nodded in response. It meant pain.

"He is bigger than you, stronger too." Jordan sounded worried, not an easy feat for an artificially intelligent hallucination.

"I'm aware," he replied, through his teeth. Jalay had watched Russo bully people for years. The guy had torment down to a science.

"Even if you beat him up, he'll just come back harder and faster."

It would never end, he agreed. Even without provocation, Russo had returned to finish what he had started at Jalay's locker. How would he react to having his ass handed to him by his weaker and chubbier cohort?

"You have to kill him."

Below, Jalay could hear the squeal of tires against the wet evercrete. Above, light thunder rumbled and shook loose the rain that was falling outside. He was stuck in the middle; nothing seemed real.

"Kill him," urged Jordan.

"Okay," said Jalay. Despite the protest in his leg, he turned and placed his hands on the column to brace himself. It would require all of his strength, every last ounce of survival instinct to get out of this.

"But what a story," said Jordan, seductively. "Can't you see it?"

Jalay's eyes snapped open and he was surprised to find a new veneer on the evercrete. Only, instead of a scene of him killing Russo, there was just a blank portal, buzzing along the edges where the black flashed gold. The next few actions were automatic.

His start page unfolded from the right side of the screen and with a mental command he was able to bring up the phone icon and a contact list of people who never called him. Wiping their names away, he expanded the number pad into full screen and actually used his finger to stub out the numbers. Nine, one, one.

"I'm sorry," he whispered to Jordan. "I can't beat him." It was a lovely idea, getting the best of Russo, but it wouldn't work. He needed help, preferably from someone with a gun.

"Easton Dispatch, what is your emergency?" asked a professionally veneered operator. She didn't have a smile on her face but she wasn't frowning either. The effect was soothing, as if her calm composure meant he could relax too.

"I have information about Russo Rivera," he stammered.

"Ru—" said the woman, before disappearing suddenly.

Jalay blinked in confusion.

The portal buzzed and sprang back to life, but this time a familiar face was staring back at him.

"Mr. Chapman," said Agent Ruiz. He was in an office, seated behind a large desk. Behind him was the Easton skyline, but completely dry and sunny. "It's a pleasure to see you again."

"I," said Jalay, unsure of how to continue. "Russo's after me."

"So *now* you know where he is?"

Was he really being that petty? "Yes! He's here and I think he's going to kill me."

"Oh, now I don't think he would do that."

"He almost killed Deron Bishop!"

The agent shrugged. "I'm not really interested in—"

"And he might have killed Eric!"

"What do you know about Agent Tavarez?"

"Russo was following him for weeks. I don't know if he found him, but…"

"Okay," said Agent Ruiz, putting up a hand. "Where are you right now? I'll send a cruiser immediately."

"I'm on Holly Street, at the Hilton parking garage." Out of the corner of his eye, he saw Russo's head appear on the stairs, then the rest of him. "He's here!" he whispered frantically.

"Got it," said the agent. "Corner of Seventeenth and Fitzgerald. Can you get out onto the street?"

"No!" yelled Jalay. "Holly Street!"

"Great. You should be safe as long as you are in a public area. Start walking towards Sixteenth. I've got a cruiser en route. Just wave them down when you see them."

Jalay banged his fists against the column. "What the *fuck* are you talking about?!"

"There's no need to thank me, Mr. Chapman. Protecting the citizens of this great city is my job. With your help, we should be able to put Russo Rivera away for a very long time."

Jalay went silent, dumbfounded. Staring at the agent in the portal, he struggled to understand what was going on. Then he heard boots sloshing through puddles and turned to see Russo approaching with a grin on his face. Jalay stood and backed away from the column, considering all options. He stopped when his back hit the low wall of the parking garage. Behind him, the rain fell close by; he would barely have to extend his hand to touch it. Taking his eyes off his enemy for a split second, he examined the view over the railing.

"Seven floors to freedom," said Jordan, her voice far away.

Stopping at the column, Russo looked down at the glowing portal. The agent was still visible, still staring into the virtual camera as if expecting Jalay to say something. Russo touched the evercrete and dragged the portal up. He nodded cordially.

"Not very efficient," mumbled the agent.

"Only pussies call the cops," said Russo, looking at Jalay again. "I thought you were better than that."

"Unnecessary banter," the agent pointed out. "Don't forget we're evaluating your performance, Rivera."

What the hell was he talking about? Were they…

"You," said Jalay, struggling to point at the portal. "You're working with them?"

Russo raised his eyebrows as if to ask, "So what?"

"Do you know who he works for?!"

"Not really," admitted Russo. "Something with a V, right?"

"Fucking *Vinestead*!" Jalay's voice broke and he felt a tinge at the back of his throat.

"You've been a busy little boy," said Agent Ruiz, shaking his head.

Jalay ignored the agent. "Do you know what Vinestead is? What they do?"

"They're going to make me a Seer," replied Russo.

It was a small opening, but it was his only angle. "Is that what you really think? You think they're just going to turn over that kind of power to a kid? To a dropout? You're a fucking loser, Russo! Why do you think they'd trust you with anything?"

Anger rippled through Russo's veneer, but it revealed a moment of consideration in its wake—a tiny crack.

"You don't know these people. You don't know what they're capable of."

"And you do?" demanded Russo. "You're suddenly an expert on agents? All you know is pizza and porn. And look where that's gotten you."

"I know how to reconcile," he corrected, "better than you and most people in this town. I can look at a veneer and tell you if someone imagined it or if they saw it for real. There's a difference that people like you could never detect. I know truth when I see it."

"And what is the truth?" asked the agent, somewhat impassively.

"Chips," barked Jalay. "Chips and wires in our bodies and brains. All controlled by Vinestead." By the looks on their faces, he knew the conspiracy theories he had dismissed one by one over the last few days were actually true. All of the things he had seen in Canvas, all of the posts on the messages boards about the history of a company once known as Vinestead International, were all true. He felt the shock as the world shifted in place, became a different version of itself in an instant.

Russo bit his lip and shook his head. The agent mirrored.

Jalay could barely ask, "What?"

"I was just supposed to beat him up, right?" asked Russo.

The agent shrugged in response.

"But now he knows."

They were talking as if he wasn't even standing there.

"And people who know," continued Russo, "are a threat to the stability of Easton and Vinestead."

"I don't abide threats," hissed Agent Ruiz.

"Me neither," said Russo.

While that was true, it was worse now that the agent was backing up his psychosis.

"I suggest summary execution." Russo obviously delighted in saying those words.

"Authorized," said the agent. "Report back when it's done and I'll send a scrub team by."

It sounded so official, so cold, that by the time the words registered in Jalay's head, the portal had disappeared from the column. All that remained was Russo and his smile. As the rain fell and the pall grew, his lips tightened into a thin line. It was the same one he had worn the night their partnership came to an end. Remembering the conversation, Jalay couldn't help but laugh. It felt wrong, to laugh at such a time, when every inch of his body was as tense as it had ever been, but the absurdity of it, the off-hand prophecy that was suddenly coming true, was too much to ignore.

"I knew you would take it too far," said Jalay.

"As far as necessary."

Jalay put his hands on the evercrete barrier; it was wet and smooth. "If I stepped on your heel," he repeated from memory. "But beating me up won't be good enough this time, will it?"

Russo took a step forward.

How long Jalay's eyes had been moist was unclear, but he finally felt the first tear start down his cheeks.

"I knew it," he said.

"Then you're ready," declared Russo.

"No." On all counts, no.

"Did you know your Guardian chip will keep operating even after you're dead?"

"Wha—" He wasn't able to get the question out before Russo charged. There was a brief struggle, which was better than a fistfight, since it gave Jalay a slight advantage. Russo seemed to have trouble with his weight, but soon Jalay felt himself go off balance. The barrier wall dug into his back and suddenly one leg was off the ground. With every ounce of strength, he tried to push it back down, tried to find something better to hold onto instead of the slick evercrete. Russo pushed with his shoulder and then he was leaning out over the alley below. Pulling his chin to his chest, Jalay got a look at Russo's face.

So much anger. So much determination.

There was never a chance, he realized. And then his other foot came off the ground and the world began to move in all the wrong ways. In the brief freefall, he heard Jordan's voice whispering in his ear.

"Seven floors to freedom."

FIFTY-SIX
ROSALIA

"The most important thing you can do is let go out of the world," said Coach Stiles. She was subbing for Coach Baird and instead of making the class run on the treadmills for an hour, she had given them the option of doing free weights or yoga. Naturally, the boys had flocked to the machine room, leaving Rosalia to join the smaller group of girls in the padded studio. There were eight of them, including Ilya, plus one Vince Covert, who took a position at the back of the room. Rosalia tried to ignore his running commentary and instead focused on the coach's dilettante mantras.

"When the mind is free from distraction, it can focus on bringing the body into harmony." She brought her hands down into a prayer pose, lifted her right leg, and placed her foot against her knee. "Tree stance," she announced. "Take your time, shift your weight. If you fall out, don't worry. Just work yourself back into position."

Rosalia lifted her foot, wobbled a bit, and then found balance. Next to her, Ilya looked serene and steady. She already had her hands in the air and an empty look on her face.

"Clear your mind," said Coach Stiles, her voice soothing. "Focus on the moment. It's just you and your body."

Ilya snickered and when Rosalia looked over, she smiled back conspiratorially.

"Don't think about all the things you have to do today. Tests, homework, lectures. None of it exists in this moment. Deep breath everyone. And switch." She waited as ten feet hit the padded mats and ten more lifted into position. "The past does not exist."

Easy for you to say, thought Rosalia. The first half of class had breezed by; the surprisingly intense yoga had distracted her from yesterday's events and last night's dreams. But when they switched to balance postures, she found she didn't have to concentrate on her body as much. As a result, her mind wandered, began to pull at the threads of memory.

"All right, is everyone feeling relaxed?"

An affirmative murmur went up from the small crowd.

"Let's take a seat and finish up with corpse pose." When Vera Delgado made a noise, Coach Stiles added, "It's just a name, people. It's also the most difficult of yoga poses. Everyone on their backs please."

Rosalia collapsed onto her butt and then reclined on the mat. Despite the coach's advice, she thought about Deron, about him waking up and discovering her gone. She hoped he didn't take it too hard.

"Put your arms by your side and flex nothing," instructed the coach. "Just let everything go limp."

A masculine giggle came from the back of the room.

"Quiet, Mr. Covert. We must have complete silence. I want everyone to visualize the silence in your mind. Walk towards it. Embrace it if you can."

Shutting her eyes, Rosalia blotted out the light from the ceiling. In the resulting darkness, she sought out the shape of silence, but couldn't imagine its form. Every time she moved in a direction, an image of Deron would appear. She opened her eyes in frustration and turned her head to the side to find a sympathetic Ilya smiling back at her.

"One more deep breath and we're done." Coach Stiles sat up and crossed her legs. "I hope you all enjoyed this. When you're with me next year, you'll do stuff like this more often." She glanced at the clock. "That's it for today, people," she said. "Except you, Mr. Covert. I'd like a word with you."

The other girls laughed amongst themselves as Rosalia stood and headed for the hallway. She knew Ilya was in step beside her, but she didn't feel like talking just yet. In the locker room, she shed her sports bra and workout shorts, felt Ilya's eyes drinking in her body as she reached to remove her underwear. The memories faded in like a liquid veneer, showcasing all the times she had caught Ilya minding someone else's business. Before, it had just seemed like the odd behavior of a quirky foreign girl. But now that she knew how much Ilya liked her, it seemed to suggest…

Rosalia shook her head and slipped out of her underwear. Pulling her towel around her quickly, she shuffled over to the shower stall and waited while the water warmed up. Naturally, Ilya took the stall beside her, stepping into the freezing water and gasping enthusiastically.

"*That's* what I needed," said Ilya, pulling her hair back. She spun it around twice and locked it into a bun with a clip.

It felt like Ilya had been trying to initiate conversation all morning, but Rosalia didn't want to talk about Deron, didn't want to try justifying what she had done. She didn't even understand it herself; her need of Deron was equal to her need of the veneer, yet she had chosen Easton over him. The admission didn't fix anything, didn't resolve his problems or hers, just brought guilt and more guilt.

"It's warm now," said Ilya, turning her chest to the falling water.

The tile partition only let her see down to Ilya's shoulders, but the image of water beading on her breasts flashed in Rosalia's head. Gritting her teeth to force it away, she wondered if her lesbian friend's habits were rubbing off on her.

"Thanks," replied Rosalia, stepping absently into the water. It was hot, making her recoil.

"You're not sunny Rosalia today."

"You're not dark Ilya," she shot back, too much bitterness in her voice.

"Why should I be dark today? My best friend got her boyfriend back."

Rosalia glanced over, tried to see past the faux sincerity on Ilya's face. She was smiling for all she was worth, but something in her eyes wasn't right, some glimmer of steely concentration. "I," she started to reply, but when the counter-argument threatened to come out, she suddenly felt out of breath.

"What happened?" asked Ilya, stepping up to the partition.

Rosalia tried to escape the question by putting her face into the falling water.

"Everything's okay, right? He's coming back…" She trailed off as Rosalia shook her head.

"He can't see the veneer," she explained, the concept still incredulous to her. "He can't see street signs or portals or anything that I reconcile." She looked up, looked for support in the Ukrainian's eyes. "He wanted me to leave Easton with him. To go somewhere where there's no veneer at all."

"What did you tell him?"

Rosalia's lower lip trembled. "I'm here, aren't I?" An aborted sob as she turned away. "I'm here at school when I should be waking up next to him." It was easy to leave him the night before, but now, several hours removed, she couldn't remember the line of thinking that had taken her away from him. She closed her eyes as if pain were a bright light that could simply be turned off.

"You left him?"

She nodded. "After everything. After all we did. But I didn't know he couldn't *see!* How could I have known that?"

"I couldn't imagine it," Ilya broke in.

"Why not? You don't even like reconciling."

"What? Of course I do," she replied. "I like pretty things, and Easton is full of them. All the streets are lit up, all the people are pretty. And you, being able to reconcile like you do. Why would you want to give that up?"

"Because I love him!" Her sudden retort got the attention of a few girls, but they kept their commentary to whispers. "Because I love him," she repeated, quieter, less sure of her answer.

"You can love him without throwing away your gift," said Ilya, matching Rosalia's tone. "Just because you didn't go with him—"

"I'm a horrible person," said Rosalia, cleaning up the foul language she had used in her head. She could only think of Deron and how he had risked so much, only to have his girlfriend abandon him in the end. He thought he could rely on the one thing that should have remained constant. And she had left him.

Unable to contain it any longer, Rosalia let out the tears she had been fighting all morning. They came out stronger and faster than she had expected, rattling her entire body and making it hard to stand. She dipped once, put her hand out on the partition to steady herself. Maybe it was that desperate grab that alarmed Ilya; in a flash, she was standing next to Rosalia, hands clasped on her shoulders. There was no way to stop her from bringing her body close to Rosalia's, no way to get a signal from her brain to her muscles without more sadness spilling out of her.

"Okay," said Ilya, pulling Rosalia's head into her shoulder. "It will pass," she assured her, speaking with the practiced patience of Nurse Hendricks. "Let it hurt," she whispered, and then a bit louder to someone else, "What the fuck are you looking at?"

I'll tell you, thought Rosalia, imagining how two naked girls locked in an awkward embrace would appear to the rest of the class.

It was such a tiny voice holding protest in the back of her mind. The rest of her didn't care, just wanted someone to hold, someone to tell her that it would all be okay. Wrapping her arms around Ilya's back, Rosalia allowed herself to be pulled further into the embrace, felt her chest collide with Ilya's. She cried harder at that, wondering how she had gone from Deron's thin but masculine arms to Ilya's gentle hands. She was softer, curvy where Deron had been jutting bones and sharp elbows.

Out of nowhere, Rosalia laughed. "Look at me," she said. "Look at us."

"What about us?" asked Ilya, pulling back.

They stared at each other for a moment before Rosalia replied. "We're hugging in the shower." Then, remembering her surroundings, she looked around. The shower room was empty; Ilya had chased the onlookers away. "Our secret is out," she lamented.

"What secret is that?" Ilya's hand had moved to the side of Rosalia's face and she routed the wet strands of hair around her ear.

"Everyone's going to think we're lesbians."

"I am," reminded Ilya, grinning.

"But *I'm* not."

"Are you sure?" she asked, her voice taking on that flirty tone again. "Have you ever even kissed a girl?"

Rosalia shook her head, tried to read the intent in Ilya's raised eyebrow. Even if it had been hiding under a veneer, it didn't take a genius to see where this was headed. When Ilya's lips moved a little closer, Rosalia retreated, shook her head more urgently.

"What?" asked Ilya.

"I… can't." It wasn't the same as being face to face with Deron. With him, there was desire, a need to join with him physically. But with Ilya, there was nothing.

Ilya's eyes glistened as her smile returned. "Your cunt is an inch from mine and you can't even kiss me?" Again, she moved, got close enough for Rosalia to feel her breath on her upper lip.

"I'm sorry," said Rosalia, meekly. She dropped her arms and gently pushed Ilya away.

The Ukrainian stood there for a moment, visibly hurt, but not without pride. She brought her hands down from Rosalia's neck, brushing against both of her breasts, and then traced lines down her stomach. The clearly erotic gesture made Rosalia think of how Deron had done a similar movement the night before. She laughed and sobbed at the same time, unsure of how things had changed so dramatically in such a short time. The tiniest pressure on her hip bones made her look down to see Ilya's hands still lingering. And again, it triggered a memory, only this one wasn't of her abandoned boyfriend. She saw her own room, dark, with back-lit veneers scrolling on the walls. Beside her was Ilya, staring back with lustful eyes, not watching where her hand moved but obviously concentrating on it.

The friendly expression disappeared from Ilya's face as a moment of recognition passed between them.

"Have… we…?" asked Rosalia.

Ilya used her thumb to trace the outline of Rosalia's pelvis while her fingers pressed into her hips.

Rosalia slapped the offending hand away and moved as far back into the stall as she could. She felt cold and cornered, afraid of what Ilya might do when pushed. Her face showed nothing but restrained amusement.

"Mellow brings out the best in you," said Ilya, taking a couple of steps back. She reached for her towel and wrapped it around her body. "Who was I to argue with a latent dyke?" Then, with a smile more artificial than any veneer, she said, "You shouldn't feel bad about Deron." She glanced down at Rosalia's legs. "I mean, he wasn't *really* your first, you know?"

Rosalia sank to the shower floor as Ilya walked away. She had been wrong about her. The girl with the pretty face did have a veneer, but it wasn't one that could be reconciled. It was all in the way she talked, the way she smiled—a completely fake persona stapled to the real her. It had come off so easily. One day Ilya was just a strange girl in the background of her life and the next she was intriguing, exotic, and friendly. No one changed that fast, not in any meaningful way.

"Fuck!" she cried, drawing out the hidden syllables.

FIFTY-SEVEN
DERON

From the safety of the fourth-floor landing, Deron watched as the agent paced the hallway outside his dad's apartment. His movements were very methodical; three steps in one direction, pivot on the lead foot, and then repeat, each stride the width of the door frame. At first, he had tried banging on the door and calling Deron's name. Then, when the pacing began, Deron thought the agent was just going to wait him out, but after a couple of hours, when the door downstairs swung open, he realized the man had just been standing guard.

The footsteps of the second agent were loud on the bare steps, though he moved with much less urgency than his partner. There was something familiar about him that Deron couldn't place until the man began to talk. Just hearing his voice brought him back to the night at the gate. He flashed on the business card and read the name easily.

"He inside?" asked Agent Memo Ruiz as he crested the third-floor landing.

The other agent completed his pivot and nodded curtly. "Yeah. I spotted him in the window and came inside, but he's not answering."

"Did you knock, Agent Fitch?" Ruiz undid the strap around his waist and shed the damp trench coat.

"Of course I knocked. I was gonna force entry, but… Memo, you shoulda seen what this kid did."

The agent slung his coat over the banister. "Which was?"

"He reconciled everything. I mean, *everything*."

"Probably just some kids messing with you."

"Yeah, him" said Fitch, gesturing to the door with his thumb. "He was doing it from the window."

Agent Ruiz sighed and adjusted the cuffs on his shirt. "Aaron, you know the sheep can't do that. Especially not some punk kid."

Deron felt something sharp poke him in the stomach; he had to look down to make sure nothing was there. He had been entertaining the idea of approaching Ruiz, explaining himself, and asking for help. After all, he seemed like a nice guy back at the gate. But now, referring to Deron as a punk kid… It didn't sound like the first time he had used those words.

"I know," said Fitch, staring at the door as if he could see through it. "He put a veneer on my car, so I changed it back." He turned to make eye contact. "*I* was touching my car. He wasn't."

So that was real. It could have all been in Deron's head, but here was proof that at least one other person saw it… whatever it was.

Ignoring his partner, Ruiz nodded towards the door. "Shall we go in?"

"Do we have enough to force—"

Agent Ruiz lifted a leg and slammed it into the door near its handle. A loud crack sounded in the hallway, but the barrier held. A subsequent kick broke it off its hinges and the two agents rushed inside, with Ruiz shouting Deron's name and ordering him to surrender.

Instantly, Deron was up and running down the stairs, taking two or three at a time in a desperate bid to get outside before the agents noticed. On the third floor, he whipped around the banisters, feeling his shoes give a little on the smooth tile. He was so preoccupied with not falling that he didn't see the blur erupting from his dad's apartment. It collided with Deron just as he was making a turn and though he tried to hold the wooden railing, his fingers slipped, and he fell to the floor. Before he could catch his breath, the blur was upon him.

"Got you, you little shit," said Agent Fitch. He pulled Deron up by his collar and forced him against the railing.

Agent Ruiz appeared in the doorway and ordered quietly, "Bring him inside."

Deron tried to go limp, but Fitch was strong and had no trouble pulling him into the apartment. The agent threw him onto the couch in front of Ruiz, who stared blankly as if lost in thought.

It was a veneer, Deron realized. He relied on it so much that he didn't even bother emoting anymore.

"Agent Fitch, please see to the gawkers."

Fitch hesitated, motioned to Deron. "Him too?"

"You got a problem with the way I do things?"

The agent shrugged in response. "You're the boss, boss."

Agent Ruiz said nothing.

"Alright," said Fitch, turning on the spot. He yelled at the onlookers in the hallway, "Back in your homes, people. This ain't no road show."

For a long minute, Agent Ruiz stood staring at the open door. Then, like a television changing channels, he plunked down into the recliner and said, "So… broken chip. What's that like?"

Deron raised his eyebrows and tried to play dumb.

"Come on," urged the agent. "I know your chip is acting up. You've been popping on and off the grid for days. So either you invented some kind of jamming device or you damaged your chip. It was the fall, right? In…" He shut one eye in concentration. "Paramel."

"How do you know about that?"

"People talk. God, do people talk. Even when they don't think they're saying anything, they're talking. Russo, Jalay, Sebo, Ilya…" He enumerated the names on his fingers. "That Sebo…"

He didn't mention Rosalia, Deron noticed.

"Or… was it the fight with Russo? I reviewed the medical scans and they *said* nothing was wrong with you, but you know doctors."

Deron shrugged, prompting the agent to sit up.

"Why did you run?"

The pristine rivers bordering Dos Presas flashed in his head. He wanted to be back there, away from the veneer and the agents, even if that meant without Rosalia.

Ruiz cleared his throat. "You went outside the walls, didn't you?"

"I got lost," said Deron.

"You know it's a crime to leave the city except through the approved gates? And I didn't see your name on any registers."

"I want a lawyer." The phrase came to him out of nowhere; he didn't even know how to go about getting one.

"Ah," said Ruiz, sitting back. "Hardball. I can play hardball. I'm the captain of the fucking team." He let the silence build, passed the time by rocking in the recliner.

Finally, Deron couldn't take the waiting any longer. "I was scared," he admitted, wondering if the ignorance defense would save him. "I couldn't see and I thought I'd be banished."

"Banished?" asked the agent, as if the word were new to him.

"Thrown out of Easton."

"Why would we do that?"

"Mr. Ficcone said—"

Agent Ruiz' laughter filled the room. "Do you believe everything that cheap-suit simpleton says? Your chip is just a device! Did it ever occur to you that we could just *fix* it? It happens all the time. People go into the hospital complaining about the veneer and they just fix 'em up."

Deron tried to respond, but his entire body had gone numb. Everything had been a waste. Rosalia, leaving him in the middle of the night, unable to give up a world she loved more than him. There was no unlearning that fact, but with time he could have accepted it, maybe even changed it.

"So I can stay?" he asked.

"Well," said Ruiz, "you can be fixed, that's for sure. Whether you can stay depends on if I can prove you were outside the city without authorization. And the penalty for that is severe." He shook his head gloomily. "Very severe."

Fighting the urge to throw up, Deron tightened his fists and dug his fingernails into his palms.

"You'll go away for a very long time," continued the agent. "Unless…"

"Unless what?"

"Let's just say I have some pull with the local authorities. I could get your desertion charge dropped, get your chip fixed up, and send you on your way."

"What's the catch?" he asked.

Agent Ruiz smiled independently from his veneer. "You know, you're not the only truant in Easton. We're very interested to talk to your friend Russo again."

"What do you want with him?"

"He's a suspect in a murder investigation. I need you to draw him out for us."

"How am I supposed to do that?" asked Deron, crossing his arms.

"That's *your* problem, isn't it?" The agent stood abruptly and walked to the window. "You have twenty-four hours. If you don't deliver Russo by noon tomorrow, I take you in for desertion. And don't think I won't find you." Turning, he tried to appear sincere. "This is your chance to go back to your life, Deron. Give me Russo and all will be forgiven." He wiped his hands in an empty gesture.

It sounded ridiculous but so did reconciling an entire street.

Standing, Deron considered his options, thought how happy Rosalia would be to know he could stay, that they could still be together. All he had to do was get Russo out in the open and the plan for that was already brewing in his head.

"I can reconcile," said Deron, "but not all the time."

The agent nodded. "Fascinating."

"So I can't call you," he explained. "Meet me at the football field at Central. Tonight, ten o'clock."

Agent Ruiz raised an eyebrow. "You sure you can get him there? You *do not* want to waste my time."

"He'll be there," said Deron, turning on the spot. When he was safely out of earshot, he added, "Either that, or I'll be long gone by then."

FIFTY-EIGHT
SEBO

"I miss you."

The sentiment appeared on Sebo's palette during lunch as he was finishing up a burrito slathered in chili and shredded cheese. He was sitting at the glass bar, essentially a line of stools under a high table that ran the length of the cafeteria's outer windows. From his vantage point, he could see the rain falling outside, waning and intensifying every few minutes. Running his fingers through his hair, he smiled at the instant message on his palette.

Sure, Jordan was only sending the message because he had configured her to do so, but it didn't make it any less important. She missed him and in a way, he missed her. Spending the night with her, watching her sleep in a bed that was ostensibly on the other side of the room, had been strangely comforting. Randomly throughout the night, she would snore a little, not enough to be annoying, but enough to get his attention. Then she'd turn on her side, the covers slipping from her naked body, and give a little moan. Sebo watched contently for a while before falling asleep, happy to know she would be there in the morning.

Jordan was doing stretches when he awoke and as he wiped the sleep from his eyes, he watched her come out of a difficult plough position. With every movement, he delighted in the detail of her body, in the skin that bunched up and released. A doll would have done no such thing. Her imperfections made her more lifelike. Though they were slight, they made her appear as an actual human being instead of a technologically advanced blow-up doll. And though he couldn't touch her, could only stand next to the wall and stare into her eyes, it was enough.

Sebo grinned and tapped the reply box with his finger. "What are you wearing?" he asked her, but there was no reply. Maybe she wasn't set up to respond intelligently to queries. He shrugged, pondered whether the omission of conversational aptitude had been intentional or not. Chewing thoughtfully, he stared out the window again, wondering how an assumed intelligence like Jordan would fare in one of his accelerated learning classes.

Outside, a blanket of gray clouds gave Easton a strange atmosphere that was accented by lightning flashing soundlessly in the distance. Sebo searched for the words to describe it.

Dreary. Miserable. That wasn't what Easton was about. That was what having veneers was supposed to prevent.

The veneer was still there, for instance, on the house across the street, but through the rain it looked muddled. The two-story townhome had been reconciled with red brick, though underneath it was likely evercrete, same as everything else. Each townhome had its own unique flair, whether it brick or siding, giving the row a disjointed feel. At least they had left room for a little natural growth in the form of a park to the right of the row, bordered on both sides by tall Cedars. They towered above the homes, their canopies providing shade for the students that lingered there after school.

A discordant splash of white caught his attention outside. Straining to see through the rain, he thought he spied someone standing in the wooded area, leaning out from behind a tree. It looked like a boy, about the same height as...

"Fuck a duck," whispered Sebo, lowering the uneaten piece of burrito and pushing his plate away. He slipped his palette into his backpack and hopped off the stool. Without taking his eyes off the aberration for fear of losing it, he made his way over to the double doors that led out to the plaza. One of the lunchroom monitors was sitting on a chair by the exit, but she said nothing as Sebo pushed on the crossbar and stuck his head outside. Without the foggy windows in his way, he had a clearer view of the ghost who resembled Deron. Uncertainly, Sebo waved his hand.

When the white flash waved back, even beckoned him, he broke free from the door and rushed across the plaza, vaguely cognizant of the lunch monitor calling his name behind him. Sprinting across the street, he watched the apparition disappear behind a tree.

"Deron?" he asked, coming to a stop a few feet away. He walked around the ancient trunk slowly until he could see the figure. Its veneer was messed up, but it somewhat resembled his long-lost friend. "Is that you?"

"Hey." He smiled, but it appeared to take considerable effort on his part.

"Are you alright?" It wasn't difficult to see the goose bumps on Deron's arms or the shiver that ran up his body every few seconds. "How long have you been standing out here?"

"Not long," he replied.

"Are you aware that everyone's looking for you? The police—"

"I know."

"Does Rosa know you're back?"

His lower jaw jutted forward. "She knows. She didn't tell you?"

"I saw her before lunch, but she was already walking into class. What about you?"

"Last night." Pain altered his voice like an accent.

Sebo crossed his arms against the encroaching cold. "What happened?"

As expected, Deron just shrugged, played the tormented soul, and kept whatever injustice he felt he had suffered inside.

"Rosa looked sad today," said Sebo, recalling the carefully reconciled veneer on her face, the one that was supposed to cover up any real show of emotion.

"We broke up," he said tightly. "Actually, she dumped me."

"That bitch!" said Sebo.

Deron laughed and shook his head in disagreement. His eyes drifted away for a moment and then he asked in a serious tone, "Would you look after her?"

Sebo felt his face scrunch up. "What do you mean?"

"I don't know. If things don't go right." He shivered at some involuntary thought. "Just keep an eye on her for me."

Listening to Deron ramble made Sebo uncomfortable, anxious. "What are you *talking* about?"

"I need to talk to Jalay. Can you give him a message?"

"He's not even here today. What would you want from him anyway?"

"Not him. Russo." His face grew dark and intense.

The new evolution made Sebo smile. Through gnashed teeth, he asked, "Do you mean…"

"I owe him," he continued. "I *really* owe him."

Sebo punched his own open palm. "Fucking yes!" He pulled his palette from his bag, grimaced at the few rain drops that made it through the canopy to land on its surface. "Wait," he said suddenly. "Why don't you—"

"I can't reconcile anymore," he explained. "Sometimes I think I can touch things in a portal, but I can't see it so I don't know if I'm doing it right. I need to get a message to Russo and I don't want him knowing I can't see."

"Is this what you were talking about on the bus?"

Deron shrugged. "It's gotten worse since then. Or better. I don't know."

Sebo nodded and brought up the Easton Central directory. He found Russo's name on the list and clicked into his mail program. "What do you want it to say?"

"Tell him I want to meet at the football field tonight. Ten o'clock."

"Excellent," said Sebo, reconciling the message onto the portal. "Though we can't be certain he even reads his school mail anymore." With a quick swipe, he brought up the instant messenger and sent the text to Jalay, instructing him to forward it on to Russo.

"Don't tell Rosie about this, okay? She might change her mind and show up and that wouldn't be good."

Sebo bit his lip. "I can't believe she dumped you. I wouldn't have expected that from her."

"It wasn't all bad," said Deron. "There was a parting gift involved."

It took a moment for him to catch on, but Sebo finally asked, "Third base?" When Deron just smiled, he added, "All the way?"

"Yar," he replied, drawing out the word.

"How was it?" Suddenly the idea of a naked Jordan writhing on his wall didn't seem as enticing.

Again, he shrugged. "It was alright. I wouldn't mind doing it again."

"Son of a dick!" bellowed Sebo, punching Deron on the shoulder. "If only you could reconcile, you could show me." He trailed off as his friend gave him an odd look in return. "I mean, not you, but Rosa…" The look changed to a glare. "Huh," he said, figuring it was as good a time as any to stop talking.

Across the street, a booming voice called out, "Mr. Kahani, you need to get back on campus at once!" It was Principal Ficcone; the lunch monitor had ratted him out.

Sebo waved enthusiastically, causing the principal to put his hands on his hips and intensify his glower. "I need to return to campus at once," he repeated. "When are you coming back?"

"Tonight," replied Deron. "Ten o'clock."

"No." Something caught in Sebo's throat; the surprise put him off balance. "I mean, back to school. Back to…" He wanted to say *us*, but Rosalia had made her choice.

A thin smile spread on Deron's face. "If all goes well, at five past ten."

FIFTY-NINE
ILYA

The interesting thing about Ramsey was that she had the most divine tan lines decorating the back of her neck. Whether reconciled or the product of actual exposure to the sun was anyone's guess, but sitting behind her in sixth period Biology gave Ilya plenty of time to argue each side. For one, it was a perfect line; a true strap would have moved around a little, creating the smallest of gradients between the tan skin and her true color. Ramsey's line simply stopped and became another color instantaneously.

It was the mark of poor reconciliation skills.

Ilya sighed, crinkled her nose at the latent scent of formaldehyde. It was warm in the Biology room, in the whole school in fact. Warm and humid such that the students had been shedding clothes all day. Even Mr. Randall had shunned his customary blazer and rolled up the sleeves of his blue button-down. He was handsome in an angular sort of way that was tragically paired with an abundance of body hair, some of which poked out from the top of his shirt.

Desiring something smoother, Ilya returned her attention to the back of Ramsey's neck. There, a few strands of hair had fallen out of her ponytail and now hung over the back of her collar. They contrasted with the white tee that was blank on the back but veneered with a pink mess of flowers on the front. Ramsey seemed focused on Mr. Randall as he droned on about the day's project, several times pointing to the microscopes huddled in the center of the lab tables. Ilya glanced over at the materials counter and saw a large beaker full of murky water. They had done this lab before at Dahlstrom, but not with such ancient equipment.

"Today, we're doing things the old-fashioned way," said Mr. Randall. "This is how young scientists before you investigated life on a small scale."

And they used to carry around a thousand little gadgets to accomplish what Ilya could do with her finger and a smooth surface.

As the teacher dismissed the students to their work, Ramsey spun around in her chair and faced the lab table. Her veneer displayed a playful smile, but it was directed at Zachary, who evidently was what passed for a varsity lacrosse player these days. Ilya ignored the longing gaze and instead focused on the two pale lines tracing over Ramsey's clavicles. They dipped under her shirt, forcing a mental reconciliation. Ilya imagined them bending towards the center of Ramsey's breasts where they expanded in elongated triangles wide enough to cover her nipples but narrow enough to expose everything else. She looked like the kind of girl who would let the world bask in the glory of her teardrop tits but at the same time drive the boys crazy by covering up the interesting parts. As if nobody knew what was under that tiny bikini.

Grinning, Ilya let her eyes drop and looked through the table to where the other tan lines would have been. She had the urge to pull out her palette and reconcile the image for posterity and for other, more selfish, reasons. After a minute of blissful daydream, she looked up and saw Ramsey fidgeting under the intense scrutiny.

"Your tan lines," Ilya said, scratching her neck. "Are they real or did you reconcile them?"

"They're real," replied Ramsey, trying in vain to get her eyes on them. "I usually lay out a few times a week."

A lie—part and parcel of every good reconciliation.

"They look good on you. I wish I could get some color like that."

Ramsey did a quick inventory of Ilya's body; the attention felt good. "You'd look great with a little more color."

Ilya's eyes drifted to the high windows dotted with rain drops. "As soon as the rain goes, maybe." She had to look past Zachary to see outside and when she focused closer, he was leering something filthy.

"What arc you looking at?" shc askcd.

Zachary licked his lips. "I heard you and Rosalia Collier were making out in the showers this morning."

Ilya didn't even blink. "So?"

"Really?" asked Ramsey. "I thought she was with Deron."

"Things change," said Ilya with a shrug. "I guess something came between them."

"I heard he died," said Zachary.

The girl next to Ramsey with horrible bangs nodded her head, putting in, "He ran away to Paramel and got killed by some gangbangers."

Gangbanged to death; it would have served him right.

"No," said Ilya, "he's not dead. Rosalia was with him last night." Then to Zachary, she said accusingly, "He tried to rape her. We weren't making out in the shower; I was just trying to console her. I'd like to see how you'd react if Deron tried to rape *you*." Inside, the laughter was tingling all of her muscles. The thought of Deron holding Zachary down on the floor and delivering the business was just too comical.

"That asshole," said Ramsey, shaking her head.

"Yes!" Ilya pointed to Ramsey as if she'd just won a prize. "That's exactly right. He's an asshole. I'm not surprised at all though. Rosalia said he's always been after sex. 'Always wanting to fool around' was how she put it."

"That's all guys," said the girl with the forehead curtain. "*He's* thinking about sex right now," she pointed out, gesturing to Zachary.

"Not with *you*," he shot back.

"You'd fuck anything that moves," said Ilya. "And maybe even things that don't move, if I know boys." With a wink towards Ramsey, she added, "And I do."

"Aw, come on," countered Zachary, "let's not fight. You and I have a lot in common: we both like fucking chicks."

Ramsey giggled and the other girl snorted.

"It's a wonder more girls in this school aren't lesbians if you're the best that we have to choose from. I'd rather bury my face in Ramsey's tits than see you without a shirt on." Ilya delivered her words nonchalantly, but she could see Ramsey flinch at the mention of her name.

"I bet you would," replied Zachary, the suggestive smile on his face again.

There was a pall as the four students considered each other. It was finally broken by Mr. Randall who expressed disappointment that they hadn't even started their lab.

"Take your slides and get your samples, ladies, Mr. Evans," he ordered.

Never cross a lumberjack, thought Ilya, as she scooted off her seat. Zachary and Bangs got their samples first and for a few moments she was left alone with Ramsey at the materials counter.

"So you weren't making out with Rosalia?"

Ilya winked. "We've kissed a few times," she admitted.

"I didn't think she'd be that kind of girl." Ramsey's voice was curious; they always started out that way.

"She's not. I mean, she just does what makes her happy. If kissing a girl doesn't make *you* happy, don't do it. But if it does…" She left the rest of the sentence unsaid as she handed a slide to Ramsey. Their fingers touched briefly under the glass.

"Don't people tease you though?"

"Who? Like Zachary? He's an idiot. If I cared what people like him thought, I'd never have any fun."

Ramsey bared her teeth in amusement.

Back at the lab table, Ilya went through the motions of loading her slide onto the microscope and staring vainly into the eyepiece. There were shapes in the water but no way to tell organism from flotsam. It occurred to her that she might be able to reconcile something on the slide, an immobile single-cell creature shaped like a horse.

"Hey, Ilya," said Zachary. "Do you want to look at my slide? It kinda looks like a little pussy."

Ilya turned her head just enough. "I'm already looking at a little pussy."

The smile on his face faded so quickly that his veneer actually stuttered.

"You're kind of a bitch, you know that?" he asked after stewing for a minute.

Ilya returned to her specimen. "You're just mad I'm not a pushover like your little cheerleader girlfriends. Empty heads and spread legs—that's all they are."

"It's not just stupid girls," Ramsey remarked. "Some of them are special needs kids, too. Why do you think they're always practicing their spelling?" She shared a private smile with Ilya.

Dump one project in first period; gain another before the day was out. Ilya regarded Ramsey carefully, examining each of her features while her attention was focused on the microscope. Her face was squarer than Rosalia's and her high forehead left something to be desired. Still, there was potential in her eyes, an unspoiled optimism that Ilya wanted to make her own. There was curiosity too, which meant she might be a willing partner instead of a girl so hung up on the socially accepted standards that she was too terrified to stray into unfamiliar territory. Besides, the mystery of the plunging tan-lines ate at Ilya, begging to be solved.

Just as a new fantasy was taking root in her mind, the classroom door opened and in walked the dreaded ex herself.

From the back of the classroom, Mr. Randall asked, "Can I help you, Ms. Collier?"

"Um, yeah," she mumbled. "I left my palette in here..." She trailed off, pointing down the row of lab tables.

"Go ahead," he replied, beckoning her into the room.

She looked rattled. The way her eyes kept darting around the room, the way her arms hung motionless at her side, all of it spoke to a deep trauma burning away inside her. Maybe their moment in the shower had been too much for her. Crinkling her nose, Ilya wondered if she actually felt remorse for hurting Rosalia like that.

The moment passed without resolution.

Rosalia avoided Ilya's gaze as she walked between the two lines of lab tables. There were already whispers spreading through the room. A squeaky voice even called out, "Didn't get enough this morning?"

It made Ilya chuckle, since in her case, it was true. It could have gone so much better, she thought. She'd had unrestricted access to Rosalia's body and that stupid bitch had messed everything up. It was her fault she got hurt. If she'd just played along and accepted Ilya's advances, then everything would have turned out okay. She'd be happy instead of sad, maybe even elated in a post-orgasmic haze.

When Rosalia reached her row, she broke right and approached Ilya, who turned sideways to greet her old friend. Without thinking, she blurted out, "Did you miss me?"

Ilya thought it would have been funny to see the reaction on Rosalia's face, but her veneer had morphed into anger even before the last word came out. The next thing she knew, Rosalia's fist had caught her square on the nose, filling her eyes with a million sparks that her body tried to counteract with a spray of tears. Dazed and half-blind, she only remembered Rosalia when the girl's hands gripped the side of her head. Long fingernails dug into her scalp and then tangled themselves in her hair. She felt herself moving sideways and then being off balance. A moment later, something hard and black was slamming into the side of her head. The lab table created an intense pain on the right side of her face. Then the hands disengaged and moved to her shoulders, to her neck, where they carved out little lines in her skin: some drawing blood, the others just stinging.

The classroom erupted into panic and Ilya felt people all around her trying to stop the fight. Someone was pulling her backwards, away from the attacker she could no longer see through the tears. Wiping at her eyes, her arms shaking badly, she cleared enough away to see two boys holding Rosalia and dragging her away. Mr. Randall was shouting, desperately trying to restore order, but all Ilya could do was stare into those hateful eyes.

It was a side of Rosalia she had never seen, a counter-balance to the mousy girl whose interests were artistic and generally passive. But this, this raw emotion, raw power, there was something exciting about it.

And despite the blood and the pain, Ilya couldn't help but want her all over again.

SIXTY
RUSSO

For hours, Russo watched the spectacle unfold from the safety of the diner across the street. Sitting in a booth by the window, he sipped water from a sweating glass and pretended to read his palette, but all he could think about was the crowd forming by the alley next to the Holly Street Hilton's parking garage. There were so many gawkers, obese Eastonians who waited in anticipation of another onlooker so they could be the one to tell the story, incomplete as it was.

The little boy jumped from the top floor.
I heard he was suicidal because he was fat.

They were all plausible, but they were all wrong.

The way Ruiz had played it up, Russo thought a covert team of black-clad agents would descend on the parking garage and cover up any trace of the incident. Instead, it was a standard cruiser that showed up first, with two uniforms that looked bothered to be there. They disappeared into the alley and a few minutes later, the smaller of the two came back to the car and retrieved a roll of yellow cordon tape from the trunk. She strung it up across the alley and then knelt on the pavement. When her hand touched the ground, a red barrier grew out into the sidewalk, flowing like water up a beach, causing the nearby pedestrians to scurry away as it approached their feet.

After that, the number of uniforms just kept growing. A fire truck got involved for some reason, followed by an ambulance. Two med techs in flashy orange vests jumped out of the back as soon as it came to a stop. Their urgency surprised Russo; did they really think they could resuscitate Jalay? It was a regular circus, far more attention than Jalay could have ever garnered when he was alive.

The show lasted only a few hours, though a solitary uniform remained for much of the afternoon, leaning against the evercrete columns and discouraging passersby from getting too close. By the time Ruiz slid into the booth around two o'clock, Russo was getting antsy. Already, the waitress was giving him dirty looks for taking up space.

There was something cold about the nonchalant way Ruiz sat across from Russo. If he had any desire to see the crime scene, he wasn't giving into it. The only thing he seemed to care about was Jalay's palette, which he had taken from

Russo the moment he sat down. He had been trying to guess Jalay's password for a while.

"You want me to try?"

"Try what?" replied Ruiz without looking up.

"I knew Jalay better than you. I could probably guess—"

Ruiz didn't smile, but there was a haughty undertone when he said, "Yeah, I'm already in." Clucking his tongue, he explained, "I know every word that Chapman has ever reconciled. All I had to do was play them back one at a time. Sometimes intelligent brute force is the best approach."

"So…"

"I'm almost done," said Ruiz, agitated. He swiped his finger a few more times before dropping the palette on the table. Pushing it towards Russo, he pulled his own palette from his jacket and began reconciling his notes. "I need you to look for information, find out how much he's leaked and to whom."

"Haven't you done that already?"

A grin in return. "Yes, but now I want *you* to do it. This is how we learn, Rivera. You'll want everyone he's talked to. That's message boards, mail, instant messages, anything that connects him to other people."

"Then what?"

A reconciled flame passed in front of the agent's pupils. "Then we close up the wound before Vinestead loses too much blood."

It was hard to see that kind of future, hard to see the consequences being as dire as the agent made them out to be. "And if it does?"

"Well," said Ruiz, standing, "then all of this goes away. You think it's bad with people like us running the show? Wait 'til we're gone, then you'll see. Or won't see…"

He left without elaborating, leaving Russo to consider all the ways the world could be better or worse without the veneer. Personally, his goal was still the same—to have a power that other people didn't, to have an advantage that would put him in another league. All of that depended on the veneer. Without it…

Looking outside again, Russo began to catalogue the reconciled surfaces, from building façades to the paint jobs on vehicles. If the fire truck didn't have a unique shape, if the ambulance weren't just a box on wheels, then without the veneer, no one would know what they were for. It might not be that shocking in the short term, but to get everything back to the way it was, to make signs useful again, to make computers replace portals, would take time and resources beyond what Easton had.

That was the point that Ruiz was trying to make by leaving him with a bleak outlook. Russo needed to believe in the veneer, believe in its necessity so that he would defend it with his life because really, it *was* his life.

Russo touched the edge of the palette and flipped the image around. Jalay's start page settled onto the screen, a mix of small icons spread unevenly around three larger ones in the center. A folder on the left read *Jubs* and when he clicked into it, a grid of smaller icons filled the screen, beige folders with photographs hanging out of them, providing a preview of their contents.

Exhibit A: Jalay had a lot of porn.

It wasn't much of a surprise; for years he had watched his late accomplice browse the network for titty pics. What he hadn't noticed was how meticulous an organizer Jalay had been, with all of the folders tagged with keywords. Along the right side of the portal was a list of those tags, followed by a parenthetical number indicating how many photos it applied to.

Asian.

Nipples.

Rosalia.

Russo smirked at the name and tapped it with his finger.

Exhibit B: Jalay had no explicit porn. All of the images tagged with Rosalia's name resembled her in some way, but they were all tame. The most objectionable thing Russo found was a folder full of girls holding skulls in front of their pussies.

Fucking Jalay wasn't even good at collecting porn.

Wiping away the harmless images, Russo returned to the start page and pulled up the instant messenger. Diving back a week, he started going through the conversations, few as they were. When he came upon Sebo Kahani's name, his eyebrow jumped. Since when did Jalay associate with Deron's crew? Curious, he pulled up the chat logs and saw that no messages had passed between them, only a file called Jordan. The conversation after that was similarly blank, except the file's name was Felicity.

Clicking on the filename brought him to a folder full of still photos that showed a young girl sitting at a desk, her oversized tits deforming against the edge of the light wood. Ah, thought Russo, the memory coming back to him. It was the Roommate software that Jalay had pirated off the network. Evidently, he had given it away to Sebo.

But why?

Russo put the palette down and looked over at the alley again. The uniform had moved under an awning as the skies resumed their downpour. Jalay wasn't the kind of guy that shared his treasures willingly. If he had given them to Sebo, then it was probably in exchange for something. Information, perhaps, or protection?

"Dumbass," whispered Russo, imagining Deron, Rosalia, Sebo, and Jalay all engaged in a big group hug, unaware that Jalay was a virus, a bug that would bring nothing but pestilence to their perfect little world.

He *was* infected, but with information that put him in danger. And if he shared it with anyone, all of them would have to die. That caused a smile to creep its way onto Russo's veneer. Even if they *didn't* know anything, he could just claim they did, say it was for the protection of Vinestead. Sitting back in the booth, Russo took a deep breath.

He could get rid of them all at once.

Letting his lungs drain slowly, he reflected on the providence of it all. Everything was coming together to achieve something he thought impossible. It even went beyond Deron's circle. Russo could accuse anyone, fake any evidence he needed, and have that person removed, banished, or even killed.

Now *that* was power.

Spurred along by the sudden euphoria, Russo picked up the palette once more and scrolled through the remaining conversations. Finally, he came upon an unread message, from Sebo no less.

"If you see Russo," Sebo had written, "tell him Deron wants to meet him on the football field at ten tonight. I think he wants to fight him."

Russo laughed loudly, garnering a strange look from the waitress behind the counter. Despite her disapproving stare, he continued to chuckle. Already he was feeling stronger for knowing what most people didn't, but this was positively magical, as if it wasn't just the veneer that bent to his will. He could actually control people and events…

Destinies.

"You just killed your friend," Russo reconciled into the message window. He sent it off and wiped the palette clean. Let Sebo chew on that for a while.

"You're going to pay for that, right?" asked the overweight waitress. She had appeared at his side and was tapping a recently reconciled ticket on the table.

"Sure," said Russo, pulling a cold french fry from his plate. He flashed his most insincere smile and thumbed the bill, sending it flittering into oblivion.

"In my day, we didn't miss school unless we were sick."

"Yeah, I know," replied Russo, scooping up Jalay's palette. "And you typed on real keyboards and watched TV with special glasses."

Outside, he paused under the awning as the rain beat down around him. The uniform across the street looked up for a moment as if standing guard at a crime scene were a major inconvenience for him.

Get used to it, thought Russo. The day isn't over yet.

SIXTY-ONE
ROSALIA

It wasn't so much that Ilya had taken advantage of her, it was that somewhere deep down, Rosalia had known what was happening and didn't do anything about it. The words, the looks, and the reconciled memories all told of a manipulative friend with ulterior motives. The veneers should have clued her in; she should have recognized them as real memories instead of just idle fantasy. A part of her had tried to argue that Ilya was bad news, but it hadn't received any acknowledgement until Rosalia sank to the floor of the shower stall and screamed until she was hoarse. Then, the doubt came back, found purchase in her conscious mind, and took over.

Out from under the warmth of the shower, shivering against the cold tile, Rosalia tried to decide what to do next, but all she saw was the moon, growing larger in the sky, its presence felt on Earth as a disruption in gravity. Buildings crumbled, but not to the ground. Every crack let loose a section of evercrete that floated up and away until it became a speck in the black night. It was just her, standing in a field of knee-high grass, watching the city from a distance as the tips of skyscrapers disintegrated. The solitude surprised her; usually there were other spectators, confused and frightened, just like her. Then the truth became clear.

The end, whatever its form, was lonely.

That's when the meaning of the dream finally materialized. She was alone because it was only her world that was breaking down, though now she could only refer to it as changing. There was destruction, sure, and that aspect had evoked such dread in her that she couldn't face what came next, couldn't imagine what horrors awaited after the Earth had crumbled. Herself broken, heaped on the shower floor, she was powerless to stop the fantasy, but the lack of resistance allowed the dream to carry to the moments after the pain. She had never considered that the universe would once again find equilibrium, that after the torment and upheaval, things would settle down into a new veneer, something random and perfect in the way only nature could reconcile.

By the time Rosalia realized that all was not lost, she had wasted away most of the school day. She came out of the haze with a newfound desire for vengeance, a desire to try her new veneer. This one, she told herself, as she simply walked out of seventh period, would be stronger than the previous revision. It would stand up for itself, exact justice where justice was due. Grand words, visions of the new Rosalia, all of it propelled her forward, through the halls, past the teachers with their stupid questions.

"To get my revenge," she wanted to say every time they asked where she was going. No one tried to stop her, not after the years of good will she had built up as a model student.

A parting gift from the old Rosalia.

Mr. Randall's Biology class was filled with a dense fog, a white haze of anger that didn't clear up until she was sitting in Principal Ficcone's office listening to him prattle on about his disappointment, each sentiment echoed annoyingly by her step-mother. Rosalia accepted her suspension with pleasure, but the ride home with Lynn was nothing short of torture. She complained nonstop about being embarrassed at work and having to pick up her delinquent daughter at school.

Not *your* daughter, Rosalia reminded her.

Just wait 'til Michael hears about this.

The threat made Rosalia wonder what her dad would think, how he would react to his daughter's sudden interest in violence. It was only an hour after they got home that he walked through the door, a stern look on his veneer that broke when he saw Rosalia sitting on the couch in the living room. His desire was to comfort her; she could see that plainly. But then the bitch started talking and her dad sighed, communicating his reluctance in a way only Rosalia understood. He sat down in the recliner opposite her and waited for an explanation.

"I'm not telling you with *her* here," she had decreed, but Lynn remained unmovable on the loveseat. Crossing her arms tightly, Rosalia leaned back on the couch and looked away.

Michael pleaded with her, made several efforts to coax the information out of her. And to his credit, she found herself wanting to spill the whole story, tell him about the seduction and the betrayal, things she couldn't imagine telling anyone, even Deron.

What felt like five seconds of silence to her must have been several minutes, because eventually her dad gave up, stood, and walked to the foot of the stairs before telling her she was grounded for two weeks. As he started upstairs, Lynn rose and trailed behind him, also pausing next to the handrail to dramatically deliver her *hope it was worth it* line.

Yeah, thought Rosalia, nodding once they were gone. It was worth it.

Relieved, Rosalia headed up to her room and shut the door softly behind her. The previous anxiety was gone, and she was surprised to find herself smiling a little. She knew that a broken nose didn't change anything, didn't undo Ilya's trespass, but the memories from that time were just veneers, just images and sounds and smells that could be reconciled over, replaced with something more pleasing to the soul.

On the wall by her desk, she reconciled a large portal. One by one, she brought up the pictures she had made that contained Ilya. And one by one, she deleted them forever, wiping out the person, the moment, and the memory. As the hours slipped by, she saw three weeks of constant worry reduced to a photo stream. Occasionally, a flash of skin caught her eye.

Ilya pretending to drop her towel.

Ilya offering to straighten Rosalia's shirt.

So many excuses for two girls to touch.

A reconciled memory showed the two of them standing in separate stalls, talking over the tile wall about Deron, about how far she had gone with him sexually. Not that it was any of her business.

"Never happened," said Rosalia, reducing the picture to a dark mess.

The next one showed the two of them on a tram, Rosalia slumping under the effects of Mellow. Ilya had her arm around her shoulder, her hand hanging to the side of Rosalia's chest, brushing up against her every time the tram rocked.

Never happened.

Then it appeared, a shadowy still from an unremembered night.

Rosalia was reclining on the bean bag chair in the center of the room, her head flung backward at an odd angle, moving with the heaving of her exposed chest. Someone had unbuttoned her shirt, unhooked her bra, and pushed it out of the way. Next to her, Ilya was on her side, using her head to pin down one of Rosalia's arms. One hand held her under the shoulder while the other rested above the unfastened buttons of her jeans.

It wasn't so much the appearance of her underwear that startled her, nor was it the proximity of Ilya's fingers. What made her stomach ache was the fact that she had reconciled the image at all, that part of her had been awake and evidently willing to participate. There were no cameras in the room, no way to see this event except from the inside. In a way, it wasn't how the moment looked, but how it felt.

Rosalia forced herself to look at the scene, to stare and wonder if she could ever forget something so horrible.

Then she remembered—it never happened.

After that, the deletions went quicker. All that remained were little candids, easily discarded moments that meant nothing to her. Time passed, the sun set beyond the windows, and soon she had banished every last picture of Ilya from her portal. True, the memories remained, but those would fade with time. It wouldn't be as difficult as trying to forget Deron, a fact that became all too clear the moment she brought up his pictures.

He was in everything stretching back for months. Deleting him would be like deleting a whole chunk of her life.

A photo flashed from the first few weeks of their relationship. It was easier then, with no soul-crushing emotions to deal with, no looming sexual tension to muddle their thinking. Minutes went by and the command to delete the picture went unheeded by the portal.

It wouldn't respond, she realized, because she didn't believe in what she was asking it to do. There was no deleting Deron. Then, more to the point, there was no leaving him.

She had made a mistake.

Panic rose in her chest as she pulled her messenger from the sidebar and brought up her contact list. She found Sebo's name and opened a window. A few seconds later, his reddened face appeared on the screen.

"Rosa," he said, wiping at the sweat on his forehead. "How's the right hook?"

She blushed, recalling the satisfaction of hitting Ilya.

"Everyone's talking about it," Sebo continued. His frame went dark for a moment and when it returned, he was sitting on the edge of the bed and pulling a shirt on.

"I forgot to tell you something today, but you can't be mad."

"Is it about Deron?" he asked, a knowing smile on his face.

"Yeah, he—"

"I know, he's back." His eyes drifted off to the left for a moment. Then, in mock accusation, he said, "I heard you guys had a *cli-mac-tic* reunion."

Rosalia groaned. It was too soon after the deed for Deron to be spreading stories. "For him, maybe," she offered, hoping her words didn't sound too bitter.

"Burn," said Sebo, scrunching up his face. "Is that why you dumped him?" He shook his head dismissively. "You owe him another chance. No one hits a home run their first time at bat."

"I didn't dump him," Rosalia asserted. "We separated for mutual reasons."

"Not likely. I've never known that boy to love anything more than he loves you. Twenty bucks says you saw something you didn't want to see and bailed. Or you saw that he couldn't see…"

"What does it matter? He's leaving and never coming back. It was either go with him or stay here. What would you have done?"

"No, no," said Sebo, putting up his hands. "I've never touched his cock. The same rules don't apply."

"Asshole! It wasn't easy!"

"He loves you." There was a strange tenderness to his voice as his eyes drifted away again. He seemed to nod approvingly at something off screen. Then he growled, "You could have at least said goodbye to him."

"I wanted to," she whispered, defeated. Wanted to, but not anymore. Now she wanted him back, wanted him to ask the question again so that she might say yes.

"I just can't believe he went to you first."

"You've never…" She choked on the words.

"Yeah, his cock, I remember," said Sebo, chuckling. "He told me he was coming back to school. After tonight… Oh, fuck!" He stood and pulled his jacket from a chair.

"What, Sebo?"

"He's going to be at the football field tonight. He's going to fight Russo."

The memory of her fingers on Deron's face flashed in Rosalia's head. Russo had beaten him to the brink of death. And now he was going back for more.

"At ten," added Sebo, looking around for something.

Rosalia glanced at the time along the top of the portal. It was already five 'til.

"Why is he fighting Russo?"

Sebo shrugged, started to fidget. "He wouldn't say, just that it was the only way back. He says he's doing it so he can be with you."

Son of a bitch.

Standing quickly, she looked at her bedroom door and wondered if she could just walk out of the house without anyone noticing. Then she realized Sebo was doing the same. "That's where you're going, aren't you?"

"Fuck yes it is," said Sebo. "I'm not going to let Russo kill him."

Rosalia didn't even bother to close the portal. As she rushed down the stairs, she heard Sebo's voice, very far away, calling her name.

SIXTY-TWO
DERON

The concession stand next to the football field was open to the elements, but Deron managed to find a spot in the back where the rain couldn't reach. The little shack couldn't keep the breezes from coming in or do anything to muffle the thunder booming overhead, but at least it was dry. He had slipped in just after dark, at what time he couldn't be sure. All he knew was that the thick clouds had brought nightfall a little sooner than normal, leading him to estimate he would spend a good three or four hours curled up on the prep counter.

Deron shivered uncontrollably for seconds at a time but not because of the weather. Each little attack coincided with his thoughts of Russo, of the impending confrontation that for all its planning could still end in a fight. The symmetry was not lost on him.

It started with Russo.

It would end with Russo.

Although a hefty price, Deron was determined to pay it if it meant putting things back the way they were. His only regret was not preparing ahead of time for another violent encounter. He wasn't sure when Agent Ruiz would make his appearance, which gave Russo anywhere from a few seconds to several minutes to beat Deron back to the first grade. Just the thought of taking another punch to the face made him cringe, made his stomach gnarl with anxiety. On a purely physical level, he was no match for Russo, which severely limited his tactics. Running was not an option; he would have to take the beating as best he could and hope that the agent showed before Russo put him into another coma.

A spike of lightning illuminated the small concession stand, exposing the gray containers on the wall. The empty bins made Deron think of food, but with football season over, all that remained were condiments and non-perishables. In his mind where he could still reconcile reliably, he imagined a dinner table full of his mom's cooking. And though it smelled great and looked appetizing, all he could do was stare at her face as she sat there smiling back at him, delighted that her efforts had brought him joy. Her expression was comforting, and it drew his thoughts towards home, then his bedroom, and finally his bed. He figured everything would be okay if he could just get back between those sheets.

The sound of faraway voices kept him from nodding off. They were masculine but indistinct, barely audible over the rain pounding on the roof. Deron sat up slowly, tried to ignore the cries of his muscles as they unwound from the fetal position. Straining to see through the downpour, he made out two figures standing at midfield. They were looking at each other and at the waterlogged grass around them. One of them was unmistakably an agent; Deron had become adept at picking out their trench coats. The other, cloaked in a hooded slicker, was slightly smaller. His forward lean, that aggressive posture, identified him as Russo. The rain was dripping from his arms like two spouts of water, curling over clenched fists. The sight of Ruiz and Russo together brought on a wave of relief, made Deron think for one beautiful moment that things might work out painlessly after all.

Emerging from the stand, Deron stepped into the rain and went from moderately dry to soaked in the span of three steps. The muddy grass squished under his feet, making the walk seem surreal, as if he would never get to the center of the field, would never see Ruiz slap the cuffs on Russo. It was sweet revenge, not the kind his enemy deserved, but revenge nonetheless. He wondered idly if he would have to participate in the trial, take the stand, and give testimony about… a murder?

It was only then the agent's words hit him. What the hell was Russo up to while he was away? It was unlikely that a thug like Russo would be capable of actually taking a life. Murder wasn't something a student from Easton Central did. Shaking his head, Deron tried to remember the last time he'd even heard of a high school student killing someone, but there was nothing. If it were true, if his archenemy had really crossed the line, then Deron's plan of capturing him had been more dangerous than he imagined. As he got closer to midfield, he couldn't shake the feeling that he should have stayed hidden.

"Deron," said Agent Ruiz. "I was beginning to think you wouldn't show."

"I got him," he replied, looking over at Russo, bewildered by the smile on his shadowy face.

"*I* got him," repeated Russo.

The agent nodded thoughtfully and looked from one boy to the other. Rain dripped down the side of his face, but it could have been blood and he would have taken no more notice of it. His eyes seemed set in determination, as if he were puzzling his next move.

Deron offered some encouragement. "Aren't you going to arrest him?"

Russo's eyes flickered, but his smile didn't waver. Speaking through gnashed teeth, he said, "I want to take care of him myself."

Again, Ruiz nodded as if considering Russo's nonsensical statements. "You're both right," he said at last, clapping once and sending a spray of water between them. "And you're both wrong."

"You said," protested Deron.

"I know what I said. To both of you. But the truth is that I only need one resolution to close this case. Either I bring in Russo Rivera for the murder of an agent or I silence Deron Bishop and stop him from exposing the veneer." He moved his hand to his chin and put on a show.

For the first time, Russo's façade faltered, showed disappointment. Had he been trying to deliver Deron to Ruiz?

Staring into the agent's eyes, Deron tried to remember the way they looked the night of Paramel. Of course, then they had been a veneer, the reconciled friendliness that Ruiz *wanted* people to see.

"I don't care," said Ruiz, waving his hand. "You two sort it out." A faux smile flashed on his face. "The winner gets my vote." Turning, he headed off towards the bleachers and sat down.

"The winner of what?" asked Deron.

"Don't worry about it," replied Russo, "you're not going to win." The raincoat slipped off his shoulders, revealing a thin t-shirt that turned transparent instantly.

Deron took a step back as Russo faked his first attack. His fist stopped midway and hung there.

"It remembers you," he said.

There was barely time to think before the real fight began, but Deron's brain crammed all it could into that microsecond. It was still reeling from the agent's suggestion that they fight it out. Did he not know how unfair that was? He knew Russo would win, so why not just take Deron away and be done with it? Another beating wasn't necessary.

What *was* necessary was to lift his arms to his face to protect his nose, but by the time the message made it to his muscles, Russo's fist had already clipped him on the chin. Deron retreated as best as he could under the barrage, but Russo had been waiting a long time for this moment and was savoring every second of it. There was pain, but Deron knew his body would overcome it eventually, settle into a numb haze. But that was a bridge he had yet to cross.

Russo laughed as he feinted with his right arm and then tested the waters with a kick to the shin. Deron felt the pain ripple up his leg and had to fight the urge to lower his hands. Surprisingly, he saw them reach down on their own, intent on rubbing away the hurt immediately. Russo picked up on the involuntary reaction and sent a left hook flying for Deron's face. It landed just below the cheek and as if to drive the severity home, a nearby bolt of lightning illuminated the world. Shutting his eyes and staggering backwards, Deron tried to regroup.

Out there, on the other side of darkness, Russo was taunting. Every part of his body was begging for a retreat, but Deron didn't listen. It was time to take control, at least put up some kind of fight. Just one hit would be nice, one moment of pain for Russo to show him that he could bleed like any other human.

Deron's eyes slid open, lubricated by tears or rain or both. He saw Russo standing a few yards off, looking different, maybe shinier. It wasn't until he noticed the school that he realized he could see the veneer again. There were lights on in the windows, reconciled strips on the ceilings that glowed night and day. Not only that, they were pulsing in time with his breathing, dimming on the intake and flaring as he breathed out angrily.

Angrily, he repeated to himself.

He imagined all the things he wanted to do to Russo, all the pain that he wanted to inflict, and with each image a little more of the world came into view. The bleachers took on their tan color, the white stripes on the football field became vibrant again, and Russo's eyes, those previously black portals, became the color of hate, a fiery red meant to instill fear in his enemies.

Dropping to a knee, Deron put a hand on the ground and tried to reconcile white veneer. At first, the grass merely shimmered, but with a guttural cry, it transformed into glossy porcelain. The change in the landscape made Russo stand out in silhouette.

Russo scoffed at the pointless display, but off to the left, the agent sat up a little straighter.

While Deron's head was turned, a boot appeared by the side of his face. Rolling to the left, he used the momentum to open the distance between them. He popped to his feet and recalled the window in his dad's apartment, the way he had reconciled the world outside without having to touch it. Gritting his teeth, Deron pushed the command out without knowing if it would truly work. To his surprise, the white field changed to black.

Russo advanced, but Deron shuffled away and turned the ground white again. Over and over, faster and faster, he made the two colors alternate until finally the agent was standing and Russo was shielding his eyes from the strobe.

"Fucking fight me!" screamed Russo.

Deron smiled at his frustration but then noticed Ruiz taking a knee and placing his hand to the ground. The original design returned; he had leveled the field again.

"Thank you," yelled Russo.

Taking advantage of the distraction, Deron rushed forward and swung his arm at Russo's chest. It made contact, but his forward momentum pushed the rest of his body into Russo and they fell to the ground. Tasting mud and water, Deron gasped for air, but strong arms already had him by the neck. His ability to breathe suddenly fell to zero.

Time slowed as his oxygen diminished. His thoughts turned to Rosalia, to what he would say to her if he didn't die right there in the mud.

Everything bathed in white, he imagined, blinking slowly to concentrate on the order. When he opened his eyes, he found not only the bleachers and the trees cloaked in pristine light, but also the rain drops that fell around him. They were encased in a white film and obscured everything behind them, compacting into two dimensions as another surface he could reconcile. Deron thought of a squad of regular uniforms, guns drawn, ready to shoot Russo to stop him from killing an innocent civilian. There was so much rain falling that they almost looked real. The question was whether Russo would believe his own eyes.

"Look," he gurgled, "They're here for you."

Russo finally looked away and upon seeing the police, his grip lessened. His shoulders bounced as if he were ready to put his hands up.

Slipping his arm out from under a leg, Deron punched up as hard as he could, knocking Russo's mouth shut in a large clap of teeth on teeth. The sudden attack sent him sprawling backwards onto the grass, dousing him in mud again. As he struggled to regain his footing, Deron unreconciled the surrounding uniforms, turning the world back to normal.

Russo stared at him, confused and angry.

Deron simply smiled in return.

SIXTY-THREE
ROSALIA

They had arrived to find Deron already wrestling with Russo and it was clear he was losing, overpowered by a bigger and stronger opponent. Now, hiding behind the end zone bleachers with Sebo, Rosalia watched in horror as Deron struggled to hold his own. She could barely stand to listen to it; his screams pierced her eardrums and each one weakened her knees. Rosalia wanted nothing more than to run to his aid, do what little she could to stem his anguish, but Sebo was gripping her tightly, had his sturdy arms wrapped around her body. That she couldn't break free was akin to torture—he was forcing her to watch Deron die at the hands of a maniac.

Then something happened, something so strange and bewildering that she stopped trying to break free, even felt Sebo's grip loosen in shock. One moment, Easton was as she knew it, sparkling veneers under a torrent of rain. The next, a circle of brilliant light expanded out from under Deron, overtaking everything in its path. It crossed the entire field in a matter of seconds, flashed past Rosalia and Sebo, forcing them to shut their eyes against the blinding glow. Like looking into the sun, it took a moment for the green and blue afterimages to fade, but when Rosalia could see again, she found a world bathed in a pristine veneer, a white canvas that stretched from horizon to horizon. Even Sebo's arms draped loosely around her had taken on the appearance of porcelain, virtually indistinguishable from her own body.

The sturdy texture bent unnaturally when Sebo let go of her to examine his arms. They stood apart, looking at their bodies and then at each other. The white had seeped into every crevice of Sebo's skin, turning his face into a featureless mannequin or some kind of doll that had yet to be painted. His eyelids moved as porcelain could never move, blinking slowly, exposing the miniature billiard balls underneath. They were so empty, so devoid of soul, that Rosalia wondered if anything still lived behind them.

His entire persona, wiped clean from his body, leaving only a blank template, a palette on which to reconcile a whole new life.

More unsettling was the fact that no matter how hard she tried, she could not reconcile herself back to normal. The foreign veneer was tenacious, preventing her from restoring her skin color. There were variations on her arm, but those were caused by the raindrops that accumulated there before flickering white themselves.

Sebo let out a croaking sound where there should have been coherent words. Staring at his face again, Rosalia watched the field of rain between them flash opaque. The new veneer moved in waves, radiating out from the school, towards the neighborhoods, towards downtown. There, pearlescent towers faded, hidden behind a curtain of veneered raindrops.

It's everywhere, she observed. Everyone in the city must have seen it.

And just like that, something sucked it back in, drew off the white sheets to let the world shine through again. As it passed over Sebo, she saw astonishment return to his face and the paralyzing confusion in his eyes. It had been a simple veneer after all; nothing underneath had changed.

When Rosalia looked back at Deron, she was surprised to see an army of uniforms encircling him. As frightening as it was to watch, she could see a stronger fear emanating from Russo. He was so distracted that Deron was able to get in a few jabs, ending with a kick that separated the two of them, left them staring at each other and gasping for air. She took a step forward and once again felt Sebo's hands around her arm.

With an angry glance backwards, she hissed, "Let me go!"

"No," he pleaded and then motioned with his head. "That's the agent who's been snooping around all week. He should be stopping this but he's not."

"Then let *me*!"

"Something is going down," he replied, spitting rain. "If we go out there—"

"It's Deron for fuck's sake!" She couldn't stop the tears from erupting.

"And you dumped him," he reminded her, his fingers tightening their grip.

Rosalia sank to her knees, immersing them in the standing water. Sebo first tried to hold her up, but when he realized that she wasn't trying to escape, that the strength had simply left her body, he went down on one knee beside her. She buried her face in his chest, wanted to stay there forever in the unlikely comfort of his arms. But over the thunder, over her own sobs, she heard the continued grunting and yelling. The fight had resumed and Rosalia couldn't stop herself from looking.

There were more than a dozen Derons standing in a loose circle around Russo. Moving as one, they rotated around a common enemy while Russo looked frantically from one apparition to the next.

A mirage, thought Rosalia. The uniforms had just been a veneer, but reconciled on what? The white raindrops flashed in her mind and suddenly she understood.

She had always considered herself a great reconciler, but it was humbling to bear witness to Deron's power. He was doing things with the veneer that shouldn't have been possible, things that went far beyond the reconciling he did while stoned or tired, the great compositions that came from deep in his subconscious.

Reconciliation without physical contact.

Change on a whim.

One of the Derons darted out of the crowd to kick Russo in the back. He stumbled forward before regaining his balance. Meanwhile, the real Deron slipped back into place with his reflections.

"What is this?" she heard Russo scream. The question wasn't rhetorical; he seemed to be asking the agent directly. "How can he do this?"

Because he's better than you, asshole!

Again, Deron struck, this time landing a right cross to the side of Russo's face. He howled in response, swung wildly with his arm, but hit nothing. Slowly, the sea of Derons calmed down, came to a standstill. They crossed their arms and in perfect synchronicity, shook their heads.

Was that laughter she heard over the falling rain, a forced celebration coming from Deron?

He broke free and charged Russo with arms flailing, but his enemy was ready. A powerful leg came up and hit Deron in the stomach, but then slipped through falling rain, sending Russo tumbling.

Something resembling a smile slipped onto Rosalia's veneer; she felt the tears run under it and pool beneath her lower lip. "Is he really doing this?" she asked, glancing at Sebo.

He shook his head in response, stunned with disbelief. "He's broken," he muttered, sounding unsure of his words. "But he's not. The rules of reconciliation don't apply to him anymore."

Over and over, the Deron clones wreaked havoc on poor Russo. He was overwhelmed by sheer numbers, even though all but one were fake, conglomerations of rain that looked real enough to fool trusting eyes. Each punch took a little bit of strength out of Russo. Each kick to the legs or groin made him dip a bit closer to the ground.

"I had a life!" came the roar above the thunder.

Rosalia's smile pulsed; she knew she was a part of the life Deron was so desperately fighting for.

A barrage of swinging arms emerged from the crowd, stood longer in front of Russo than any other attacker. All Russo could do was block, hold his arms to his face, and hope it would end soon. Or maybe something else. The possibilities came to Rosalia one by one, filling her stomach with dread.

Then it happened, appeared in Russo's hand out of nowhere, a glinting length of pipe that Rosalia had never seen but so often imagined after Deron's stories. His arm was slightly behind his back, hiding the weapon from view.

She wanted to scream out, warn him, but it was too late. The pipe started on its course, arcing in a wide circle, bound for Deron's head. From everything she had seen in movies, Rosalia expected time to slow down, that the moment of Deron's undoing would drag on. Instead, it all happened in an instant, less than the entire lifetime of a bolt of lightning.

The pipe swung, but Deron dodged.

He kicked his foot up and leaned back dangerously. Somehow, his shoe caught Russo on the chin, sending him onto his back. Stunned, he tried to bring himself to his knees.

That's right, thought Rosalia. You pray, motherfucker.

The pipe sloshed through wet grass and came to rest at Deron's feet. He considered it for a moment.

Sirens broke over the constant beat of the rain, their headlights peeking out from behind houses, from behind the school, until they squared on the football field. Judging by their proximity, Rosalia guessed they had driven right up on the school grounds, ruining the expansive mall that separated the field from the main building. It wasn't until they dimmed the beams that she realized their flashing blue and red lights weren't like those of the Easton PD. All the cars were dark, with a single stripe that alternated the alerting colors.

"Agents!" whispered Sebo, as the car doors opened and three men in trench coats emerged. He pulled Rosalia further into the shadows of the bleachers, his heart beating hard against her back.

"Look at me!" she heard Deron yell. He was standing over the exhausted Russo, pipe in hand. A pulse of white shot out from his feet in a tangle of ribbons before fading away.

Poor Russo—he couldn't even lift his head.

Rosalia didn't know where to look. The newcomers were approaching, heading for the suddenly restless Agent Ruiz, but Deron had the pipe raised in the air, threatening to strike at any moment.

"LOOK AT ME!" screamed Deron, his voice breaking on the last word.

A flash of lightning illuminated the field and when it faded, it took the rest of Easton along with it. The grass lost color, along with the bleachers and the school and downtown beyond. The agents that had been so confident the moment before stopped in their tracks. All around them, the veneer crumbled, broke free of the surfaces it was supposed to enhance, falling to the ground like bits of paint, until they absorbed enough water and became transparent, then invisible.

Silence. Except for the rain. Except for the thunder.

This is how Deron sees the world, Rosalia told herself. This is what drove him away. For a fleeting moment, she understood why he had gone. They both had the same choice to make: accept a world without color, an empty, cold facsimile of reality, or break free for a place that still had some vibrancy. And while he had let her decide, chance had decided for him. Russo had decided for him. But now everyone in the city could share his handicap. The towers of downtown were dark, a shapeless gray lit only by the storm.

One boy had seen the truth and run away.

How would the whole city react now?

"That's enough, Memo!" barked one of the agents.

The voice drew Rosalia's attention back to the field, just in time to hear the gunshot ring out, just in time to see Deron's body flailing about unnaturally. He was spinning in the air, his screams not reaching her until he was halfway to the ground.

"Oh, fuck me!" said Sebo, scrambling to his feet. "Come on, we've gotta go!"

Rosalia sat there, dazed. There was no denying what had happened, not with the extended arm of Agent Ruiz pointing to where Deron had once stood, not with the gun's barrel still glowing.

"Der—" she tried to say, but all the air had gone. When Sebo began pulling her away, she protested by latching onto the bleachers. "He shot…" The words barely trickled out.

"And they'll do the same to us just for seeing it." He grabbed her face to get her attention. "There's nothing we can do now."

Rosalia slapped him as hard as she could with her open palm. Turning to run, she felt his arms grip her waist and then a feeling of weightlessness. Sebo stumbled under the added weight, but the football field receded nonetheless. She called out to Deron, her cries muffled by the wind.

The four agents approached midfield, came to stand near the fallen Deron and fatigued Russo. Agent Ruiz raised his gun in one slow and agonizing movement.

As Rosalia screamed her protest, beating her hands against Sebo's back, a rolling thunder boomed over Easton, drowning out the gunshot, drowning out the end to the boy she had known and loved.

The moon burst through the clouds and crashed into the Earth, erasing the possibility of reconciling with Deron.

There would be no reunion.

There wouldn't even be a goodbye.

SIXTY-FOUR
ILYA

The petite fist came flying out of the darkness, but Ilya was able to get a hand up and deflect it, sending Rosalia stumbling to her left. She regained her balance and reached out with razorblade fingernails, trying to rip the flesh from Ilya's bones. The only option was to retreat while the blood-tipped claws flailed about in front of her. Ilya took a deep breath and waited for Rosalia to press forward again.

Synapses that had been well-trained but seldom used sprung into action, directing her defensive parries in a delicate ballet that spread Rosalia's arms wide and opened her torso for attack. She brought a knee up and it landed with a dull thud between Rosalia's legs. The shock gave Ilya enough time to twist her body and catch her assailant on the chin with a right elbow cross. Blood splattered into the air and hung there for an eternity, Rosalia's cries echoing all the while.

Ilya opened her eyes to find moonlight filling her bedroom. In the shadows it created, she saw Rosalia's face, saw the anger and fire she remembered so clearly.

It was called a rage fantasy. They were considered a type of therapy at Dahlstrom Academy.

In all, there were seven psychiatric counselors at Easton's most prestigious and secretive school; Ilya went through three of them before being paired with a woman who gave her name only as Roberta. She had a refined veneer that exuded confidence, and unlike others in her field, she didn't take any of Ilya's bullshit. Roberta was brutally honest at times but could also be empathic. She taught Ilya not to deny her inner fury, but rather to channel it in another way, one suitable for the civilized world. Between those weekly sessions and Practical Applications of Eastern Philosophy, Ilya wasn't sure what she hated most about sixth grade.

Dahlstrom had taught her so much, but it was only useful as a student. As a normal person, the rage fantasy technique led nowhere, only served to fuel an anger that would just find some other way to come out. It didn't take long after getting kicked out to realize how different the worlds were, how the children of the academy were being trained for something else entirely.

Ilya sighed and winced.

Rosalia had broken her nose and shattered it so completely that the doctors were forced to put her under while they reconstructed it. Ilya awoke to the same face, the same flawless veneer hiding her true identity, but she could feel the change underneath. It was the throbbing that gave it away. Where she saw clear skin in the reflective portal, there were really bruises. Where the light bent awkwardly, there were scars, gashes from fingernails that had drawn blood. It had taken time to adjust her veneer and had it not been for the lingering pain, she might have considered going to school. No one would have known how bad the damage was, not unless they got in close and listened to her breathing.

She told her grandmother that she deserved a day off and got no argument. What she really wanted was time to think. To plot.

It wasn't the first night she had medicated herself into sleepy submission, but this time there were a couple of Oxycodones chasing half of a Mellow tab. The combination gave her strange dreams that alternated between past transgressions and future retributions—mostly drug-fueled rage fantasies. Rosalia was there, sometimes playing the victim, sometimes the aggressor. She went from swinging her fists to cowering nude in the corner of the shower in the blink of an eye. The alternating fear and contempt roused Ilya from her sleep throughout the night. Between the dreams and the pain, there was little rest to be had. Sometime in the early morning, the pills wore off and Ilya got up in the dark to find more.

Babushka had left the bottles on the dresser along with a glass of water. It was warm, but the pills went down just the same. On the second dose, Ilya grazed her nose with her hand, and it felt like someone had pressed a mask of hot pins into her face. She recoiled and tried to crinkle her nose, but that only brought more agony.

A sort of laugh escaped her lips.

Somewhere on her desk was half a tab of Mellow just waiting to be placed under her tongue. Ilya crossed the room, confident no one could see her walking around in her underwear through the open window. Though the desk was bathed in soft light, she could not find the tab amongst the clutter. More illumination would help, so she placed her hand on the wooden surface. In her mind, she thought about a thin veneer of Birch wrapped around a glowing orb with just enough yellow light bleeding through to bring out the grain in the wood. Then, like a song changing key, the orb broke apart, spread across a single plane. Through it rose a desk just like the one in her room. It took only a second to visualize the desk with its new color, but it would take the veneer even less to translate the command.

Ilya waited. Nothing happened.

She took a step back and then reached for the wall. The alternating stripes of white and red she imagined failed to materialize. It was then that she realized all the little touches were gone from the room. The soft glow of the baseboards for navigating the house at night, the dim amber of the analog clock on the wall by her bed, and the blue ambiance of the bathroom: all gone. Ilya looked from one surface to the other, searching out any sign of life. When her gaze fell on the window, she hurried towards it and scanned the outside world.

Everything was dark, even the porch lights on the houses across the street. No path guides glowed on the sidewalks. It was just the moon and the stars and a spark of red at the end of the street.

Ilya did a double take and pressed her cheek against the glass. She could barely make them out, twin lines of red fireflies stretching into the distance. It was the only color in the world.

Her robe was draped over the footboard and she pulled it on as she headed down the stairs. It looked different now, no longer the mix of emerald and topaz, but rather a dull white, almost gray. Not that she could see it well; the living room and foyer were both pitch black. Ilya navigated the room slowly until she was standing at the front door. Opening it allowed a breeze into the foyer, reminding her to tie the sash at her waist.

Though the rain had passed, the ground was still wet and puddles dotted the street. Gusts of wind tore at Ilya's robe, exposing her legs to the cold. She held the ends down as she walked, winding around the deeper wells, her feet becoming wet and numb within seconds. At the sidewalk, she turned right and headed towards the light. As she got closer, she noticed shadows moving down the street. Two of them walked in unison, pausing at the same time while a red flash exploded in front of them. Ilya could hear the sizzling from a distance.

"Excuse me, Miss," said a voice from her right.

Ilya jumped at the sound. She hadn't even seen the large man approach.

He was dressed like a uniform, but his clothes were gray and lacked the designatory stripe. From what she could see of his face, he was a younger guy with a crooked smile and some kind of rash on his cheeks. The image was intriguing and repulsive at the same time.

"Are you okay?" he asked. Something slipped from his sleeve, a short tube that glowed neon green. He held it up to her face.

Ilya raised her hand, but not before noticing his eyes go wide. "I'm fine," she replied, squinting against the light.

"I need you to return to your home. There is a dusk 'til dawn curfew in effect."

"What time is it now?"

He glanced at his wrist. "I don't know. I'm just here to keep the streets clear."

"And them?" Ilya gestured to the line of flares. "What are they doing?"

"Marking the road for emergency services."

Ilya shook her head. "But *why* are they doing that?" She felt emotion spill onto her face and tried to cover it up with a veneer.

The uniform cocked his head and studied her face. "Are you sure you're alright?"

"Why do you keep asking me that?" She pushed past him and walked as quickly as her bare feet would carry her.

"Miss!" Footsteps sounded behind her, closing fast. "You need to return to your home."

Ilya yelled over her shoulder, "Why?"

"For your safety!"

She stopped, turned, and put her hands on her hips. "From what? From who?"

The uniform squirmed; he wasn't used to being disobeyed. Maybe it was Ilya's appearance that gave him so much trouble. He could hardly resist staring at her, couldn't keep his eyes from scouting the curves of her breasts under the thin robe. Had she the energy, she would have used his lecherous nature to get her own way. As it stood, the Oxycodone had a hold of her system now, giving the world a dreamlike quality.

She remembered the bandages and cringed. The uniform wasn't ogling her; he was captivated by the assortment of cuts and bruises on her face. Except the only way he could have seen them was if Ilya chose to allow it. As far as she knew, she had spent more than an hour the night before reconciling the evidence away. Either the uniform possessed some kind of magic that allowed him to see under the veneer or…

Gravity doubled, then tripled, and Ilya felt herself falling. The uniform grabbed her before she hit the ground.

"Careful," he said, pulling her arm around his shoulder. He tried to stand her up, but the height difference was too much. With a grunt, he leaned her back and slipped his other arm under her leg.

Ilya took her first breath in what felt like minutes and found herself being carried back to her house. The stars were twinkling and multiplying in the sky, occasionally disappearing behind a fast-moving cloud. Out of the individual points formed larger patterns, even belts. There was so much detail and on such a large canvas.

"Which house is yours?"

She turned her head to the sound and saw the uniform's face again. He was smiling. Ilya resisted the urge to smile back.

"Miss?"

"Two down," she slurred. It was the kind of side effect she'd expect from Mellow, but not from just one dose of Oxy. Or had she taken two? Two down.

"You don't have to be scared. I've got you."

Ilya frowned. Her veneer should have been blank.

"Aw, don't be sad either."

"How are you doing that?"

The uniform returned his attention to the sidewalk. "I'm not doing anything. You're the one making faces."

"But how can you see my face? My veneer…"

He sighed. "I suppose there's no harm in telling you. There's going to be an official announcement in the morning."

Ilya felt the world dissolving around her. Stay awake, she told herself.

"Something happened to the veneer last night," he said, whispering.

Her heart stopped as they climbed the front steps. "What?"

The uniform nodded to the door. "I'd like to speak to your parents. Can you knock for me?"

"Just press the doorbell."

"There is no doorbell."

"Yes there is," she replied, trying to lift her arm to point to the portal beside the…

"No, you don't understand. There's no doorbell… there's no veneer at all."

SIXTY-FIVE
ROSALIA

Rosalia stood on the corner at the end of her street for fifteen minutes before she realized that the trams weren't running. Dawn had just broken over Easton and the usually busy street was empty. Friday mornings meant commuters heading to work and kids in the neighborhood heading to school, but neither graced the sidewalks or the benches at the tram stop. Instead, it was quiet, with nothing in the streets except spent flares and glow sticks that looked inert in the glare of the sun.

Everyone was still in shock.

She nodded to herself. It explained why people were hiding in their homes, unable to come to terms with the absence of the veneer. Rosalia was not immune to the uneasy adjustment; had Deron not prepared her for what it would be like, she might have run screaming into her closet and never come out. But then what was the loss of the veneer against a human life? Against Deron's life? The context lessened the blow and allowed her to accept what she believed in her heart to be a temporary setback. If it all came down to chips and computers, then they would find a way to bring back the veneer. Just send a guy down to replace a fuse.

The image made her laugh, but it was cut short by Deron's face merging with the overweight man in tight coveralls. It was that face alone that propelled her forward, made her feet move despite the distance involved. If she had to walk all the way downtown, then so be it. There had been enough time wasted screwing around. It was time to involve the police.

Sebo had tried to talk her out of it, but nothing he had said the night before made any sense. He stayed with her a long time, let her cry on his shoulder even as the color drained from the veneer. He left her with a promise that if she waited until morning, he would be at her door at dawn so they could go to the police together.

Rosalia didn't know why she had bothered believing him.

Still, his lack of commitment wouldn't stop her, nor would the tram service's inability to function without the veneer. So she walked and took solace in the smell of fresh rain, of dew-covered grass that refracted the sunlight in a million little sparkles. Deron had been right; there was so much to see in the world, if you knew where to look.

Crossing Marsh Street, Rosalia noticed a man walking down the sidewalk towards her. The way he moved suggested middle age, but his head swung from side to side like a child discovering a toy store for the first time. Though he smiled, his eyebrows pitched at the middle, as if he were going to cry. When he saw her, he froze for a moment before turning back the way he had come.

Another street down, she found a couple walking hand in hand and pointing to various plants and birds that had reemerged after the storm. They were dressed like the man, just like Rosalia, in gray clothes. They looked like they had both escaped from the same mental hospital.

Rosalia laughed, though she didn't understand why she found it so amusing. Maybe it was the justice of it all. Agents had taken Deron away from her and he had broken their precious veneer in return. Now everyone would feel the same fear. She certainly had.

Her mind wandered as she turned the corner towards Gillock Pond. She replayed the night in his dad's apartment, of her sneaking out of bed and out of Deron's life. She shivered. Had it really happened? Or had it all been some terrible dream? Looking down at her hand, at the bruises dotting her knuckles, she knew it had all been real—real enough to scar beneath the veneer.

Voices carried on the wind, mixing in with the sound of insects. It sounded like a crowd and sure enough, Rosalia discovered several people gathered together in the park.

She suppressed outrage at their presence. The intruders had trespassed on her special place, the only piece of Easton where she and Deron had ever felt together and alone. It was where they had shared their first kiss and first touch and…

So many firsts, thought Rosalia, unable to recall anyone interrupting their time together. What had changed that made people so interested now? Was Gillock Pond hiding something under its veneer?

"Look at you," said a woman in a nightgown.

"I know."

"Marshall, my hair! Why didn't you tell me?"

"Reflections," whispered Rosalia. They were all looking at their reflections in the pond. Mirrors were nothing more than reflective portals built in the veneer. With those gone, the only place to see a reflection would be…

It was so low-tech, yet so effective in altering a population's mood. The wonder on their faces made their eyes dance and their mouths curl. Deron had ripped out the backbone of an entire city and its people were reveling in it.

Nightgown woman noticed Rosalia and beckoned to her. "Come here, dear. Pretty thing like you has no reason to be afraid."

"I'm not afraid," she replied, trying to steel her veneer out of habit.

The woman's husband stepped aside and gave Rosalia room at the edge of the pond. After a deep breath, she leaned over and looked at her reflection.

Freckles—dotting her cheeks. Deron had never mentioned those. And her hair wasn't completely blonde; there were streaks of brown that set off the golden color. Reconciliation had changed the shape of her mouth over the years, adding contrast to define the edges. In the smooth water, she saw that her lips weren't as full as she had made them out to be. The difference was small, but Rosalia couldn't shake a decade of self-image so quickly. The girl in the pond looked like a long lost relative, someone known in childhood but sent away only to develop into a woman in the interim.

Then it hit her. The reflection was what Deron had embraced on the sidewalk after coming back for her. He saw her for what she really was and still wanted her.

"She's speechless." A wrinkled hand appeared on her shoulder. "You were expecting someone else, maybe?"

"Not really," she admitted, though it certainly wasn't the same girl she had seen in the mirror the day before.

"Well, at least you don't have any gray in your hair."

"I like it," said her husband. "It matches your clothes."

They tussled playfully behind Rosalia's back. All around her, people where shaking their heads at the aberrations they saw in the water. Some looked pleased; a few pressed tenderly at old wounds or unexpected wrinkles. Within minutes, there were was no free real estate left around the pond. The crowd grew and Rosalia gawked at the variation, at the imperfection of natural humans.

Ugliness has returned to Easton, she thought. If nothing else, it would make school more interesting.

"What is it, dear?" asked the woman.

Rosalia remembered herself. She had to get used to her emotions betraying her. "I just realized… I mean, everyone I know. I might not recognize them."

"Well, just think of it as a second chance to make a first impression."

"I've done that already," said Rosalia, thinking of Deron on the sidewalk.

"Oh. And how did it go?"

The memory made her smile. "He said I was beautiful."

"He sounds like a smart boy."

"But I don't know what he looks like."

The woman shrugged and looked at her husband. "Will it matter?"

The dagger in Rosalia's heart twisted. "Not anymore."

She withdrew from the crowd without waiting for a response. It was time to leave Gillock Pond and continue towards downtown, but Rosalia felt another attack coming on. They had plagued her all night, each one trigged by some lingering memory of Deron. This one spawned from the appearance of the swinging chair at the edge of the park; she was sure that if she sat down on it, she would keep to one side and leave Deron enough room to sit beside her.

Her heart pounded. Only one thing stopped the attacks: progress. So long as she kept pursuing justice, kept working towards the goal, the pain lessened. But then downtown was so far away, even by tram.

A sound Rosalia hadn't heard all morning broke out over the relative quiet. It was as much a surprise to everyone else; they all turned together to look at the gray cruiser creeping up the street. A uniform was hanging out of the passenger window with a bullhorn held to his mouth.

"This is a city-wide notice. A mandatory meeting will be held at Easton Central High School this morning. Please proceed to the school by foot. Do not attempt to drive as all traffic lights have stopped functioning. All of your questions will be answered by city officials. The Easton Police Department has no further information at this time."

He repeated the message twice before noticing Rosalia and her new friends. The cruiser stopped in the middle of the street and both uniforms got out.

"I haven't been to Central in ages," said the nightgown woman. She had drifted towards Rosalia out of some ingrained maternal instinct.

"What happened to the veneer?" shouted one of the men in the crowd.

The driver of the cruiser put his hands up. "Ladies and gentlemen, please proceed to the high school. Everything will be explained to you."

"Why can't I reconcile anything?!"

"Listen, we don't have anything to tell you. All we know is that the mayor has mobilized a response team and they are handling the situation."

"Are they going to fix the veneer?"

"They…" The uniform hesitated and looked around at all the faces. "They will answer that question at the school. I suggest everyone heads there immediately."

There were murmurs in the crowd, but almost everyone wanted to know whether the veneer would come back. Rosalia felt her own curiosity, but all she could focus on was the idling cruiser in the street and the providence of its arrival.

The police had come to her.

As the group broke up, Rosalia approached the uniforms.

"Excuse me," she said.

The driver looked her up and down. "Don't I know you?"

Rosalia recalled the lewd smile of the uniform standing guard in front of Deron's house. He had looked so official the moment before, but now there was no mistake.

"Aren't you the dick that tried to keep me from seeing Deron's mom?"

His partner laughed. "Well, she knows *you*, Aguilar."

"Whatever," continued Rosalia. "I want to report a crime."

"A crime? What kind of *crime* do you want to report?" They laughed in unison.

"Murder. There was this agent—"

Aguilar's smile broke. "What did you say?"

"An agent."

His partner crossed his arms and inched closer. "What about this agent?"

"He… he shot my boyfriend last night. I saw it happen."

"You're sure it was an agent?"

Rosalia nodded and tried to read the anxious looks on their faces.

The uniforms shared a glance.

Aguilar stepped to the side and motioned to the cruiser. "I'm going to need you to come downtown with us."

Relief rushed over Rosalia like a steady breeze.

Finally, she thought.

SIXTY-SIX
RUSSO

"Then what happened?"

Russo groaned and arched his back against the irritating tingle that was running down his spine. He had been on his side since they brought him in, unable to put pressure on his fractured shoulder blade. The nurses were alternating hot and cold, coming in every thirty minutes to adjust his bandages. Russo counted four different women, two wrinkled in the face and the others young but hardened. They all had the same humorless demeanor and despite their rehearsed concern, they seemed to share the same bad mood. It wasn't until the haggard uniform walked in and sat in the chair across from his bed that Russo joined the women in their agitation.

"I told you," he replied. "I don't remember."

The uniform looked uncomfortable with his little notebook and pen. His large hands held it awkwardly, unsure of how to write without slipping off the page.

"So you were out for a walk in the middle of a storm and the next thing you know, you wake up here?"

"Exactly."

The uniform scoffed. "With multiple contusions on your face and a broken scapula? You like look someone tried to hamburger you, son."

The image of Deron feeding Russo's broken corpse into a meat grinder flashed in his mind.

"Not to mention the shift nurse tells me you were pushed out of an agency cruiser in front of the ER. Care to explain that?"

Russo looked away from the spot he had been burning into the wall. "Agents dropped me off?"

"Oh, now you remember something?"

"Where are they now? Where's Ruiz?"

The uniform flipped to a new page and scribbled the name. "Who is Ruiz?"

"*Agent* Ruiz. He's the man that'll have your job for hassling me."

He laughed, exposing his yellowing teeth. "You really think an agent is going to protect you from me? You think I'm afraid of those Vinestead thugs?"

"You should be…"

"If anyone's going to protect you, it's good ol' Detective Pierce." He tapped his chest where his badge should have been. "So you tell me what really happened and I'll make sure everyone gets what's coming to them."

The tingle had turned into a full-on itch and Russo bucked in the bed, unable to find relief. He thought about asking the detective to scratch his back, but figured the man would take it metaphorically.

"I'm not talking to you," said Russo, gritting his teeth. "I'll only talk to Agent Ruiz."

"Why's that?"

Russo narrowed his eyes at Pierce. "It's above your pay grade."

"That's probably true. I don't get paid nearly enough to deal with pieces of shit like you. I'd take agents over juvenile delinquents any day of the week. At least they have some sensibility. It's just too bad there aren't any left." He paused, a smile on his face. "You haven't heard the news, have you?"

"Like I wouldn't notice the veneer is down?"

"Yeah, that." Pierce put the pen in his mouth and chewed it for a moment. "But no veneer means no portals and that means information is flowing slower than my morning piss. We've got cops rounding up people like cattle and herding them to the schools. Smarter people than you have already asked themselves: why aren't agents handling this?"

There was a fog where a cogent answer should have been. Logical thinking gave way to pride; the agents weren't helping because that kind of work was below them. They were the elite of Easton and had no business interacting with the commoners except to put them down or bring them up. Let the uniforms worry about the citizens. A good agent would only be concerned with Vinestead.

"I'll tell you why, son. Because every one of those fairy bastards skipped town overnight. There's a convoy half a mile long on its way to Sonora right now. And in case you haven't reconciled two and two, that means there's no agency oversight in Easton anymore. The guns are down and the gates are open. The bad times are back, Russo, and it's only gonna get worse unless I get these people under control. To do that, I have to know why Vinestead decided to jump ship. And from what I'm told, you're one of the last people to even see an agent. So be straight with me. How is all this connected?"

I have no fucking clue, thought Russo. He remembered everything before the fight, but the event itself was a blur. It was possible that he had been losing, that for one terrible moment, he was at his lesser's mercy. The image of Deron standing over him with a pipe raised in his hand lingered as the last frame of an unfinished memory. Something had happened to defer the pain and defeat. Something loud.

Russo recalled sirens in the distance, hard to pick out over the rain and the thunder. Though Deron screamed at him, he heard the shouting of older men arguing about something. The pipe went up.

Then a flash from the left—a gunshot.

Deron fell out of sight and the world trailed after him.

Agent Ruiz had saved him only to abandon him later? It made no sense.

"Are you aware that Jalay Chapman killed himself yesterday? He was your friend, wasn't he?"

Russo blinked away the questions.

"Strange thing though; I can't find any record of an Easton PD investigation. For some reason, all we have on file is an open-shut jacket signed by one Agent Memo Ruiz." He flipped through his notebook. "Now where do I know that name from? Oh yeah, he's the one that's going to protect your ass from my foot."

The detective paused as one of the older nurses came into the room. He stared at Russo as the woman injected something into his drip.

A warm sensation grew out from Russo's elbow. Within seconds, he felt the general awareness of his body dim, though the tingle remained.

"But you must know him better than I do, don't you, Russo? After all, you've spent a lot of time with Agent Ruiz. From what I can tell, you're the first person he talked to after Jalay's body was found. You two shared a table at Late Andy's Diner for an hour. What did you talk about?"

"Since when do you follow high school students?"

The detective sneered. "That's your true veneer, isn't it Russo? Your file says you suffer from an undeserved ego, but I thought the desk sergeant was just being flippant. But you *are* a little egoist aren't you? The whole city and everyone in it revolves around your wants and needs, right?"

"In a perfect world," replied Russo. He flexed his muscles under the blankets. If it came down to a fight, he wanted to be ready.

"No," said Pierce, chomping on his pen again. "In a perfect world, we wouldn't have to set aside an entire department just to keep tabs on Vinestead's goons. We tolerate them because we have to, not because we trust them. They're company men, Russo, every goddamn one of them. Type A personalities across the board: focused, goal-driven, and willing to do anything inside and out of the law if it serves Vinestead's interests. And every once in a while, we get a real sicko like Ruiz who treats Easton as his personal playground. I've tailed him personally for two years now and have never been able to make anything stick. But now I have you."

"You have shit," said Russo, smiling.

"What I have is footage of you pushing Jalay Chapman out of a parking garage."

Someone poured a bucket of ice down Russo's back.

"Do you know what the penalty for murder is, son? They don't kill you nice and easy; you're too valuable for that. No, they ship you off to Mexico where you'll eat beans and maggot rice for the rest of your meaningless life. I'm talking twenty-three hour lockdown in a six by six cell, not even a bucket to piss in. And that one hour a day you get to leave your cell? Best case scenario's that one of the bigger guys claims you for his own. Otherwise, they'll be passing you around like a tube sock, if you get my drift."

Detective Pierce glanced towards the open door, which Russo could barely see from his vantage point. He lowered his voice a bit as the footsteps of nurses rushed by.

"Are you feeling me?"

"Fuck you," said Russo. "I haven't been scared of uniforms since kindergarten."

He laughed, though it sounded forced. "No, Russo, I'm not trying to scare you. Like I said, that's all best case scenario. But if you keep up with the attitude, you might just end up in the ReTread program." Pierce waited a beat. "Never heard of that?"

"You're gonna tell me anyway."

"It's a complicated legal process, but after you're shipped south of the border, the Mexicans sell you back to Vinestead as cheap labor."

"And if I don't want to work?"

"You won't have a choice. That's where the ReTread part comes in. They'll wipe you clean, Russo. All your memories, every thought you've ever had, pretty much anything that makes you the little shit you are today: gone for good. After they blank slate you, they'll crate you down to Peru to build all of their little gadgets. On the books, Russo Rivera would be dead, but down south, you'd spend the rest of your life working your fingers to the bone."

"Bullshit." He tried to dismiss the idea. The way Pierce talked about it was too rehearsed, as if he'd given this speech before.

The detective shrugged. "Maybe. Maybe not. But I've seen that look on many a veneer in my time. Whether you want to admit it or not, you're scared of the possibility. Embrace that fear, Russo. No one will blame you. I'd be shitting the bed if I were in your shoes. Luckily for you, it doesn't have to end that way. We don't even have to take a single step down that road."

Russo felt a new pain radiating from his hand and realized he was digging his fingernails into his palm. He had just done the same song and dance with Ruiz; now the Easton PD wanted to cut in.

"What do you want?" he asked, his lips barely moving.

"Ruiz. The Agency. They've bailed on us, and I want to make sure they never come back."

"Don't you want your veneer?"

Pierce pointed a thick finger at Russo. "Don't *you* want to be free? Or are you content to live the rest of your life with their greasy fingers around your brain stem?"

He had a point. The only reason for joining up with Ruiz had been to gain advantage over the commoners. With the veneer gone, that advantage counted for nothing. That's why all the agents had left town; the system that supported their power had collapsed. But how? What the fuck had happened to the veneer?

"Tell me why I can't reconcile anymore."

"I don't know," said Pierce.

"Then no deal."

Frustration passed like a ripple over his face, making Russo smile inside.

"Look, if I knew what caused this, I would tell you, because from the looks of it, the veneer isn't coming back. That's the reality now. You can either accept it or we can give you a crash course in Spanish. It's your choice."

The notebook disappeared into his chest pocket and he stood up slowly, favoring his right knee. He groaned as he stretched, his eyes looking past Russo, presumably at the windows.

"It's going to be one of those fuck-all days. And after that, when the lights go out... Mexico's looking better every second, huh?"

"If I tell you what I know, you'll make sure I don't end up there?"

Pierce glanced at Russo. "I'll do what I can."

"Not good enough. I want all charges against me dropped."

"Right," said the detective. "My offer is to keep you out of Mexico, but you'll have to take some token punishment for what you've done. I can't just make that go away."

That was the difference between agents and uniforms. One had power, and the other was a uniform.

"Ruiz could do it."

Pierce nodded. "I'm going to give you the morning to think about it. We'll talk more about Ruiz this afternoon when I come back for your friend." He gestured to the space behind Russo.

"What friend?" he asked, but the detective ignored him and left the room with a smile on his face.

Russo strained to hear over his heartbeat monitor, but there was definitely someone else in the room with him. The drugs helped soften the blow as he twisted and lowered himself onto his back. The pain in his shoulder was immediate and overwhelming. Lines danced in front of his eyes, reminding him of the way Jalay used to reconcile expansive murals, driving color in from different angles until they formed the image of Deron fucking a dead goat. He wanted to laugh, but instead concentrated on his breathing.

When his vision cleared, he turned his head to the side.

"Son of a goat-fucking bitch."

SIXTY-SEVEN
SEBO

Given the position of the sun and the lingering rain on the bleachers, Sebo figured it was somewhere between eight and nine in the morning. The cruisers had come around just after dawn, barking out their orders as if Easton were some kind of military state. He had been standing at the door, waiting for a little bit of light before venturing off to Rosalia's house. Had his parents not been roused by the uniforms, he might have gotten away. As it stood, his father had forbidden him from leaving their sight, at least until their sight returned.

It appeared that most of the students of Easton Central High School had suffered the same fate, not that Sebo could pick them out as they climbed the bleachers and sought out a dry place to sit. They were all his age, and he had probably sat next to them in classes for years, yet he recognized no one. Only their voices gave them away, like aural fingerprints. He had entertained the idea that maybe Rosalia's parents had similarly forced her to attend the so-called town hall meeting but now realized that unless he talked to every girl with a ponytail, he probably wouldn't know if she sat down beside him.

"Ladies and gentlemen, if we could all quiet down."

The man from the city was standing on the sideline; someone had brought him a small riser to keep his expensive shoes out of the mud. His bodyguards weren't afforded the same luxury, not that they seemed to mind. Their attention was outward at the throngs of people shifting nervously on the metal benches. Sebo noticed more uniforms loitering in the end zones. They pretended not to be interested, but there was a pattern to their occasional glances.

"Now, we've all had a rough night."

Sebo yawned and stretched in place. The man from the city was right; last night had not given him the rest he needed. He had felt contentment for only a few seconds after waking as he thought of Jordon starting her day with a quick masturbation session before taking one of her signature forty-five-minute showers. He hadn't needed to look at the wall to know she wasn't there. The veneer was gone long before he fell asleep, fading with each step as he dragged Rosalia home. The descent into the gray world lasted for what felt like hours, undulating in waves, each time failing to reach the previous brightness. Sebo watched Jordan disappear, unable to give her anything else to do besides sit in her chair and stare into the fourth wall. At the very end, she smiled. It didn't help much.

"My name is Andrew Greene and I'm a community liaison. The mayor has asked me to come here today so that you will be informed about the current crisis. Unfortunately, we do not have very much information at this time. I am not here to speculate, so I will only tell you what we know for sure."

Mr. Greene had to shout to be heard by the crowd. Sebo would have made a sarcastic comment had he not been straining to hear the man over the ambient chatter.

"The veneer has suffered a catastrophic failure."

"No shit," said Sebo, garnering a stern look from his father.

"At the moment, we do not know what caused this, only that we were dropped from VNet around ten-thirty last night."

"What's VNet?" someone whispered.

"Once the uplink was disabled, the veneer began to degrade and became nonfunctional within hours. We're not exactly sure of the timeline, as no one on the mayor's staff has a mechanical watch."

A chorus of snickers went up from the crowd, followed by laughter. No one seemed to understand how serious the situation was. Even Sebo's father had a grin on his face.

Mr. Greene began to pace the riser, looking from one end of the crowd to the other. "As soon as we noticed the problem, city officials were dispatched to Sonora, Paramel, and Ventura Heights. The Paramel runner returned this morning and we are happy to report that the veneer is fully functional there. We expect to hear the same news from other cities." He spread his hands. "Whatever has happened, has happened to us alone."

The atmosphere changed in an instant.

Then the man from the city made it worse. "All indications point to a speedy resolution, but the mayor wants to be ready just in case."

No one had to ask *in case of what*. Sebo was already imagining the worst scenario possible, that the veneer would never come back. At that point, there'd be no reason to remain in Easton, not with modern life continuing as normal in nearby cities. His father would move them in a heartbeat if he thought for one second that his son might grow up in a primitive world. Sebo wouldn't be the only one; a lot of families would pack it in. Maybe that was for the best.

Sebo scanned the grass behind Mr. Green, focused on the muddy spot at mid-field. There were too many bad memories in Easton anyway.

"To that end, we are asking for your cooperation during this critical first twenty-four hours. Whether or not we make it safely through to tomorrow will depend on you and every other citizen of Easton. A police officer will be stationed on every major intersection. Should you have any emergency, they will be your primary point of contact. Emergency services are being strained, so we recommend taking extra precautions. Stay in your homes if possible and refrain from dangerous activities. There will be another meeting tonight, here, before sunset. Last night's curfew will be in effect again tonight, for your safety."

Mr. Greene paused as if to say something else, but then nodded to his bodyguards. As he stepped off the riser, someone shouted, "Is that it?"

"That's all I have," he replied, shouting into a crowd that grew more animated by the second. Questions rained down with sufficient force to make him seek refuge behind the two large uniforms.

A few people in the front row stood up, but when the uniforms drew their guns, they reversed course quickly.

The appearance of weapons silenced the crowd again.

"Please," said Mr. Greene, touching the uniforms, "put those away." He stepped forward again. "I understand that everyone has questions. But we all know that people smarter than us have already asked those questions. The top engineers in the city are working towards a solution. I don't know about you, but I'd rather they focus on fixing it rather than take the time to explain every step to me. The city cannot survive without the veneer. We all know that."

Sebo nodded his head along with everyone else. He had no doubt the city knew more about the veneer than most of the population. What they didn't know was what had happened just a few yards from where one of its liaisons now stood. Sebo thought of the trouble he could cause by standing up and telling his story to the crowd. It didn't look like there were any agents around to stop him.

The man from the city said nothing else, despite the voices trailing after him. A small group of uniforms left the end zone to form a barrier between Mr. Greene and the families on the bleachers. It seemed like a lot of effort for a few moms and dads. What did they really expect?

The assembly ended so abruptly that a majority of the crowd stayed seated for several minutes until all but one of the uniforms had left.

"You can go see your friend now, but check in at lunch," said his father.

Sebo wondered whether Rosalia would still be at home or somewhere else entirely. She wasn't the kind of girl to wait around on him.

The crowd dispersed and Sebo was caught up in the flow of people off the bleachers. Unlike everyone else who turned right or left at the bottom, he continued forward, headed towards mid-field, his shoes sloshing in the wet grass. The white line that marked the fifty yard mark was gone, but Sebo didn't need it to pick out the small circle where the grass had been torn up and replaced with mud.

Footprints. Everywhere.

Most of them were crowded around two thick lines; Sebo imagined Deron's body being pulled away and cringed. Where would they have taken him?

"I'm sorry," said Sebo, trying not to think of how things could have ended differently. The proper thing would have been to join the fight, maybe take down Ruiz before his backup had arrived. But that was a fantasy, a type of battle plan only applicable in Destined 4 Death. The cold reality was that he couldn't get involved with agents, no matter whose life was at stake. His presence probably wouldn't have made a difference anyway. They would have killed him and Rosalia without hesitation.

He couldn't believe Deron had really brought down the veneer. It probably wasn't premeditated or even conceivable in his mind. If it had been part of some master plan, he would have failed miserably. As an accident, it exposed the weak link that none of them had ever considered: the network. Taking down the uplink meant dissolving the shared hallucination. The whole thing just crapped out. Without any feedback from the network telling it that a stop sign was red, it simply gave up trying to render it.

That was the kicker.

All this time, people believed they actually had control over the veneer. They thought that anything in the world could be theirs if they only reconciled it. But they weren't really telling the veneer how to be; they were asking it. As a magical force, it would defy explanation, but the veneer as a simple technology would be a program that took input from millions of sources. It listened to all of them, but only after checking with the network, with VNet.

Sebo narrowed his eyes as the gears and cogs came tumbling out of the black box. He laughed at himself for not figuring it out sooner.

"Sebo?"

He turned to find an older woman standing next to him. Again, if it hadn't been for the voice, he wouldn't have known it was Deron's mom.

"How are you?" she asked, squinting in the sunlight.

"I'm fine," he replied, then paused. "Sorry, I didn't expect to see you here."

Ania shrugged. Just like Deron. "I had to get out of the house. It's so empty now." She looked at the mud but recognition eluded her. "Deron still hasn't come home."

Fuck, thought Sebo, looking away.

"I knew you wouldn't be surprised by that. You don't seem surprised by anything that's happened today."

"What do you mean?" He imagined a blank face, but then remembered there was nothing he could do with the mental image.

"I was watching you, on the bleachers, when that guy was feeding us his bullshit. Everyone had moon eyes except you. And I tell you Deron hasn't come home and you act like it's old news."

"I'm not…" Sebo bit his lip. In his mind, the fuck-fuck-fuck train ran steady.

"You know something, don't you? About all this?"

He looked down at the mud again. Was it his imagination or was that blood pooling at the bottoms of the little puddles?

"Tell me, Sebo. Please."

Even with his expansive vocabulary, Sebo could find no combination of words that his mouth could utter. There was simply no way to tell her what had happened. But if he didn't, when would she find out? The city was in turmoil; it would be days before anyone cared about one little boy gone missing.

"On the way back from Paramel," he said, looking at the sun. The light burned his eyes, made them water. "Deron said he couldn't see the veneer."

Ania nodded. "Is that the last time you saw him?"

"I saw him yesterday."

"Where?" She stepped in front of Sebo and gripped his arms. "Where is he?"

"He was here at the school. He showed up at lunch and told me he was going to fight Russo." The terror that flashed across Ania's eyes made him pause, but it was clear she wanted to hear more. "And then last night, I was here when they fought." He looked at the mud and Ania followed his gaze.

"Did Russo hurt him?"

Sebo shook his head. "It wasn't like that. Deron was winning. I actually thought he was going to kill Russo."

She didn't try to hide the hopefulness in her eyes.

"So where is? Why doesn't he come home?"

"I don't know where he is now. We ran after the shooting started." Sebo grabbed Ania's hands as she tried to move away. "They shot him, Mrs. Bishop. Deron is dead." He braced for the hysterics, but they didn't come.

Something flashed on Ania's face, like a resetting of her expression. It wasn't clear what she was feeling until she spoke.

"Why?" she asked. "Why would you say such a thing?"

"I'm sorry. That's what happened."

The slap was as painful as anything Sebo could remember. His eyes began to water.

"How dare you! You don't say those things to a mother!"

Another slap, this one on his shoulder, followed by another. Each word he tried to get out only resulted in another attack. He wanted to tell her about the agents and describe in detail the timeline of her son's death, but she wouldn't allow it. Maybe she believed the truth could be beaten out of him; maybe it was the punishment she thought he deserved for allowing it to happen.

Either way, Sebo couldn't bring himself to stop her. His arms went numb, there was shouting from behind, but no part of him felt wronged. It was the retribution Deron should have paid him after being deserted by his only friend. This was what he got for not helping.

It was nothing in the grand scheme of beatings, but if it provided some measure of comfort to Ania to see him suffer, then so be it.

SIXTY-EIGHT
ROSALIA

Rosalia noted the change in the buildings as the cruiser approached downtown. In the neighborhoods, the houses had all been gray, though they still resembled homes. The skyscrapers were a different story. Their materials didn't come from a lumber mill on the outer rings; engineers had to import from a city that likely didn't have the veneer. It was the only explanation she could think of for the markings on the paneling: words, serial numbers, and even joint designations. The rough design made it look like she had walked behind a set piece in a play and seen the boards held together with duct tape.

With the tall condominiums came the hordes of people spilling into the street to share their stories about how they were surviving one of the worst disasters in Easton's history. Some of them were not prepared for the loss; they wandered slack-jawed in the crowd trying to understand the ashen world, their eyes jumping from one splash of natural color to the next. A few stood in front of windows to scrutinize their reflections. Others congregated around the decorative trees that grew out of the sidewalk and examined their leaves as if for the first time.

"Look at them," said Aguilar, to his partner. "It wasn't this bad this morning." He rolled down his window to get a better look at the people. Some of them turned and stared at the only moving vehicle on the street. "I hope nobody does anything stupid."

His partner nodded and reached for a blank panel on the dash. He made it halfway before remembering himself. "This would be easier with a siren."

Rosalia recognized some of the naked buildings as they turned onto The Drag and came to a stop. The street was packed with people; even a bicycle would have had trouble getting through. In the distance, Rosalia could see the police headquarters shrouded in the shadow cast by the TNC Bank. Both buildings looked like they had passed through a nuclear war and come out the other side with their paint blasted off. Between the buildings, a line of uniforms had most of the intersection blocked off. They hid behind riot shields as confused and angry Eastonians tested the borders.

Aguilar whistled. "Twenty bucks says someone bites it today."

"Shit, I'd play fifty for a dozen."

"We gotta get these people under control or we're going to lose the city. Once they start killing each other, it's going to be hard to stop."

His partner hit him on the shoulder and gestured to Rosalia. She looked away, pretended not to be listening.

"She's got bigger problems," said Aguilar. He put the car in park and killed the engine. "You know all the agents have gone missing, right?"

Rosalia shook her head.

"Yeah, real convenient. The Chief is pissed as all hell." He looked over his shoulder and saw the lack of interest on Rosalia's face. "I'm saying, if there ever was a time to tell him about an agent shooting a citizen, it's now. Any other day and he might write you off. But today..." The sound of glass breaking nearby made him turn away. "Today is different."

"His name was Deron, not *citizen*."

Aguilar nodded and shared a look with his partner. He banged his hands on the steering wheel. "Well, looks like we walk the rest of the way."

A scream erupted from behind the cruiser and both uniforms turned in unison. Rosalia looked out the back window and saw a fight breaking out between two men. One of them already had blood on his face.

"Typical Friday in Easton," said Aguilar. Then to his partner, "Think you can handle that yourself?"

"Pepper spray don't need no veneer," he replied, pulling two canisters from the glove box.

Aguilar laughed and looked at Rosalia. "You ready for this? We're gonna have to move fast and I need you to stay on me the whole way." An ugly smile spread on his face, a reminder of the vulgarity lingering just below the surface.

The crowd noise was a dull roar inside the car, but once Aguilar jumped out and opened her door, Rosalia felt the weight of the collective shouting press down on her. The next second, she was in the street and drowning in a sea of panicked voices. Aguilar held her by the wrist and guided her hand to a loop on the back of his uniform. Once she had a firm grasp, he drew his gun with one hand and his blackjack with the other. With the baton held threateningly above his head, he carved a path through the agitated congregation. Rosalia couldn't help but feel ashamed under the angry glares.

Things got easier once they passed the line of riot shields. Alone in the middle of the intersection, Rosalia snuck a look back at the chaos in time to see a bottle fly into the air. It crashed on the street several feet away, making her heart jump. She was scared, but she understood. Their world had been turned upside down and no one was telling them why. Aguilar's words replayed in her mind, and she wondered how bad it would get when the scales finally tipped towards anarchy. People were going to die. One already had.

The popping of tear gas launchers announced their arrival at the top of the steps. Rosalia watched the smoky trails for a moment before Aguilar pushed her inside. Though unsure of what she had been expecting, she knew it wasn't the serenity that greeted her as they walked into the lobby. It was packed with uniforms from wall to wall, some sitting on benches while the others milled around on their feet. Her own heart was trying to escape her chest, yet none of the uniforms even seemed aware of the riot outside.

Rosalia shot Aguilar a questioning look.

"They're Zoned," he explained, pointing to a woman who was handing out pill cups. "People are scared of agents because they think there's something magical about them. But I don't know any magic that'll stop a Zoned police officer." He smiled at her confusion. "Never count anyone out of a fight. People always find a way of surprising you."

Before she could respond, an older man with bushy eyebrows and an intense glare stepped in front of them.

"Aguilar, I thought I put you and Harris on neighborhood patrol. What the hell are you doing here and who is this citizen?" He glanced down. "And *why* is your blackjack out, Officer?" He took a breath, barely. "Answer me."

"Captain, this is Rose. She has something the Chief needs to hear."

"Is that so?" The eyebrows turned towards Rosalia. "Are you a Vinestead programmer, Ms. Rose? Do you know how to get the veneer up and running again?"

"No, I—"

"The Chief has real problems to worry about. I don't know if you've been outside lately, but Easton is on the precipice!"

Aguilar looked a lot younger standing across from the Captain. It was in his eyes, the way they avoided the other man's gaze. "It's about an agent," he tried to explain. "She saw—"

"I don't give a greased shit about agents."

Rosalia noticed a few looks from the other uniforms around them. The woman who was handing out pills locked eyes and flashed an understanding smile.

"Agents are yesterday and you will be too if you don't get back to your post. Take this girl home and do the job you were ordered to do."

"Sir, I must insist."

The Captain moved in closer and put his nose inches from Aguilar's. "Now, Officer? You want to do this *now*? The way I see it, you have two choices. Either you get your good for nothing ass back out on patrol or you step to the other side of that riot line. Either way, I don't give a fuck what you insist!"

Aguilar looked broken. He shied away as the Captain turned in place and stormed off, disappearing behind a partition.

Rosalia didn't know what to say. She wanted to reach out and lift the uniform's chin so that he didn't look so sad. Instead, she placed a hand on his arm to comfort him.

"Is he gone?" he whispered.

"Yeah, but…"

Aguilar looked up and smiled. "I thought he was gonna bust a tit or something." He held up two crossed fingers and shook them angrily. "Maybe next time."

"What about Deron?" asked Rosalia.

"Don't worry. The Captain has been up all night. Soon as he crashes, I'll get you in front of the Chief."

"How long will that be?"

She got a shrug in response.

"Are you okay, dear?"

Rosalia hadn't noticed the woman approach. Close up, she recognized the nurse's uniform.

"We're fine," Aguilar assured her.

Without breaking her smile, the nurse replied, "I was talking to the young woman. Are you a young woman? I didn't think so." Then to Rosalia, "Aren't you one of Susan's kids?"

It took a moment to make the connection. "You mean Nurse Hendricks?"

"Yes. I'm Kaitlyn, Dr. Blake's assistant. And you're… Rosalia, right?"

"Yeah, how did you know?"

"You don't forget such a pretty name. You saw Susan just a few days ago, right?"

Rosalia nodded and looked around. Conversing with the nurse wasn't progress; the tremors would be back soon.

"I'm not supposed to do this, but would you like something to calm you down? I can break one of these in half."

"They're not bad," said Aguilar.

"Come on," said Kaitlyn. She led Rosalia to a bench by the wall. "Here, have some water."

Rosalia downed the pill despite not knowing what it would do to her. All she knew was that the anxiety was building. No one wanted to help her with Deron. And if the agents had vanished, then Ruiz had probably vanished with them. How was she going to get justice for Deron's murder? Her head dipped.

"What's the matter?" asked Kaitlyn.

Aguilar cleared his throat. He seemed reluctant to leave Rosalia's side. "Her boyfriend got shot last night."

"Oh my God," said the nurse, her face bunching up. "Is he alright?"

Rosalia couldn't raise her eyes, couldn't even shake her head.

"She's not sure."

"I saw him get shot," said Rosalia.

"Yeah, but you didn't see the body, right? I've seen a dozen men take slugs to the chest without any armor and still get up the next day."

"Really?" She looked first to Aguilar and then to Kaitlyn. "What is it?"

"Nothing," replied the nurse, shaking away the fog. "It's just, I was at Easton General last night and we took in two teenage boys."

"Deron?"

"I didn't see them. I just heard about it in the halls. There was talk that they had been dumped at the ER. By who, I don't know. They couldn't ID them before the veneer went out."

"Could be your boy," said Aguilar.

Kaitlyn put up a hand. "I don't want to get your hopes up. It was hectic last night. All I know is that they were in pretty bad shape. Dr. Blake assisted on the surgeries, but I haven't spoken to her today."

It was impossible. She had seen him go down. She had watched Agent Ruiz fire a second shot. There was no way he could have survived, not at that range.

"You know, the Captain really wants me to head out. I bet I could swing by General on the way."

Seeing was believing. Deron was dead. Optimism was not going to change that.

"It's going to be a madhouse down there," said the nurse. "Modern medicine isn't designed to run without the veneer."

"Shit," said Aguilar, tightening a strap on his uniform. "That'll be nothing compared to getting back to my car." He glanced at the front entrance. "They're probably eating each other out there."

Rosalia stood and followed his gaze. When he turned to her, she asked, "Will you take me?"

"Yeah, I'll take you. Maybe we can borrow something from the motor pool. It's probably not as crowded out back." He smiled and collapsed his blackjack. "Still won't be cake though."

"Nothing ever is," said Rosalia.

Kaitlyn stood and put a hand on Rosalia's arm. "You be careful out there. I'll be praying for you."

She nodded politely and followed Aguilar across the lobby. They went through several doors and hallways that all looked the same. Along the way, they passed more Zoned uniforms, all with that steely glimmer in their eyes. No one stopped them or asked what they were doing. That would have been inefficient.

The uniforms needed to be in the Zone, the same one that Rosalia could feel herself slipping into.

In the motor pool, Aguilar led her to a beat-up cruiser parked near the exit. He studied it for a moment before saying, "These things look shitty without the veneer."

"You could say that about anything," said Rosalia, unsurprised to see his eyes scan her from head to toe.

He started to reply but caught himself. "We should go. Midday traffic in this city can be a real bitch."

"Is that a joke?"

"Not funny?"

She shook her head.

"You must be fully Zoned now, because that shit was hilarious."

Rosalia pulled back for a moment and looked closer at the world around her. Everything had a new shimmer to it, yet was in perfect focus. It was crisp and undulating at the same time.

It wasn't the veneer.

It was something… different.

SIXTY-NINE
ILYA

Father had gone to the school while Ilya slept, but now he was back and standing in the front yard with a baseball bat and his best scowl. Not that he came off as threatening; nobody in their right mind would look at his socks and sandals and tremble with fear. Then again, nobody *was* in their right mind, certainly not her father. If he had been thinking clearly, he would have put on some jeans and shoes instead of a gray shirt and matching shorts that looked like boxers. Everyone was a little off, but there were no roving bands of looters or teenagers with Molotov cocktails for her father to be worried about. At least, not on her street.

Downtown, with its rising plumes of smoke, was a different story.

Babushka had sat outside for a while, overseeing her domain from a regal folding chair on the porch. Every once in a while, she yelled something at father that sounded harsh, though it might have been the rough sound of Russian playing tricks on her ears. Their arguments were cut short by passersby. Father would get very quiet and very still until they had passed on, at which point Babushka would start in again. During one argument, father gestured with his bat to Ilya's window, looked up, and saw her watching him. He said something sharp to grandmother and sent her inside. He smiled before returning his attention to the street.

A few minutes later, there was a knock at the door. Before Ilya could invite the visitor in, Babushka entered the room with a serving tray. She didn't offer a greeting, opting instead to nod her head as if already engaged in conversation. She stopped beside the nightstand and set the tray down. Again, silence as she offered a cup to Ilya.

Ilya sipped quietly, tried to ignore the uncomfortable sensation of steam rising past her face. From the look on Babushka's face, she was busy translating some pre-rehearsed speech from Russian to English.

"This tray," she said, placing a finger on it, "has been in our family for five generations. One hundred percent silver." Her accent suggested she should be dropping an article now and then, but Babushka spoke English well, albeit very slowly. "It was my grandmother's. American businessman bought it for her. *Iz Praha.* Very beautiful."

Ilya examined the tarnished tray. It was decades from beautiful.

"It survived two wars. Even Yuri Lyakhov could not take it."

The details of the Lyakhov Insurgency came up automatically, pulled from a brain cell that had been programmed in seventh grade.

Babushka motioned to the window. "This is nothing. If this tray could talk, it would laugh at us." Her smile was full of stained teeth. "When I left Ukraine, it was just me and tray. My grandmother told me to sell it, but I could not."

"You're saying I should be more like tray?"

"No. *The* tray is just a thing. You are a person, Ilyushenka."

She liked it when Babushka used the long form of her name. The Americanized version had nothing on the Russian pronunciation.

"The tray does not notice the world as we do. Look at Petter; he thinks someone will take the house. Do you think he cares about the veneer?"

Ilya realized her father had bigger problems. She clenched her eyes and felt the pull of the stitches in her skin. "Let it hurt, right?"

"There is no choice. We come and go. The world stays. The tray stays."

The words swirled in Ilya's head. "What the fuck is that supposed to mean? You sit there and say this is nothing, but you have no idea how much I need the veneer." She felt her voice break. It was the first time she had ever spoken so rudely to her grandmother and the worst part of it was that she couldn't stop herself. "Look at me," she shouted. "Look what she did to my face! How am I supposed to live with this?"

Babushka studied the swirls in her cup.

"Nobody cares what this tray *used* to look like. All they see now is how ugly it is. You carry it around like it's the most valuable thing in the house, but it's not. I don't want to carry my scars around forever. I want to reconcile them into oblivion and never think about them again. That's my right! And if that means no one can ever touch my face, then fine. The world has to see me as I want to appear, not how I am."

"It's not that bad."

Ilya swung her feet to the floor and leaned forward. "Then why won't you look at me? All this time, you've been staring at that stupid tray."

Babushka shook her head.

"If you love me, if you've ever cared for me, look me in the eyes." She felt bad forcing her grandmother's hand, but she needed to know. There were no portals left in Easton that could tell her what she looked like. Seeing Babushka's reaction was the only way.

Sure enough, there were tears in the old woman's eyes. She held her gaze for all of three seconds before turning away again. The hand on her mouth barely contained a sob.

It was all Ilya needed to see. She stood and left the room. At the top of the stairs, she debated going down to the living room, but her mother was probably on the couch making love to something alcoholic. Instead, she walked past the master suite and her grandmother's room to the door at the end of the landing. It went up to the attic and there she found the lack of veneer less jarring.

This was where all the old stuff was kept; even the serving tray had spent most of its life up here. Ilya wandered from one shelf to another, looking at the ancient and colorful things that had once been Babushka's prized possessions but were now relegated to a dusty vault. They might have filled an entire house at some point, been the backdrop to a life that she thought would never wind down, would never finish out its days as a third wheel in her son's guest bedroom.

Ilya didn't find it on the shelves or in the boxes that were stacked near the back of the house. There was a mobile wardrobe that held only fur coats that had long since been made illegal in Easton. Sports equipment stood guard at the top of the stairs; a small tennis racquet reminded Ilya of the fifth grade, of a passing fancy that barely lasted a summer.

What looked like a pile of old jackets actually concealed a hope chest and it was there that Ilya focused her search. She lifted the wooden lid and squirmed at the sound of the rusted hinges opening. The dust had not intruded into the chest, leaving the old trinkets and costume jewelry in good condition. The object of her desire sat on a shelf that rose with the lid. It was trying to hide under a yellowing handkerchief, but Ilya would have recognized the Revlon font anywhere.

Like the tray, the compact had seen better days, but inside, the untarnished mirror reflected the world as well as any portal. Ilya held it at an angle at first and looked at the stairs behind her. She took a deep breath and rotated her hand.

"It's not that bad," she said, her lip trembling. "It's not that bad." Even as the sobs climbed her throat, she couldn't stop repeating her grandmother's lie. "It's not that bad!"

In fact, it was worse than she had imagined. Even as she turned away, she couldn't escape the memory of her bandaged face. She saw it in her mind, her perfectly reconciled face with a veneer that wouldn't hold, that kept slipping away to reveal the carnage underneath.

It wasn't her; it couldn't be.

"It's not that bad," she whispered.

Ilya threw the compact at the wall and collapsed on the floor, her cheeks already damp. She wanted to curl up into a ball and disappear, but the pressure against the side of her face made her yelp. Instinctively, she put her hand to her cheek, but even that was too much to bear.

"It's not that bad," she screamed.

It's just my face, she thought. Who even looks at people's faces?

No, it wasn't her face. It was someone else's, someone's sick joke, like Russo making shops of Deron.

Except it wasn't funny. She hated it, just wanted it to go away.

A hand came up and slapped her gently on the cheek. It stung, but Ilya hit herself again. More pain, she thought. More pain would make her forget about the end of her social life. There would be no more friends, no more Ramseys to seduce or Rosalias to fondle in the dead of night. The window of possibilities had slammed shut and Ilya couldn't think of anything she wanted more than to drown in the pain.

Another slap on the cheek, followed by a closed fist against her forehead.

"It is that bad."

The next shot caught her on the nose and made her cry out. The sound attracted Babushka and Ilya opened her eyes as footsteps climbed the stairs.

"Ilyushenka!"

Not so comforting this time.

Blood covered Ilya's hands and most of the floor, but she barely recognized it as her own. All she could think about was how she had been wrong. She didn't want to suffer forever. If anything, she just wanted it to go away.

The pain. Easton. Everything.

Ilya recoiled when Babushka tried to help her up. She pushed past her and ran down the stairs, smearing blood on the handrail and the walls. Her fingers slipped on the doorknob, but she managed to lock her bedroom door behind her. She fought through the throbbing in her head to the dresser. There, she had wisely left the cap loose on the clear bottle. She turned it over and dumped the remaining Oxycodone pills into a small pile.

"Be enough," she prayed.

Be enough water to down the pills, enough pills to drown the pain.

Just be enough.

SEVENTY
DERON

Deron thought about the tunnel leading out of Easton.

Down where the light couldn't reach, he saw nothing, only an infinite blackness that had no shape yet crushed in on him from all sides. At the time, he had been more concerned with bugs and spiders hanging from the ceiling or crawling up his legs, but in the days after, he remembered only the silence, not of sound, but of light. The lack of stimulus did not make him feel empty; it felt more like stillness with no one pestering him to move. Nothing vied for his attention and nothing stood in the way of his imagination. The spiders he saw with his mind's eye were more vibrant and alive than anything in the real world. As consolation prizes went, it wasn't bad.

It was that silence that Deron thought about as he writhed in the muddy waters of the football field. He had overwhelmed Russo with reconciliation and was seconds from putting an end to the nightmare. Then, his shoulder exploded and a jet of red liquid spewed into the space in front of him. The impact put him off balance, but it was the resulting pain that brought him to the ground. He watched Agent Ruiz approach, the gun still steaming in his hand. He realized Ruiz had never intended for him to win, that it was all some sick game that ended with Deron bludgeoned to death and Russo made into a full-blown killer.

He tried to ignore Ruiz and focus on the storm roaring overhead. The rain fell in tiny explosions in the water around him. He heard the sound and tried to push it away. Closing his eyes, he thought of the tunnel, of an unstoppable darkness that could wash over Easton like a tsunami. Where everything had once been white, it would now be black. The field, the school, and even Russo who he could hear on the ground a few feet away crying out like a wounded dog; they would all be in shadow. Deron imagined it and pushed the command out with a guttural scream. In the resulting emptiness, he found a moment of silence.

Then, a crack of thunder and a searing pain in his gut.

Deron had been there before, had suffered through the interminable stage of thinking himself dead but knowing his brain still functioned. Death was the lack of all input, not an awareness that something was missing. This was not death. This was a gradual reinsertion into the world, a series of switches being thrown in the back of his brain. The voices came first, distant and muddled as if shouted from a moving vehicle. Later, the feeling in his body returned, a sensation that rivaled a warm bath but which quickly turned to pain. He tried to cry out, and for all he knew he did. The only feedback was a sting in his throat.

How long it went on, he wasn't sure. At one point the hospital room came into view, and he saw a nurse doping him with something wonderful. It quieted the pain for a while, but the crawl back to the light became more difficult. The line between dream and reality shimmered like a bad veneer. He kept seeing the ceiling, kept trying to shroud it in black, but it only disappeared when he closed his eyes. The ceiling didn't respond to his commands and lacked any decoration.

His ability to reconcile remotely was gone, but it didn't matter. The veneer had gone with it.

It was supposed to be over. Ruiz had offered him a way back. All that was left was for Rosalia to realize she still loved him. The fight would have taken care of all that—had he won. And yet here he was, back at the start, worse off than ever before.

Deron spent the morning drifting in and out of the drug haze. He listened to the panic in the hallways and the shouting of doctors that grew worse as the day wore on. There was a window to the left and he could hear disorder outside. Breaking glass and gunshots broke up what was otherwise a continuous rumble of discontent. It was the shooting that made his heart race, that caused his shoulder and stomach to throb in remembrance. He could think of nothing but the memory, even when a man named Detective Pierce came into the room, even when he revealed that Russo was in the next bed.

Then Pierce had gone and for a long time, no noise in the room competed with the crowd outside.

"Hey, asshole." It was Russo's voice, less muffled than before.

Since kindergarten, Deron's body had developed an automatic response to Russo's presence that included increased heart rate and the release of life-saving adrenaline. He had become accustomed to the feeling, but not so much that he couldn't recognize its absence. Deron imagined Russo and tried to make him a shadow. His mind answered with a fifty-fifty split, as if someone had dialed the brightness down.

"Answer me, faggot."

The fear was gone, Deron realized. There was just nothing left for Russo to threaten short of death. With the drugs in his system, it wouldn't even hurt that much. He would lose the war, but at least the battles would end.

"What do you want?"

"I want to strangle you."

"Why?" Deron couldn't see Russo's face, but the pause told him his question was one rarely, if ever, considered.

Russo groaned. "I…"

"Do you even know why you want to kill me?"

"I know why." Russo spoke slowly, steadying his voice. "Do you?"

Deron opened his eyes and saw the dim ceiling staring back at him. His ears perked up and caught the sound of the metal guardrail on Russo's bed collapsing into its folded position. He resisted the urge to look, though there was no mistaking the movement of the bed and the scraping of tubes across the sheets. The monitor that had been belting out the tempo of Russo's supposed heart increased to a frantic pace and then plummeted to a dull monotone. Bare feet hit the floor and Deron's own monitor took up the second verse.

"Does not get along well with others. Do you remember that? When they pulled me out of Bowie? They told my mom I was bad for the other kids." Footsteps brought his voice closer. "They made me wait outside. They thought I couldn't hear them. That bitch teacher told them I was tormenting a boy named Deron." His voice took on a high, mocking pitch. "It would be in *Deron's* best interest if Russo was transferred." He groaned again, breathed in sharply. "Do you know what they do to little boys at Glenmore? Do you have any fucking idea?"

Unable to fight it anymore, Deron turned and looked at Russo. The sight of blood still caked on his face made him happy, but the moment was lost as he looked into his enemy's eyes. On Halloween, it would have made a decent costume. But today, out of context, Russo's eyes made him look supernatural. The whites were completely gone, replaced by blood that had stagnated into black.

Russo shook his head; blood dripped from his nose onto his gown. He wiped it away and examined his finger. "I bet you thought you were going to win, didn't you?"

"I did win. You cheated."

"No. I just had the better backup plan."

"I guess Jalay should have planned better too."

He sniffled and tried to rub his nose. "You heard that, huh? I can't believe all this time I've wanted to end you and I never realized how easy it would be. All I have to do is reach out and put my hand on your throat. Then I get to watch you die. Very slowly. And if it's anything like throwing that fat fucker off a building, then I'm really going to enjoy it."

Deron felt pressure on his neck as Russo's fingers dug into place. At first, he thought he could still breathe, but as the residual oxygen ran out, his lungs panicked. He felt the contractions in this throat, but Russo's grip was too tight. The gray ceiling faded down even further.

"I would hate to suffocate to death," said Russo. "It's even worse than drowning. All I have to do is let go and you'd be saved."

The pressure relented and Deron gulped down air.

A gunshot echoed outside, closer than the others.

"Sounds bad out there. The pigs have their hands full. No one to save little Deron Bishop."

"Fuck you, Russo. You getting sent to Glenmore was the best thing that ever happened."

Russo grabbed his neck again. "Not for me! The kids they send there…"

His voice trailed off in time to the dimming of the world. Deron prayed it would keep going so the true black could take over, but it didn't.

"Poor… little… Russo," sputtered Deron.

"Yeah, poor little me." Russo let go and straightened up. His black eyes surveyed the room, coming to rest on the IV bag hanging on a metal stand. "I saw this in a movie once. You pull this line here and drain the fluid."

Deron couldn't see if he was actually doing it, but the dripping on the floor backed up his narration.

"Then you plug it back in and squeeze." He came back into view. "Once the air hits your heart, you die instantly."

"Bullshit."

"We'll see. For now…" Russo didn't finish his sentence, though maybe his hand returning to Deron's neck was intended as punctuation. "We're going deep on this one. Your lungs will be so deprived that they'll start working against you. And when you wake up, it'll be in the worst pain of your pathetic life."

Darkness rose like the surf in Rosalia's dream. Each wave brought a measure of release. Deron felt himself sinking beneath them, felt the world retreating.

A scream rang out in the hallway, followed by deep voices shouting. Somebody came into the room and tackled Russo, ripping his hand away from Deron's neck. It was the man from before, Detective Pierce.

"Hold him!"

"I'm trying!" The other voice sounded younger. He grunted as he wrestled with Russo.

A woman's voice shouted, "You can't go in there!"

"Keep her back," said Pierce.

There was so much activity that Deron didn't notice the darkness persisting. He felt his eyes blink, but the voices never grew bodies.

"Cuffs are on."

"You can't do that," said the woman, possibly a nurse. "This boy is a patient!"

"Fuck that," said Pierce. "He's a murderer and a danger to society. I'm taking him back to HQ. Help me get him downstairs, Aguilar."

"Dr. Blake won't allow that."

"Dr. Blake isn't the law around here."

"Now just relax," said Aguilar. "Nurse, can you check him?"

"I have to tell Dr. Blake…"

"I can't see!" Deron tried to bring his hands to his face, but he was tucked in tight.

"Stand that piece of shit up. We're outta here."

"You can't take him out *there*," said the nurse. Her voice shifted as she came closer and soon Deron felt her thin fingers on his face. Seeing the tears in his eyes must have made her abandon her argument. "Don't worry, I'm here. Now, I want you to follow my finger."

"What finger?"

He had been wrong. He thought it couldn't get any worse. Being blind to the veneer was one thing, but going all the way down to nothing…

"Deron?"

That voice.

Even in the darkness, he could see her. Deron imagined her standing just outside the room, half-hidden by the doorjamb, concern on her face. The last time, they wouldn't let her come into the room because they weren't married or related. If only she had come a few minutes earlier, he could have glimpsed her face before the world shut off for good.

"Rosie?"

It was enough of an invitation; footsteps hurried across the room.

Something dug at the blanket around his arm and then Rosalia was holding his hand. "I'm here," she said.

Deron turned his head to the sound of her voice. "I can't see you."

"It's okay. You're gonna be okay."

"I need to find Dr. Blake. You'll stay with him?"

"I will." She squeezed his hand. "I'll stay."

Deron felt his lips reposition into a smile. Somewhere in the unending gloom, he imagined Rosalia smiling back at him.

SEVENTY-ONE
SEBO

Parker Avenue was shut down, but that didn't stop people from milling around in front of the shuttered businesses, using their outdoor seating as a place to congregate and discuss the latest happenings. Stories from downtown were trickling out with each public servant that managed to escape the chaos. They told of riots and unrest, of cops shooting people dead just for getting too close. For those that lived in the neighborhoods surrounding Parker, such talk of violence was enticing and they drank it down like a strawberry-banana smoothie.

Sebo glanced at the front windows of Perrault's and wondered how long the pristine plate glass would last before someone put a chair through it. He listened to the rumors too, but where a commoner would abhor the tragedy, Sebo could only focus on the hysteria, the driving force that would ultimately cause the most damage. A few decorations had come off, yet people were behaving as if the heavens were crashing to the ground. Even the other men and women sitting at the tables around him looked agitated, as if at any moment they might stand up and start murdering each other.

"I hear buses are lined up at South Gate to take people to Paramel. North Gate too."

It was a common rumor that people were not just leaving Easton, but fleeing in droves, intent on waiting out the crisis in a city that still had television and computers. A few days in Paramel didn't sound so bad, but the people waiting at North Gate would be heading to Sonora. Sebo couldn't imagine why anyone would want to go there.

"The hotels are gonna double their rates, you watch."

Yeah, thought Sebo. Someone was always waiting to profit from a disaster, severe or not. If anything, the lack of veneer was only a minor inconvenience. There were still basic services: food, water, and electricity. The worst thing that had happened so far was that everyone got a day off from school. He smirked and wondered what the hell was wrong with people.

"They make you sign a contract. On paper."

"Who does?"

"The bus people. You have to sign an I.O.U. saying you'll pay them back when the veneer is back up. Don't know how much they're charging though."

"Shit... I'd expect that from Paramel types, but it doesn't seem right to do that to your own people.

The man sighed. "Those people aren't from here. Those buses are with a Sonora company. You ever notice those agency mini-tanks following you on the way to Paramel?"

"I just thought agents were nosy."

"They're psychotic assholes," said Sebo, under his breath. They were cheats and rogues, but they didn't take an interest in anything without reason. Whoever ran the buses controlled the flow of people from one city to the next. Sebo had heard stories of ambushes in the outland, so hiring muscle that could travel freely between cities made sense.

"You know it's not just the veneer thing," said one of the men. "If those riots spread out here, I'm taking Rebecca and the kids and getting out of here."

Sebo nodded his head thoughtfully. What did it take for neighbors who had lived together in peace for years to suddenly look upon each other with distrust?

"What gets me is the lack of a plan. Did no one ever think this might happen?"

"They had a plan," said Sebo, turning in his chair. "Cut and run."

The men looked at him with curiosity.

"The veneer is too big to fail." He conjured up the appropriate maxims. "We put all of our eggs in one basket. And then the basket disappeared right out from under us and all the eggs fell on the floor." He pointed to the ground and the men followed his gaze. "They're all broken now, see? Social services, communications, the fucking network; all gone."

"I don't see anything," said one of the men.

"They're not real," said the other. "He's just saying."

"Oh."

"But that doesn't mean we have to freak out," Sebo continued. "I don't think the agents abandoned Easton because of a little thing like the veneer. And I don't think they're going to let it stay down permanently."

A couple at a nearby table looked at Sebo, as did a few other interested people. He smiled at the attention.

"If anything, they left because of that." He gestured to downtown and was surprised to see half a dozen heads turn at his instruction. "They knew some of us wouldn't be able to handle even twelve hours without TV or e-mail. But they'll be back. You can't keep agents out of Easton forever. Once the veneer is back up, they'll come riding into town like fucking heroes. And we'll love them for it."

That got a few nods.

"We should be fortifying the walls," he concluded. When one of the men scoffed, Sebo went after him. "Would you rather see the city burn? You really want your family to get caught up in *that*?" He pointed to downtown again, only this time, he didn't see the smoke. What it was, he couldn't put his finger on. It reminded him of a shadow cast by a high cloud moving quickly overhead. It flowed out from downtown and passed over in a flash. No one else seemed to notice it.

Could it have been a veneer?

Sebo put his hand down on the table; it shimmered at his touch. Multiple theories came hurtling out of the darkness. He had just seen an artifact of reconciliation, which meant…

"You alright?" someone asked. They were all looking at Sebo.

"Did you guys see that?" He looked to the couple, as they were closest to his table.

"See what?"

"I thought the table changed."

"Oh, I've been seeing that all morning. I thought it was just my mind playing tricks on me."

A hand came in from Sebo's left; it was a younger boy, maybe a few grades down the totem pole. "I don't see anything," he said.

"The veneer is down," said Sebo, repeating Mr. Greene's words from earlier. "We've lost our uplink to VNet."

"Why would we need an uplink?" asked the boy.

Sebo's head shook minutely, stuck in a nervous tick. "It's too big to fail. And too big to fit in one person's head. You have to trade information. You reconcile a portal, but it's only real to you. It has to get to me somehow. We're all part of a network of reconcilers, but if we disagree—"

"Someone has to be the authority."

"Yes!" He pointed to the man in recognition. "A master control that reconciles reconciliations. You make something blue, but I make it red. Who is right?"

"But…"

"Exactly!" Sebo could no longer bear the shaking of his leg. He stood and looked over his congregation. "There's too much data to be processed remotely. They have to have a local server, something keeping the city's veneer consistent. Maybe the uplink is there to spy on us." He cocked his head. Something was shouting at him from the back of his brain, but the words were unintelligible.

"I thought the things we reconciled were private."

Sebo looked at the couple; they were nodding in unison.

"Some of the things we've sent each other," continued the girl, "well, you know."

Sebo imagined their late night chat sessions and the racy messages Jordan had sent him before it all went to hell. That was reconciliation into a portal, into software. How did it get from Jordan's program in his wall to his palette during lunch? There was more software at work than he realized and all of it was built around one purpose: reconciling conflict.

He pushed his chair away and beckoned to the people around him. "Everyone stand up," he said. "Get around the table."

The older men hesitated, but soon Sebo had seven people surrounding the small, plastic table.

"Put your hand on it." He pointed to each person in turn. "You're blue, red, orange, green, purple, and… yellow. Now, reconcile the table."

Nothing happened.

"Harder," he commanded. "Try harder."

It took a few minutes, but eventually someone gasped and the voices around them became excited. The table was still gray, but its surface was shimmering as if it wanted to be anything but the lifeless color.

The younger boy's face was scrunched in concentration. His fingers were splayed on the table and under them, trickles of blue were blinking on and off.

All around the table, false starts erupted from the seven hands. The colors faded quickly once they appeared, but some lasted longer, swirling with the hues around it. They were flashes of a world that everyone desperately wanted to go back to, but it always ended the same way, with a gray film overtaking everything.

"Okay," said Sebo. "That's enough." The murmurs in the crowd made it hard to think.

"What does that mean?" asked one of the men.

Sebo found they were all looking at him again.

"Conflict," he replied. "Everyone wants to see a different color. Something in the way the veneer works says there can be only one version. Whoever wanted it more should have won out."

"Nobody won," said the boy. "It's still gray."

Tooth. Gap. Sebo's eyes went wide.

"Come on," he yelled. "We need to try it on a bigger scale."

He led them to the street and used the newcomers to form a large oval. There were thirty or more people, all of them feeding off of his excitement. Some were already kneeling and placing their hands on the ground. Sebo followed their lead.

"What color should we think of?"

"I've got blue!"

"I'm green!"

"No!" Sebo put his hand up. "We all need to think of the same thing. How about bright red?" There were nods all around. "Alright, fill in this circle. Shut your eyes and concentrate."

More people gravitated towards the group of maniacs kneeling in the middle of the street.

Sebo stood and watched for any signs of reconciliation. The gray was constant, but again the shimmer took hold. Everyone saw it at the same time.

"More!" he yelled.

Around the edges, people kneeled down and closed their eyes.

"Keep going!"

Sure enough, the hue was changing. A dull red flickered beneath the gray fog. It grew and grew until a fiery crimson filled the entire circle. Shouts went up; some even clapped.

"Open your eyes!"

Those that had been kneeling removed their hands and stared at their creation.

Sebo couldn't believe his hunch had been correct. The red was holding. The veneer was still there.

"The veneer is back!" someone shouted.

No, thought Sebo. It had never left. Everyone could still reconcile, but something—

The red flashed and disappeared, dialed down to black in an instant. Then it returned with the same quickness. Back and forth, it alternated between the two extremes. Some people looked away, but not Sebo. He kept his eyes focused, for in the oscillating colors he saw something more, some familiar pattern.

He wasn't sure if it was really there; everyone else was too busy panicking at the strange light show. If only they had looked closer, had pushed through to the image hidden within, they would have seen her, seen the muddy portrait of one Rosalia Collier.

It ended with an audible gasp from the crowd. The gray street returned, yet the people didn't react as Sebo expected. Instead of disbelief, there was jubilation. The man who had been sitting at the next table grabbed his arm.

"You did it! What's your name, kid?"

"Sebo," he whispered without thinking. "Sebo Kahani."

Rosalia's face… it meant something.

"Sebo Kahani!" shouted the man. Cheers answered him. "We have to tell everyone!"

Sebo didn't like hearing his name shouted as if he were some kind of hero, but he couldn't bring himself to object. The puzzle was too intense, the outcome too optimistic. Yet there was no denying what he had seen.

The crowd split in half. Some of them headed back towards the neighborhoods while the other, smaller, group started for downtown.

"You know, don't you?" It was the underclassman again.

"Know what?"

"You said it yourself. Conflict. We all wanted red. So who wanted black?"

Sebo looked towards downtown. He hadn't imagined the shadowy wave, just as he hadn't imagined the whitewash from the night before. They had both originated from the same person.

"His name is Deron," answered Sebo.

"The missing kid?"

Ania. She had been right.

Sebo didn't respond. He turned in place and began walking.

The boy called after him. "Aren't you coming downtown?"

Part of him wanted to go, but finding Deron in that mess would have been impossible. It wasn't something in his power, even if the people of Easton came to consider him a hero. The only thing he knew he could do was find Ania and let her know her son was still alive.

He smiled and looked around.

Alive and still causing trouble.

SEVENTY-TWO
RUSSO

Don't be a little bitch.

Those were the words Detective Pierce had spoken after jamming a syringe into Russo's leg. It wasn't so much the sting of the injection as the element of surprise that had made him cry out. Up until that point, they had just been sitting quietly outside the hospital under a carport watching a parade of ambulances drop off casualties of the Easton Panic. That's what Russo was calling it. After all, every significant event needed a name.

The Collapse of the Veneer.

The Easton Panic.

The Botched Assassinations of Deron Bishop.

Russo squeezed his hands into fists and tested the strength of the zip ties that Pierce had used to secure him to the wheelchair. They didn't budge, nor did his legs when he tried to wiggle them. At first, the plastic had dug into his wrists, but whatever Piece had pumped into his thigh had made all the pain disappear. Even his anger faded away, leaving Russo light-headed.

"You really fucked that up, didn't you?" asked Pierce.

Russo looked up and squinted. All he could see was the man's silhouette.

"It's one thing to work alongside an agent to subvert the law, but to go it alone? Did you think just because you knew this Agent Ruiz that somehow you had his immunity?" Pierce kicked at Russo's left wheel. "You think you're an agent now?"

"More than you'll ever be," he replied.

Pierce scoffed. "Shit. You're nothing. You're just a little punk who thinks he's hard because he put down a classmate."

"I have no idea what you're talking about," said Russo, looking into his lap. The sun stung his eyes and produced patterns when he closed them.

"Yeah, you keep that up. Like it or not, you're going down for Jalay's murder. You're lucky you're so inept or you'd be getting a double dose of homicide."

"Fuck you."

Pierce laughed and crossed his arms. "What went wrong up there? Why couldn't you do it?" When Russo didn't answer, he continued, "You toyed with him, didn't you?"

Russo tried not to acknowledge the accusation.

"Yeah, you did. That's emotion fucking with you. One thing you should know about agents is they don't have any emotions, nothing to get in their way. They'd kill their own mothers as easily as they'd kill you. You just don't have what it takes, do you?"

"I have what it takes to kill *you*."

Pierce took a step towards the curb and looked down the street. "We'll see about that. But from where I'm standing, you're tied to a wheelchair. I could push you into traffic and that'd be the end of it."

"No one can drive today, dumbass."

"No plebes, but those ambulances have been tearing in and out of here all morning." He laughed again. "At least if you get hit, you'd be near a hospital."

On cue, another gray box on wheels came roaring around the corner, taking full advantage of the suspension before screeching to a halt in front of the automatic doors. Two EMTs jumped out of the front as the back doors popped open on their own. A third tech emerged from the back and began pulling out a stretcher.

"Looks like someone's having a worse day than you."

Russo watched the men push the stretcher into the building. They were gone only a few seconds before they came running out again without their cargo. Before Russo could blink, they were back in the ambulance and peeling out of the carport.

"Lots of people getting hurt today," said Pierce.

Russo wasn't sure if he was talking to himself or not.

As the ambulance turned the corner, a cruiser appeared in front of it. The driver swerved hard to avoid a collision and managed to navigate the narrow alley to pull up in front of Pierce. The door opened and the uniform from earlier stepped out.

"You're bleeding, Aguilar."

The uniform touched the side of his head and examined the blood on his fingers. "It's just a scratch. Someone hit me with a rock. Kinda makes me want to take this uniform off. All people see is a target."

"Then we'd be no better than those damn agents, would we?" asked Pierce. Then, after giving the car a closer look, "This isn't my cruiser, Officer."

"No, uh…"

"I asked for mine."

"All the cars in B lot were trashed. I had to get mine from over on Elm. But I can give you a lift downtown."

"No," said Pierce. "I need to meet up with my partner. You can take us to the inner loop."

"Which direction?"

"North."

Aguilar rubbed his face. "Alright. I gotta swing out east anyway and find that kid's mom."

"Why?" asked Pierce.

The uniform stared back at him for a moment.

Pierce shook his head; his laughter sounded hollow. "Fuck, it's been a day, hasn't it? Yeah, okay. You take us out to the loop and then let Ms. Bishop know you found him. And that's no minor accomplishment, Officer. Stronger men have tried and failed."

Russo looked up and caught Pierce's eye.

"I think we're gonna have to cut him loose for the trip," said Aguilar.

Pierce pulled two ties from his back pocket. "Bind his hands. That should be enough."

"Really? He doesn't look like much of a threat."

"Never trust a person by their veneer."

Aguilar cut Russo's hands free and then bound them together with the ties. Russo thought about head butting him while he was struggling with his ankles, but he knew his shoulder wouldn't support it. Instead, he let his body go limp and forced the uniform to carry him into the cruiser and buckle him in. Once he was secured, Pierce pushed the wheelchair into the wall and then hopped into the front passenger seat. Aguilar joined him a moment later and started the engine.

"Alright, Easton General to the loop. This shouldn't be a problem."

Pierce nodded and pulled a gun from his jacket. He pulled the slide, inspected the chamber, and then let it click back into place.

"You think you're gonna need that?"

"Some things change, some don't. You need to make sure you're prepared, Officer."

"Yessir," said Aguilar.

They rode in silence for a while. Aguilar kept to the side streets and alleys, avoiding the crowds when possible. A few times, rocks or chunks of evercrete hit the side of the car, but the glass on the windows held. If it was strong enough to stop a bullet, then a few pebbles weren't much threat. Crossing out of downtown proper, the crowds thinned out and became small groups of people milling around news kiosks or sitting at outdoor patios. They weren't fully engaged with the riot, but at the sight of a cruiser, they started yelling and throwing things.

It was glorious.

Russo wanted nothing more than to be out there with them. The uniforms deserved a taste of their own injustice. Had he been healthy and not shackled, he could have helped take the riots to a whole new level.

It was such a waste of civil unrest.

"You been working this case long?"

Russo guessed the quiet had been making Aguilar uncomfortable.

Pierce seemed to have no trouble with it and took his time replying. "Couple weeks now."

"Not a bad turnaround."

"I guess." He looked over his shoulder at Russo. "I really wanted state's evidence though. All he had to do was agree to testify against an agent."

"And now?"

"Too late for that. I've got witnesses that saw him try to kill Deron Bishop. On more than one occasion."

"I don't know," said Aguilar, guiding the car into a tight turn. "That depends on the DA. Who'd you get, Orchard or Kasabian?"

Pierce laughed. "Neither."

"So you didn't have approval?"

"I figured it would be easier once I had some dirt on an agent."

"You fucking asshole," said Russo.

"Whatever, kid. I could've protected you. Now you're fucked beyond all saving."

"That's not SOP," said Aguilar. "The Chief's gonna shit a plum."

"Well it doesn't make much difference now, does it?"

Russo could see the annoyance on Pierce's face. "Is the big bad detective gonna get in trouble?"

Pierce simply smiled in return.

"So what's your interest in agents?" asked Aguilar.

"Gotta put 'em down. They run around like the own the place. The one I'm after is a monster, just a real psychopath, you know?"

"He'd kill you just for saying that," said Russo.

"See what I mean? We can't have people like that walking our streets with corporate immunity. Look what they're doing to our kids. Before this, Russo was just a delinquent who cut school and trespassed in office buildings. Now he's an attempted murderer."

"I thought it was two?" asked Russo.

"I can make it three if you'd like," replied Pierce.

"Then I'll make you my fourth."

There was a flash in Pierce's eyes, but he said nothing.

Outside, the streets were nearly empty. There were no street signs, but Russo recognized a few landmarks. The world looked so bland. He wondered how the agents could stand it.

"See that alley on the next block?"

Aguilar nodded. "Kind of a strange—"

"Back entrance," explained Pierce.

The cruiser rumbled into the alley and the high buildings blocked out the sun. Russo wondered if he could use the darkness to make his move. The ties were still tight; thirty minutes of working his wrists hadn't produced any results. If he could just get the door open, he could make a run for it. When the time is right, he told himself.

"Up there on the right, there's a loading dock."

"What is this place?"

"Safe house," said Pierce. "In case things got hot."

"I don't see any other cars. How are you going to get him downtown?"

"My partner's cruiser is in the garage."

Aguilar pulled into the small driveway and put it in park. "This doesn't feel right."

The engine sputtered to a stop and Aguilar looked over at Pierce. The shadows made both men look more sinister.

"I don't appreciate you staring me down, Officer."

"How did you know Deron's last name?"

Pierce scoffed. "What?"

"Deron. You said you hadn't questioned him yet. So how'd you know his name?"

"The kid told me." Pierce gestured to Russo.

"No I didn't."

Aguilar tensed up. "You're not wearing your badge, Detective."

"It's in my jacket." Pierce's voice was equally tight. "Would you like to see it?"

Both men moved at the same time. Aguilar drew his gun but couldn't get it leveled before the back of his head exploded, spraying blood and brain matter everywhere.

Russo felt it coat his face. "Oh shit! Shit!" He tried to grab his head, partly to wipe the blood away, but mostly out of a need to hold his ears. The gunshot still echoed in the cabin. Despite his shoulder, he flung himself to the seat to avoid the crossfire. Mumbling curses, he waited and prayed.

"Stop being such a little bitch," said Pierce. Then, as if nothing had even happened, "Well, this jacket is ruined."

Russo opened his eyes and tried to spit out the blood that had collected on his lips. He looked down and saw his hospital gown had changed from gray to red.

"What are you doing down there?"

"Why… why did you shoot him?"

Pierce snorted. "He was asking a lot of questions. You know how I feel about questions."

Russo sat up and looked at the carnage. Aguilar's head was little more than a stump of pulsing flesh.

"Come on, my partner is waiting." Pierce got out of the car and came around to Russo's side. He opened the door and gestured.

There was no avoiding dragging his ass through the fragments of bone and flesh on the seat. When Russo was finally standing outside the cruiser, Pierce whistled at him.

"You're gonna need a shower before we go."

"Go where?"

Pierce started up the loading dock ramp without reply.

Russo tested the ground with his bare feet; the bits of gravel slowed his climb, but he made it onto the landing as Pierce approached a service door.

It opened before he could knock and a man stepped out with his gun drawn. "What the fuck was that?" When he saw Pierce, he put the safety on and holstered his weapon.

Russo didn't recognize him, but he looked too lanky to be a detective. He looked like someone Russo would have beat the shit out of between classes.

"Little speed bump," said Pierce.

The man caught sight of Russo. "Jesus. What did you do to him?"

"That's nothing. You should see the other guy." Pierce winked at Russo and then pushed past his partner.

Russo followed him inside to find a sterile apartment that lacked color but looked modern and comfortable. Three duffle bags sat on a table, along with multiple handguns and extra clips.

Pierce rummaged in the side pocket of one of the bags and then beckoned to Russo. "Come here so I can cut those things off you."

"Who are you?"

"You haven't told him yet?"

Pierce reached out and grabbed the ties. With the flick of his knife, he cut them loose. "Feel better?"

"Look at his face. He's scared shitless."

"Shut up, Fitch. I want to see if he figures it out on his own. What do you say, Rivera?"

Russo stared back at the smug face, but nothing in its lines or curves looked familiar. He ran it against everyone he had encountered in the last few weeks but found no match. It took a glance at Fitch for him to remember the room and how everything lacked a veneer, even people. Comparing Pierce's face would do no good, not if…

"The suspense is killing me," said Fitch.

It wasn't until Pierce smirked that Russo made the connection.

"Ruiz?"

The agent smacked Russo on his good shoulder. "What took you so long?"

"It was you the whole time?"

Ruiz shrugged and folded his arms. "I had to know if you were gonna fuck us. That was the last test."

"How did he do?" asked Fitch.

"Fucking defiant to the end. We got interrupted, but I'm sure he would have kept his mouth shut. Right?"

Russo nodded. He didn't have to ask what Ruiz would have done had he talked. Plug the leak. No loose ends.

Ruiz motioned to the bathroom. "Get cleaned up so we can get the fuck out of here. There are some clean clothes in your duffle bag."

"Where are we going?"

"Sonora. You're way behind on your training."

"Is the veneer still working there?"

Both agents looked at each other and laughed. Fitch gave Ruiz a questioning look and got a nod in response.

Russo watched with wide eyes as they both began to shimmer, first their skin and then their clothes. Ruiz got there first, bringing up a full veneer in just a few seconds. Fitch followed close behind and soon both men were smiling at him and chuckling. Against the drab background of the room, they looked almost ethereal. Ruiz took a step closer.

"You don't get it, Russo. The veneer can't be stopped. It'll always be here. And so will we."

SEVENTY-THREE
DERON

Rosalia wasn't wearing perfume, but Deron could smell her just the same. The scent he had become so familiar with over the last few months had been absent from the room for a long time while the doctors and nurses worked in vain to figure out why he couldn't see. They argued sharply amongst themselves for a bit, which only made Deron more anxious. A nurse whispered into his ear that she was going to give him a sedative, blocking out the sound of the doctors as they talked in the hall. They were too far away, the sound too muffled.

They said something about a conversion disorder, whatever that was.

His senses dulled after that; moving from reality to dream without sight was an easy transition. It wasn't until he smelled Rosalia that he realized he was awake again. For a few minutes, he said nothing and simply took inventory of his senses. There were all kinds of noises around him: a nearby heart rate monitor, a more distant rattling of gurneys being pushed down the hall, and most importantly, a quiet kind of sobbing he had heard too frequently in the past week.

It was Rosalia, of course; the sound was unique to her. Deron thought of the reasons why she might cry. His current physical state was certainly depressing. The fact that he almost died might have made her realize how important he was to her. Or maybe it was that he was confined to a hospital bed, echoing the last days of her mom from so many years ago. The tears he imagined running down her cheeks might not have been for him at all.

"What's the matter?" His throat was dry, making his voice raspy.

Rosalia stirred, sniffled. "You're awake."

"You're crying."

"Maybe," she replied, following it up with a forced laugh. "I'm just happy."

"That I lived?" Of the reasons he could think of, it seemed the least passive-aggressive. He almost wanted to ask if she was happy he was blind.

"No." Her voice got a little closer. "I'm happy they let me sit with you. Last time, they wouldn't even let me in the room."

Deron tried to swallow and coughed.

"Do you want some water?" She moved without him having to answer.

He followed her footsteps around the bed, listened to the change in the ambient noise as she passed in front of the door. On his right, he heard water being poured into a cup. A hand slipped behind his head, helping him up slightly.

"Does that hurt?" she asked.

"Yeah." There was no use being brave.

"Open."

Deron tasted plastic on his lips and then relief as the water ran into his mouth. He swallowed enthusiastically until his throat was coated again. Rosalia was patient, holding his head and the cup until it was empty. When she lowered him back to the pillow, he sighed contently.

"Feel better?"

He turned in the direction of her voice as she walked around his bed again. It was as she returned to her chair that he felt a change in the warmth coming from the left. He recalled there had been a window there. If it was giving off heat, then it was still light out.

"What time is it?" he asked.

"I don't know. It looks like the sun is going to set soon."

"It'll get dark out there without the veneer," he said, thinking about the tunnel leading out of Easton.

"Yeah," she replied. Her voice sounded close by and Deron imagined her resting her chin on her arms and her arms on the bed.

"You're not very talkative," he observed, challenging her.

Rosalia huffed. "What do you want me to say?"

She could have said sorry, Deron thought. She could have apologized for abandoning him after what he considered the night that finally brought them together. But then he thought about what he would say in response. He would tell her that he forgave her, that he understood why she did it. So why the empty ceremony?

When she didn't reply, Deron said, "I missed you." He felt her fingers brush against the side of his cheek. Though the skin was tender, the pressure felt good.

"Me too." Her fingers hesitated at the border of his bandages. "I wish we could start over, you know?"

The awkwardness of their first kiss flashed in his head. "From the very beginning?"

"Not like kindergarten. Maybe Valentine's Day, remember? We had fun that day."

Deron recalled a late night at Gillock Pond and a large coat that hid his hand as it fumbled under Rosalia's shirt. But could they really reset? It was while waiting in the concession stand by the football field that he first wondered how they would ever reconcile the events of the past week. Even if he had beaten Russo, would she have run back into his arms? Would everything have been okay?

"It wouldn't be the same," he said at last. "Even if I could get your shirt off, I wouldn't be able to see your boobs."

She laughed and put her hand on his arm. Her fingers nestled around his bicep. "You don't remember them from the other night?"

In truth, his memories seemed blurry, but that might have been from the medication. Telling his girlfriend that she didn't have memorable tits probably wasn't a good idea. He didn't even know if he could still call her his girlfriend.

"I remember the other night." The words came out more solemn than he had intended.

Rosalia's fingers stopped moving. "If I wasn't sorry, I wouldn't be here."

"I know." He wanted to see her face, wanted to see the sincerity.

"If I didn't love you…"

"Yeah."

"It wasn't easy getting down here, you know that? Everyone's gone crazy without the veneer." She took a deep breath and turned her head politely to exhale.

"They should try going blind." Or being shot, he thought. Or having a tube in their nose blasting oxygen into their lungs. They didn't know how good they had it.

"Nurse Hendricks is here, did you know that?"

He shook his head minutely.

"She said Dr. Blake said you have hysterical blindness."

The laugher bubbled up through his chest and stung his wounds.

"It's all in my head?" Since when did a doctor's inability to diagnose a condition mean the patient was making it up?

"It's not like you're imagining—" She stopped midsentence. "Have you tried that? Reconciling in your head?"

"What do you mean?"

Her hand withdrew and he heard her stand up. He tried to follow the footsteps around the room, but lost her. Somewhere in the mix, the door closed and shut out the voices in the hall. In the resulting quiet, he locked in on the rushing of air through vents in the ceiling, the unintelligible grumbling from the streets below, and the movement of Rosalia's body around the room. He heard her clothes rustle as she walked, as she swung her arms. Her footsteps returned to his side, blocking out the fading warmth of the window again.

"What do you see in your head?" she asked.

Her inflection suggested she wanted a specific answer, but Deron answered truthfully. "Nothing."

"Okay. You're in a hospital room."

"I knew that—"

"Try to picture it. There are two beds about six feet apart. The other is empty. Yours is covered in white sheets. There is a thermal blanket rolled up by your feet. The mattress is gray, but the bed frame has some silver in it."

"Why are you telling me this?"

"I just thought… I mean, you know all those paintings I've done? They're all gone now, but I can remember them, so they're not really. You can't see me right now, but you could remember what I looked like and imagine me. It's a start."

"It's not enough," he told her. The images in his head were fuzzy. Just thinking about Rosalia standing in front of a window wasn't enough to sharpen the lines.

She continued undaunted. "By the bed is a table with a pitcher of water on it. On the other side is a chair. Next to the chair is a pair of shoes. The owner of those shoes is a young girl in bare feet standing in front of the window. She has on that blue shirt you like and jeans."

"I thought everything was gray?"

"Imagine it's blue. Visualize her shirt and her chest. You can really see her boobs because she's not wearing a bra."

"Yeah right," said Deron, unable to stop himself from seeing it in his head. Unlike the room, it was an image he wanted to reconcile. Somehow that made the idea more tangible.

"She's wearing the kind of ponytail that makes you smile. She can't keep her bright green eyes off of you."

"Your eyes are blue."

He heard rustling.

"Now she's taking off her shirt. Can you see it?"

Deron wanted to respond negatively, but realized that his mind had been filling in the pieces as Rosalia spoke. He went back in his memory, to the night in his dad's apartment, to the last image he had of her: the hair he knew well, the same for her eyes. But to imagine her topless meant remembering what he had seen in those brief flashes of lightning. He felt silly for trying so hard.

"You're not really taking your clothes off, are you?"

"Why do you think I closed the door?"

Deron smiled. Because I can't see, he thought. She was taking advantage of his handicap.

"She's standing in front of the window. She doesn't care who can see her. The sun is almost gone and the shadows are very long outside. The buildings are all gray, but the sky is full of pinks and purples."

He recognized the sound of her jeans unsnapping.

"Her pants are on the floor now. She is wearing fancy lace panties that she got at Victoria's Secret just for you." Rosalia almost giggled. "You've got a look on your face, Deron. Do you see her?"

In his mind, Rosalia's avatar had crystallized. It was easier to maintain once he realized he wasn't simply testing his imagination. He truly wanted to see her. And that desire only made her more real. It provided backdrop in the form of a window that showed buildings silhouetted by the fire of a sunset.

"She's putting her thumbs in her waistband and pushing them down her legs."

There was something in the way she said *legs* that made him imagine her turning away, looking out the window perhaps. He could hear her breathing, but her narration had stopped.

"What's the matter?" he asked.

"Are you doing that?"

"Doing what?" He didn't like the alarm in her voice.

"I thought I saw something out there."

"All I see is you," said Deron.

Rosalia replied in a distant voice, "How does she look?"

"Beautiful. But in my version, your hair is down."

"You have some kind of fascination with hair." She slipped back into describing herself. "I'm taking out the tie, I mean, she's taking out the tie and letting her hair fall to her shoulders. She's whipping it around like they do in movies."

It was the twist of her neck, he realized, that was putting pressure on her voice box that in turn, made her voice sound different.

"What's she doing now?" he asked.

"Looking outside. She doesn't understand what she sees."

"I see you and a window." The desire to see her had changed to a full-blown need. As she had tried to say, she wouldn't have been there if she didn't love him. No matter what she did, he was compelled to reciprocate.

In the new world he had created in his mind, he smiled at the image of a naked Rosalia standing against a sunset. He reveled in the detail and thought about how proud she would have been to see him reconcile so well.

"What else do you see?"

Deron brought up the lights to find more to talk about. "It's a small room. The far wall is empty, but there's a frame where a picture should be." He turned his head to explore his imagination. "I see the door you closed. There are people walking by. I can see them in the little window."

"What about the girl?"

"She's gorgeous."

"Describe her." There was urgency in Rosalia's voice.

"She's leaning against the window. Her skin looks soft—"

The texture shifted unnaturally. Rosalia's long legs suddenly looked like fabric. As hard as he tried to push the detail away, it kept coming back and even expanded. The next moment, she was wearing jeans. Deron looked to her chest but her breasts had disappeared under a blue t-shirt. Then her hair morphed into a ponytail, as did the shadows that seemed to be overwhelming everything. He tried to get a handle on his imagination, but it was no longer listening to him.

It turned her around, made her look at him with such joy on her face that it broke his heart. He thought it might be his subconscious screwing with him, the dormant creativity inside him that only came out when he was messed up.

"Deron…"

It was when Rosalia spoke that recognition set in. Somehow, her lips moved right along with the pronunciation of his name. Not even on his best day could he have reconciled something so complex. She put her hand to her mouth— another command he hadn't sent.

Deron grasped for some clue that would show her to be nothing more than his imagination, but found none. He could see again, but he couldn't believe it. Believing it would have made the impossible real.

Rosalia ran the short distance to his side. "You can see me!"

"In my mind, yeah."

"No," she said, kissing him on the forehead. "For real!"

Deron looked at the far wall, at the picture of a clipper ship navigating rough seas. "If this was real, there wouldn't be a veneer."

Rosalia touched her face; new color rippled over her skin. She hurried back to the window and put her palms against the glass. "You have to see it!"

He *was* seeing it; the veneer climbed Rosalia like a billion little vines all joining together to cover her from head to toe. Only when it was over did he chance a look around the room. Then he understood why she was so excited.

The veneer was back.

"I knew it," said Rosalia, shaking her head. "Last night, when the whole city turned white, that was you, wasn't it?"

"I think so."

"And today, the whole city was gray."

"I didn't mean to," he said, even though he still questioned his ability to reconcile all of Easton at the same time.

Rosalia turned and faced him. "Do you hear that?"

She was right; the voices in the halls had calmed down. Beyond the hospital, Deron could no longer hear the people in the streets.

"You…"

She didn't finish her sentence, but Deron understood. He had brought the veneer back. He had saved the city. As the solution to and cause of the original problem, it was a hollow victory.

"Now we can start over, right?"

Rosalia approached the bed and put a hand on his chest. Her eyes darted to the nearby bullet wound. "If you want to."

He didn't waste any time before saying, "I do."

She kissed him and held her lips against his for a long time.

When she finally withdrew, Deron said, "I knew you weren't taking off your clothes."

Rosalia let the reddening of her cheeks trickle to the surface. "If that's what it takes for you to get better, I'll never wear clothes again."

He smiled at her, let his imagination churn out the possibilities.

"You don't believe me?"

Deron shook his head.

"From now on, whenever it's just me and you, I'll be naked."

He looked over her face; she truly believed her own words. But if she went through with it, they wouldn't really be starting over. Their night together in his dad's apartment would always be with them. And if either recalled that memory, it would always end with Deron sitting alone on the edge of the bed.

There was no starting over, but they could continue. Their relationship had survived two trips to the hospital, a city-wide disaster, and the meddling of agents. What else could there possibly be?

Deron laughed to himself. He had drifted away in thought, but his eyes returned to Rosalia's. She was still looking at him expectantly, maybe hoping he would balk at her offer to spend their time together nude. It wasn't that he expected her to do it forever; even once would be something to look forward to. It was just a matter of finding something beyond her veneered flesh to hope for. Something more than boyfriend and girlfriend. Something more than sex.

As he stared into her eyes, he couldn't imagine what those things might be.

Deron cleared his throat and replied, "I'll believe it when I see it."

EPILOGUE
MEMO

When Memo got to the end of the report, he scrolled back up to the top and read it again. And again. After the fifth time, he tossed the palette onto his desk and watched as it slid dangerously close to the edge. Not that it would have mattered. Destroying the palette wouldn't change the fact that the impossible had happened, had been witnessed by more people than he could silence cleanly. For the briefest of moments, he considered the idea that it was all a joke, that someone higher up the chain was jerking his.

A level five event—that's what they were calling it upstairs.

Memo turned in his chair and looked out over the Sonora skyline. There had only been three level five events in his lifetime. The most recent had come at the hands of a young boy with a malfunctioning Guardian chip. To have another one so soon suggested a problem with the system, something in hardware or software that was breaking down. Or was there just a problem with the supply to Easton?

Two troublemakers from the same city. Not very likely.

Without looking back, Memo reached for his desk and reconciled a portal. When a chime rang out in the room, he said, "Get your ass in here."

A few minutes later, he heard the door open and close behind him.

"You wanted to see me, boss?"

"Have a seat," said Memo. "There's something on my palette you need to see."

"What am I looking at?"

"Scroll to the end. Take a look at the eyewitness veneers."

A stunted laugh echoed in the office. "Nice try, Memo."

Memo smiled. The apprentice was becoming more like the master every day.

"It's real," he said. "It's a level five event."

"Bullshit. There hasn't been one of those since…"

"Deron Bishop," said Memo. He flashed on the football field and Deron's body motionless and bloodied in the mud.

"Fucking Deron."

Memo turned to find a dispassionate veneer on Russo's face. His control over his emotions had improved steadily over the years, or at least, he had finally learned proper control over his mask.

"Is he our prime suspect?" asked Russo.

"A person of interest," said Memo. "But I'm not convinced."

"Who else is there? He's the only sheep we know of who can reconcile remotely."

Memo shrugged. "If he even *can* anymore. His file at Easton General says they flashed his chip." He considered the lapse for a moment. "I thought that would have taken care of it."

"It should have," said Russo, examining the palette again. "He's gotten a lot better at reconciliation. I don't think even I could do a portal on this scale."

"I don't buy it." Memo touched the desk and brought up the pictures from the report. Easton appeared under his hand; at the horizon, the image flipped, showed the streets and buildings hanging from the sky.

"I only know of two people that could reconcile this kind of detail," said Russo. "And I killed one of them."

"And the other?"

Russo looked at the wall and reconciled an image of Rosalia in the halls at school.

"And there's the tricky part," said Memo, standing and walking to the wall. He reconciled a similar image of Deron standing in front of a bus. "Two people gifted in different ways. One is a modern Da Vinci; the other doesn't require physical contact. So either Deron has learned to reconcile like his girlfriend or…"

Russo's mouth went slack. This time, a hint of anger rippled through his veneer. "That son of a cock," he said, slamming his fist into his open palm. "He taught her how to reconcile remotely. How is that even possible?"

"Fuck," said Memo, wiping out the wall and replacing it with the mirrored Easton. "How the hell is *this* even possible?"

Russo considered the question but said nothing.

"It's spreading, Russo. It's not supposed to be spreading, but it is. If he can teach her, they can teach others. And so on until the entire city is in chaos."

"Again."

"What was that?" asked Memo.

Russo cleared his throat. "Until the city is in chaos *again*."

"We're not gonna let that happen."

"So what do we do?"

Memo turned to the window. In the distance, he could almost make out the border walls of Sonora. Somewhere beyond the dip of the horizon was Easton.

"We stop the infection at the source," he replied.

"You mean, we go back to Easton?"

Memo nodded.

"For Deron and Rosalia?"

Again, he nodded. Memo watched carefully for a reaction on Russo's veneer. "You think you can handle that?"

Russo looked away for a moment. "Do I really get to kill him this time?"

"That'll be up to you," said Memo.

"I'll take care of it," replied Russo, patting the bulge under his right arm.

"Then pack your shit. We leave for Easton tonight."

AUTHOR'S NOTE

If you've already read *Xronixle*, you may have seen the note I included there about what it means to revisit early work. *Veneer* came a few years after that first effort, and in many ways, it represents the first time I tried to grapple with deeper themes—identity, perception, and the masks we wear to survive our world. But even so, the distance between who I was then and who I am now remains significant.

Since writing this book, I've continued to grow as a storyteller, and there are choices I made in *Veneer*—in dialogue, character, and especially certain actions— that I would approach differently today. Some moments are overly clever, others unnecessarily cruel. I see the seams in the writing now, and more importantly, I understand why they're there.

This second edition includes only minor grammatical fixes and formatting updates for wide release. No major content has been changed. Like *Xronixle*, this book remains a snapshot of the writer I was at the time—flawed, ambitious, and just beginning to understand how to write stories with heart as well as edge.

Writing is a journey, and *Veneer* was an important step in mine. I'm grateful you've picked it up.

Thank you for reading.

Daniel Verastiqui
April 12, 2025

THANK YOU

Veneer is the second book of **The Vinestead Anthology**.

If you enjoyed this book, please consider leaving a review.

Each standalone novel in the Vinestead Anthology tells a small part of a larger epic: the rise and fall of Vinestead International, the exploits of a rogue artificial intelligence named Lassiter, and a seemingly endless stream of idealistic hackers—each convinced they're the hero of the story.

Enjoy them in any order.

Xronixle (2007)

Veneer (2011)

Guardian Angels (2012)

Perion Synthetics (2014)

Por Vida (2017)

Brigham Plaza (2019)

Hybrid Mechanics (2020)

Vise Manor (2022)

House of Nepenthe (2025)

To learn more about the Vinestead Anthology and explore additional titles, please visit:

danielverastiqui.com

www.ingramcontent.com/pod-product-compliance
Lightning Source LLC
Chambersburg PA
CBHW070558300726
48975CB00006B/1626